OUTSTANDING

Also by Kathryn Flett

Separate Lives

Outstanding

IN THE SCHOOL OF LIFE, NOT EVERYONE CAN WIN A GOLD STAR

KATHRYN FLETT

Quercus

First published in Great Britain in 2016 by

Quercus Editions Ltd
Carmelite House
50 Victoria Embankment
London EC4Y 0DZ

An Hachette UK company

A CIP catalogue record for this book is available
from the British Library

HB ISBN 978 1 78429 824 1
EBOOK ISBN 978 1 78429 322 2

10 9 8 7 6 5 4 3 2 1

Typeset by Jouve (UK), Milton Keynes

Printed and bound in Great Britain by Clays Ltd, St Ives plc

For Jackson and Rider

'If you choose to represent the various parts in life by holes upon a table, of different shapes – some circular, some triangular, some square, some oblong – and the person acting these parts by bits of wood of similar shapes, we shall generally find that the triangular person has got into the square hole, the oblong into the triangular, and a square person has squeezed himself into the round hole. The officer and the office, the doer and the thing done, seldom fit so exactly, that we can say they were almost made for each other.'

Sydney Smith, 'On the Conduct of the
Understanding' (1804–6)

PROLOGUE

Eve Sturridge sat at the desk in her attractively appointed and spacious office at Ivy House Preparatory School, scrolling through status updates on her Facebook page. It was 2:46 p.m. on a pleasantly warm Friday afternoon in June and, with the school week all but over, Eve was allowing herself a little time to search for a link to a newspaper article somebody had posted that morning but that, what with one thing and another, she hadn't yet had time to read.

Nor would she now. There was a knock and then, without pause, Gail Prince, her PA, poked her head around the office door and hissed, 'Your three o'clock is waiting in the hall!' Eve smiled; Gail's conspiratorial hissing was a regular default.

'God, is it that time already?'

'The Sorensens are absolutely charming. And fully loaded. You'll have noticed they arrived by *helicopter*.'

'I thought it was a bit windy over by the rugby pitch. Tell them I'll be right there.'

Eve turned to the bookcase behind her chair from

which she pulled out a well-thumbed copy of the *Sunday Times* Rich List. There they were: Stefan and Anette Sorensen, number eighty-six – which meant, were she to bag them for Ivy House, they'd hurtle past her current richest Rich Listers, the Dershowitzes, at number one hundred and two. She had the Dershowitzes to thank for recommending Ivy House to the Sorensens in the first place.

After a couple of minutes, Eve got to her feet, quickly checking that she passed muster in the small gilt-framed mirror by the door. Tucking one side of her neat blonde bob behind an ear, revealing a discreet pearl and diamond stud, Eve headed out through the maze of school offices and into the wood-panelled entrance hall where, she noted with satisfaction, sunlight was streaming through a stained-glass window and glancing off the well-polished sporting silverware in an adjacent cabinet.

'Mr and Mrs Sorensen, how good to meet at last. I hope your journey was pleasant?' Eve extended her hand to Mrs Sorensen – it was important to get the wives onside straight away. Classic new money and loads of it, thought Eve, but very tastefully done.

'Twenty minutes from Battersea in the whirlybird; here before we knew it.' Eve picked up a mid-Atlantic twang alongside the native Danish in Stefan Sorensen's accent. He smiled, partly with his shrewd blue eyes but mostly with his mouth, Eve noted, as she gave Stefan a swift, imperceptible once-over: beautifully cut, unstuffy navy suit jacket, clearly Savile Row; dark indigo jeans and a pink, tieless, shirt – Jermyn Street, obviously; a pair of brogues and an unshowy but expensive-looking wrist-watch peeking out from his cuff. In short, the very model of a modern master of the universe.

'Y-*es*. It is so much easier and quicker to fly than it is to drive down the A21,' said Mrs S with just a hint of Nordic sing-song.

'Absolutely,' said Eve. Despite being the spit of *Mad Men*'s Betty Draper, there was an aura of warmth about Mrs S, and it was she rather than Mr S who was wearing a suit – cream and, Eve decided, looking a lot like Stella McCartney – which she'd teamed with a pair of baby-blue loafers. Eve liked to see attractive women wearing flats in the daytime; it said, 'Comfortable in my skin.' And the evidence indicated that, despite Mr S's bank balance, in this context at least, it was his wife who wore the trousers. Eve allowed herself a moment to congratulate herself on her wives-first handshaking strategy.

'I wasn't sure if I would be meeting –' Eve paused, it was all about the pronunciation – 'Aija and Petrus today?'

'No-oh, we decided against it. Children dislike change, don't they?' said Anette Sorensen. 'We think that if we present their new school to them as a fait accompli it will be much easier.' Easier for whom? thought Eve. 'Anyway, right now they are at the Natural History Museum with their nanny. They can't get enough dinosaurs.' Anette smiled, the sun came out, glaciers melted.

Eve was conscious of Anette Sorensen's 'new school' comment but restrained herself from making an air punch. And, despite disagreeing with Anette's 'fait accompli' concept, she said, 'So true – and frankly I can't get enough dinosaurs either. Now, would you prefer to start the tour in the gardens or inside?'

'Inside,' said Stefan Sorensen firmly. 'Then we can finish up by the 'copter. Are we due at Heatherdown at five, honey?'

Ah! thought Eve. Heatherdown . . . Heatherdown School was, in Eve's opinion, a very un-Sorensen sort of choice. Admittedly the Sorensens were Nordic, so Eve suspected they probably went in for a bit of free-range *Hello, trees! Hello, sky! Let's build a yurt!* stuff, along with skinny dipping and entire days spent doing 'art', but if it was proper British prep school box-ticking they were after then she felt that Heatherdown was, for all its touchy-feely 'family' ethos, not going to be quite their ticket. Fingers crossed they'd find that out for themselves – probably by about ten past five.

'Y-es,' said Anette, who turned towards Eve wearing a subtly empathetic, sisterly expression. 'We are seeing other schools.'

'Of course,' Eve said enthusiastically, 'and so you should. These are not the kind of decisions one rushes into.' Eve infiltrated herself comfortably between Mr and Mrs Sorensen and, placing a proprietorial hand gently on the small of their backs – a trick she had learned by watching

US presidents 'welcoming' foreign (invariably less power-ful) heads of state – ushered them through the entrance hall. 'A delightfully idiosyncratic school, Heatherdown, and always very much a reflection of its Principal – though I'm sure you're aware that he recently passed away?' Eve didn't wait for an answer; it was enough to plant the seed and then water it a bit. 'So who knows what will become of the school now? Anyway, let us start with our marvellous new library, which I'm sure you know all about since it was so generously endowed by Mr and Mrs Dershowitz.'

AUTUMN TERM

1

'Mum. Mu-*um*!'

Seeing her mother's brand new and extremely expensive handbag still sitting on the kitchen table, Zoe Sturridge hurried down the hall in her dressing gown and opened the front door. Not wanting to negotiate the wet gravel drive in bare feet, she hopped up and down on the equally damp front step.

'Mum! Your bag! First day of term and you've forgotten your satchel.'

At which Eve re-emerged from the Volvo. 'Thanks, darling. Every bloody year, eh?'

'Just as well the staff don't know how heavily you rely on a seventeen-year-old, but your secret's safe with me. Have a nice day, Mum.'

'You, too. Shouldn't you be off soon?'

'Nothing till eleven today.'

'OK. Well, when you leave, wrap up – chill in the air.'

'Dur! I'm not *seven*.'

Zoe shut the door, went back to the kitchen, rummaged

in the fridge for yoghurt, padded up the stairs to her bedroom and opened her wardrobe. Staring at the rails she
decided she was feeling skirt – *short* skirt – far more than
she was feeling skinnies, and started looking for some
black opaque tights before settling on a clean purple pair.
As she slipped on her favourite old pink Converse high
tops, Zoe heard the *beep-beep* of an incoming text on the
phone beneath her pillow.

I ♥ U. Coast clear? XXX

♥ U2. Yeh! XXX

Round in 5 XXX

!!!XXX

Zoe removed the Converse and peeled off her tights, put
her dressing gown back on over her second-best bra and
knickers and went downstairs where, having checked that
her mother had actually left the premises for the entire
day, she set the front door open on the latch and went back
upstairs to wait until Rob arrived on his Honda. She hoped
he didn't rush too much – not in this rain – yet, with an
anticipatory tingle, she couldn't help thinking, Hurry up!

Zoe believed herself to be fairly sensible, even allowing
for being seventeen. Nonetheless, she knew it wasn't particularly sensible to be bunking off half a day's school – she

was in the upper sixth of a highly sought-after girls' grammar – in the first week of the autumn term and preparing to shag her boyfriend at home – but, hey. Zoe was unfazed by the prospect of removing her sensible handbag-spotting head and replacing it with her sexy-for-my-boyfriend head. That stuff was simply part of the game of growing up. And she was, for the most part, enjoying growing up.

She heard the slam of the unlatched front door, a pounding on the stairs and then there was Rob in his leathers, bike helmet under his arm, grinning at her in the doorway. Zoe had, along with most of her mates, watched sufficient online porn to know that, if the opportunity presented itself, sex should probably always start with a bit of burlesque-style flirtation before you got down to the serious stuff, so she let the silky pistachio-coloured dressing gown slide off her shoulders and thrust out her right hip.

'Morning, babes.'

'Sick!' said Rob, appreciatively. 'How long we got?'

'How long do we need?'

'Not long.'

He launched himself at Zoe, fumbling with his leathers.

'I'll do it.' Zoe knew it was important to be in control. Men liked that stuff – even nineteen-year-old boy-men.

Rob groaned. 'Go on, babes.'

Zoe went on, falling to her knees, unzipping Rob's leathers.

'Yeah, like that; more like *that* – please?' Rob's voice

dived up and down an octave or two as if it were still breaking, so Zoe carried on. It didn't take long. If she was honest, she didn't really like this bit of the proceedings but she was very good at pretending she did.

'Love you, babes.' Rob sounded spent but happy. What's not to like? thought Zoe. But the truth was she enjoyed making Rob happy.

'You're good at this, babe. Do you want me to make you come?'

'I'm all right. I'm a very giving kinda girl.'

'Fucking right you are! Kiss?'

Zoe got to her feet, rose on her tiptoes and kissed Rob full on the lips.

'You'll make me hard again.'

'Make the most of it. One day you'll be fat and forty and needing Viagra just to do it *once*.'

'Ha! Not me. Never. Now I wanna fuck you. Slow.'

'Right. Bang goes the eleven o'clock lecture then.'

Rob cocked his fingers, pistol style. 'Bang *bang*!'

Beep-beep: her phone.

'Wait a minute,' said Zoe, moving over to the bed. 'You can fuck me while I read a text.'

Rob raised an eyebrow. 'Sex-y! Whosit?'

Zoe fell back on the bed, pulling off her knickers. She started texting her reply. 'Mum. She wants me to make sure I walk the dog before college.'

'Ha! Tell her you'll walk the dog, doggy style! Fuck, I fancy your mum.'

'You're gross!' said Zoe with a grimace, but she didn't mean it. Rob had said this sort of stuff before about her mum. She thought it was funny, the idea of Eve being hot, but it also made her, weirdly, slightly proud. A hot mum was better than a not-hot mum, surely? She touched *Send* on the iPhone as Rob sat on the bed next to her, watching.

'And I bet she'd be so proud if she could see you now.'

'Sarky!'

'Sexy!'

'Fuck me!'

And then, after that particular distraction, Zoe posed for some more pictures for Rob – pouty, porny, very obviously boyfriend pleasing and designed to be something for Rob to revisit on those occasions when Zoe wasn't around. And Rob posed for pictures for Zoe, too – which seemed fair, even though Zoe felt that pictures of naked men alone always looked a bit, well, *gay*. And then both of them took selfies together. This was the most fun because they looked as good as they felt – maybe even better. A little bit Rob Pattinson and Kristen Stewart, thought Zoe. Cool.

2

Eve stood in Ivy House's entrance hall, welcoming the new intake. Having learned over time that you could never assume any decision by the super rich was a done deal until the evidence was in front of you, she was satisfied to note the intake included Aija and Petrus Sorensen. Eve had previously seen children delivered to their first day at school by nannies, so on this occasion she was pleasantly surprised to see the children with both their parents.

'Mr and Mrs Sorensen, Aija and Petrus –' Eve was pronunciation perfect – 'welcome!' She extended her hand to Aija, the eldest, first. The girl shook it solemnly and seemed very likely to curtsey. Though she did her best to disguise it, Eve always found it impossible not to favour the school's more attractive children, especially those with impeccable manners. And despite having the off-spring of three ex-models on the school roll, with their matching white-blonde hair and huge cornflower eyes the junior Sorensens were not only beautiful children but apparently had manners to match. When Petrus shook

Eve's hand there was, too, a perceptible nod – a bow – of his head. Eve was charmed. 'So, let's go to the classrooms where you can meet your teachers and fellow pupils. Each of you has been assigned a special classmate to show you around the school and tell you where your pegs and lockers are. I guarantee that by lunchtime you'll be so settled you'll feel as if you've been here a week!' Eve glanced at the senior Sorensens. 'Mummy and Daddy are very welcome to come with you to the classrooms, or we can leave them right here and you can say goodbye now.'

'We'll come today,' said Anette, firmly. 'Just to see where you are.'

'But don't come to the class every day,' said her daughter, equally firmly. Aija was ten and therefore about to go into Year Six – aka 'Beethoven'.

'Come every day to my classroom, Mummy!' said eight-year-old Petrus, who was going to be in Year Four – 'Brahms' – where he'd be taught by Eve's favourite Ivy House teacher. At thirty-one, with a modish angular haircut and a bubbly head-girl's personality, Ellie Blake – a former head girl, albeit not at Ivy House – would almost certainly have blanched at the description but was, in Eve's opinion, the definition of diligent and methodical, yet without being dull. Yes, Eve thought, you're both in very safe hands . . .

Anette smiled at Petrus. 'If you want me to – though I know you won't when you see that I'm the only mummy who does.'

He's her favourite, noted Eve. And Aija is a chip off her mother's block, which is probably why.

'OK, so I shall come every day, Aija – whether you like it or not,' said Stefan Sorensen, smiling.

And she's his favourite. Same old same old.

Aija pulled a face. 'Don't be silly, Daddy. Even if you wanted to, you couldn't. You're hardly ever here.'

Stefan Sorensen shrugged and carried on smiling. 'You're right, of course, *pølse*, though I'm here now, aren't I? Come on, let's go.'

Anette turned to Eve. '*Pølse* – Danish for sausage.'

'Well, thank you – *tak*! The addition of *pølse* has just improved my Danish by precisely one hundred per cent.'

Smiles all round; ice duly broken. Fifteen minutes later, Eve was standing on the school's front steps, assuring the Sorensens that everything would be 'fine, just fine! They're in very good hands. Rest assured, we've done this rather a lot.'

'I'll be back at four o'clock,' said Anette. 'Though not every day – Birgitte looks after the children when I can't, so she will deputize quite often. I have a lot of commitments.'

'Of course! We look forward to seeing you both whenever you're able. In the meantime, don't ever hesitate to pick up the phone.' And with that Eve turned her attention to the remaining parents. Even if the Sorensens were on the *Sunday Times* Rich List, it wasn't good to be seen to be devoting her entire attention to them when they were paying pretty much the same fees as everyone else. Though none of the other hovering couples and a few singles – all of whom, Eve noted, had spotted the Sorensens' waiting Bentley and driver – seemed to mind. Indeed, a few of the fathers looked particularly impressed – *If Ivy House is good enough for the Sorensens . . .* – while several mothers wore expressions Eve could easily read: *How many children do they have? Boys or girls? What years are they in? How soon can we arrange a play-date for Milo/Tiffany? Right, I'll be back at 3:55 . . .*

Some things, Eve noted, didn't change much, even though the style in which they were carried out clearly did. For example, in Sorensen circles, peaked caps and ties for one's driver were obviously déclassé. This driver leaned casually on the bonnet of the car, wearing jeans and a hoodie. From a distance he could easily have passed for David Beckham on the school run. Eve turned to the nearest pair of parents.

'Mr and Mrs Brooks! Was Lauren excited this morning? I know that the girls in Bach are going to thoroughly enjoy welcoming a new member into their little gang!'

By ten a.m. the last angsty and nervous parents had departed, ushered soothingly out of the door by Eve ('Really, there's no need to worry. Lauren's EpiPen will be very clearly labelled in her locker and we have six other children in the school with peanut allergies . . .') and she was back in her office, putting off the paperwork that had piled up on the desk while she'd been on meet-and-greet duty in favour of catching up with an education blogger she'd found on Mumsnet. She scanned the article:

Against a challenging economic background, fee-paying schools have continued to grow. New figures released by the UK Independent Schools Conference show that among the 1,222 schools that took part in their survey this year and last, there are now 25,690 non-British pupils with parents living overseas, compared to 23,529 the year before.

Yada-yada-yada. Eve suppressed a yawn and ploughed on.

In the same schools, the number of British pupils fell to 476,007 from 478,932 in 2008. In the past five years, the biggest growth in overseas pupils has come from Russia, Spain, India, Pakistan, Sri Lanka, Bangladesh and China . . . The Schools Conference says that the rise in numbers of non-British pupils 'highlights the attractions of an education at an independent British school to the global market'.

'Thought you might need this.' Gail Prince entered the room without knocking, but bearing a large mug of proper frothy coffee from the new mini Gaggia that had been installed in the staffroom over the holidays.

'Marvellous, thanks – you are a total treasure. What a morning, eh?'

'How'd it go? Sorensens OK?'

Eve pulled a mock-reproachful face. 'We do have several *other* new parents, Gail.'

'I know, but none of them were on the cover of last Sunday's *Telegraph* magazine.'

Eve shifted a few of the papers on her desk and pulled out the magazine.

'No, indeed. Nice cover: "Sex and the City, Sorensen style".'

She appraised the amusing, stylish portrait: Stefan in his trademark jacket-and-jeans, facing the camera squarely with one arm draped over Anette, who leaned into him while looking into the lens in semi-profile, wearing – distractingly – a high-cut red and white swimsuit that was clearly intended to evoke the Danish flag, plus her old beauty-queen sash ('Miss Denmark 1995'), vertiginous heels and a tiara. This one's probably not paste, thought Eve. And those legs . . .

It was an arresting image even without the added visual 'joke': in his free hand Stefan held a large bouquet of flowers while Anette held a MacBook Pro. The message was, presumably, that Stefan Sorensen was a master of the universe who was also in touch with his feminine side, and that there was far more to Anette than met the eye – despite the fact that what met the eye was more than enough to be going on with.

'Handsome couple,' said Gail.

'To say the least. And the *children*! Do you remember that old film from a thousand years ago, based on John Wyndham's *The Midwich Cuckoos*?'

'Oh, yes – *Village of the Damned*. They did a remake a while ago.'

'That's the one. The Sorensen kids are like that – all blonde and blue-eyed and "Tomorrow Belongs To Me".'

'That's awful, Eve. You are *so* bad!'

Eve knew that Gail was thoroughly enjoying her badness. 'Any resemblance is purely physical. They are charming children and both lucky enough to have one parent each who loves them the best, which is at least fair. Also, I think Aija, the ten-year-old, is probably very bright, while Petrus is . . . well, he's a boy and yet to make eye contact with me, so it's a bit too soon to say. He's his mother's favourite, clearly, so probably a bit of a handful. We'll see.'

'Can't wait. Can I borrow that mag for a mo? Everyone in the staffroom is gagging to see it.'

'Sure. Not too much passing around, though. If people want to read all about the Sorensens, tell them I've said to do it online, and preferably in their own time. Now, Mrs Brooks says she'll call me at midday to check how Lauren is doing. I'm in a meeting, obviously – and Lauren is *fine*, obviously. And thanks for that coffee.'

As Gail left, Eve logged on to her computer and checked Facebook: two status updates already from Anette Sorensen with whom she was now 'friends' (Eve had been surprised but undeniably pleased when the request had come from Anette):

Dropped the kids off at their new school today – both are happy and excited. Meanwhile, I'm still sharpening my pencils!

And:

> Beloved husband is already en route to Geneva. Guess that leaves me with the rest of the unpacking!

Eve recalled recently reading something about the Sorensens' new house but couldn't remember where; however, Google revealed it was a two-week-old article from the Sunday *Courier*'s property supplement. Eve pored over the accompanying picture; now that really *was* a house and a half.

SUSSEX AND THE CITY – SORENSEN STYLE:

> Danish power-couple Stefan and Anette Sorensen last week moved out of their Mayfair town house to be nearer their children's new school in East Sussex. They have a daughter, Aija, ten, and a son, Petrus, seven.

Wrong, thought Eve – he's eight.

> A spokesperson for the Sorensens, who married in 1998 and made London their home in 2005, says they 'currently have no plans to sell their London house'. However, it is thought that the family will be spending the majority of their time at the Grade I listed Palladian mansion with 7,500 acres, including its own river, woodland and home

farm, all of which was formerly owned by the Russian oligarch Pietr Brezinsky, who has now relocated to New York.

The Sorensens' nearest neighbours, Mr and Mrs Percy of Eastdene Farm, with whom they share a boundary –

Now that should be interesting, thought Eve.

– say they are 'delighted to have such charming neighbours'.

'We were charmed when Anette turned up on the doorstep with the children and a bouquet of very beautiful flowers and said that she hoped the building of the family's new helicopter pad – for which they have full planning permission, I might add – wasn't too noisy,' says Richard Percy. 'I'm sure they will be an asset to the neighbourhood.'

Meanwhile, the Sorensens have been on something of a property spree recently, adding a house in the Hamptons, a Manhattan triplex and a Spanish villa to their portfolio, so it remains to be seen whether they will manage to spend much time at their new local, the Red Lion, or attend a service at their parish church, St Mary's in Eastdene.

Anette Sorensen has a MSc in Economics and is a former Miss Denmark.

Not just a pretty face, then, thought Eve. And then, with a start – Bugger! I wonder if Zoe has remembered to walk Barney? She reached into her bag and extracted her phone.

3

Gail had never imagined she'd live in a bungalow – at least not before she retired and started consulting Stannah catalogues. Yet, back in April, when her parents had decided to move into sheltered accommodation in Bexhill, Gail had sold her pretty first-floor, two-bed flat on the edge of Battle and moved herself and her ten-year-old son, Harry, into her parents' house.

The bungalow, a long, low, 1950s build on a large plot with a detached garage and what estate agents describe as a 'carriage drive', hadn't been Gail's childhood home – her parents had moved into it in the mid-1980s when their daughter had first flown their cosy thatched nest – thus Gail hadn't felt quite as repelled by the idea of moving in as she might have. For a start, her parents were effectively handing over their legacy early, which was typically generous, with the result that, after a decade of living with a bijou balcony heaving with tubs, she and football-mad Harry would now have the best part of half an acre of garden to play with – and in.

The bungalow had been built as a sort of dower house in the old orchard of the solid Victorian villa next door, which meant it had a walled garden so gloriously laden with horticultural 'period features' it might have been planted by Frances Hodgson Burnett. It also had a lawn the size of a football pitch, a vast magnolia and a bed of peonies. Of all trees, Gail loved magnolias the best, and of all flowers, she liked peonies the most; there was, she thought, something especially fragile, even sad, about their extravagant size in relation to their lack of longevity. God, I must be going soft in my nearly middle age.

A glance at her watch revealed that it was 4:16 p.m. Gail could see her son through the window, on the Xbox. She sighed, felt the habitual stab of maternal guilt over Harry's latch-key lifestyle. But in truth he'd been back for less than an hour, having walked with a bunch of his classmates and their mothers for the three minutes it took to get home from Eastdene Community Primary School – unless he detoured via Londis for a quick fix of Chilli Heatwave Doritos.

Gail had decided many years ago, back when she had been a pupil at Eastdene herself, that autumn was her favourite school term. It still was; spring term was invariably about being stuck inside during rain-lashed breaks, longing for the passing of the vomity bugs and the arrival of, well, *spring*. It always felt like a long haul. Meanwhile, the summer term was exam-stressy and then, post-May, it was all about the stroppy, sap-rising Year Sixes swaggering around, knowing their primary work was all but done. And that'll be Harry in a heartbeat, thought Gail, wistfully.

This term, however, was all about new shoes and pristine pencil cases and optimism, with a balmy Indian summer segueing into crunchy piles of leaves and then all the Halloweeny bonfires followed by the crush of Nativity rehearsals and Christmas fayres, themselves hot on the heels of fundraising mufti days and lunchtime Christmas card designing workshops. At Ivy House School, autumn was especially full of the pupils' top-of-the-year enthusiasm. And it was always so good to see Eve after the long holiday, mused Gail, who (as her mother often, and correctly, observed) spent more time alone with Harry than was probably good for either of them.

After moving into the house in April, Gail had spent the summer transforming it from a home fit for septuagenarians into something just right for a single mother very much on the 'right' side of forty-five. She was quietly rather proud of the result – a space into which she and Harry could expand indefinitely, or at least until he upped sticks.

In the meantime, however, Gail's home was the frontline of defence against the chaos of life outside. When she had read in a women's glossy about David Beckham's penchant for neatly lining up the cans of Coke in his fridge so that the logos faced the front, Gail had wryly noted her own ongoing battle against incipient domestic meltdown.

For example, after cooking and washing up for herself and Harry, she would never allow herself to sit down with her favoured Sauvignon and watch TV until she had made sure that every single jar lid in the kitchen was screwed on sufficiently tightly, that no stray cereal packets had somehow insinuated themselves on to a shelf in the larder (on entering the house, all cereals and grains, from brown rice to Cheerios, were immediately decanted into labelled Kilner jars), that every ice-cube tray in the freezer was full . . . *even in January*, and that both loos not only contained a plush cushiony roll but that its end was folded into a tidy point, as in posh hotels.

Gail knew that this was an exhausting, even potentially debilitating, way to live, not to mention pretty tough on Harry, who was as averse to tidiness as any ten-year-old boy. It is, thought Gail, very much to Harry's credit he's respectful of my domestic agenda. But then we only children often are . . . She explained to the therapist she had started seeing a few months ago: 'I never drink to excess. I have never smoked or taken a drug in my life. I'm just a perfectly ordinary middle-aged woman who is rather keen on cleanliness and tidiness. That's not going to kill anybody, is it?'

The therapist's response had been a shrugged and smiling, 'No, of course it isn't.'

Gail had nodded and smiled, gratefully. 'Look, I know that *you* know why I'm like this. And I know it's because I'm busy trying to control the things I can control, having been made to feel out of control by the things I clearly *can't* – I see that.' The therapist nodded her assent. 'But where's the harm if it keeps me on the straight and narrow?'

'No harm at all,' said the therapist. 'None whatsoever,' she reiterated. 'So, how is Harry?'

Gail said that Harry was 'absolutely fine, thanks.'

Which, of course, he was.

'Hi, Hazza,' said Gail to the back of her son's head as he negotiated his way around *Fifa 2010*.

'Hi, Mum.'

'Good day?'

'Yeah. You?'

'Aw!' She felt a tiny stab – a pinprick, really – of maternal love for his touching ability to, just occasionally, think of people other than himself. 'Yes, fine, thanks, love. So, what do you make of your new head teacher?'

Harry shrugged. 'Dunno. OK, I guess. Didn't really see him much today.'

Gail was, parentally, professionally and personally, very interested in Eastdene Community Primary School's new head teacher, Mr Browning. Indeed, such was Mr Browning's reputation in educational circles that she and Eve had been discussing him only that afternoon:

'And how is Mike Browning settling in at Eastdene?'

'Well, you only have to Google his name to know that he's a fan of big changes, but as far as I can tell he left London precisely because he didn't want that kind of pressure again. Didn't ever want to wake up – and I'm quoting him here – "to find myself being discussed on the *Today* programme or invited to defend myself on *Channel 4 News* and *Newsnight*".'

'Yes, that must have been onerous.' Eve raised an eyebrow.

Just like every other Eastdene parent, as soon as Gail had learned that their new head was going to be the infamous/fabulous (depending on one's political stance) Mike Browning, she had burned up her search engines finding out more about the man who, the previous year, had been effectively 'outed' by a newspaper as Britain's highest-paid primary school teacher, earning an annual salary 'more than £50K higher than the Prime Minister's'.

Mike Browning had thus gone from being a hardworking head teacher known only in education circles, highly respected for his ability to turn around schools in special measures, to the media's whipping boy. A year later, when he pitched up in Eastdene, the media storm may have subsided but, like every other Eastdene Community Primary School parent, Gail had pored over any scrap of information to be found on Mr Browning. How, for example (and this, from the *Courier*, when Browning had still been in London), 'grateful parent, Mrs Anita Mukherjee, said, "every parent and child at the school loves Mr Browning. He treats the children as individuals and the staff with the respect they deserve. And yes, he deserves his pay cheque because he works so hard and inspires so many."'

'Christ, we'll want to watch out,' Dave Donald, landlord of the Bell, school governor and father of three Eastdene Community School pupils, had said to Gail as he'd pulled her first half of a lager and lime of the summer. 'Mr Chips is going to be running the Dead Poets Society before we know it!'

Gail hoicked herself on to a bar stool. 'Yeah, Dave, but will he cut it with the PTA?'

'Apparently so,' said Dave. 'Look –' he groped under the bar and pulled out a crumpled copy of the previous week's *Courier.* '"Within a term of arriving at Highfield Road Primary School in Tower Hamlets, Mr Browning informed staff that up to twenty jobs would probably be lost in order to tackle the failing school's £150,000 debt."'

'Irony doesn't come close, really, does it?' said Gail. 'And why on earth would he want to come here when Ofsted already rate the school "Good with Outstanding Features"?'

'Had enough of all the attention, apparently,' said Dave. 'Thought that he shouldn't have become the story when the real story was the success of Highfield – so he resigned. Apparently parents turned up at the school gates in *tears* when they found out.'

'I'm not surprised,' said Gail. 'Can I have a packet of cheese and onion?'

Yet, despite all the inauspicious media coverage, when Mike had turned up to meet, greet and flesh-press in July, it had taken about fifteen minutes for everybody, including Gail and Dave, to be completely charmed. For once it seemed you really could believe what you read in the papers; Mike Browning was effortlessly likeable, self-effacing and funny. But above and beyond all of that, he was, as Gail told Eve at work the next day, 'Completely and utterly drop-dead bloody gorgeous. And apparently single.'

'In which case, if there's a sudden exodus of Ivy House pupils to Eastdene, I shall know why,' said Eve.

While Harry spent his last hour pre-homework on the Xbox, Gail got the pasta bake with the extra-creamy béchamel sauce that Harry loved into the oven. After which there was still time to pop upstairs and see that the lights were on in Mr Browning's house – something that, aside from cooking, needlepoint and consulting interior-decorating magazines for breaking news in soft-furnishing trends, was rapidly becoming Gail's favourite hobby. Although the house was a bungalow, Gail's 'study' was a small room tucked up into the eaves and overlooking the garden. Aside from always getting three bars on her broadband signal up there, Gail had a near-uninterrupted view of Mr Browning's big old Victorian house next door – and his equally big and old, not to mention verdant, garden. At some point in the future, she knew she would probably have to give up the luxury of a study-eyrie in favour of creating a small private bedroom-den for a teenage boy who would need more personal space, but not quite yet.

It really was absolutely *lovely*, thought Gail, that that big old house, which had been a bit of an eyesore until Mr Browning – *Mike!* – and his sister, who was apparently a fashionable London architect, had got their hands on it. But it was also an awful lot of house for just one man. Since Mike had moved in, in August, he had been very busy; there had been a new roof and replaced windows and some serious repointing. From Gail's upstairs office vantage point it had been like watching an episode of *Grand Designs* happening right on her doorstep. And while obviously there had been no Kevin McCloud, you couldn't have *everything* – and, anyway, Mike Browning was enough distraction.

'Mu-um.' Harry was coming upstairs. 'It's maths home-work. Can you help?' Gail appraised her son as he stood in the doorway making actual eye contact: the freckles, the upturned nose, the set of his jaw, the messy cowlick of dark wavy hair – good-looking boy, image of his dad.

'Of course I can, Haz. The thing is, though, you're prob-ably much better at it than I am. You've always been good with numbers.'

Harry shrugged. 'C'mon. Let's go. What's for dinner? And can Ryan come round after school on Friday?' Gail wanted to think of a reason to say no – Ryan was a bit wearing – but she wasn't quick enough for Harry. She sighed and shrugged. 'Brilliant! Thanks, Mum.'

4

As she arrived home and opened the front door, Eve could smell Simon's aftershave before she either saw or heard him. A nice smell, of course – unmistakeably her ex-husband. Simon glanced up, smiling, as Eve entered the kitchen and she noted the bottle of Merlot and cheerful Tesco 'seasonal bouquet' on the kitchen table and thought, not for the first time, how lucky she was to have such a thoroughly decent ex-husband. Decent, not to mention handsome . . . And looking particularly nice today because that green shirt brings out his eyes. Eve occasionally forgot why Simon was an ex-husband; nonetheless, it had been ten years now and they'd not only all moved on, they'd stayed close while they'd done it. It was quite a feat – was, in fact, one of the achievements of which Eve was most proud.

'Hello, dear! Good day at the office?' said Simon. 'Hope you don't mind but I was sort of passing so I texted the daughters to see if they were around. Thought you might appreciate this.'

'Thank you, Simon, that's very kind. In fact, you

wouldn't mind opening that right now, would you? It's been a classic first day back at school.' Eve handed Simon the corkscrew. 'Where are the daughters, anyway?'

'Number One has just gone out with Barney – I was gifted a very nice life-the-universe-and-everything-in-fifteen-minutes chat – and Number Two is upstairs, allegedly tackling homework but far more likely to be on Facebook.'

Eve sighed theatrically. 'It's a bugger to get Alice to do homework these days. GCSEs *and* bloody A levels in just eight months' time. Why didn't we leave a bigger gap between them, Simon?'

'Because we weren't planning that far ahead?' Simon shrugged. When Eve and Simon had bravely bucked the living-in-sin trend and married at twenty-six, weddings among their peers had been so unfashionable that theirs had looked like some kind of perversely groovy statement, while the possibility of having actual children was still a long way from being even a hint of a twinkle.

'No, we weren't planning much beyond Friday night, as far as I can remember. Well, at least Zoe has always been nose-to-the-grindstone under pressure. I'm not panicking about her A levels yet. But Alice!' Eve tipped her head to one side. 'Could you be a darling and have a word?'

Simon nodded. 'It's already done. I've played good cop *and* bad cop and then incentivized her with the prospect of a practically bottomless pit of Abercrombie and Whatsit at half-term if she can prove to me that she's putting in the hours. But I said I needed proof. Essays, marks, the works.'

Simon tipped too far back on his chair and locked his hands behind his head. Eve always hated it when he did that; one day she knew he'd go all the way on to the flagstones.

'You are great, thanks. And it's not that I'm not doing any whip cracking, it's just that sometimes it's better coming from you. And of course this year is shaping up to be . . . well, *interesting*, with or without bloody exams.'

Simon grinned. 'Yes, please tell me about the Sorensens – it's the real reason I'm here. In my experience, the first thing those sort of people want to do when they buy a bloody great pile full of history is to leave their own architectural mark – tricky when your pile is Grade One.'

Eve went to the freezer and extracted one of her super-sized foil-covered lasagnes, often prepped on quiet Sunday afternoons for occasions such as this. 'You'll stay? Look, it's vast; I could go into catering.' Simon nodded approvingly. 'Well, the Sorensens – that is, Stefan and Anette, to those of us who actually know them – have already built a helicopter pad, according to the *Courier*. Of course, if I discover they're thinking about a funky ha-ha or a mad modernist folly or a lovely new garage made of glass, I'll let them know you're available, shall I?'

'Thanks, Evie, though of course it will never happen. They'll probably go straight to David Chipperfield – or maybe Zaha. Wine?'

Eve liked it when Simon called her Evie; he was the only person who did and it whisked her straight back to freshers' week – which, she suddenly realized, had been very nearly . . . 'Simon! I've only just realized, it's been *thirty-five years* since we met.'

Simon started. 'Blimey, you're right. And never a dull moment either, so cheers to that.' He raised his glass of Merlot. 'Maybe, in retrospect, we could've done with a few more dull moments, eh?'

They were still laughing about Edinburgh University in the late 1970s ('You'd hand-stitched your jeans into a pair of drainpipes . . .' 'You can talk – in your shoes made of actual bricks . . .') when they heard Zoe arrive home with Barney.

As she hung Barney's lead in the hall, Zoe paused for a moment, listening to the exceptionally pleasant and slightly unexpected sounds of her mother and father laughing together. It was a good sound, the *right* sound – and it made her happy. However, being seventeen, Zoe was also old enough to appreciate that, were they still married, they'd be unlikely to be laughing together over a glass of red at six p.m. on a random Thursday. They'd probably be a lot more like her friends' parents – at least the ones that were still together – who, if they weren't sniping, were mostly just ignoring each other. For several years when she was younger, Zoe had longed for her parents to get back together – they'd split when she was seven and Alice was five – but now she knew that, even if they had, it could never have worked, and not just for the obvious reasons. They were happy being together now, her mum and dad – just not *together* together. But that was good enough.

'Hi, parents.'

Mid-anecdote, while topping up their glasses, Eve and Simon turned and smiled at their eldest daughter.

'Hello, darling! Good day? I really do wish you'd wear more clothes,' said Eve.

'Yeah. Y'know, kind of a Thursday? And I'm not, like, Scott of the Antarctic. How are the Sorensens?'

'Ha! They're fine; but, as you well know, it's not all about the Sorensens.'

'No, just most of it. Can I have a glass of that, Dad?'

Simon glanced at Eve, Eve raised an eyebrow at Zoe, Zoe hopped from foot to foot and Alice materialized in the doorway. 'If she's having one, I want one too.' A pout.

'Neither of you can have one. Not on a school night. High days, holidays and occasional long, dull Sunday lunches with the grandparents only, I'm afraid,' said Simon, surprisingly firmly.

'You're not the boss of us!' protested Alice.

'I believe I am, actually; another two and a half years for you, young lady, and the best part of a year for *Madam*. After that, for all I care, you can both mainline WKD for breakfast in your respective crack dens.'

Which prompted a noisy duet of '*Shuddup Da-ad!*'

'Can I just say –' Eve paused; everybody turned – 'I do love you lot.' Three pairs of eyes, three smiles . . . 'Simon, is

Ed lurking nearby?' wondered Eve. 'Is he hanging in the pub with a Sudoku, or something? If so, he really ought to come and help us out with this lasagne.'

Simon smiled. 'Actually, he *is* in *Le Lion Rouge*; we were going to have pie and chips and a pint. He thought you might be a bit whelmed, what with it being the first week back at school, and stuff.'

'So text him immediately and tell him to get over here right now. Don't tell me he's not *gagging* to hear about the Sorensens?'

'Of course he is. I was merely doing discreet research on Ed's behalf.' Simon reached for his phone. 'Are you sure there's enough lasagne?'

'Tell him the bloody lasagne will end up inside Barney if he doesn't come. And that Zoe will be scooping up the result of *that* in the morning.'

Zoe pulled a face. 'Gross. Get Ed over here right now *purleeese*, Dad.'

Eve started laying the table. 'Oh, and Simon, tell him to pick up another bottle on the way.'

'Ooh!' said Alice.

'No, Alice,' Eve said firmly. 'Well, OK, maybe a *sip*.' She noticed Simon's raised eyebrow.

'You're in a suspiciously good mood, Mum,' said Zoe. 'So is it, like, OK if I see Rob later?'

'Actually, would you mind very much if we just kept you chained to the dining table for the rest of the evening?' asked Simon.

Zoe looked nonplussed and shrugged. 'Whatever – but why?'

'Actually, Ed and I have some, uh, *news*. I wasn't planning to hit you with it just yet, but seeing as you're all here and in such fine and fabulous fettle, well . . .'

Eve was intrigued. 'Go on. Renewing your vows, are you? Do I need another bloody fascinator?'

Simon laughed. 'No, I think the vows are new enough and feathers aren't really your thing, are they? Let's wait until Ed's here and we'll both get you up to speed.'

Much later, in bed, at the end of a day in which the envelope of her life had been pushed into new and unanticipated directions, Eve couldn't sleep. At 11:56 p.m. she turned on her bedside light for the second time, picked up *Wolf Hall* – after three weeks she was, despite her best efforts, still only on chapter two – and managed another paragraph before giving up again. Try as she did to push them away, seasick thoughts and emotions made her head and stomach heave.

It had been a fine evening. And Eve knew she had been right to make Simon invite Ed – though not just because Ed was one of those rare, special people whose positive presence somehow set the temperature to 'warmer' in any room he graced; an enviable skill, Eve had always thought, and one Ed didn't seem to be remotely aware he possessed. Eve had often wondered if, for Ed, life was simply a series of joyous rooms in which he just happened to be present – and, if so, how wonderful it must be to live so unselfconsciously. Yes – it had been a predictable pleasure to see Ed, whom Eve had, quietly and undemonstratively, come to love almost as much as her husband loved him. This hadn't happened overnight, of course. You couldn't be a red-blooded woman *d'un certain âge* and have your husband of seventeen (mostly) happy years leave you and your children for anybody, much less another man, without some shouting, a few slammed doors and (Eve blushed to recall it now) a bit of chucked crockery, too – though, because she wasn't actually *insane*, nothing that would be missed if it were broken.

However, all the drama hadn't lasted very long because, although she and Simon had long since lost the sexual intimacy (and indeed fidelity) by which so many couples – *most*, presumably – set such store, they had also somehow never quite managed to stop being the best of friends. Thus, when the sobs and screaming matches had finally subsided, and Simon had explained to Eve yet again that he hadn't fallen in love with men per se, he'd fallen in love with somebody who happened to be a man, and that that had been in and of itself entirely disarming ... after they'd thrashed that one out, over wine, loudly at home and *sotto voce* in restaurants, Simon had somehow persuaded Eve that meeting Ed was not only a good idea, but essential. Eve had resisted for several months but eventually allowed the girls to meet him and then – because, as seven-year-old Zoe had exclaimed, 'We LOVE him! We do! You will too! You WILL!' – she took her emotional cue from her

37

daughters and met Ed, four months after Simon had moved out, on neutral territory.

She had been disarmed when Ed's first words were, 'I am so sorry, Eve – but actually I only want the bits of him that you don't need.' As Eve had burst out laughing, so Simon had looked relieved – while Ed, as it dawned on him precisely what he'd said, looked horrified and tried to backtrack speedily, to no avail.

'No, please don't say a thing – that is just *perfect*.' Eve hiccupped, laughing. 'Believe me, you are *very* welcome to all the bits I don't need!'

After this, not only were Eve and Simon able to salvage the best 'bits' of what was left, they managed to reconfigure them in an entirely different, and arguably much better, way. What *was* left, it turned out, were all the best things they'd shared since freshers' week: the uniquely Simon-and-Evie things they'd managed to build together – the successful careers, the (mostly) happy marriage – and of course their girls. So, it wasn't the past that was eating Eve as she lay in bed, it was the present, and, by extension, a future that had changed as a result of Simon and Ed's news. Or 'the totes *amazeballs* news!' as Alice had swiftly and delightedly dubbed it.

Eve replayed the moment in her head when Simon had said, 'So, the thing is, uh, Ed and I are going to *adopt*. We've been thinking about if for a while and then we started looking into it and now the process has advanced – and rather more quickly than we'd expected or we would have told you sooner, I promise – so, anyway, by mid-October we will be –' Simon had paused and locked eyes with Eve in an attempt to gauge her feelings beyond Eve's speedily assumed and very headmistressy poker face – '*parents*. Again.'

'Speak for yourself, old man,' said Ed. 'This parenting thing is a new one on me.'

Meanwhile, the girls – jaws slack, forks poised mid-air – were silent for several entire moments consecutively before simultaneously exploding.

'A BABY!' squealed Alice.

'Oh. Em. Gee-*sus*!' said Zoe. 'My dad and his husband are having a *baby*?!'

'Steady on, guys,' said Simon. 'It's not a baby. *He's* not a baby. He's a six-year-old boy and his name is Jordan – after Michael, apparently. Who is an American gentleman who played some sort of *sport*.'

Zoe rolled her eyes. 'We do actually know who Michael Jordan is. We weren't born, like, yesterday.'

'I don't know who Michael Jordan is,' said Alice, 'and I don't care.'

'That's because you are so savagely stupid. He's, like, *Air Jordans*!'

Alice ignored Zoe. '*Wow*. A little brother.'

Meanwhile, Simon ignored the nascent sibling squabble at the end of the table and looked closely at Eve, narrowing his eyes. 'Say *something*, Evie. Anything?'

Eve was in fact very keen to say something, but not just anything. And she wasn't feeling particularly 'Evie', either.

Nonetheless, she did the right thing, as she invariably tried to do. 'That is the most completely wonderful news. I am so happy for you both and for, uh, Jordan. He couldn't have two better dads in the entire world, even if he doesn't yet know it. And of course we will be delighted to find a space for him at Ivy House, too, if that's what you'd like?' At which, when Eve saw Simon's affirmative nod and expression of warmth – *love* – it was impossible not to . . . yup, here they came . . . 'And, look, now you've made me cry.'

'Right. I'm going to get that bottle from the car,' said Ed, standing up.

Clever Ed, thought Eve, who stood up at the same time as Simon. 'That's great, but if we even sniff the cork of another bottle I'm definitely calling you both a cab later. Or you can crash here? So many questions and so little time. If only it were Friday.'

Simon walked round the table, took his ex-wife in his arms and hugged her. Both were aware that the girls were watching them intently. 'You are the most magnificent ex-wife an idiot like me could ever have. Thank you.'

'Why are you thanking me? For what?' Eve buried her face into Simon's chest – the part of him, incidentally, of which she was probably most fond, physically speaking.

'For being you. We've sprung this on you on a day when you probably didn't need things sprung, but of course you wouldn't let that show.'

'Yeah, well done, Dad,' said Zoe dryly, 'it's a massively big deal to upstage the *Sorensens*.'

'Family hug?' suggested Alice, sweetly.

So they did.

But now, getting ready for bed, having long-since dispatched Simon and Ed the five miles home to Battle in a minicab, Eve's head was full of *Jordan*. Who was he? She was pleased for Simon and Ed, and the girls. But everything had been absolutely fine just as it was, really . . . and now this.

Maybe it's a sign of incipient old age – a bit of dotage slippage – that I feel so much resistance to change? Eve wondered about this while she squeezed a pipette's worth of Estée Lauder's Advanced Night Repair and massaged it gently into her neck. Though maybe life won't change much at all? Perhaps everything will be fine? It's probably just that I'm fifty-three . . .

Now, in bed, having temporarily given up on Hilary Mantel, she selected instead a thriller set inside an ant colony, which had been recommended to her by Zoe. However, Eve soon recognized, with relief, that being fifty-three – and therefore practically a grown-up – meant that life was far too short to bother reading novels about insects when she was really only interested in people. Thus, having established that she shared her daughter's taste in jeans' brands but not books, Eve decided to give Hilary Mantel another chance and eventually fell asleep close to one a.m. with a head still full of unanswered questions.

5

The following morning – a Friday – saw the first proper Ivy House autumn term assembly. Though Eve usually enjoyed assemblies, today she was very slightly on autopilot, with her head full of last night's news.

Having reluctantly given up teaching English Lit to the brightest kids in Years Seven and Eight three years previously, since when her days had become increasingly consumed by paperwork and PR, Eve felt strongly that assembly was the best opportunity to make eye contact with as many of her charges and staff as possible. As usual, this morning Eve stood at the entrance to the school theatre (thank you, Mr and Mrs Dershowitz) saying, 'Good morning,' to every pupil by name and preparing to deliver a short, punchy speech that might just raise the pulses of the cleverest kids and (one lived in hope) kick them up a gear or two. Even a head teacher responsible for Ivy House's highest ever number of scholarships to independent secondary schools couldn't, Eve knew, rest on her laurels. The irony, of course, was that the more Eve's pupils achieved, the higher the proverbial bar was raised and therefore the harder it became to jump.

Anyway, despite having half her head still stuck in last night, and without either notes or hesitations, today Eve talked warmly about effort and attainment, the unique knots of friendship that could only be tied at school; she talked about teamwork and co-operation, a bit of meta-phorical bar raising – and jumping as high as one could . . . though ideally not off 'The Mound'. This was the old Second World War air-raid shelter that had long since been attractively and expensively landscaped and fenced off, but which nonetheless, despite a great deal of woodchip and *Keep Out* signs (or, probably, because of them), remained an essential extra-curricular rite of passage for pupils in Years Three to Five. Then Eve welcomed every single new and crisply uniformed – navy with red accents – pupil individually and fixed as many of them as possible with her most headmistressy look. It was the look she'd given Simon the previous night and it was an essential part of Eve's professional, and occasionally personal, armoury.

Eve surveyed her audience. 'Now, I'm sure you are already all aware we have four school Houses here – Shakespeare, Milton, Dickens and Austen – and you will all now know to which one you belong. You will stay in your House until you leave the school and, as the name implies, it will be your school-time home from home.' Then Eve went on to explain how, for the last decade, the Houses had been nicknamed: Shakespeare was now also known as Sly,

Milton as Puff, Dickens was Gryff and Austen The Claw. Eve suspected that Harry Potter's on-screen reach was so great that even the children in Reception and Year One understood the references – or pretended they did. 'So, despite the best efforts of several consecutive Year Fives and Sixes, we have failed to provide a Sorting Hat for the first day of term, though one does now often make an appearance during Upside-Down Day – along with a few owls!' At which news some of the smaller pupils looked so excited that Eve hoped she hadn't set off a domino-effect series of impromptu lavatory breaks.

'Upside Down' was Ivy House's red-letter day, held post-exams towards the end of the summer term, during which the school was 'run' by its pupils. It culminated in a performance by the brave/foolhardy staff in which they lightly roasted each other and then spoofed various much-loved school traditions. Instigated by Eve, Upside Down was now in its ninth roaringly successful year and there was every indication it would run as long as *The Mousetrap*. Eve sometimes suspected that Upside Down could be her Ivy House legacy and, depending on whether she had had a good, bad or indifferent day at the office, the thought either delighted or slightly depressed her.

Eve always tried to be positive, had been fundamentally a glass-half-full person all her life. Yet on her emptier days it struck her that, increasingly, there was a great deal to feel uneasy about. In the past, when her girls were younger, Eve had joined in with all the more fashionable mothers making their just-the-right-side-of-dark jokes about, for example, the 'horrors' of 'endless' school holidays. By the end of the summer, indeed, it had often seemed to her as if every woman she knew was publicly bemoaning the monumental misery/boredom of it all. The intended blackly comedic refrain – these were, after all, rather privileged women whose 'eight weeks of hell' generally included at least a fortnight poolside in Provence or Tuscany – was 'the bloody kids have gone feral – can I handcuff them to the radiator without social services finding out?' In other words, it was an in-joke – inasmuch as the relentlessly consuming business of modern parenting was, Eve thought, ever really a 'joke' these days.

When Eve and Simon had one of their post-break-up 'parenting summits', they tended to want to congratulate themselves on the things they'd got right rather than berate themselves for their mistakes. 'I mean,' one would invariably say to the other, 'y'know, for the most part, the girls are fine. Well done us!' That proverbial 'fine'. However, if she and Simon were being really honest with each other, which took courage fortified by wine, they were forced to admit their daughters weren't always paragons of perfection and limitless founts of kindness and generosity, were indeed often a bit rude and somewhat lazy, prone to cheeky backchat or a Berlin-style Wall of Indifference rendered with Contempt.

Eve would sometimes catch sight of Zoe – preferably when Zoe didn't know she was being watched – and fleetingly see signs of . . . well, what? Eve knew there was a certain 'something' in her eldest daughter – a narcissism that perhaps exceeded the entirely predictable teenage vanity and self-absorption. Her own late mother would probably have described Zoe as 'a piece of work' – an expression Eve loved because it sounded like something Rosalind Russell's Hildy Johnson might have *rat-a-tatted* at Cary Grant's Walter Burns in *His Girl Friday* – a film Eve had first seen on TV on a rainy Sunday afternoon with her Edinburgh room-mate-turned-oldest-friend, Cathy, and which had instantly become one of her favourites. So, yes, Eve knew that Zoe was probably 'a piece of work', just as she knew that Alice was, somewhat mysteriously, rather lacking in brightness and occasionally overcompensated for it with a slightly cloying sweetness. Eve knew all this just as she knew there was nothing she could do about it.

In her darker moments, few and far between though they were, Eve sometimes wondered whether her career was the cause or the effect of her own failings as a parent – and whether it was also the compensation. Eve knew that the largely unspoken despair that freighted the middle classes of her generation had never troubled her parents' generation, who had apparently bred, fed and shed their offspring without suffering from any of her own generation's non-specific *parentitis*. Eve thought that kind of ignorance-is-bliss approach was to be envied.

But then Eve didn't like to dwell in the dark for too long. She was by nature a 'do-er', so she would tidy away heretical thoughts on the grounds that failure was no more of an option for her than it was for the children in her charge. Failure was fundamentally an expression of weakness, just as weakness was necessarily a failure. Onward and upward!

So this morning she stood in front of the lectern, voicing her hopes for Ivy House's pupils and felt the usual sense of something approaching pride prickling with another, less easy to define, emotion. Not quite a feeling of foreboding, precisely, but certainly a sense that all things must come to pass. However, before the 'things' could 'pass', the moment passed. Like a senior officer surveying troops, Eve watched as the children filed out of the assembly hall, line by line, and she mentally placed a tick in one of the day's many boxes.

By 9:23 a.m. she was back in her office and Gail was announcing that, 'There's head lice all over pre-prep already, apparently. Oh, and you've got a twelve forty-five today with Lula and Charlie Fox's mother – Susie-thingy? Sorry about that but she said it was urgent.' Eve listened to Gail with one ear and nodded, while inwardly steeling herself for her first meeting of the school year with her boss, Tony Salter – Ivy House's owner and self-styled Principal.

'Is *Tony-Tone* in "Da House" yet?' Eve gave it her best ironic R&B shot, waggling her fingers as air quotes.

Gail giggled. 'Yup, Jay-Z. He just got here and gave Ellie a bollocking for parking her Polo slightly too close to his new black Range Rover with tinted windows. So he has a matching "gangsta" mood.'

Eve tut-tutted. 'Be very careful, Gail, you know these walls have ears.'

Although slagging off the boss was something she and Gail greatly enjoyed, Eve knew she mustn't overstep the mark. At the end of the day – and indeed right now, here, at the beginning – Eve was Gail's boss but Tony was Eve's boss and, in the workplace game, it didn't do to move too fast around the board.

Meanwhile, her eighteen years at Ivy House had more than demonstrated to Gail that for every ladder there were at least a couple of snakes lurking in the long grass. Yet Gail still loved her job, especially as she was privy to most of the school's secrets. There was virtually nothing worth knowing that hadn't long since been gleaned by Gail on the subjects of, for example, the PE teacher who had run off with one of the school's MILFier mothers, which had been the talk of 2007. Tony had been a great deal less annoyed about losing a popular and charismatic teacher than he had been about losing MILFy's three sporty kids to nearby prep school rival, Hartsmere.

'I hear you. But, anyway, Tony says he's ready when you are, baby – apart from the "baby", obviously. I'll bring in a couple of frothy coffees, shall I?'

Eve snorted. 'You bet. Tell him I'll be there in five. And I think I might need two sugars today. By the way, I've been meaning to ask – how is Hazza enjoying being a king of the primary universe in Year Six?'

'Loves it, of course. Look –' Gail pulled out her phone

and handed it to Eve, who scrutinized a recent snap of Harry, in his football kit, flushed with success after scoring a hat-trick.

'Quite right too,' said Eve, noting the boy's broad cheeky grin and distinctive messy cowlick. 'Growing up to be a handsome lad.'

'Thanks! I'm obviously a tiny bit biased but I think he is.'

Eve handed back Gail's phone. There was a momentary silence; though professionally close, there were some things between Eve and Gail that remained undiscussed – not least the issue of Harry's parentage. When Eve had first arrived at Ivy House, Gail had recently returned from maternity leave and all that Eve really knew – or indeed needed to know, at that point – was that Gail was clearly not in a relationship with her son's father. Eve had heard some comments on the subject over the years, of course, but habitually didn't ever give much credence to office gossip. As she'd glanced at the picture on Gail's phone, she'd realized it had been a long time since she'd seen Harry in the flesh; it came as a surprise to see him so grown-up.

As she was about to knock on Tony's office door, Eve steeled herself, breathing in and exhaling deeply. Tony Salter was the price she was forced to pay for having a job she mostly loved and, though over time Eve considered that she had successfully negotiated the price of her soul upwards to counteract Tony's negative impact, a one-on-one with the Principal was often a prospect to be endured rather than relished.

'Come in, come *in*! Darling! You look marvellous! That hair is magnificent! Cracking summer, I hope?'

Tony's speech was invariably a series of articulated exclamation marks. Even if he asked the time of a casual passer-by, he'd chew the scenery like an am-dramatist in a Ray Cooney farce. He was completely exhausting – *vampiric*, as Gail had once memorably described him – and though very firmly heterosexual, he was also slightly camp. Nonetheless, Eve was brilliant with him, assuming a kind of fake cheerfulness verging on that of a CBeebies presenter.

'Lovely summer, Tony – inasmuch as we had a summer! And you? Portugal fun? New motor too, I hear!'

'You know I live for summer, darling. A month on the golf course thrashing pensioners in the Al-*grave* –' Tony delighted in a play on words – 'equals a whole new me, fit for purpose and raring to go. And yes, *my* new satchel is a gorgeous new motor, but my parking space isn't big enough. I'll get Gail to sort it. So!' Tony leaned back into his Eames chair, locked his fingers behind his head and stuck his very large feet on the pristine blonde wood of his stylish 1950s desk; he may have come slightly late to mid-century modern design, but when he finally arrived Tony had embraced the concept with all the obsessive-compulsive enthusiasm of a Year Four pupil collecting Match Attax cards. Unfortunately, Eve was not in a position to confiscate any of it. 'So! Well bloody *done* with the Sorensens, darling! Gold star to the Principal's pet.'

Eve shrugged. 'I like to think we're at the stage where the school does its own selling, but thanks.'

'Nonetheless, you are – as we both know – a marvellous saleswoman. Double glazing's loss was our gain.' Tony leaned forward. 'Are they absolutely horrendous?'

'Far from it – they're charming and there's probably nothing they don't know about . . . er –' Eve clutched at names – 'Arne Jacobsen?'

'*Yes!* Make sure they come to the Principal's A-list Christmas drinks, there's a doll. Or at least make the hot one come –' a beat – 'as it were.'

Eve raised an eyebrow. 'I take it you're talking about Mrs Sorensen?'

'Obviously – I'm not a fag!' Tony paused. 'No offence intended, obviously.'

'None taken.' Eve made it a point of principle not to take offence at the Principal, what with the Principal often making offensiveness his raison d'être. Her predecessor, in his first headship, had been far more thin-skinned, conceivably more principled and had lasted precisely two terms simply because he hadn't known how to play the boss. Eve, on the other hand – Kent born-and-bred and grammar school educated – had been acting head in her previous job at a small Kent prep school, Wealden Girls', the owner of which, in his intrepid and single-minded pursuit of absolute and total intransigence, made Tony Salter look infinitely reasonable. This had turned out to be very good preparation for the Ivy House headship. Eve had been perfectly satisfied when, within a year of her departure, Wealden Girls had shut up shop.

'So, I'll hit you with a quick need-to-know on the bottom line, darling.'

'I can barely wait. Fire away!'

'Look, don't panic, we're not completely up shit creek, but we *are* strolling towards the pontoon with a G&T in our hands while admiring the sun setting over the turds.'

'Beautiful picture you're painting there, Tony.'

'So I'm bunging up the fees in January.'

Eve looked slightly startled. 'But—'

'Please don't "but" me – needs must. I held off in July on your say-so, but if we hit them with an increase in January we're unlikely to lose too many because the old parental guilt shtick will kick in and they'll start bulk buying Rollover Lucky Dips, or whatever. And as for those who do offer the statutory two terms' notice, well –' Tony paused and rocked backwards in his chair, entirely relaxed – 'we'll have a brand new shiny Ofsted "Outstanding" soon enough, won't we, darling? So after that we can market hard? And when I say hard, I mean *bloody* hard.'

Eve shook her head. 'But—'

'No, hear me out. I'll be doing quite a bit of travelling between now and Chrimble – Moscow, Hong Kong, Beijing, that sort of thing. We need all of them onside, especially since we'll be offering the boarding option from Year Three next September.'

Eve considered her half-formed response, thought better of it and said, instead, 'OK, Tony. It's your call. And of course I do see the need for more overseas pupils. I've been reading lots of stuff and talking to people over the summer and it's clearly the only way to go, long term, because numbers are down and dropping – I *know* that. But I still don't think we should put the fees up too dramatically this year.' Eve knew that if they did put up the fees they'd immediately lose the borderlines, especially the recent redundancies eking out their pay-offs, while any potential new locals – the farming set, particularly – would head for Hartsmere. She told Tony this.

'Bloody *Hartsmere* is crap!' Tony pronounced it with the emphasis on *smear*.

Eve nodded. 'I wouldn't disagree with you but they also offer scholarships for showjumping and, for all I know, street dancing.' She shrugged. 'And there's no escaping that it costs an average of just under four grand a term – under three, actually, in the pre-prep. And the girls wear sort of *St Trinian's* boaters and the boys *Just William* caps, and—'

'You've lost me. What the hell have their bloody *hats* got to do with anything?'

'Actually, rather a lot, but I'll save it.'

'Whatever. Hartsmere offers scholarships for spelling the child's name correctly on the application. It really is an absolute crock.'

Eve shook her head. It was no use – Tony really couldn't see that Hartsmere offered entry-level independent education with enough of the trendy bells and whistles (and boaters) to appeal to a pushy parent's petit-bourgeois sensibilities.

'The thing is, Tony, they've nailed their market. They've just built an indoor manége and the upper school is offering a GCSE in PE with a horse-riding module. Who even knew?' Eve shrugged. 'Anyway, my Alice would *kill* to have a GCSE in *My Little Pony* Studies. Oh, and they do a lovely perfect-bound prospectus, too. *Look* –' Having arrived well armed, Eve pushed a copy of Hartsmere's latest brochure across Tony's desk. It was American-A4 sized with thick matte paper, a gatefold cover and pages of cheerful 'lifestyle' shots – lots of pillow fights and pizza nights and air punching on the rugby pitch – with very little text but *lots* of (alleged) quotes from the school's happy band of international pupils. Next to Hartsmere's glossy brochure, Ivy House's sober, accurate and frankly *academic* prospectus suddenly looked a lot like 1990.

'Christ, they've make it look like PGL!' said Tony, flicking through the brochure, eyes widening.

'Better known as *Parents Get Lost*? Precisely my point – it's basically a brilliant work of fiction, and salesmanship,' said Eve. 'Look, Tony – we're not in bloody Gloucestershire; we're in a fairly socially disadvantaged corner of Sussex and you know that for every Sorensen there are fifty mortgaged-to-the-hilt middle managers on the brink of redundo who are killing themselves to send their kids here precisely because we get the results which make it all worthwhile!' At which point Eve surprised herself by thumping Tony's sleek Scandi-woodwork with her fist. 'But for that we cost six grand more than Hartsmere. And, by the way, there are more Billingses on the roll this year than you may be aware.'

'More trailer trash?' Tony shrugged.

'God, Tony, you are appalling. The Billingses may live in a mobile home but you know as well as I do that it is so they can send Chanelle *here*. And hats off to them. It's called *wanting the best for your child*.'

'Ha! Poor kid; she'd be much better off at, I dunno –' Tony paused – 'Eastdene Primary, where nearly everybody gets dropped off in a white van. The only thing Ivy House can probably do for Chanelle Billings is ensure she goes through the rest of her life carrying a monumental chip on her shoulder engraved with the words *Lack of Entitlement – and Angry*. And of course she'll probably resent her relentlessly self-sacrificing parents, too.' At which point Tony paused. 'Is Chanelle Billings by any chance in the same year as the oldest Sorensen – the girl?'

'Aija? She is indeed. In fact, Chanelle is her new-term buddy. And I wouldn't bother slagging off Eastdene. Not now Mike Browning is the head.'

'Dene, schmeen; Browning, schmowning. Whatever. Jesus, Eve – are you conducting some sort of experiment in social engineering?'

Eve shrugged. 'Maybe, in a manner of speaking. Anyway, they're the smartest and – for what it's worth – *prettiest* girls in their year, so they'll either be best friends or hate each other on sight.'

'Be it on your own head. I'm all for shaking things up a bit but this one might just backfire.'

'Actually, I think it'll be fine. And do you know why?'

'Go on.' Tony seemed genuinely intrigued.

'Because I guarantee Jayne Billings will be the only mother who won't be hovering in the car park at four fifteen in an attempt to bag the space closest to the Sorensens' Bentley just so that she can strike up a casual conversation with Anette. And that, because of this, Jayne Billings will probably be the only Year Six mother that Anette Sorensen will actually want to speak to!'

'Brilliant, Sherlock! And then what?'

'Christ, Tony – who knows? It's hardly up to us.' Eve smiled. 'But I like the idea of it.'

'Fine. And I like the idea of increasing the fees after Christmas, so we'll be doing that.' At which point there was a knock on the door and Gail appeared with frothy coffees.

'Sorry these are a bit late. Slight crisis in Year Four.'

'Anything I need to know?' said Eve.

'No, all under control, but I got distracted from my barrister duties for a moment.'

'I think you'll find it's pronounced bar-*ista*, Gail,' said Tony, wrinkling his snub, freckled nose and raising his eyes to the heavens. 'Because you don't need a thousand years of law school to learn how to make a fucking *latte*.'

While Tony relished a little light ritual humiliation with his elevenses, Eve hated it, particularly when he belittled Gail, which he did often, but she was also impressed by how exceptionally unrattled Gail always remained. Like now, for instance.

'Ba-reee-stah. Bareeestah! *Barista!*' Gail enunciated. 'By Jove, Mr Salter, I think I've got it!' She winked at Eve. Eve grinned back. And Tony, apparently still transfixed by Hartsmere's prospectus, missed all of it.

Back in her office, Eve considered Tony's news. Despite many ideological differences, Eve and Tony usually found common ground. This had been much easier pre-recession, when each had got precisely what they wanted without very much in the way of compromise. In the early years of the new century, for example, Ofsted had pronounced Ivy House 'Outstanding'. After that, the roll was up year on year, there was a waiting list for places and Eve had been empowered to make the kind of changes she felt the school needed, turning it from a so-so prep with an intake of round pegs stuffed into round holes, who were in turn dispatched to second- and third-division independent secondary schools, into a non-selective yet academic destination for the area's smarter kids. Given that she'd also managed to keep the less able children (and their deep-pocketed parents) onside too, it was no surprise that Tony Salter had been so grateful to Eve that she'd had a substantial salary increase every year in the decade since she'd started. It was a very cosy arrangement all round.

Gail reminded Eve that she had a 12.30 with Susie Poe, Lula and Charlie's mother, which Eve in turn hoped wouldn't stray past one p.m. because she wanted to grab a lunchtime sandwich in a quiet corner with Ellie Blake. Ostensibly, this was a casual professional catch-up, though of course it would also involve finding out more about that 'crisis' referred to by Gail earlier. These days, one really couldn't be too careful – and obviously not *just* because Year Four equals Petrus Sorensen.

'Ah, hello, Ms Poe! Do come in and sit down. How *are* you?'

'Hello, Mrs Sturridge,' said the fortyish blonde with the feline eyes. 'Please call me Susie.'

'In which case, I insist on Eve. Now, I know it's very early days, but are Lula and Charlie finding their academic re-entry a bit less painful than they maybe expected?'

Susie Poe smiled thinly. 'Actually, I think they're probably just relieved to be back at school. It's been a testing summer . . .' She tailed off, shrugged and then met Eve's searching gaze head-on.

Ah . . . thought Eve as she looked properly at Susie, noticing not only that Lula and Charlie's mother had lost quite a bit of weight since, well . . . whenever it was she'd last seen her, probably Sports Day . . . but also that, for someone who was usually very well groomed, Ms Poe had a large mascara smudge under her right eye, which indicated either a very hasty application or maybe . . . God, yes, of course – stupid me! Eve knew exactly which way this conversation was headed because she had been there many times before. She also knew that the appointment would stray well past one p.m. and involve tea being fetched for them both by Gail. She was pretty sure she'd need the box of Kleenex in her desk drawer, too.

At 1:15 p.m., crumpled tissues now littering her bin, Eve stood up. 'I am *so* sorry, Susie; the last thing I want to do is hustle you out – and of course you are absolutely welcome to stay here for as long as you need – but I'm afraid I have another meeting to fit in elsewhere before the end of lunch.'

Susie hopped nervily to her feet. 'God, is that really the time? I am *so* sorry – but thank you.'

'No need to apologize or thank me.' Eve lay a hand on Susie's arm. 'In fact, I insist that you don't.'

Susie blushed. 'Sorr— God, there I go! Anyway, thanks *very* much for all your help.' She paused. 'And, um, on a totally different note, is it true that the *Sorensens'* kids have just started here? Only, I'd heard a bit of muttering and Lula tells me there's a new girl in her year?'

Of course, thought Eve, you're a journalist. 'Yes, charming couple, delightful children, and yes, Lula's quite right – Aija Sorensen is in her year, though not in her class. In fact, there are two new additions to Year Six, the other being Noah Peck.'

'OK – I'm afraid boys tend to be slower to make it on to Lula's radar.'

'Well, you probably have a year or two's grace in that respect – three, if you're exceptionally lucky. And I speak as a mother of teenage daughters.' Eve offered a hand. 'Have a good weekend, Susie. And don't worry about the children. However, if you *do*, please don't hesitate to pick up the phone.'

As Eve shut the door behind Susie, she decided that *Please do not hesitate to pick up the phone* would probably be inscribed on her headstone – or, more likely, scribbled in red Sharpie on the lid of her cardboard eco-coffin. But before *that* eventuality, it was time to find out about whatever it was that was going on in Year Four. Ringworm, probably, mused Eve. Or threadworms. She grimaced; it was impossible to imagine a Sorensen harbouring a threadworm.

6

Gail was sprinkling chocolate on to the top of a frothy coffee in the staffroom when, to her surprise, Eve sidled up, reached over her shoulder for a digestive and said, 'So how's Harry's new head teacher getting on, then?'

Gail smiled. 'Mike Browning is definitely a hit. Quite aside from being an awesome head teacher –' she noted Eve's slightly raised eyebrow – 'he's a handsome, charming, middle-aged bloke who is not only good with kids but apparently genuinely likes the little blighters.' Eve laughed. 'I know – I don't get it, either.'

'And have you met Mrs Browning?'

'There is no Mrs Browning. I suppose there might be one missing-in-action somewhere, but . . .' Gail shrugged.

'Bloody hell – he must be fighting off Eastdene's mums with a stick. Or maybe he's gay? Either way, judging by the pictures I've seen, he looks like George Clooney's younger, better-looking brother.'

'No, he doesn't. He looks like a George Clooney *lookalike*.'

'Well, roughly ninety-nine point nine-nine-recurring per cent of womenfolk would probably settle for that.' Eve paused. 'But seriously, I should probably know the Blairite poster boy Mike Browning much better than I do – if only as a fellow local *educationalist*.'

'He's not only a "superhead" –' Gail wiggled her fingers as air quotes – 'he *has* a super head.'

'Ha!' Eve laughed. 'Though I do wonder why he's at Eastdene. It's already Ofsted "Good with Outstanding Features" and I'm pretty sure rural primaries aren't paying superhead salaries. What is the going rate for a superhead, anyway? Perhaps we ought to get one?'

'I have no idea. But I can tell you – and it has to be true because I read it in the *Courier* – that he earned two hundred and seventy-something thousand pounds one year. And that's more than the head at Eton, apparently.'

Eve glanced at Gail, shaking her head. 'Two hundred and seventy-something thousand quid? I am clearly in the wrong job!'

'Well, I suspect he's probably worth it,' said Gail, adding quickly, 'Not that you're not, of course! Right, I'd better crack on.' And she was halfway to the door when the penny finally dropped. She turned around. 'Ah, Eve? I'm on the Eastdene PTA. Do you want me to ask Mr Browning if he'd like to meet up, informally *and* educationally – and down the Bell?'

Eve smiled, glanced quickly and theatrically around the

empty staffroom and, nodding, said, 'I would, actually, Gail – if you can arrange it. But *shush*! These walls have *ears*.'

Gail grinned. Obviously Eve was joking, though sometimes it was hard to tell.

7

When it came to communication with parents, Eve knew she was the yin to Tony's yang, the metaphorical cheery chintz to his chilly minimalism. She was good at everything he wasn't, including *people* – while Tony's skillset lay more behind the scenes in a string-pulling, Wizard of Oz sort of role.

However, there were a few annual occasions from which Eve could not keep him away, and during which Tony liked to make it quite clear that he was the boss. One was Sports Day, where he made himself useful by pinning blue ribbons on to polo shirts. Another was Upside-Down Day, during which he liked to 'send myself up' by cross-dressing as – in so far as anyone could tell – Alastair Sim's headmistress from the old *St Trinian's* film. On Speech Day, Salter enjoyed presenting the trophy to the year's winning House, and at Christmas he liked to host a pleasantly forgettable – to the guests, if not Tony – drinks party. Originally this had been conceived as a party for all the school's parents; however, over the years, two separate parties had evolved after Tony had initiated an intimate A-list soirée for those parents whom he perceived to be far too bloody important/rich/posh/all of the above to have to mingle with, for example, the *Billingses*.

As far as Eve was concerned, every child at Ivy House was treated equally, but, when it came to Tony, some of their parents were considered just that bit more equal than others. Eve had noted on numerous occasions that Tony was perfectly happy to take the Billingses' cash – and they did sometimes pay fees in cash, for which they received a ten-per-cent discount (and the fewer questions asked about *that*, the better, frankly). However, accepting that cash did not, in Tony's eyes, equate to any kind of endorsement of the Billingses' lifestyle choices, social mores or, more specifically, what he described as their 'trailer'. Unlike Tony, Eve had actually once been to the Billingses' 'trailer', for Christmas drinks. It was in fact a very high-end log-cabin-style 'park home' with three bedrooms, an en-suite, an attractive cedar-clad exterior and gorgeous rural views, especially from the hot tub on the deck. Not only had Eve considered it to be about as far from 'trashy' as a prefabricated home could be – not a burning tyre in sight – it was also, rather ironically, positively Scandi-chic. However, Eve knew that Tony would never discover this for himself because he was a screaming snob. Given this, the fact that Tony's own front doorstep featured a pair of anodized zinc pots with dwarf bay trees, just like the Billingses', had made Eve smile.

So, on the eve of half-term, Tony summoned her to his office to discuss (she thought) this year's A-list parents' Christmas drinks party – which, due to the A-list parents' relentlessly hectic social schedules, had, over the years, slipped back in the calendar from its original mid-December spot to its current position in November. Now apparently Tony was thinking of rebranding it, losing the Christmas bias, and bringing in fireworks, mulled wine and hot dogs on the lawn. Big wow, thought Eve as she knocked on Tony's door and entered without waiting for a response. Silence. Tony was lying at full stretch, shoeless, on one of the sofas, reading matter perched on his comfortable stomach.

'Right. I'll sit, shall I?' Eve didn't wait for an answer but took her place on the slightly-too-hard sofa perpendicular to Tony's.

'So anyway,' said Tony, as though they were already in mid-conversation, 'we'll be slipping a little letter in with the, uh, *glowing* reports at the end of this term, and I'm entirely optimistic that that is the very best thing to do. In future, I'll make sure we won't be forced to rely on our local parents. After Christmas, I'm straight off to meet with –' Tony waved a sheaf of papers – '*this* lot.'

'Who are . . . ?' Eve leaned forward and peered. Nothing doing – having expected to discuss firework-display budgets, she'd left her reading specs on her desk.

'InterEduSol: "Innovative marketing and internationalization strategies for global education providers".' Tony hauled himself up to a sitting position and started to read:

' "In a world of constant change and challenges, how can you ensure your academic institution triumphs over competition and quality concerns? How willing are you to accept that expanding into overseas markets, commerce and convergence are essential for those twenty-first century global education providers intent on succeeding – and prospering – in the future?" '

'Oh, God. What does any of that actually *mean*?'

'Who gives a shit? This is the future and I can tell you that intensive undercover research reveals our good friends over at –' Tony paused, wrinkled his nose – 'Hartsmere, are fully-paid-up members of the InterEduSol –' Tony wiggled his fingers, air-quote style – ' "community". So, anyway, as I was saying – "InterEduSol is a B2B consultancy with more than twenty years' experience in bringing schools, colleges and universities together with new students, education partners, technology and fresh and exciting revenue sources from abroad. We are committed to providing international student recruitment strategies for a twenty-first century market." So there we are, darling – the future's bright, the future's—'

' "Fresh and exciting revenue sources from abroad"?'

'Exactly – pots of lovely cash from your Russian oligarchs and Far Eastern potentates who are very sensibly wishing to buy into the considerable benefits of a world-renowned British independent education. I hope you're not going to come over all sentimental, Eve? This is the future.'

'And of course, if that future's so "bright", we'd better buy into it?'

'I don't see how we can avoid it. And even if we *could*, why would we want to?'

'Because . . .' Eve paused. There was a point she very much wanted to make but she also wanted to make it in the right way, lest it be lost, unheard or simply bludgeoned by Tony's bombast. 'Because we might be punching above our weight? Here we are, a happy, successful little prep school, relatively under the radar, all things considered, and now we're having to engage with, what the hell is it again? Twenty-first century international student recruitment strategies?' Eve sighed. 'You're making me feel really old, and I'm not ready to feel old just yet.'

'You're not old, darling – you're just grown-up. Totally different thing.'

Eve shrugged. From where she was sitting, which was quite literally on the edge of a very uncomfortable sofa, it was hard to tell the difference. 'The world is changing, Tony – and that's not necessarily a bad thing. It's just the *speed*.'

'Leave the speed stuff to me, darling – I'm built for it.' Tony stood up, stretched, ran his fingers through his hair, making it stand up straight like a fifties rocker's DA, and started throwing fake punches, shadow-boxing an invisible opponent. He looked utterly absurd, though in his own mind presumably he was floating like a butterfly, stinging like a bee. Not for the first time, Eve marvelled at

Tony Salter's complete lack of self-consciousness – with all that that implied.

'Fucking –' *puff* – 'Hartsmere –' upper cut, jab, *puff* – 'bunch of –' *puff-puff—*

'Yeah, you take 'em down for us,' Eve interrupted. 'Meanwhile, I'm going to drink coffee and eat stollen and fine-tooth-comb a few reports, if that's OK?'

Shutting Tony's office door quietly behind her, Eve didn't wait to find out because her head was already halfway out of the building; twenty-first century international student recruitment strategies could wait. She was looking forward to a half-term working mostly from home and, more importantly, catching up with the girls. She was a mile from home before she remembered she'd had an informal meeting booked in with Ellie Blake, who had wanted to talk to her about Jordan. Damn and blast and bugger . . . How could I forget *that*? Eve berated herself and put her foot down. She'd call Ellie from home, before the girls got back . . .

Simon and Ed had, of course, told her quite a bit about Jordan. His background wasn't, to all intents, horrifically tabloid-headline-grabbing, but it was clearly confused in a contemporary sort of way. There were lots of siblings and half-siblings and step-siblings and he seemed to have got lost in the middle of them all, somehow, and then there were a succession of parents, step-parents, 'uncles' and 'aunties', and his mother had had alcohol problems and a breakdown, and the children had been removed from her, for a period, and then she'd got them back and had seemed to be 'on top of it'. However, after this, Jordan had never quite fitted in, had started displaying 'behaviours', so (and Eve didn't quite know how these things worked and didn't really feel she needed to, frankly, given that her professional life was already full of other people's children) Jordan had been put up for adoption by a local authority, after which, Simon and Ed and Jordan had all found each other, miraculously.

And somehow, now that he was a pupil at Ivy House, Jordan had become her problem, too. This was a situation in which it was unfortunately hard to separate the personal from the professional. Eve felt a twinge of regret for having ever suggested that Simon and Ed send Jordan to Ivy House in the first place. And then, of course, she felt guilty for thinking that. So much guilt, so little time.

8

It was a mercifully quiet half-term. Harry was at his football club for five consecutive mornings, which allowed Gail to get on top of things domestically. Then, in the evenings, he was in bed early, properly physically exhausted. 'Run boys out like dogs. They'll be tired and you'll be happy,' her dad – one of four boys himself – had often said. It may have been an old-fashioned approach but there was no denying it worked.

So with Harry sound asleep by 8:30 p.m. Gail spent her leftover evenings home alone with her boxed sets. A crime buff, Gail had seen enough episodes of *Silent Witness* and *Wire in the Blood* to know that serial killers often created a shrine to their victims in some dank basement or claustrophobic attic lined with newspaper cuttings and pictures downloaded from the internet – in the corner of which the poor victim might often be found alive (albeit cowering, gagged and chained) by the police, in the fifty-ninth minute of the eleventh hour, especially if that victim were female – and preferably a female child that bore a passing resemblance to the young Cosette from *Les Misérables*.

Gail had occasionally wondered if these creepy 'shrine' scenes were based on fact or had originally been invented by a thriller writer, after which the idea had caught on among *actual* serial killers so that eventually the whole elaborate construct had become a kind of media invention that had eaten itself. Gail was extremely interested in this kind of thing – though not in any particularly sinister way, much less as a thriller-writer *manqué*. No, Gail was interested because, at some point in the future, when Harry was older, she secretly hoped to do a degree in criminology, maybe even forensics. However, she had also read that these courses now attracted large numbers of students, presumably also lured by consuming boxed sets of *CSI*. Not that Gail believed you could ever consume too many boxed sets of *CSI*.

In the meantime, Gail honed her super-methodical, neat-freak approach to all aspects of her own and Harry's life by resisting the urge to turn her attic office space into a kind of shrine to forensics and criminology, mostly on the grounds that to do so would make her look bonkers. In fact, she had veered so far in the opposite direction that the effect was maybe even more sinister . . . After all, what could be scarier than your classic scary cinematic cliché? Answer: its antithesis.

When surfing YouTube in order to discover yet more nerdy gamer-boys who narrated their way through their *Minecraft*ings, Harry preferred to use their shared laptop downstairs in the kitchen or (much to Gail's irritation) on the coffee table in front of the telly. However, occasionally he'd venture into her eyrie, pull a face and say, 'I don't like your office, Mum – there's nothing in it.'

It was true – the room was a wipe-clean magnolia-tinted shrine to blank canvases. Other than the louvre blinds, which cast a moody *CSI* sort of light, and a 1990s-looking computer table with a Sony VAIO (a member of the Walkman rather than the iPod generation and all but oblivious to fashion trends, Gail was Sony brand-loyal to the point where she would happily have bought a Sony car), there was nothing in the room to distract the eye from whatever might be the business at hand. Mind you, look out of Gail's study window and it was an entirely different story. Even in autumn one could see that Mike Browning's garden was coming on beautifully – he'd achieved that outdoor room in the garden that everybody seemed to aspire to these days, all bifolding doors and a chiminea and patio furniture that Gail felt was perfectly good enough for her lounge. Yes, it was truly a pleasure to overlook Mike's house and garden – just a shame she couldn't strike up a conversation about his work on the house without making herself look as if she was, well, if not a *stalker*, precisely, maybe somebody whom he might decide was slightly too close for comfort, twenty-four/seven. Gail felt that the only thing worse than Mike believing her to be in any way stalkery would be for Mike to move away.

However, as both an Eastdene Community Primary parent and his next-door neighbour, Gail seized upon any legitimate interactions with Mike wherever and whenever she could. For example, they often bumped into each other arriving or leaving their houses, and then Gail was an active member of the PTA, so she'd seen him during heavily chaperoned chats about the cost of replacing the woodchip near the monkey bars with some of that hardwearing foam. Then she'd very nearly engineered a casual collision at the pub when she'd seen Mike leave his house on a Sunday at 12:45 p.m., swiftly and inaccurately interpreting this as a stroll-to-the-pub-for-a-pie-and-a-pint manoeuvre. Harry was out, so Gail had hastily gathered her own belongings and emerged from her front door just in time to see Mike's back moving away from her in what was, even if you chose the scenic route, unequivocally the opposite direction to the pub.

Eventually, however, it was less a case of Gail's persistence paying off as it was the law of local averages coming into play when Gail bumped into Mike, not in Eastdene, but, of all places, in the wine aisle in their nearest Sainsbury's on a Saturday morning. Gail laughed when she spotted they'd both chosen the same white wine – on a very good offer so not exactly the coincidence to end all coincidences – and then again, a few minutes later and largely, it must be said, engineered by Gail, when they found themselves in the same checkout queue.

'Ah, hello, *neighbour*!' said Mike. Firstly, it was all professional business ('So, is it best for the PTA to spend on foam or save on woodchip?') and then, much to Gail's astonishment, he'd suggested a cuppa in the supermarket's café.

'So,' said Mike, stirring his latte, 'I'm very glad I moved to Eastdene. Proper community and a proper community school.'

'Are you a Londoner?' Gail enquired politely.

'No, born in the Midlands – Walsall, to be specific. But I left at eighteen and, apart from flying visits to see Mum, I've never really looked back.'

'You don't have a Midlands accent.'

'According to friends, it does occasionally emerge after a drink or two, though happily not –' Mike glanced down at his latte – 'after a coffee. Are you local, Gail?'

'Yes, very local.' She glanced at Mike, and then could feel a blush rising so she stared at her tea. 'I couldn't really envisage being anywhere else.'

'You work at Ivy House, right?'

Gail nodded. The last thing she wanted to do was talk about work. 'Yes, I'm the head's PA. Been at Ivy House eighteen years now. Unbelievable, really.'

'I bet you're a great PA. Sadly, my budget will never run to one.' Gail wondered if this meant that, if he had a budget, he'd be asking her to be his PA. And then she swiftly dismissed this as overthinking. Mike, necessarily oblivious, carried on. 'Seeing as you've been in and around it for so long, did you never think about maybe teaching?'

Gail started, surprised. 'Well, er, yes – I *am* actually qualified.' She could feel herself stumbling, 'I was a teacher for my first seven years at Ivy House.'

'OK. So . . . ?'

Gail rushed to fill the gap. She had her reasons but she wasn't going to share them with him. Or anyone else, for that matter. 'I, uh, decided it wasn't really for me.' This seemed a bit vague, so she elaborated. 'I felt that my skills lay, um, elsewhere. So I was lucky to be able to make that change while staying at Ivy House.'

'Teaching's loss, clearly!' Mike smiled and got to his feet. 'Right, I have a lawn to mow. It was nice bumping into you, Gail. Have a great weekend.'

'Yes, yes, you too. I will, thanks!' She watched approvingly as Mike tidied the contents of his tray into a rubbish bin. And then she remembered what she needed to do and hopped to her feet in order to catch him. 'Mike?'

He turned around. 'Yes?'

'I wonder if you'd be interested in meeting my boss, Eve Sturridge? She mentioned you the other day, just before half-term, and as fellow –' Gail made air quotes with her fingers – '"local educationalists" she thought that you should probably get together sometime, so I said I'd ask you if I got a chance. We were thinking about an academic summit in the Bell?'

Mike smiled. 'Why not? Yes, that would be fun. My evening schedule is bound to be less hectic than Mrs Sturridge's, so why don't we let her choose? Take my number and text me.' As Gail rummaged in her bag for her phone, Mike said, 'And thanks, Gail.'

9

In the event, the A-list parents' drinks party fell on a random Tuesday in mid-November, plans to 'rebrand' it having been put on hold until next year. What with December being a non-starter for the alpha crowd, for whom it was chock-full of charity fundraisers, big corporate seasonal bashes and the occasional intimate soirée in New York with their best friends from the World Economic Forum meeting in Davos, the mid-November date effectively chose itself.

Ivy House's parental heavy-hitters numbered about twenty couples, from the super-rich Sorensens to the relatively impoverished local landed gentry, the Percys, generations of whom had been prep-schooled through various Ivy House incarnations, mostly because their farm adjoined the school. Just like their forebears, the current crop of small Percys – four of them, aged between three and eleven – arrived each morning via a stile on the far side of the coppice.

While she contemplated the guests milling around

chatting politely to one another, Eve noted that the drinks party attracted mostly the A-list wives, their husbands presumably busy mastering the universe elsewhere. Mrs – *Dr* – Anna Dershowitz was, Eve recognized (not for the first time) properly *classy*: mid-forties, sharply featured and elegantly elongated, she was wearing a barely there, yet also intriguingly demure, black cocktail dress with some sort of clever draping around the neck and sleeves and the kind of complicated and painfully architectural-looking shoes that Eve understood aesthetically if not practically ('She's wearing *hooves!*' Gail hissed at Eve as she passed by with the canapés. 'No,' Eve replied, 'she's wearing McQueen').

In short, Anna Dershowitz was both daunting and exciting in pretty much equal measures; ferociously clever and famously witty, she was your classic power-behind-the-throne Alpha Wife: an ex-academic with a laser-guided missile of a brain that, Eve knew, habitually turned the Tony Salters of the world into microwaved Ready Brek. On the outside, however, Eve noted that, even if microwaved, Tony usually managed to behave quite normally in her company, greeting Anna warmly and in a manner that was entirely seemly and appropriate. In recent years the Dershowitzes had contributed a considerable percentage of the school's excellent facilities, but now, sadly, with the youngest remaining Dershowitz a third of the way through Year Eight, all good Dershowitz-related things were coming to an end. Nonetheless, Salter and the Dershowitzes had been on first-names terms for the best part of a decade. On the edge of the group, Eve watched their interaction, intrigued by the juxtaposition.

'Delighted you could make it, Anna,' said Tony, leaning forward for the obligatory brush of cheekbones.

'Delighted to be here, Tony. It was rather touch-and-go whether either Mr D or I would be able to come, but in the event he drew the short straw and went to the J. P. Morgan do, while I've joined forces with Anette, here – which is, of course, so much more fun.'

Eve watched Tony turn to Anette Sorensen, whom he was meeting for the first time. Anette was thus spared kisses and received Tony's extended hand – clammy, no doubt, thought Eve. While Anna D was scary-chic, Eve supposed that, to Tony, Anette Sorensen was as scary-sexy as photographic evidence always suggested. And she smelled divine. 'A great pleasure to meet you, Mrs Sorensen,' said Tony, just this side of unctuous. 'I hear that, uh, Ai-jaa and Petruuus –' the exciting but unfamiliar conjunctions of vowels and consonants stuck to the roof of Tony's mouth like a claggy crumble – 'are settling in marvellously well. Obviously we're *delighted.*'

'As indeed are they.' Anette Sorensen was wearing another clever cocktail-frock-and-challengingly-cantilevered-shoe combination; however, the dress was the palest dove-breast grey against her white-blonde hair, so that she and Anna looked like each other's negatives. 'They are both enjoying school very much, which is great news for their father and me. In fact, it seems we did all the worrying on their behalf!' Anette continued, apparently oblivious to Tony's goldfish expression and stunned silence.

It was her job, Eve felt, to step in and rescue things. 'We find it's very often the way: all parents are naturally concerned about how well their children will adapt to a big change – and then the children themselves invariably take it all in their stride.'

'Ah, but only if the parents have made the right choices on their behalf,' said Anna Dershowitz. 'And, as it would seem that you and Stefan have done exactly that, you can presumably relax and start to enjoy your new English country lifestyle.'

'Yes, and how are you finding our neighbourhood?' said Tony, mostly recovered by now. 'I do hope we've given you a warm welcome?'

'Very warm, thank you. Stefan is here, there and pretty much everywhere other than where we'd like him – so not very relaxing for him – but when we *do* have him, we're having such a great time together. We're all very excited about our plans for the future of the estate – we have some building to do – and very keen for the children to learn just how much work it takes to run it all.'

Building! Eve couldn't resist. 'Well, if you're planning any building, I can recommend an excellent architect. The fact that he's the father of my children is, frankly, entirely by-the-by.'

'Your husband's an *architect*?' said Anette. 'I am all ears.'

'Ex-husband – but we're on extremely good terms. Have you seen the Dershowitzes' marvellous glass tree-house? It made the cover of *ELLE Decoration* in the summer. That's Simon's. Though the majority of his buildings don't tend to be suspended twenty feet in the air.'

'You know how much I *adore* your tree-house, Anna! How stupid of me not to have made the connection that Simon Sturridge was Eve's husba— *ex*-husband!' exclaimed Anette, slapping – albeit very gently – her smooth forehead with an elegantly manicured hand.

'Obviously I'm biased, but Simon is a marvellous, imaginative modern architect – though not so imaginatively modern that his buildings actually scare you,' said Eve. 'You wouldn't cut yourself on their edges, for example. They're ... uh ...'

'Organic?'

'Well, yes, but not in a mulching-the-allotment sort of way, more of an eco-sustainable sort of way. But, even though I'm a fan, I'm not the best person to talk about Simon's work ...' Eve tailed off, conscious not only of having potentially overstepped the mark but of having evoked *allotments*. However, Anette's enthusiasm seemed entirely genuine.

'No, and of course there's no need for any of us to do Simon's PR – is there, Eve? – given he's actually terribly good at it himself,' said Anna.

'Well, I shall speak to him. And I have a particular project in mind, too,' said Anette, firmly. 'So you have children, Eve?'

Eve nodded, grateful for the shift of subject: 'Yes, two daughters – seventeen and fifteen. Simon and I regret not having left a larger gap between them because next year we shall all be coping – or otherwise – with A levels *and* GCSEs. And I for one am not looking forward to that.'

'No, I can imagine! And are the girls either budding architects or head teachers?' asked Anna Dershowitz.

'Hardly!' laughed Eve, just as she caught sight of Richard Percy wandering the room, ignored by the rest of the staff. If not as lonely as a cloud, then he was as lonely as any other florid-faced, jug-eared middle-aged man who had never entirely shaken off the prep-school nickname Dick Cock. 'Tony, um, Mr Percy seems to be all at sea . . .'

She watched Tony following her gaze and suspected he was calculating, correctly if reluctantly, that there were more young Percys than there were minor Sorensens and Dershowitzes at Ivy House, thus . . . 'Ah, now do please excuse me, ladies,' he said, peeling away.

'God, no – not architects *or* teachers!' Eve continued, 'Alice considers her GCSEs to be some sort of largely irrelevant qualification she has to fit in between dressage tests, while Zoe is doing Maths, Politics and Economics for her As and desperately wants to go into the City.' Eve shrugged. 'To do exactly what, I have no idea, but then I'm entirely baffled by finance.' At which point, Eve became very conscious of sharing this information with a couple of women who presumably weren't *remotely* baffled by finance and felt the rising heat of an uncharacteristic blush of gaucheness. Though she wasn't sure how much of a role, if any, Anette actually played in her husband's hedge fund, it was fairly safe to assume that Dr Anna Dershowitz (PhD in Economic Research from Cambridge) had more than a working knowledge of whatever it was – venture capital? – that went on at the Dershowitz & Dohenny Group. Either way, if Eve hoped the subject would be changed, she was disappointed.

'Well, if Zoe would like to have a taste of the financial life, I know we have some very sought-after work placements at Odense Holdings – and I am sure the same is true of D&DG? There is quite a bit of coffee purchasing. But then it's a very caffeinated kind of environment, isn't it, Anna?'

'And how! But yes, if Zoe's interested, do let either – or both – of us know, and we'd be delighted to put her in touch with the right people,' said Anna.

Eve felt slightly flustered by this pincer movement. Even without the possibility of a commission for Simon, this was a lot of generosity and, if there was one thing Eve hated, it was feeling beholden. It actually panicked her, the sense that she was being given gifts she could never return. 'That's incredibly kind of you both, but—'

'No buts necessary,' said Anette, surprisingly firmly. 'You're educating our children, so the very least we can do is offer a tiny bit of vocational training to one of yours.'

OK, fair enough, when you put it like that, thought Eve. 'That's enormously kind of you both and I know Zoe will be particularly thrilled. And of course I'll be delighted too because it means she'll be able to come home and tell me what a hedge fund actually does. It's a major gap in my knowledge.'

'And meanwhile my Latin is easily as bad as my French, which is pretty terrible, so we're probably all square,' smiled Anna. 'Now, if you don't mind, I'm going to whisk Anette over to see one of her neighbours.' Anna leaned forward and whispered into Eve's ear: 'Is it true that locally everybody refers to him as "Dick Cock"?'

Eve grabbed Anna's forearm to steady herself while suppressing a snort of laughter before assuming her faux-stern headmistress face. 'We have educated several generations of the Percy family at Ivy House, so I couldn't possibly comment.'

A few minutes later, Eve noticed that Mrs S and Mrs D had left, just after their brief chat with Richard Percy, which had in turn been chaperoned by Tony. Nonetheless, Eve dutifully and methodically spent another forty minutes working her way around the room, ensuring she spoke to everybody who wasn't on the Ivy House payroll, by which time there were only a couple of handfuls of parents and staff remaining. She tapped Tony on the shoulder and made her excuses, after which Gail tapped Eve on hers: 'I've ordered you balti lamb, saag aloo and a peshwari naan. Hope that's OK? It'll be ready to pick up in ten minutes. Night!'

'You are an absolute bloody *angel*, Gail,' said Eve, greatly cheered by the prospect of not having to eat a microwaved supper while standing up and, possibly, arguing with a teenager.

Twenty minutes later, at home, eating the delicious balti while – luxury of luxuries – sitting down, Eve attempted to tear her thoughts away from the first half of her evening in order to listen to her daughters competing for her attention with tediously increasing levels of whini-ness. 'Could you please both just shut up! You know I can stand almost anything but I do draw the line at *whines*. On the subject of which . . .' Eve paused and extracted the remains of a three-day-old bottle of white from the fridge. 'Right. Who wants to go first? How was your day, Alice?'

Eve sipped and sort of half listened while Alice raced through a quick précis of a Year Eleven school day, with which her mother was au fait, what with it not being wildly different to, say, a Year Ten or Twelve day, apart from the dreaded looming GCSEs.

'Any kind of prep being undertaken this week – maybe? Any chance that my delightful youngest daughter won't cover her parents and herself in ignominy?' Eve knew that not all mothers spoke to their children the way she spoke to hers; nonetheless, at her instigation, sarcasm had become a conversational keystone among the female mem-bers of the Sturridge family.

Alice nodded. 'Yup; I've done precisely ninety minutes of French and that was after I'd done an hour with Monty, too.'

Monty – or, to give him his proper name, Montague Verona – was a 15.2hh thoroughbred bay gelding bought by Simon for his horse-mad youngest daughter's thirteenth birthday and bankrolled not only by the Dershowitzes' tree-house commission but by the business accrued from its high profile and design awards. As soon as Alice had fallen for ponies, Eve had known this was not going to be a cheap hobby; however, she had been both astonished and slightly terrified by the expense – and grateful the tab was mostly being paid by Simon. On the other hand, she'd also been secretly rather impressed by Alice's horse-related work ethic: fifty per cent of Monty's livery fees were now sucked up by Alice shovelling horseshit from A to B every Saturday and three evenings a week at the yard. The impact of this fairly thankless manual labour on her daughter's GCSEs was, of course, yet to be seen.

'Great!' said Eve. 'And Zoe – have I got news for you!'

Zoe didn't look up as she replied to the *ding* of an incoming text on her phone. 'Yeah?'

'Yeah, *yeah*. So how is Rob?'

'Yeah, cool.' Zoe carried on staring at her phone. 'S'what's the news?'

'If you deign to make eye contact, I'll tell you.'

Zoe looked at her mother blankly. 'Sorry, what?'

'Thanks for joining me. So, I had a chat with two of the more high-profile mothers this evening – the fathers off being fabulously high-profile elsewhere.'

'Mrs Sorensen!' said Alice.

'*Indeed*, Mrs Sorensen,' said Eve.

'And Mrs Dershowitz?' Even Zoe was intrigued by this double whammy of high-financial glamour.

'You bet. They're big mates, anyway, of course, but you may be interested to hear that we talked about you.'

'Me?' Zoe scrunched up her (lovely, Eve noted) nose. 'Like, really *me*?'

'Yeah like, really *you*. In fact, when they heard what you're studying, they both offered you the possibility of work placements. Practically fell over each other to do it, too.'

'You are kidding me, right?'

'No; though I hope you realize how lucky you are, young lady, because an internship at either of these businesses must be extremely sought after.'

'God, *yeah*. So what do I do?' Zoe hopped from foot to foot; Eve couldn't recall the last time she had seen her daughter looking so unequivocally thrilled.

'They'll tell me who to contact and put in a good word, and then you can do the rest yourself, by email. But please make sure I see it first. After that, it's over to you.' Eve smiled at her eldest daughter, who smiled back before glancing down when her phone *ding*ed again. 'Oh, and here's a tip. No random texting during conversations in the high-powered office, yeah?'

'That's a bit like saying, "No breathing," Mum – but whatever. And thanks!'

'I meant no texting *Rob*, really. Can you even conceive of the fact that my generation went for many, many years without –' Eve wiggled a pair of air quotes with her fingers – ' "breathing". Kind of miraculous, in retrospect.'

Zoe shrugged. 'We all know your life was basically ten thousand kinds of tragic.'

As she soaked up Zoe's insouciant cheekiness, Eve briefly recalled herself at seventeen, recalled the intensity of it all via a series of mental snapshots – of being drunk on cider at parties, where something mournful by David Bowie always seemed to be playing in the background whenever the wrong boy made a lunge for her, invariably at exactly the same time as the right boy was busy lunging at her friend. It seemed – indeed was – *a long, long time ago* . . . And Eve suddenly found herself humming the rest of 'The Man Who Sold the World' as it occurred to her that, back then, no seventeen-year-old girl would ever have told her mother that her life was 'tragic', even as a joke.

'Right,' said Eve, as casually as she could manage, 'I'm off out to the Bell, for a drink – with Gail.' She felt this announcement was unusual enough to provoke a question or two from her daughters; however, there was not the slightest flicker of interest. To have her life perceived as relentlessly dull by her children was, of course, the inevitable parental lot. Eve sighed and picked up her keys.

'Bye, Mum. Have fun. Don't drink and drive,' said Zoe, glancing up from her phone.

To be perceived as dull and patronized, too . . . thought Eve, who planned to drive, anyway.

In the event, it was a very short evening – considerably shorter than either Eve or Gail had expected. Gail arrived first, and was already sitting in the corner with two glasses of Sauvignon when Eve joined her. When Mike arrived five minutes later, Gail introduced Mike to Eve and vice versa, apologizing for not buying him a drink: 'I know Eve's tipple but I would have got yours wrong, I'm sure.'

'Yes, I don't know how handy the Bell is at knocking together a margarita.' Mike held out a hand. 'Good to meet you, Eve. And thanks to Gail for bringing us together for this, uh, educational summit across the political divide.'

Gail grinned; however – and entirely unexpectedly – Eve smiled a very tight little smile and said, rather grandly, 'I wouldn't necessarily bother making any assumptions about my politics, Mr Browning.'

Mike looked surprised. 'I'm so sorry. I didn't mean to offend.'

Eve shrugged. 'The thing is, it's very easy to assume that a parochial prep school head teacher must be, at the very least, small-c conservative, if not actually large-C.' Mike raised an eyebrow as, to Gail's astonishment, Eve carried on. 'However, I think that would be both lazy and presumptuous. A bit like assuming that, for example, an inner-city superhead teacher on a whopping great salary is always going to vote for the hand that wrote the cheque.'

Eve took a sip of her Sauvignon. 'Except, of course, that he *is*.'

Mike looked suitably astonished. 'Well, *now* who's making assumptions? Goodness, that's a start to the evening I hadn't anticipated.'

Gail was crestfallen; it was so unlike Eve to be socially prickly. What on earth could be the matter? For her part, however, Eve appeared unfazed.

'So, why on earth *did* you take what must have been a huge pay cut to move to Eastdene, Mr Browning? It's hardly at the epicentre of things. I would've thought a big urban state secondary in special measures would've been more your thing?'

'It's *Mike* – please. We may not have got off to the best start but I do think we can salvage something of the evening, especially if we're on first-name terms,' said Mike Browning easily.

Gail was impressed by how hard he was trying to turn things around, though she suspected it was in vain; in her experience, whenever Eve got into one of her (admittedly rare) bad moods, it tended to take time to work itself out.

Which is exactly what came to pass. In the hope the mood would shift a little quicker in her absence, Gail excused herself to go to the loo while Mike (presumably) answered Eve's question. And though the atmosphere had been marginally less awkward by the time she returned, it was clear the evening would be truncated to some tetchy small talk over a couple of drinks. Gail was embarrassed and a little annoyed; both Eve and Mike been keen to meet each other and so, having arranged it, she resented feeling compromised. She sipped her Sauvignon and waited for Eve to offer to buy the next round, but that didn't happen. Instead, having drained her glass, Eve stood up and said in her in briskest, most head-teachery tone, 'Well, thank you, Gail, for arranging this and I'm sorry it turned out to be so brief. However, just as Margaret Thatcher wasn't for turning, turns out I'm not really one for patronizing. Good luck at Eastdene, Mr Browning.'

Gail noted that Mike shared her father's old-school decency, standing up as Eve left – even if this gallant manoeuvre was lost on Eve, whose rather swooshy coat enabled her to sweep grandly – Thatcherishly, even – out of the Bell.

Gail dived into the silence. 'I am *so* sorry, Mike. I had no idea that would happen. It's entirely unlike her. I just don't get it at all.'

Mike shrugged. 'No problem, Gail – and thanks for trying. It was rather unexpected, though, especially as I have only heard great things about, um, Mrs Sturridge. Still, everybody's entitled to an off day, not to mention a difference of opinion. Now, can I get you another glass of wine?'

Gail nodded. 'I think I need one, thank you. And please can we steer clear of politics?' Mike had the good grace to laugh. They had quite a pleasant chat after that, albeit mostly about the PTA, which had in turn allowed for a little local gossip, too. They were both home in time for *News at Ten*.

By which time, back at the Barn, Eve was already in bed with *Wolf Hall* and a glass of Merlot on the bedside table, attempting to distract herself from replaying the disastrously brief events at the Bell over and over again in her head. She really had no idea why she'd taken against Mike quite so strongly and suddenly over a comment that, while ill judged, was clearly not intended to be malicious. All Eve knew was that she hadn't felt this strongly, negatively or positively, about anybody for . . . well, *ages*. I'll apologize to Gail first thing, she thought. No, hang on . . . Eve reached for her phone and tapped out a text.

> G. So sorry about tonight – really. For some reason
> Mr B pushed buttons I didn't even know were pushable.
> My pet hate (one of!) is people who drag politics into
> conversations before you've even made eye contact.
> Another is people who make sweeping assumptions
> based on . . . nothing! But I concede I could have been
> more polite. Not least for your sake. And yes, he's very
> handsome – but sometimes that's not enough! Night. E x

Eve made a note to buy Gail one of the posher supermarket bouquets on the way to work; she knew she owed her wingwoman rather more than this. However, flowers would have to do as a gesture, for now.

One more chapter . . . one more . . . Yet Eve fell asleep while her bedside light was still on and *Wolf Hall* still in her hand. It slipped to the floor as her phone beeped with Gail's reply:

It's FINE, E! Sleep well! G x

10

Eve's lack of enthusiasm for all things Yule-related did not extend as far as Ivy House. You couldn't, she had long since reasoned, be the headmistress of a school with 'Ivy' in its name and not embrace a few seasonal traditions. Somewhere back in the mists of recorded time the lyrics to 'The Holly and The Ivy' had, for example, been reimagined ('Of all the trees that are in the wood, the *ivy* bears the crown . . .').

There was the Nativity, too, of course, and, though visually he was a shoo-in for the angel Gabriel, this year's performance starred Petrus Sorensen as the least Semitic-looking Joseph in the school's history – a casting decision made on talent alone and one that bore very little relation to the Sorensen family's generous gift to the school of a thirty-foot Norwegian spruce. On a thrilling morning in early December, this magnificent tree had been delivered to Ivy House's front door by Denmark's leading Christmas-tree supplier, then craned into position in the middle of the school drive's turning circle, where it sat proudly in its own specially designed super-tub, festooned with lights that Anette had been invited to turn on during a spontaneously arranged late afternoon event.

Until this point, Eve hadn't known that Denmark was the world's largest exporter of Christmas trees – though, other than (presumably) the people of Denmark, who did? However, as soon as Anette had informed her of this fact, Eve had been inspired to write a special assembly on the subject of Christmas trees and their history and provenance, after which every child in the school – and by extension their families – knew *all* about the marvellous work of Pedersen Inc, which grew and distributed 30,000 Christmas trees annually, and in which it turned out Stefan Sorensen was a majority shareholder. As Gail commented to Eve in a whispered aside during the switch-on event, 'This makes Stefan Sorensen the closest thing we'll ever get to a real Santa – albeit a very buff, beard-free, gym-bunny Santa.'

'Gail! *Shush!*' said Eve.

'I shall. But doesn't Anette make a beautiful Santa's Little Helper?'

Eve took in the sight of a smiling Anette Sorensen, resplendent for the occasion in a mink-collared white coat with matching Russian *ushanka*. 'Yup, she does. Now, be quiet, Gail. I *mean* it.'

Gail sighed. 'Where would we be without the marvellous Sorensens?'

'Clutching a G&T at sunset on the pontoon overlooking shit creek – apparently.'

'You *what*?'

'It was something Tony said to me a few weeks ago, as a result of which our parents will be receiving a little wake-up call with their children's reports this Christmas. Fees up in January, Gail, I'm afraid.'

Gail shrugged. 'I guessed something was up, if not the fees. There have been some mutterings in the staffroom about yesterday's internal email.'

'Look, I really don't want people to misinterpret that email. Is that what's happening? You will tell me, won't you?'

'I think there's been a bit of basic *two-plus-two* stuff going on – yes. I think, if you send an email asking staff to err on the side of – what was it? – "accentuating the positives" in reports, then you're bound to get a bit of internal feedback.'

Eve looked alarmed. 'I wasn't looking to *whitewash*, Gail. I don't want staff to *lie*. I'm just looking for their words to be particularly well chosen this term – and, yes, OK, maybe contain some positive spin while they're at it. Look, if there are any genuine problems with any of the kids then they need addressing, obviously, but for the majority of children who are doing just fine then I really don't think it would hurt anybody, this term, to say that they're doing better than expected. Do you see my point?'

'Of course I do. And we are indeed fortunate to have jobs

we enjoy –' Gail broke off, raised an eyebrow and looked squarely at Eve – 'and which we would, ideally, like to *keep*.'

'Exactly that – and now it looks as though . . . Ah!' Eve broke off as Anette approached her, smiling. She noted that, backlit by the light from the twinklingly white tree, Anette's Russian hat looked like a soft furry halo. 'How absolutely stunning your – *our!* – tree looks. We really can't thank you enough, truly.'

Anette nodded (Eve couldn't help noticing) ever so slightly regally. 'Believe me, the pleasure is all ours. We have a tree delivered every year from our forest so that we have a little piece of Denmark with us wherever we are living. As we were having a tree delivered to the house anyway, it made sense. I think it's –' Anette paused, a teeny frown struggling to manifest on her taut brow – 'a BOGOF?'

Eve suppressed a giggle; if ever there was a woman who didn't do BOGOFs, it was surely Anette. 'Marvellous. Well, we're all thrilled.'

'No problem. Oh, and I've been meaning to email but this time of year is just so insane. Anyway, I have here the information for your daughter. If she's still interested, our London office manager is expecting to hear from her.' Anette handed Eve a proper old-fashioned paper business card. Eve couldn't recall when that had last happened but guessed the card had probably started life as a Sorensen tree.

'Oh, she's very interested, trust me. I know she'll be thrilled. You've been so generous, Anette – we do appreciate it.'

Another tiny queenly nod. 'Family and community are very important. Having joined your community, we are keen to play our part.'

Eve assumed Anette did actually have a sense of humour, even if she had yet to see much evidence of it. Perhaps now was the moment to find out? 'Well, in that case, your neighbours in Eastdene will expect to see you for a pint in the Bell on Boxing Day.'

There wasn't much to go on other than that brow furrow, a quizzical tilt to Anette's mink-haloed head and a slight, tight little smile. 'We should so love to do that, but we are dashing over to Denmark on Christmas Day – lunch with Stefan's mother – and then we're straight off to Vail after lunch.' Anette shrugged. 'Stefan gets to spend a little quality time with Mayor Bloomberg and the rest of us spend some with the snow. We Scandinavians need to have a lot of snow around us at Christmas and there's no guarantee we'll have any here.'

'No, far more likely to be January or February, though I suspect you could import some?' Even as the words left her mouth, Eve was conscious that she might have overstepped the mark. Generous though Anette Sorensen undoubtedly was – not to mention whip smart, stupidly beautiful and possibly even quite good fun after a glass or two of Carlsberg – she was not a friend, would *never* be a friend.

'Hm,' said Anette, narrowing her eyes and putting one finger to her lips. 'Imported snow? You may just have something there. I will *definitely* speak with Mr Sorensen.'

The intention, Eve suddenly recognized, was to be Dr Evil in *Austin Powers*, however the overall comedic effect was slightly undermined by Anette's beauty. Either way, this was the point when Eve decided she didn't just like the *idea* of Anette Sorensen, she liked the *actuality* of Anette Sorensen. And she liked her even more when Anette said, 'We'll be back here on December thirtieth and we have no plans for New Year, on purpose. Of course, something is bound to come up, but if it doesn't I am hoping to persuade Stefan to come out to the pub for a drink.'

Eve still thought Anette might be joking. 'Seriously?'

'You *bet*, seriously.' Anette leaned closer to Eve. 'Stefan and I didn't grow up around the kind of money that has quite so many noughts, you know.' At which point she put an arm round the shoulders of Aija and Petrus, who had been standing beside her, bickering with each other in Danish. 'Unlike these two. Right, off to the car, kids – Daddy will be home tonight!'

I wonder how many noughts? thought Eve as she watched three-quarters of the Sorensen family walk towards the car. Nine, probably. Which is a lot. And Mayor Bloomberg is a lot of power.

Eve had had sufficient dealings with the extremely wealthy to know that their world ran parallel to everybody else's, sharing just enough similarities to allow them occasional interactions with the civilians, however charmingly Anette Sorensen may pretend otherwise. Eve attempted to explain her new theory to Gail after assembly the following day.

'So, imagine that three empty lanes of the M25 were inhabited by a few cars that were allowed to get to their destinations as fast as they liked, while normal traffic was consigned to the hard shoulder –'

'OK.' Gail held out a frothy coffee for Eve.

'– and everybody trying to drive on the hard shoulder is sharing it with all the breakdowns waiting for the AA or the RAC or whoever, while the super-rich speed right past, apparently quite close, but actually entirely separate.'

'Uh-huh, I get it. That's *good*,' said Gail.

'Thanks. Anyway, occasionally the drivers of the fast cars in the three empty lanes glance over and wave at us, but mostly they're just oblivious. We're all heading to the same destination but our journeys are entirely different.'

'That last bit – is that an actual *philosophical* observation? At 9:23 a.m. on a busy Thursday morning in December, are you actually talking to your long-suffering assistant about *death*?'

Eve laughed. 'I might be. You can dump the death stuff if you like but I think the rest of it stands up pretty well. We're stuck on life's hard shoulder while the Sorensens and the Dershowitzes are –' she shrugged – 'whatever.'

'Hurtling down a ski slope in Colorado beside the mayor

of New York? They're welcome to *that*. On Boxing Day, I for one am looking forward to pouring a Baileys and working my way through a large tin of Quality Street in front of whatever it is I've Sky-Plussed.' Gail warmed to her theme. 'And, actually, the idea of being forced to ski among the world's powerbrokers really does make my blood run cold – and not just because I'd end up totally Sonny Bonoed on the grounds of not being able to ski. Now, drink this –' Gail pushed the mug of coffee towards Eve – 'and stop confusing me with your best friend. The food chain is, basically, me, you, Tony, followed by the Sorensens and the Dershowitzes, who I'm sure would eat the lot of us if we ever all happened to be on a plane together that crashed in the Andes.'

Eve assumed a pitying expression and tipped her head to one side. 'I really hate to think of you at the bottom of the food chain, Gail.'

'I'm not. If the worst came to the worst, I suppose I would eat the cats. On the subject of which, sort of, I'm off to the dentist today at – and frankly I can hardly believe it myself – two thirty!'

'No! Really? I'd assumed dentists' receptionists only ever booked appointments for two twenty-five, never your actual *tooth hurtee*. Please tell me your dentist is Chinese?'

'No, but he is devastatingly good-looking.' Gail grinned.

'Well, I hope you need a root canal and it takes forever.' There are, thought Eve suddenly, possibly many things I don't know about Gail.

Like the majority of schools, during the last week of the Christmas term, Ivy House abandoned any semblance of teaching and/or learning in favour of chocolate, tinsel-decorated mufti, a tangerine-flavoured Christingle carol service at Eastdene's St Mary's – Eve enjoyed its cheerful paganism – and regular deliveries of the internal Christmas-card post throughout the day. Even the cur-mudgeonly caretaker, Mr Dodd, wore a Santa hat while he raked gravel and tut-tutted about divots on the lawns, and thus all was positively ding-dong-merrily. When, in the midst of this festive, familial atmosphere, Tony 'Scrooge' Salter called a quick meeting with Eve on the penultimate day of term, to 'discuss upcoming developments', her heart sank.

Eve knocked on Tony's door and entered without wait-ing for a response. 'Nice Santa hat you've got there, Tony. Been taking style tips from Dodd?'

'Nah. Don't be fooled. In order to drown his sorrows, the Ghost of Christmas Future has just popped out to the Co-op to pick up a small bottle of gin, but he'll be back. Like the Terminator.'

'Chin up, Tony – only ten more sleeps until Christmas. I'll sit, shall I?' Eve didn't wait for an answer but took her place on the aggressively modernist leather sofa, at right angles to the one on which Tony was once again lying at full stretch, shoeless, with some reading matter perched on his proud stomach.

'Or, to put it another way, only five more sleeps till Barbados,' said Tony. 'So anyway, we'll be slipping this little letter in with the, uh, *glowing* reports tomorrow.' Eve glanced at the letter and did a double take. Fees up by a thousand pounds a term?! Dear Lord and Father of mankind, hummed Eve, forgive his foolish ways . . .

11

Two days before Christmas and Rob noted that Zoe was *very* excited. Though apparently not by Christmas.

'So, I'm going to be staying at Auntie Sonia's, which is awesome because her flat is like totally amazing, and I'll be working in Bond Street, which is basically the street containing every single shop in the world you would ever want to visit.' Zoe rolled on to her back on her bedroom floor and brought her knees up to her torso, clenching them tightly in a ball. Meanwhile, Rob, who didn't seem to be quite as thrilled by Zoe's work placement as he might be – *ought* to be, frankly – watched her very intently. He had a good poker face; it really was impossible to read.

'No. That *you* would want to visit.'

'Are you proper *jealous*, Bobby?' Zoe sat up and fixed her boyfriend of eighteen months with a look that was half stare, half pout and wholly mesmerizing. The physical effect on Rob was instantaneous; however, he would have to disguise it because this was a conversation he'd been putting off having ever since Zoe had first told him, breathlessly, about her work experience, and he knew he needed to have it now, distractions permitting.

'Jealous of *what* precisely?'

'I dunno. Me, out there alone in the Big City . . . ?' Zoe tailed off.

'Nah. It's not the *alone* bit that bothers me.' Fuck. What a giveaway.

Zoe grinned. 'Aw, babes. That's so *sweet!*' She gave Rob a semi-brisk kiss on the cheek and a business-as-usual sort of 'Love you, babes'.

Rob leaned back on a beanbag and watched Zoe for a moment or two, and then, inevitably, out came his iPhone. He tapped the camera icon, swiped to *video* and pointed the lens at his girlfriend.

Rob was in his second year at uni, studying Broadcast Media, and wanted to become a film editor, preferably Ridley Scott's film editor. In the meantime, however, he would settle for editing advertisements for discount sofa warehouses. Rob loved his course but he slightly less loved the fact that, once acquired, his skills would probably have to be deployed in London. The only upside to potentially living in the capital was the chance that Zoe may just choose to go to a London university. However, before that, she had to sit her A levels and then probably have a gap *yah* – and, before either of those things, she had to spend a fortnight hanging out in *Mayfair*, with, like, *complete tossers*.

As ever, the prospect of sustained happiness with the woman he loved seemed to Rob to be some way off. And then there was the fact that he just didn't like the idea of Zoe being in London *at all*, much less staying with her aunt for a week – even a *working* week. From what he knew of Zoe's Aunt Sonia, whom he had met just once, she was less 'auntie' and more like a cool, very much older sister, who worked in some sort of incredibly high-up position doing God-knew-what in retail and earned a fortune, was happily unmarried and child free, and apparently holidayed on a semi-professional basis, the sort with heli-skiing and horse-back African safaris. She was, Rob had noted, hot in a cougar-y kind of way – could easily pass for ten years younger in the right light. Whatever, Rob didn't like Londony life-style stuff. He felt entirely out of his depth. And yet, London was a city of opportunities, he could see that . . .

'Hurry up, Zo. Yeah?' Rob put away his phone.

'Posh coffee in the kitchen, babes,' said Zoe, applying a gunmetal grey varnish to her big toe, 'if you're bored.'

'OK,' Rob said flatly; even the poshest coffee in the world was a very poor substitute for sex with Zoe. Rob drank the coffee very fast and was halfway through a second cup when Zoe padded delicately into the kitchen, strips of loo paper separating her toes.

'They just look like someone's stamped on them,' said Rob. Zoe grinned. He was now buzzing with caffeine – caffeine and *lust*. Zoe read his expression and shook her head.

'No time, babe; *soz!*'

Rob shrugged and tipped the rest of his coffee down the sink. 'Right then, I'm off.'

Zoe was surprised. 'Already?'

'Yeah, stuff to do.'

'OK, love you, babes.' Zoe went on to her tiptoes to kiss him on the forehead.

'Yeah. You said that.' Rob noted Zoe's crinkled nose, quizzical expression. 'Love you too.' He surprised himself by how suddenly he wanted to leave. He'd had an idea. A *plan*.

'You could call it a kind of insurance policy,' he explained much later that night to his flatmate, Nev, a fellow Broadcast Media student, as they both watched Rob's phone footage of a naked – *beautifully* naked – Zoe on Rob's laptop.

'Man. That is a seriously hot girlfriend you have there. Remind me why she's with you again, yeah?'

'Because I have a lot of charm and an enormous cock?' Rob moved his cursor over the image, clicking, improving very slightly on the near perfection. No woman in her right mind ever objected to a nice bit of 'photox'.

'Uh-huh, yeah, the ginormo-dick – that'd be it.' Nev knocked back the dregs of a can of warm Stella. 'More beer?'

Rob didn't take his eyes off the screen. 'Yeah, good idea – it might be a long one. No pun intended.' And then he started humming as he watched the ancient footage of his girlfriend, filmed just a fortnight after they'd started seeing each other. All that giggly mugging by Zoe for the camera and the *panting* – did anybody other than dogs ever pant during sex? wondered Rob – was obviously porno inspired and a little too stage managed; all about performance and not much about the feeling. Nonetheless, even eighteen months after the event, he still watched the footage several times a week, sometimes alone, sometimes not. And whenever they got the chance to see it, Rob's mates – and Nev was a particular fan, now practically a Zoe connoisseur – were invariably very appreciative. Whatever – Rob *liked* the fact that his mates appreciated his girl. Her all-round glory reflected pretty well on him.

Nev grinned – 'OK, yeah, I get it!' – and he joined in on the chorus of the song: 'Don't cha wish your girlfriend was hot like me . . . ?'

12

During the last week of term at Eastdene Community Primary, when word flew round the playground that one of the teaching assistants whose remit included After-School Club had phoned in sick, Gail surprised herself by volunteering to run it. With Ivy House already broken up, her seasonal shopping completed and something approaching boredom kicking in, she suddenly quite fancied the idea of corralling thirty-odd faintly feral kids. Indeed, so relaxed did she feel that, when a trio of Year Four girls asked if they could 'do some art', she resisted the impulse to steer them towards the felt tips and not only cheerfully acquiesced but suggested they get busy with the glitter and gluesticks.

It was, then, a pleasant afternoon spent mostly designing frocks for princesses, with only minor skirmishes elsewhere: an altercation over whose turn it was to go on the PlayStation and a disagreement over the ownership of a water bottle between a pair of the more challenging Year Twos. A good bunch of kids, thought Gail with an involuntary burst of pleasure. She watched Skye Davies and Nancy Robertson, the daughters of near neighbours, whom she'd known since they were foetuses, failing to persuade Rufus King – a Year Three heart-throb ever since he'd landed a job modelling school uniforms for George at Asda – to join in. Rufus looked horrified, however, and shook his head vigorously before running outside to play keepy-uppies with Harry – who was, in turn, clearly so happy to escape being mothered in public by Gail that he could countenance hanging out with a Year Three. Gail smiled fondly at her son's retreating back. It had been a good term, mostly, and today was a good day and Christmas was round the corner. And if there was one thing Gail appreciated, it was the school holidays, when it was possible to abandon oneself, guilt free, to the lure of the boxed sets for *days* at a time.

So, by five p.m. and with only fifteen minutes of After-School Club left to run, Gail was in a good mood and had already successfully tidied away the art table and announced the countdown to the PlayStation switch-off. She went to the lavatory and took a moment in the cubicle to rub off the strings of glue that had attached themselves to the knees of her trousers. Just as she was doing this, she heard the sound of adult female voices entering the Ladies. And because she didn't feel in the mood to make small talk with other mothers, Gail decided to sit this one out, quietly, and see if she couldn't get rid of the rest of the glue while she was at it. Meanwhile, it took her a moment or two to work out how many women there were. And *who* they were – Gail was not a PTA stalwart for nothing.

The posh one was Nancy's mum, Sam, thought Gail, and the un-posh one was Jill, Skye's mum, and the one with the accent somewhere between the two was easy to identify because Gail had known Joanna King, Rufus's mum, since their first day at secondary school. Of course, thought Gail, Jill and Joanna have known each other since Reception, if not longer, and Sam is a relatively recent down-from-Londoner, so probably doesn't know either of them very well at all. And even though Nancy and Skye had just been bonding over their glittery princesses, they weren't normally particularly close, while Rufus was a boy. So, thought Gail, this is a triangle of expedience rather than intimacy. I'm not crashing anything.

And it took her another moment or two to adjust to the dynamic of a three-way conversation between people she couldn't see, and another second or two after that to realize, with an unpleasant seasick sensation in her stomach, that one of the women was in the midst of some cheerful bitching about . . . *Gail.*

'This morning, Gail said –' Joanna assumed a high-pitched, patronizingly sing-song tone – ' "So, Harry, we're going to be doing lots of hard work for our SATs over Christmas, aren't we?" You know, as *if!* God, that woman has such unrealistic expectations of a ten-year-old that I sometimes forget she's actually a mum and not a maiden aunt.'

Gail's cheeks burned. She felt both slightly sick and *very* angry, not least because what she'd actually said to Harry was, 'You've come on really well this term, so let's keep it up for the next one, because that's the SATs term, yes?' And what the hell was wrong with *that*? However, there was nothing she could do except sit very still and button her lip – bite it, even.

'Poor Gail!' It was Sam, who paused mid-sentence. 'She's quite, er . . .'

Go on, thought Gail. What sort of a 'poor Gail' am I, then? However, it appeared that Sam wasn't trying to assume an intimacy she hadn't yet earned.

'Spinsterish? Is that the word you're after?' asked Joanna. 'That's what I always think of her. A little bit Miss Jean Brodie, despite the highlights and the great legs. There's a sort of chilly primness to her. But, to be fair, that's probably just because of her, um . . .'

Now it was Joanna's turn to search for the right word. Gail hardly dared breathe; surely the women could hear her heart pounding as loudly as she could? And did 'great legs' cancel out 'spinsterish'? Gail thought that, on balance, it probably didn't.

'Circumstances?' said Jill helpfully.

'Circumstances! Exactly,' said Joanna.

'OK, so what are her "circumstances", if you don't mind me asking?' asked Sam.

'Ah, well, y'know – a terminal single mum. It's no good for the boy.'

For fuck's sake! thought Gail.

'Is Harry's dad not around, then?' said Sam.

Gail put her head in her hands, then her fist in her mouth – and bit down on it, *hard*. She felt absolutely nothing. Meanwhile, the conversation continued.

'No, he's never been around. One day Gail was just . . . y'know, six months pregnant. Harry's not only never met his dad, he doesn't even know who he is,' said Joanna.

And how the fuck do you know that, precisely? thought Gail.

'Oh dear. It might be old-fashioned of me, but I do think kids need some sort of a relationship with their same-sex parent. No sign of a stepdad, then?' Sam again.

'No, not that anyone's ever noticed. Like I say, a terminal singleton. Makes Bridget Jones look like . . .' There was some door-banging as the women emerged from their respective cubicles and reconvened by the basins. Gail held her breath. There was the sound of running water and hand-dryers, and she felt a furious, impotent tear slide unbidden down her cheek, wiped away angrily with the sleeve of her – spinsterish? – blouse.

'And I never understood why she gave up that great teaching job at Ivy House and settled for being the head's PA. I hear she was a very good teacher.' This was Jill.

Yeah, go on – try and be fair, Jill . . . thought Gail.

The loo door banged as the women departed, though Gail could hear them loud and clearly in the corridor. 'Ah, hello, Skye! There you are! Have you been playing nice with Nancy?'

Nicely, you silly bitch – not *nice*, thought Gail, who took a deep breath and counted to ten in her head before emerging from the cubicle. And only then, with an internal lurch, did she realize that she wasn't alone in the loos – Nancy's mum, Sam, was still there, loitering by the basins, inspecting her phone. Gail wanted to hide or run. Either – or both. Instead, she tried to breathe. Sam started at the sight of Gail, who was studiously avoiding eye contact as she washed her hands carefully and intently, concentrating on removing all the remaining traces of glue and glitter from beneath her nails. Gail then moved over to the hand-dryer.

'Um . . . Gail?' Sam coughed.

Gail turned around to face Sam reluctantly, willing herself to brazen it out. 'That's me, yes. What do you want?'

'I am so, *so* sorry.'

For what? wondered Gail. For being party to the things that were said? Or for seeming to endorse them by staying around? Or – most probably – just sorry because I overheard? 'Well, I really hate gossip. But, in fact, she's wrong – Harry does know his dad. He knows him really well.' Gail paused. And I should stop now . . .

Sam shook her head. 'There's no need to explain, Gail. As I say, I'm *so* sorry. It's none of my business.'

Too right, thought Gail. Too fucking right it's not. And this is the moment when I turn on my heel with my head held high.

Twenty minutes later, as she tidied up the sports hall

after the last child had left, she quietly congratulated her-self on her choice of words when she'd spoken to Sam. It was, indeed, perfectly true that Harry knew the man who was his father and had known him all his life – he just didn't know that that same man *was* his father. Harry had asked Gail who his father was on no more than half a dozen occasions – and Gail's answer had remained con-sistent each time: 'Someone who didn't want to be a father.'

13

As far as Eve was concerned, Christmas was a reminder of loss. Her mother had died on Boxing Day and, although that had been nearly twenty years ago, this remained very much her least favourite time of year. Thus, on an annual basis, Eve would rant at Gail about how the season had become a protracted, expensive and nauseatingly idealized 'lifestyle' which had surely never existed other than in the final scenes of *It's a Wonderful Life*. No, Eve didn't believe in a Hollywood – or even John Lewis TV ad – sort of Christmas any more than she believed in bloody Santa. There was a kind of co-dependent relationship between that fantasy and the 'ghastly, retro, Betty Crocker vision of domesticity which, from the beginning of November, completely takes over the media and results in *at least* nine hundred different Christmas Specials featuring every TV cook demonstrating how to baste a *fucking* turkey, as if Christmas dinner – and fucking *turkeys* – have only just been invented!'

And every year, Gail, whom Eve knew loved Christmas, would simply smile, nod and put the kettle on.

But though Eve resented Christmas's intrusion into the rest of her life, she did (secretly) enjoy dressing a tree and doing all the cooking; thus, this year, it was eight for Christmas lunch. As far as Eve was concerned, this was the perfect number; any more and she might lose track of her internal portion controller, but eight she could easily both cater for and conduct proper conversations with in-between basting duties. The guest list was pleasingly straightforward, too:

Eve

Eve's father (Edward – aka, to all members of his
 family since the mid-1990s, 'Father Ted')

Zoe

Alice

Simon

Simon's mother (Grace – aka 'Gramma Grace')

Ed (thankfully never confused with 'Father Ted' Ed)

Jordan (Simon and Ed's newly adopted son)

At seven a.m., as Eve hit the snooze button on her alarm, she contemplated the day unrolling and felt . . . comfortable, largely because any surprises her guests might spring were, she knew, likely to be comfortably familial surprises. Vaguely functioning families, such as Eve's, were, she felt, a kind of trellis through and around which each individual's story grew and merged; this was what families were for. This was why they existed. This was the *point*.

But six-year-old Jordan was an entirely different proposition: nothing to be *scared* of, exactly, but (according to Ellie Blake) he was increasingly challenging in the classroom, probably on the autistic spectrum. There was no doubt that, right here, in Eve's home, this little boy was the variable quantity in her family Christmas equation. As she lay in bed, half listening to the hiss and pop of a bedroom radiator (perhaps Simon would bleed them if I ask him very nicely . . .) the word 'interloper' settled in her brain. She pushed it away. That's unfair, thought Eve – even if it's true. And so she got up and braced herself for the day.

Seven hours later, then, it was Christmas business as usual. The house smelled good, Simon was carving the goose – Eve disliked turkey and felt that not serving one was, as hostess, entirely her prerogative – and Ed was doing useful things with the corkscrew. Meanwhile, Father Ted and Gramma Grace were joint favourite in the traditional Christmas Day deafness stakes. Having both attended the Tate Modern's exhibition earlier in the year, they were currently arguing good-naturedly about – as Zoe described it to her mother – 'whether, like, Futurism is all that'.

'And is it "all that"?' Eve asked her eldest daughter wryly, as she sieved flour into her thickening gravy over a low simmer.

'Not sure – I think the oldster jury's out.'

'And what do you think of Futurism?'

'I thought it was, like, a 1980s music thing? But then I figured Father Ted and Gramma Grace were unlikely to be talking about, like, Kraftwerk, or whatever.' Eve raised her eyes and grimaced. 'Aw, c'mon, Mum. I'll lay the table if you tell me where the crackers are. Also, Rob's coming round later, if that's OK?'

'Sure, and sure. How are you two getting on? Crackers are in the cupboard in the utility. And if they're not in that cupboard, they're in the other cupboard.'

Zoe frowned slightly. 'Dunno. OK. *Ish.* Maybe.'

'Oh dear.' Eve would have pursued this line of questioning, subtly; however . . .

'Mum?' Alice appeared, slightly breathless, by her side. 'I think Jordan may have had a, like, *accident*?'

Eve spun round, maternal buttons duly pushed. 'Where is he? What sort of accident?'

'No, not a sort of *blood* accident, Mum; a kind of –' Alice wrinkled her nose – '*bottom* accident, maybe? He's been in the loo for, like, ages.'

'Really? Well, we're about to dish up. Could you ask one of his fathers to sort it out, please? Which loo is he in, anyway?'

'Upstairs. He asked me where it was and went in about ten minutes ago – with, like, a bunch of Lego?'

'Well, he's probably just playing. Simon?' Eve turned to her ex-husband. 'Can you check on Jordan, please? He's in the loo with his Lego, apparently.'

Simon glanced up from his goose wrangling. 'Ed?'

'Sure.' Ed went into the hall. 'Jordy? Where are you, Jordan?'

'He's mad for Lego,' said Simon. 'Fine by us. You know they do architectural Lego, Evie? Ed bought me Frank Lloyd Wright's Fallingwater for Christmas, and when Jordan saw the box this morning he said, "That's *bad* Lego."' Simon shrugged. 'I see his point. It is a symphony of beige bricks.'

'But it will give you hours of pleasure! How are you doing with that goose?'

'Great. I'm pretending it's a turkey. We're nearly there. OK, everybody, *seats!*'

Ed came back downstairs, hand in hand with Jordan. Not for the first time, Eve was struck – as indeed was everybody – by the boy's beauty. He really was arrestingly lovely: long-lashed, dark brown eyes, snub nose, a slightly surprised arch to his brows and close-cropped curls with streaks and flashes of what looked like expensive blonde highlights. Extraordinarily beautiful kid, thought Eve. And she noted, too, that he had a startlingly self-contained sort of air and a kind of preternaturally knowing, almost adult, look in his eyes that spoke of . . . well, intelligence, definitely, but something – *what*? – else.

So everybody took their places around the dining table, on which a freshly dismembered goose sat, attractively accessorized by a small landslide of roasted carbohydrates. Plates were decorated with crackers and there were abundant glasses, for red wine and white and water (apple juice for Jordan), alongside several layers of cutlery and the old Sturridge family silver candlesticks with guttering beeswax candles. The lights were dimmed while the candles were lit, and everybody was *oohing* and saying, 'How *lovely* that table looks, Eve – you really have done us all proud, as usual,' and Eve remembered, just in time, to decant her gravy into the boat and wedge it in between the bowls of stuffing balls and red cabbage, just as the guests started bickering fondly about the seating arrangements.

Everyone, that is, apart from Jordan, who (everybody else noticed simultaneously) was standing, apparently rooted to the spot, shaking his head and refusing to sit in the seat reserved for him, between Simon and Ed. The more he was cajoled by Simon and Ed ('C'mon, matey, choose a knee instead!'), the less likely it looked that he would sit at all.

'No,' said Jordan, firmly, shaking his head, staring at the floor.

'Go on. We're all hungry! Aren't you?' said Alice.

'NO.' More forceful; much louder.

'OK, well, I tell you what, Jordy – we're all going to start and you can come and join us when you're ready. OK?'

'No. NO. No, no, no, NOOOOOOOOOOOOOOOOOOO! Fucking NO. Fucking FUCKING. I HATE YOU! FUCK OFF! FUCK, FUCK, FUCK, CUNT, CUNT, CUNT!'

At which, a red-faced Jordan lay down on the floor and started pounding the boards with his fists and his head, howling a primal cry of – what? Rage, apparently. Or maybe fear?

'Good Lord! Did he just say what I think he said?' said Father Ted.

'Yes, that's what he said!' said Simon, conceivably furious with both his ex-father-in-law and Jordan.

'Is it some sort of *culture shock*?'

'No, it's not bloody culture shock, for God's sake! Or at least not in the way you're defining it! Now, please, let us try to sort things out? Just carry on and start without us; we'll be back,' said Simon, as Ed hoisted a writhing Jordan into his arms and the three of them silently left the room.

So everybody else did start, albeit in stunned silence. It was Eve's job, she felt, to break the ice and, in particular, soothe the entirely baffled oldsters.

'We – that is, his class teacher, Ellie, and his dads and I – we think he might be on the autistic spectrum, somewhere. Possibly Asperger's.'

'Very rum,' said Father Ted.

'Indeed. We can help him a lot if we know what to do with him. Unfortunately, Ivy House may be the wrong school for him. We're not big on special needs.'

After a minute or two, somebody asked somebody else to pass a condiment, and then everybody tucked in and somehow a normal conversation asserted itself and, after a few minutes, Simon reappeared and sat down and, a minute or two later, Ed joined him and there was a muttered *sotto voce* conversation between them, to which nobody attempted to contribute, at which point Eve couldn't restrain herself and said, 'Look, this is all ridiculously British. Is he OK? Where is he? Will he come and sit with us or should we make him a tray to eat in front of the telly next door? Would that be more comfortable for him? It probably *is* a kind of culture shock, surely?'

Simon turned towards Eve with a wan smile. 'Actually, the tray might work. One of us will sit with him. He seems very distressed but he says he wants to be on his own. I'm not sure if he really does. It's happened a few times.' Ed shot Simon a glance and Simon shrugged. 'OK, a lot of times.'

'I'm sure it has.' Eve gave Simon a knowing look. 'Have you been keeping track?'

'Yes. I started a diary the day he arrived. It was meant to be something I would be able to show him one day. Now I'm not so sure. And I also have –' Simon paused, sighed deeply – 'something his mother wrote.'

'Will you show it to me?' Eve spoke gently, but not so quietly that Gramma Grace didn't hear.

'It's probably a phase,' Gramma said. 'Boys are such terribly volatile creatures.'

Simon raised an eyebrow. 'Thanks for that, Mommie Dearest.'

Eve got up from her seat and started putting together a small plate of food.

'I'll sit with him first. We can do shifts,' said Ed. 'With a bit of luck, he may even want to come back and join us.'

'Well, bully for him,' said Father Ted cheerfully. 'In my day, behaviour like that would have meant a stripe on the arse and being sent straight to one's room for the rest of the day without lunch or supper. How on earth do six-year-olds even learn that sort of language? And I rather think you don't have to answer that!'

Simon sighed again. 'Well, he didn't learn it here.'

'I think it's all about context, really,' said Eve. 'But perhaps we could move on from this topic for the moment, seeing as it's Christmas? And may I just take this opportunity to say how lovely it is to be surrounded by most of my delightful family. And I trust my beloved, if exceptionally spoilt – and I blame the parents – little sister is having a fairly decent time in Grenada.'

'She is. I spoke to Sonia yesterday,' said Ted, clearly relieved by the conversational shift.

'Excellent!' Eve raised her glass. 'Well, here's to family and friends – and even small boys who are clearly very upset to have their traditional turkey swapped for a goose, *and* little sisters with far too much disposable income, slumming it on Caribbean beaches. Oh, and to Zoe finding out what a hedge fund is, so that *we* don't have to. Merry Christmas!'

There was a chinking of glasses. Eve glanced around the table and decided that, even with the two temporarily empty chairs and the disruptive arrival in her home of a difficult little boy, it was, nonetheless, still mostly Christmas as usual.

14

I shall be very pleased to get back to work, Gail thought on Boxing Day. She'd had a quiet Christmas – though this was not for lack of offers. Several friends had invited her and Harry over but Gail preferred not to play gooseberry with other people's families and declined most of the invitations. On Christmas morning, however, she and Harry went to visit her parents in Bexhill.

Gail's mum and dad were in their early seventies and, while Gail knew this was not even remotely ancient these days, they weren't the kind of metropolitan, silver-surfing, theatre-going, frothy-coffee-quaffing, Hampstead-dwelling septuagenarians she imagined, say, Sam's parents to be. Instead, they were proper provincial *old people*. Her mum, Iris, was in fact more like a nan; she wore pale grey elasticated shoes in extra-wide fittings that could only be bought mail-order from small ads in the *People's Friend*. Iris had given up her secretarial job the week before she'd married and currently volunteered at the same church in which her own parents had been married. She had travelled overseas just three times in her life and, after the third occasion, declared that 'I don't like *abroad*' – as though (as Gail said to Eve) 'abroad' was sprouts, or Les Dennis.

Meanwhile, Gail's dad, Ronnie, had wholeheartedly agreed with Iris when she'd decided, in 1975, that she didn't care for 'abroad' and wouldn't be bothering with it again. Since then, her parents had led safe, comfortable local lives without either of them recognizing, much less caring, that there might have been another kind of life to lead. Iris was content even as she struggled with her arthritis and Ronnie had failing eyesight and an increasingly slippery memory. At the same time, after the initial shock of becoming grandparents – having bypassed not merely an engagement and a marriage but indeed knowledge of anybody who might conceivably be their daughter's long-term partner – both took enormous pride in Gail and Harry.

So, all the members of the Prince family were pleased to see each other, for about three or four hours. After that, it became a little wearing when Iris started asking her usual questions: 'Has Harry seen his dad over Christmas? No, not yet? Do you think he will? Anyway, Gail, love, are *you* seeing anybody? No, I don't mean to pry – none of my business – sorry!' And so on. Gail . . . rhymes with 'fail', thought Gail.

She and Harry took Iris and Ronnie out to lunch at their preferred pub before dropping round to Auntie Ruby and Uncle Den's properly *bungaloid* bungalow in Bexhill, where they stayed long enough for a slice of Battenberg and a cuppa you could stand a spoon in, enquired politely after Gail's cousins and then made their excuses. Later, Gail briskly helped Iris tidy up, ran the vacuum round the flat, loaded some rubbish into her boot for recycling, and then whispered to Harry, 'You've done brilliantly with Nan and Grandda. You're a total star. Tomorrow, we'll stop by Game and you can pick up *Fifa 2011* with your Christmas money, yeah?'

So despite being a fan of Christmas, this year it would be a relief to get back to work. Yes, Gail was very much looking forward to the second week of January.

And then it started to snow and both Eastdene Community Primary School and Ivy House Preparatory School were closed. Meanwhile, beneath its pristine white duvet, the village hunkered down to a few consecutive inset days of its own. The silence is astounding, thought Gail. After the snowball-throwing novelty had worn off (somewhat quicker for Gail than it had for Harry, granted), there wasn't much to do except wait, and slide over to Londis to stock up on Heinz cream of tomato soup. Then, in the evening, at Harry's suggestion, they tossed a coin as to whether Gail should stay in for yet another boxed-set binge or leave him to *Fifa 2011* for an hour or two and slip, quite literally, across the road for half a lager-and-lime – or even, sod it, a vodka tonic. Tails, it was telly; heads, the pub . . .

'Gail! *Welcome*. Quite the Blitz spirit we've got going here!' said Dave.

Gail glanced around the heaving pub. 'Understatement, Dave. Is Penny around?'

Dave pointed out his wife. 'Over there, by the dartboard, in a huddle with some school mums you'll know. And a new one, but you'll probably know her too – Susie some-one, whose son and daughter were meant to start at Eastdene last week, all bright eyed and bushy tailed, freshly squeezed out of the Ivy House sausage factory.' Dave grinned. 'If Eastdene was private, we could bung up the fees. Anyway, pop over and say hi. Penny was asking after you just this morning. We were going to send over a search party.'

Gail smiled. So, it seemed that Tony's little Christmas treat for the Ivy House parents had gone down badly with Susie Poe. 'Yeah. I will say hi.' She glanced over, spotting Penny, in conversation with Susie herself. On cue, both women turned and looked towards the bar. Seeing Gail, Penny smiled and beckoned and Gail waved back before making fleeting eye contact with Susie, who also smiled, although less warmly. She either can't quite place me – invisible PA that I am – or she can place me and would rather not, thought Gail. Interesting woman, Susie Poe. Also, very blonde and attractive. Gail recalled that Susie didn't live in Eastdene but somewhere just out of the school's catchment, so she had been particularly lucky to get places for both her kids at such short notice. Mike had mentioned at his first PTA meeting that he liked it when the children came from outside the immediate area, 'because parents who are prepared to drive a few miles on school runs are parents who demonstrably care about their children's education.'

Recalling this, she suddenly spotted Mike himself, tucked behind a pillar with a pint and a copy of the *Guardian*. He raised his hand in acknowledgement when he spotted her and she nodded back. She and Mike hadn't spoken since that last evening in the Bell and Gail decided it might be worth losing her spot at the busy bar in favour of seizing the moment to say something. And then, seeing the over-stretched bar staff, she thought better of it, waiting to be served and taking her vodka and tonic with her. There was just one chair at Mike's table, so Gail hovered awkwardly by the pillar.

'Sorry, I'd ask you to join me, of course, but –' Mike jerked his head in Susie Poe's direction – 'that lady, there, one of Eastdene's new mums, needed a chair so I figured that was politic . . . no, sorry, definitely not *politic* – polite!'

Gail laughed and looked more closely at Susie Poe. With her pale grey skinny jeans and expensive-looking creamy cashmere layers, she was very much the kind of stylish woman who made Gail feel frumpy – frumpy and spinsterish and overly reliant on Matalan. She turned back to Mike. 'No problem; I'm table-hopping, anyway. I really just wanted to say hi again, after . . . y'know?' Gail grimaced. Then she followed Mike's distracted gaze, which was still fixed in the area of Susie Poe who, she noted, had angled her chair in such a way as to have an equally uninter-rupted view of Mike Browning. Well, yeah, *that* makes sense, thought Gail. They'd make a very attractive couple.

'So how's your prickly boss?' asked Mike.

'Ha! Well, actually, she's on top form at the moment. You *really* didn't see the best of Eve.'

'I hope not, because if that was the best I'd dread the worst. Anyway—'

At which point they were interrupted. 'Ooh, hello, Gail! Isn't this absolutely unbelievably insane weather? I'm afraid I'm AWOL from the Home Front! I knew we had snow chains on the old Land Rover, so I just spontaneously decided to let Mr P get the juniors up to Bedfordshire while I popped over to the pub to meet the girls.'

Leonora Percy, aka Mrs Dick Cock, waved a hand at a huddle of practically identical ruddy-faced middle-aged women wearing waxed jackets and the kind of wilfully ugly sweaters that made Gail itch just to look at them, accessorized by a selection of wet retrievers. She knew all of them by sight, if not name, and waved cheerfully. As Leonora leaned closer, the better to shout into her ear, Gail noted that *eau de chien mouillé* invariably clung to members of the Percy family, of whom she was terribly fond. 'And I fear,' stage-whispered Mrs P, 'that I may not get back until terribly late. Dave is threatening a lock-in.'

Gail grinned. 'Go for it, Mrs P. Now, Dave, let me give you a hand with those glasses.' Gail turned back to the bar, but Dave wasn't listening; he was staring at the door – as, by now, was nearly everybody else in the pub. Though palpable, this near-silence only lasted a second or two. Gail swivelled around awkwardly, attempting not to spill her drink and took in the entirely incongruous sight of a very beautiful blonde woman wearing a fur coat and hat and standing in the doorway on the arm of an absurdly handsome man in a fabulously expensive-looking cashmere overcoat. Both were stamping snow off their feet.

'Blimey!' whispered Gail. 'It's the Sorensens!'

'Goodness, my next-door neighbours – how super!' said Mrs P.

'Yes, you can see why they're very good friends with Brad and Angelina, can't you,' said Gail.

'Brad and Angelina who?' said Mrs P.

'Do you think they'll expect *waitress* service?' wondered Dave.

Gail raised an eyebrow. 'Actually, I'm pretty sure they won't.'

Meanwhile, Gail noted that the entire pub was pretending not to be straining to overhear the conversation currently taking place between Stefan Sorensen, standing at the bar, and Dave, who was breaking the habit of a lifetime and actually smiling at a stranger. Dave then rang the ship's bell that calls time and the hum instantly became a hush.

'Laydeez 'n' genelmen! I know you will be delighted to hear that Eastdene's newest residents, Mr and Mrs Sorensen, here, have very kindly just set up a tab, so feel free to order what you like. But before you all start getting ideas, I can tell you straight away that I'm fresh out of nebuchadnezzars of Moët.'

At this, there was much laughter, shouts of, 'Thanks!' and, 'Cheers!' and some of the more well-oiled locals went over to the Sorensens' table to offer their thanks in person. Gail watched all of this wide-eyed. 'Bloody hell, Dave! If the Bell's going to be this glamorous then you'd better start stocking posher crisps.'

SPRING TERM

15

'Thanks for a typically generous Christmas, Evie.' Simon exhaled and patted a non-existent stomach while Eve watched him, tracing her finger round the sugary rim of a tea mug. They were in her kitchen, alone, at three p.m. – a small miracle on Boxing Day in a house that should have been full of people. Ed had taken Jordan for a walk with Barney and Alice, and they were detouring via Monty's stables; Zoe was upstairs in her room with Rob (while both her parents pretended not to be unnerved by the quietness) and Gramma Grace was having a lie-down ('I do believe there is something in poultry – a *hormone* – that makes one *terribly* sleepy'); meanwhile, Father Ted had slipped quietly off to the pub with the *Telegraph* and Eve emptied the dishwasher as Simon continued singing her praises. She had absolutely no objection whatsoever to being praised for delivering a successful Christmas, which always felt like a familial duty rather than an unmitigated delight.

'And I bet you have no idea how much it meant to us all,' said Simon.

'All, except possibly Jordan.' Eve folded a tea towel excessively neatly, as if to briskly delineate her all-round domestic goddesshood.

'No – *especially* Jordan. Look, last night, Ed and I had a very long conversation – till about two a.m., I think, like *young* people – and we both agreed that, at the risk of upsetting Jordy's precious routine too much, we should remove him from Ivy House, for all the reasons you've already suggested.' Simon looked at Eve hopefully. 'Fortunately, via our "connections", we think we might be able to pull this off without being penalized too heavily.'

Simon was referring to Ivy House's standard private school get-out clause: a full term's fees for the sudden removal of a child. Or, thought Eve, in the case of Susie Poe's swift withdrawal of both Lula and Charlie at the end of term, *two* full terms. Expensive business, spontaneity.

'Well, look, I'm sure we can work something out if I catch Tony in the right mood.'

'Thanks. The point is that we – the *three* of us – agree that Heatherdown is probably the right sort of school for Jordy. Having said that, I am also quite pro Eastdene Community Primary School. Apparently it has some sort of new superhead.'

'Yes, the famous – or infamous, depending on your view – Mike Browning.' Eve was polishing the smears from wine glasses with an attention to detail that surprised her. She had a sudden mental snapshot of herself as a full-time retro housewife, complete with gingham pinny and a rolling pin. She smiled to herself – where had *that* come from? Mum. Mum had a gingham pinny . . .

Simon continued. 'Well, we took your point that state schools are often brilliant with special needs while prep schools tend to tackle "bad" behaviour by dishing out detentions and hoping the kids sort themselves out on the rugger pitch.'

'Yes. I'm afraid some of us are very much stuck in the twentieth century. It's bothering me, frankly, that we don't have a full-time Special Educational Needs Co-Ordinator – SENCO, to you. Because, the thing is, of course, that I'm not teaching anymore. I'm not on the frontline, just busy recruiting new square pegs for our old round prep schooly holes.' Eve paused. 'You know, Jordan has been a real eye-opener, but we've got a few Jordans.'

Simon looked intrigued. 'Really?'

'Yes, lots of super-bright, tricky kids, a bit autistic spec-trumy without any proper diagnosis. And Tony couldn't give a monkey's.' Eve shrugged.

'Tony is always going to be about the bottom line. He relies on you for the ethical judgement calls. Too much, in my opinion.'

Eve reached for a tin and extracted a dark and dense-looking Madeira cake, steeped in alcohol, which smelled like something one might choose to kick-start a lost week-end. 'Fancy some over-the-limit cake?'

'*Grace's* over-the-limit cake? Try stopping me.'

Eve cut Simon a slice. 'So, anyway, I'm still slightly

concerned about Heatherdown's ability to stay in business long enough – there are *rumours* – to provide some consistency and continuity for Jordy, for whom routine is probably everything. Ellie says it's not so much that he *dislikes* change, but that change seems to kind of unplug him from his mainframe. Does that make sense?'

'It makes perfect sense. Here . . .' Simon reached into a new, very smart leather manbag, a Christmas present from Ed, and pulled out a large brown envelope. 'I should have shown you this ages ago, really, but for some peculiar reason I felt that it would be a betrayal of trust. I have no idea why, in retrospect.' Simon handed her the envelope. 'It's basically *The Jordy Diaries*. Brace yourself, it was written by his mother and fills in at least some of the gaps. By the way, Mum has really excelled herself this year – the cake is awesome.'

There was a cake-fuelled silence for a few moments. Then Eve said, 'Oh, gosh, Simon – I'm suddenly thinking about my ma.'

Simon patted her hand in an avuncular sort of way. 'Of course you are.' He raised his tea mug. 'In loving memory of the most excellent Charlotte Eva Amelia Wharton.'

Eve raised her tea mug. 'To Mum – who would have bloody loved this cake.' A pause. 'I think I might just send Sonia a text, actually. Dad's fine; he's in the pub.' She glanced at Simon. 'I'm talking to you like you're my husband, now, like a mad old woman. I'll be sitting around watching telly in my wedding dress before you know it.'

'You were always a mad old woman in waiting, Evie. It's

sexy. It suits you.' A beat. 'Do you really think you can still get into that dress?'

Eve punched him – and not quite as gently as she'd intended.

The twenty-seventh of December, the day after the anniversary of her mother's death, and Eve was alone, right in the middle of the twilight zone. Although still technically only lunchtime, it was gloomy outside, the Barn was empty of daughters and Eve's day stretched ahead, unformed. Yet, even with a lack of demands on her time, she wasn't quite ready to read the contents of the brown envelope marked *Jordy*. Instead, she visited Tesco Extra and started stocking up for New Year – despite the fact she wasn't expecting guests for New Year – and even if she decided to invite some over, the freezer was already full, anyway.

So it was at 3:30 p.m., post-Tesco, with *still* no sign of any daughters but an unexpected amount of new stationery, soap and light bulbs, that Eve finally sat down with a cup of tea as proper darkness encroached, and opened the envelope.

MY JORDY

My beutiful Jordy is six and goin to live somewere else now so I decide to fihgt the DYSLEXIA (!) and write few words down that will ecsplan who he is to his new dads. He is his own (litle) man from the start. After first few week & months (I hav mastites he hav colics = I watch lots of

Big Brother!) Jordy sleept through the night (coinsidens?) on the first night I bottelfed him when he was 3 month. He sleep well thro nihgt ever since. But its not the nights its Jordy when hes awake that keeps ME awake at nights!

BABY JORDY

He was strong newborn baby – real bruser not lik brothers & sisters. J lift his head, clench fists like a boxer and go all stiff when you held him when he was only a few weeks old. He felt all 'redy to go'! My other babys was more soft like babys! Jordy was like grown up INSIDE a baby.

Eve read on; there were ten more pages, charting Jordan's life from birth to, as far as she could tell, about six months ago. It would have been an exhausting – and exhaustive – document for any parent to create, never mind one who was also dyslexic. But what these words revealed most clearly to Eve was the fact that Jordy was not only loved, he was understood. Eve paused: Can I honestly say that I know Zoe and Alice as well as Jordan's anonymous mother understands her son?

But perhaps that was best left as a rhetorical question. Either way, Eve reached the final page:

Her are things what Jordy does.
– Hes righthand but hold his FORK in his rihgt-hand and NIFE in left. No way to make him change!
– He refuse to ever wear coat.

- He walk on tiptos nerly always. I think it must hurt
  but J say it don't.
- He get angry and stressey with shoe he has to put on
  with his hands. He hate lases!
- He take off T-shirt as soon as he come into the house
  becuss he say 'I am a WWE champ!'
- He has never sit in his seat thro a meal.
- He is clever at lots but isn't bothered about doig well in
  things

I love him so much tho. I wil ad more things to this list
wen I think of them soon.

And that's where it ended. When she'd finished reading,
Eve curled her feet beneath her and stared out of the window into the gloaming, enveloped by the profound silence
of a biggish house in the country that was, quite suddenly,
very empty.

'Barney! You stupid old hound, where *are* you?'

At the sound of Eve's voice, the old dog heaved himself
dutifully and waggily from his basket in the hall and sought
her out, curling himself up like a giant furry comma at her
feet. At which point, Eve finally allowed herself to cry – non-
specific crying that could nonetheless be apportioned fairly
equally amongst ... well, Jordy, yes, but also her dead mother,
her rapidly disappearing daughters, her happily-married-to-
someone-else ex-husband, a career that no longer consumed
her and, finally, being fifty-fucking-three and alone again on
the twenty-seventh of December.

16

'So, no texting in the office, please. And don't bite your nails. And always make eye contact. And don't assume people are just going to *tell* you things – they will all be wildly busy so you will not only have make yourself as useful as possible, you will have to do it by stealth.'

'And how do I do *that*, Mum?' said Zoe.

'Haven't the foggiest. I've been the general for so long that you can't really expect me to remember how to be a foot soldier.' Eve grinned; Zoe grimaced. 'Now, have fun and text me at lunchtime.' Zoe nodded while Eve paused on the driveway and peered closely at her daughter who, though presently leaning against the door jamb chewing a length of hair, nonetheless looked gorgeous. 'And I'm not sure those trousers are tight enough. Maybe you could try cling film?'

'Shut *up*.'

'I'm totally shutting up. I'm actually *off*. Have a fabulous time.'

Rob turned up exactly five minutes after Eve had left.

Zoe knew that he would try to have sex, but the timings were all wrong, even for a quickie. Anyway, Alice was mooching around upstairs somewhere, probably waiting to steal Zoe's make-up.

'Sorry, babes – we've got to go in, like, five – and, anyway, Alice is around.'

Rob pretended not to care. 'S'OK. What time you back, then?'

'Not *tonight*.' Zoe glanced over her shoulder. 'Didn't I tell you? I *did* tell you. I'm away all week – back Saturday. You did know that? It's too far to commute to, like, Bond Street from here, and Auntie Sonia lives in Notting Hill.'

'Which is close to Bond Street, right?'

'Close enough.' Zoe reached up on her tiptoes and planted a kiss on her boyfriend's forehead. 'You are so *local*, Rob.'

Rob shrugged. 'Nah. I don't do London.'

'You do. You go up to take pictures!'

Rob looked nonplussed. 'That's different.'

By the second week of January, the novelty of a white New Year had entirely worn off. Having exhausted all the googleable Inuit descriptions of snow and constructed a passable igloo on the lawn with Harry, Gail was delighted to learn that Ivy House's car park and grounds had thawed sufficiently to ensure it no longer contravened health and safety legislation.

I'm sure I never brought this much stuff home when

I was at school, she thought as she rushed to ready herself for work, rifling through the fistfuls of paper she'd extracted from Harry's school bag before he'd left for the second day of his term, Eastdene having reopened the previous day. Gail glanced briefly at Mike Browning's *Welcome To The New Term!* letter ('And we give a warm Eastdene welcome to Charlie and Lula Fox, who join us in . . .', blah blah blah) before sticking it to the fridge with her favourite magnet, which read *BECAUSE I'M YOUR MOTHER, THAT'S WHY!* She screwed up the rest of the paper and, guiltily, shoved it into the recycling bin before heading outside. Fingers crossed the Micra would start. And, though Gail briefly pondered whether or not her ten-minute drive at thirty miles per hour was doing its bit to accelerate the deterioration of polar icecaps, in the middle of the current bleakly arctic East Sussex midwinter, she hoped that the sooner this bloody snow thawed the better, frankly.

Twenty minutes later she was sharing her frustration with Eve. 'So, all this bloody paperwork came home with Harry last night. You'd think they'd have had better things to do at Eastdene than stuff bags full of paper on the first day of term, wouldn't you? Why does being the parent of a primary school-aged child feel like being the manager of a small business?' She plonked Eve's first frothy coffee of the spring term on her desk and wiped the inevitable spillage with her sleeve. 'Surely every parent hates this stuff?

Even the smug mummies whose lives revolve around it? Would some sort of future-proof paperless school be a complete pipe dream?'

'And a happy new year to you too, Gail!' Eve smiled. 'You are dangerously close to *ranting* – and, in answer to your question, yes, it *would*. It is quite clearly our job as educators, whether working within the state system or independently, to make parents feel they're getting their quid's worth and, these days, that means bombarding them with information they will almost immediately forget and then feel guilty that they've forgotten – and preferably several times a week.' Eve raised an eyebrow. 'I am very well aware that when *we* were children, weeks, months, possibly even *years* could go by without any interaction between a parent and their children's school. If only it were still the case!' Eve sighed mock-theatrically as Gail laughed. 'Got any more important questions you suggest I raise with Tony?'

Gail smiled and shook her head.

'Sure?' Eve was feeling bullish. 'No – silly me – why on earth would you?' She noted that Gail narrowed her eyes very slightly and shrugged, but said nothing. 'Well, anyway, rant over! Now, catch me up on what's happened so far this morning'.

Ten minutes later and Eve had learned that twelve children had left Ivy House between Christmas and New Year. While the majority of their parents had invoked financial pressures as a result of the fee increase (including Susie

Poe), a small but nonetheless troubling minority had talked – again – about Ivy House 'failing' their children. As Eve listened to Gail, she considered the idea that children could be 'failed' by even the best schools and decided it was all a bit fashionable; nonetheless – and despite being her own school's staunchest fan – she instinctively knew there was something awry. She wasn't particularly bothered about the falling numbers – which were set to rise again in the autumn, after Tony's international-pupil recruitment drive started paying off – however, she *was* bothered about the reasons behind some of them. She knew that what the parents said was, in some respects at least, right – some children had been failed by Ivy House ... and perhaps in ways they had never been failed before.

Eve sensed that the children in her charge were becoming somehow (and it was hard to put her finger on something so nebulous, but ...) *different*, more *complex*. She had attempted to raise her hunch with Tony last year but had predictably been given short shrift. ('They're children, Eve, ergo they're difficult. After all these years in teaching, do I really have to break this to you quite so gently?'). But Eve knew she was right; there were more problems – from relatively straightforward peanut allergies to outbreaks of bad language via an increase in Tourette's-ish behavioural tics and a veritable rash of attention-deficit-type disorders – and the children were unable to be easily diagnosed or supported by Ivy House for the simple reason that one hundred per cent of the Ivy House staffroom remained entirely unqualified in any special-needs capacity whatsoever, despite the fact that the latest statistics – and Eve enjoyed ferreting out statistics – claimed that as many as one in five school children displayed some sort of Special Need.

Yet, try as she might to join the dots, Eve had failed. On top of which, she was preparing to go along to her boss with only a bunch of hunches in order to beg for new staff. Eve hated begging – and she *particularly* hated begging Tony.

'Darling, come and keep my lap warm!' said Tony as Eve entered his office without knocking.

'Actually, shut up, Tony – this is serious.'

'And so are those *heels*. Wow. I can tell you mean business.'

But Eve was having none of it. 'Really, Tony, I mean it!'

'OK.' Tony sighed. 'I'm all ears. What do you want? More money?'

'It's not so much what *I* want as what *we* need.'

And so Eve explained, at considerable and conscientious length, how, for reasons she could not really begin to explain, the school's demographic was changing – and not so much socially as, for want of a better word, *emotionally*. (At her use of 'emotionally', Tony perceptibly and predictably flinched). And so, in order to continue to cater for these invariably bright but occasionally challenging children, the school would simply have to (deep breath) up its game.

'Up our fucking game, Eve?' Tony clearly couldn't

contain himself. 'How much of its *game* does an Ofsted "Outstanding" school need to *up*, precisely? Or is there some secret Ofsted category we should be aiming for? Something beyond "Outstanding" that, for some inexplicable reason, I don't fucking well know about? Maybe "supercalifragilisticexpialidocious-standing"?'

At any other time, Eve would have been laughing – but not right now. 'Stop. You sound just like that Alastair Campbell-ish character in *The Thick of It.*'

'I *love* that show. Malcolm *Fucker*. Anyway—'

'Look, I am absolutely, one hundred per cent completely *serious*. Unless we get new SENCO-qualified staff – or train up some existing staff – I –' Eve paused; she surprised herself by how very fast things had moved even though she had thought she was completely in control, which just went to show how elusive a concept 'control' could be – 'I would very seriously think about . . . about –' and Eve surprised herself too by how fast she arrived at this outcome, but here she most definitely was – '*resigning*.'

Silence. The moment felt filmic enough for several bars of a theme tune by Ennio Morricone to play while metaphorical tumbleweed rolled down Main Street, sunlight glinted off the protagonist's spurs and beads of sweat were wiped from brows. Though it was 9:47 a.m. it could just as easily have been high noon.

'Right, so that's your dry-run resignation, is it?' said Tony, sarcastically. 'It needs a bit of work, to be honest. Any other business?'

'Tony!' If she hadn't been sitting, Eve would almost certainly – and bugger the new heels – have stamped her foot.

'*Darling* Eve, I am not interested in running an educational establishment for society's marginals and ferals. I am, however, very interested in running a school for fundamentally nice middle-class children, or indeed nice *wannabe* middle-class children, who –' Eve recognized a rant coming on – 'despite dressing their Barbies – and Kens, for all I know – in *Porn Star in Training* T-shirts and swapping their Subbuteo for on-screen drive-by shootings, are still children we recognize as our own kind.' Tony briefly paused for breath. 'Do you see, Eve? They're our *breed*? On the other hand, all the other ADHDivas and arsing dysmorphic-o-praxial-lexias and autistic-spectrum whatevers – *they* are fundamentally *not* our kind.' Tony thumped his desk. 'So, to reiterate, I don't want Ivy House to go there, Eve. Because we most emphatically do *not* do special needs!'

And as Tony again thumped the beautiful blond Nordic wood with the palm of his hand, Eve thought, I can do that, and thumped it too, recognizing that Tony's rants were the outpourings of a man thoroughly terrified by the prospect of change. Secure in this insight, she ploughed ahead. 'Right, you can huff and puff and blow Ivy House down if you want to, but I am roughly ninety per cent sure that we have at least fifteen to twenty children – maybe five per cent of our intake – with some sort of

special-needs *something*, one of whom, you may be interested to know, is almost certainly Petrus Sorensen, whom
Ellie Blake thinks may even be Asperger's. And there's
probably double that of dyslexics and dyspraxics, many of
whom are already getting help privately because *we can't
help them*.' Eve was warming up now, flexing her head-
teacher muscle. 'And then there's the stuff I don't even
know about yet: the kids with problems and issues lurking
just under the radar, waiting to surface – and I can tell
you there are going to be several of those.'

Surprisingly, Tony seemed to be rather touched by Eve's
passionate soliloquy – but first things first. '*Petrus Sorensen?*
What's wrong with Little Lord Fauntleroy?'

'Well, it depends what you mean by "wrong", doesn't it?
He is displaying *behaviours—*'

'And what the fuck does *that* mean? And since when did
you become the expert? And, while I'm at it, don't you *dare*
go saying anything to Anette Sorensen without . . . without
–' Tony paused, floundering slightly – 'without running it
by me first, yeah? This needs a proper *strategy*, Eve.'

'But there is no strategy, Tony! We have a kid – *kids!* – who
needs our help, which is part of our duty of pastoral care.
I'm already organizing a series of meetings with all the
form teachers, both individually and in groups, to work
out our –' Eve wiggled her fingers in the air, Tony Salter
style – ' "strategy".'

'Fine, but I still don't know how you suddenly became
an expert on kids with special needs?'

And this, thought Eve, is the moment for the big reveal: 'Because Simon just adopted one. And he only found out after the event. And, even though it isn't confirmed, it's extremely likely that Jordan—'

Tony interrupted Eve: 'This is the Jordan who joined our Year Two when I was schmoozing the Far East?'

'Yes, that's the one.'

'So we have a bunch of fruit-and-nuts on our roll. Is that what you're telling me?'

'Not in quite so many words, Tony – but your offensive-ness is nothing if not predictable.'

Eve knew that Tony disliked being predictable rather more than he disliked being offensive. He frowned, seemed to be considering a different tack.

'What do you need, then? And more to the point, how much will it cost?'

Victory! Eve seized the moment. 'Right, so we need a designated special educational needs co-ordinator, full time *and* on a proper salary, starting September. And then I'd like three existing members of staff to be trained, on a voluntary basis, to screen for dyslexia – bill to be footed by us.'

'And all this will keep you quiet, will it?'

'I doubt that, Tony, but it *will* help Ivy House become the very best school of its kind it can possibly be.' Eve leaned forward and met Tony's gaze. 'Which would be nice, wouldn't it?'

Tony rolled his eyes. 'You know what I mean.'

But Eve, as usual, was already halfway towards the door before her boss could change his mind.

Once back on safer ground in her own office, Eve re-ran her meeting with Tony and marvelled again at just how quickly things had progressed. It was not so much that she appeared to have got her own way – at least for the moment – but the fact that she had expressed just how passionately she felt about getting it. And yet, for the first time, Eve also allowed herself to think that, even if she acquired all the SENCO staff she'd ever dreamed of overnight, her days at Ivy House were still numbered. It wasn't so much that Tony would want her to leave, it was that, once she'd achieved what she needed to achieve, *she* might want to leave. Not that she planned to breathe a word of any of this to Gail – yet. Gail was a glory in every way, but she was also a *gossiping* glory: tell her, and Eve would effectively tell not only Eastdene but a sizeable chunk of East Sussex, too. She stopped briefly by Gail's desk.

'Mine in ten? May involve dictation.'

'Dictation? Is it 1986? And you're *hissing*,' hissed Gail. 'What's going on?'

'Tony's what's going on. And I'm going on, too.'

'On the subject of which, he just went out, face like a wet weekend in Folkestone.' Gail's tone was light. 'Have you just *resigned*, or something?'

So much for my resolve, thought Eve. She sighed. 'Not properly, not yet – but I might.'

'Right. That's *totes oh-em-gee*, as I'm sure Zoe and Alice would never dream of saying. May I ask why?'

'You may ask but I haven't got long enough to answer. If I tell you, though, you mustn't breathe a word. But first – 1986.'

'Scout's, Cub's, Brownie's, Guide's honour. And, look, I've even brought my special 1986 pen, the Parker my dear old dad gave me when I got my shorthand and typing certificate.'

Gail saluted and Eve grinned. Ultimately, it didn't really matter if Gail gossiped. In fact, word getting out might be a good thing; it wasn't as if Eve could afford to be a lady of leisure, after all – or would want to be one, even if she could afford it.

'Come on, then. It's a job ad. No, don't look at me like that – we're getting a SENCO.'

Gail held up her hands, jazz style. 'Hallelujah! It's all I ever hear about in the corridors of the powerless: "special needs" this, "spectrum" the other. "Why don't we have any specialist staff?" Blah-di-blah . . .'

'Really?' Eve raised an eyebrow. 'Why didn't you *tell* me, Gail? This is *important*.'

Gail looked nonplussed. 'I would've thought you'd known me long enough to know that I'm not a gossip, Eve. But, hey, I'm telling you now, aren't I?'

17

Zoe pressed the buzzer on the entryphone of the discreet black door that had taken her a nervous fifteen minutes to locate and which turned out to be at the Piccadilly end of Bond Street. *Old* Bond Street – the posh bit. Where else?

'Hello?' said a tiny, tinny voice.

'Ah, hello, my name is Zoe Sturridge and I, ah . . .'

But the buzzer had already buzzed and, as no instructions had been forthcoming, Zoe headed up the stairs. On the first floor, there was another black door with a discreet brass plaque: *Odense Holdings*. As far as Zoe was concerned, this may as well have been a rabbit hole and she might have been Alice – the fictional one, that is, not her dumb kid sister.

'Good morning, Zoe; welcome to Odense.'

At the sight of the exceptionally beautiful blonde woman standing in the foyer, Zoe instantly dreamed of being matter-transported away from Odense Holdings. Despite its being ostensibly a chic office ranging over three storeys of a Bond Street townhouse above a fashionable cobbler's shopfront, it was, Zoe knew in her marrow, a parallel universe to which it was inconceivable she could ever belong.

I mean, Zoe thought to herself, how can anybody this awesome be, like, a receptionist?

'Hi,' she said in her smallest voice; a voice so small, indeed, that, until now, she hadn't actually known she'd possessed it. 'Thanks. I really hope I can be of some, er, help?'

'I'm sure you can. We are always grateful for another pair of hands.' The blonde woman held out her own hand. 'I'm Anette Sorensen. You are absolutely the image of your mother and, believe me, that is *definitely* a compliment.'

Zoe felt herself start to blush. 'Wow, thanks. And, er, thanks very much for having me, Mrs Sorensen.'

'It's Anette and it's a pleasure. And I know exactly what you're thinking: "But I thought *Mr* Sorensen ran Odense." And, despite feminism being well into its fifth decade, you wouldn't be the first and, sadly, you won't be the last. And Stefan *does* run Odense – at least, fifty per cent of it. We're a double act, but we just don't shout about it.'

'That is *so* cool.' At which, of course, despite her new black spray-on skinnies and buttoned-up crisp white blouse and the moss-green cashmere cardigan she'd borrowed from her mum, Zoe herself felt very uncool. 'I mean . . .'

Anette smiled. 'I know exactly what you mean. Now, come and meet the team. We'll start at the top – that is, upstairs with my husband, who is off to New York soon – and then work our way back downstairs, by which time you'll probably be ready for coffee.'

And so Zoe followed Anette up four more flights of stairs ('Of course, we have the lift, but this is such good exercise . . .'), which gave her just enough time to contemplate the fact that, although she clearly knew nothing much about anything important in the grown-up world, she would endeavour to be a very fast learner. By the time she'd reached Stefan Sorensen's top-floor office suite, Zoe had already vowed to (a) learn as much as she possibly could about hedge-fund management during the next few days – obviously – and (b) never again (if she could help it) judge a book by its cover. Somehow, (b) already seemed to Zoe a far greater challenge than (a).

Either way, forty-five minutes after arriving at Odense Holdings, Zoe Sturridge found herself in the loo, attempting to tame a few escapee fronds of hair into something appropriately groomed while gathering her thoughts – which, despite her best organizational efforts, kept scattering around her head like a flock of ditzy sheep. It was important to corral them, though, because life was moving *extremely* fast.

As she washed her hands, Zoe replayed her introduction to Stefan Sorensen and the three-way conversation with Anette and Stefan that had followed:

'So, Anette, I've just spoken with Richard – you know

how much he loves those five a.m. wake-up calls – and if
we're going to nail the Dersh and Dohenny, uh, situation,
then I gotta get over there before the NYSE closes.'

Anette glanced at her watch. '*Very* tight. I'll get Tina to
make a call; so, OK, whatever, off you go. Of course, I can't.'
She shrugged.

Zoe's eyes moved from Anette to Stefan and back again.

'I know, honey,' said Stefan. 'Get home for the kids. So!'
He glanced at Zoe and, hopping to his feet, grinning, he
banged his hand on the desk. 'So, young lady, you fancy
some *work experience*?'

Zoe smiled and nodded. She had absolutely no idea what
was unfolding; however, Stefan Sorensen seemed suitably
adrenalized by whatever it was that she did her level best to
match his mood. 'Yeah! I mean, yes, *please*.'

Anette laughed, then, eyes widening, clasped her hand
to her mouth. 'Oh, *Stefan*. Oh my word! She barely has time
to ask her mother's permission!'

'You do the asking, Annie, yeah? You two get on great.
Is that OK, Zoe?' Zoe nodded, though she had absolutely no
idea for what her mother was going to be asked permission. Then there was a swift and staccato exchange in
Danish between Anette and Stefan, which Zoe obviously
had no hope of understanding, so she jigged from foot to
foot nervously, wondering what was going on.

Anette turned to her, smiling. 'So, Zoe, have you ever
flown to New York by private jet?'

Yeah, course I have, thought Zoe, in my dreams. 'Er, no.

155

But then again –' brightly, confidently, though, she hoped, not too smart-arsey – 'I've never been to New York!'

Anette smiled at Stefan, Stefan smiled at Anette, and both of them smiled at Zoe. 'Well, this is definitely the way to do it for your first time!' said Anette. 'And now I'll call your mother.'

And so, as she dried her hands, Zoe rewound this conversation and replayed it again, just to make sure she hadn't made it up, after which she realized that, yes, she would in actual fact be (a) accompanying Stefan Sorensen to (b) New York (c) today. And that, after being phoned by Anette, her mother had (d) (astoundingly) already agreed to this absurdly bonkers thing, and that (e) one motorbike courier was at this very moment being dispatched to East-dene to collect her (f) passport, while another was (g) picking up her suitcase from Auntie Sonia's and that (h) both would be waiting at the office of something called *Execujet* – Zoe googled this in the loo and discovered it was 'The World's Leading Purveyor of Premium Business Travel Solutions for a Demanding and Discerning Clientele'. She fished in her bag for her lip gloss and then dexterously started applying it while texting:

> Babes!!!! Am off to New York in a min wiv MR
> SORENSEN + his PA!!!! Yeah, NYC Concrete Jungle
> where dreams are made of there's nothing you can't do
> now you're in Nu York! Back Thurs a.m. Love you!!!! Z xxx

*

As he read the text in the student canteen between lectures, Rob suddenly, painfully, already felt a long way away from Zoe *indeed* – and so much faster than he'd expected. He went to the loo and locked himself into a cubicle and re-read the text, noting that there were more exclamation marks than kisses – and then came out, blew £1.50 on a filthy-tasting *vomaccino* from the vending machine, read the text one more time and, finally, replied:

Gr8, babe! Think ul go2 applestore?!!!! Xxx

Rob touched *Send* . . . just as he realized this text didn't sound quite right. He sent another:

luvu2!!! Xxxxxx

Despite his deep discomfort with using multiple Xs, Rob hoped this one more successfully disguised how he really felt.

18

Eve returned to her office after her weekly walkabout around Ivy House's nursery wearing a thunderous expression, which Gail intuited probably shouldn't be challenged, especially not in her habitual cheerfully-joshing, bubble-bursting fashion. Eve's subsequent meeting with Mrs Charteris, head of the nursery, and her deputy, Miss Short, was brief, especially for Miss Short, who exited after precisely (Gail was keeping count) three minutes and sixteen seconds, in tears. Mrs Charteris, meanwhile, emerged after a further four minutes, twenty-three seconds, looking even more stony-faced than usual, after which Gail counted to thirty before knocking on Eve's door and presenting her with frothy coffee. She was, of course, desperate to know what had gone on.

Eve nodded a 'Thanks' and avoided eye contact, yet it was impossible for Gail not to notice that Eve was *in tears*. This was so rare as to be tectonic-plate-shiftingly seismic. Nonetheless, as a PA at the top of her game, Gail resisted the temptation to ask proper questions.

'Biscuit?' said Gail.

'Please,' said Eve. 'Thanks.' Which was the precise moment when Eve's mobile chirruped.

'Shall I go?' mouthed Gail silently, but Eve shook her head vigorously, indicating she should sit.

'Anette!' said Eve brightly, professionally. This greeting was, Gail noted, followed by a conversation lasting two minutes and twelve seconds, of which Eve's final words were, 'That's tremendously exciting. I'm sure she's thrilled. Do *please* get her to call me on her mobile before she leaves!' After which, Eve leaned back in her chair, closed her eyes and muttered, 'Jesus fucking H Christ on a stick.'

'Eve, are you sure you don't want me to go?'

'No. Stay a minute, please, Gail.' Eve reached for the phone again. 'Simon! Hi! So, I thought you ought to know that our eldest daughter – and you'd better sit down – is literally about to jet off to New York for three days with her new boss.' A pause. 'Yes, indeed, the, uh, not entirely below-the-radar hedge-fund billionaire, Stefan Sorensen. And I'm sorry to spring this after the event, but do you think that's OK?' A pause. 'OK, uh-huh – as long as you're *sure*, because I just sort of let her go without asking many questions. Yes ... Yes ... No ... I'm sure they can be trusted *completely*. His PA is going too, of course.' Eve sighed, 'I've got to pop home in a mo, to pick up Zo's passport.'

Gail's eyes widened. 'Wow,' she mouthed silently at Eve.

'I know!' Eve mouthed equally silently back. 'OK, Simon, thanks for that. Better shoot. Crazy day ...'

'And Zoe's day sounds like the plot of a 1980s bonk-buster,' said Gail. 'I mean, *wow.*'

Eve laughed, gratefully. 'I don't think they've called them "bonkbusters" since *Lace*. But the good news is she's not travelling alone with the handsome billionaire. Anette told me Sorensen's PA, Tina, is going too. She's a sensible fifty-six-year-old mother-of-three with an empty nest, and, according to Anette, she will be "treating your daughter as her own" –' Eve's Danish accent was abysmal – 'even as she sends her out on errands in –' Eve paused – '*Manhattan!* God, Gail – New York!'

Gail braced herself. 'And, before that call – what was going on with the nursery? Or do you not want to talk about it?'

Eve leaned back in her chair and threaded her hands together behind her head. She exhaled deeply. 'No, I *do* want to talk about it. I want to talk about *all* of it very much.'

So Gail listened as Eve told her how she'd visited the nursery and, after Eve had stuck her head round class-room doors and heard busy-looking small people chanting, 'Good morning, Mrs Sturridge,' she made a point of visit-ing the lavatories, where, of course, somebody was usually marshalling the not-quite-toilet-trained.

The school's nursery department – the Tree House – had a policy of insisting that children older than three were toilet-trained before they entered the Reception class in Ivy House's pre-prep department, where none of the teach-ers were prepared to tolerate pull-ups and even accidents were frowned upon. This meant that, as the deadline approached, there was often an air of panic amongst the more recalcitrant children(usually boys) and their mothers, and the staff. A particularly longstanding nursery staff member, Miss Short, had taken the bulk of the toilet-training upon herself – or possibly had it thrust upon her. 'And so,' Eve explained, 'as I approached the loos, I could already hear Miss Short in full cry: "Pants down *before* we poo, Michael!" Obviously, this was a bad moment, so I just said something like, "How are we all doing here, then?" ' Eve paused and wiped her eye. Gail waited. 'And then Miss Short barely missed a beat. She said, "The little sod'll get the hang of it soon, *won't you, Michael*? Cos he knows what happens if he doesn't. *Don't you, Michael?*" '

Gail's eyes widened. Eve was ashen-faced. 'And I just hoped I had somehow misheard, *please, God*. So I said to Andrea Short, "*What* did you just say?" And she said, of all things, "I . . . uh . . . I'm sorry, Mrs Sturridge. I thought you were Mrs Charteris!" To which the only response was, "Right! And that makes it better, does it? Do you say things like that to Mrs Charteris – or, indeed, Michael – very often?" '

'My God, Eve. I don't know what to say.' And, for once, Gail genuinely didn't.

Meanwhile, Eve was still close to tears, her voice catching in her throat. 'And, all the time, Michael Percy was just sitting on the loo with his fat little legs swinging back and forth.' Eve wiped her nose with the back of her hand. 'And all he said was, "Miss Short is stressy." '

Gail listened as Eve told her how she'd gently asked if Michael, who was three, had finished his business, and if so would he like to wipe his bottom and wash his hands and then she would take him to the cloakroom, because it was very nearly break, so he may as well get his hat and coat and gloves on and play outside – but to please be very careful on the equipment because it was still a bit frosty-the-snowman. To all of which Michael Percy, Richard's youngest son, had apparently nodded very seriously. Like all the Percy offspring, Gail considered Michael to be endearingly sweet and biddable – a fact that shouldn't have made Miss Short's behaviour any more appalling, yet somehow did.

'So,' said Eve, 'I told Charteris and Short that I'd see them in my office in fifteen minutes and I took Michael by the hand and led him to the cloakroom and waited while he dressed himself, painfully slowly, before taking him outside where several nursery staff were huddled by the climbing frames, stamping their feet and warming their hands on their mugs.' Eve rolled her eyes. 'So I told them I'd prefer it if hot drinks weren't brought out to the play-ground, and I'm pretty sure one of them shrugged, so I sort of lost it a bit and said, "In fact, it's not so much an 'I'd prefer it if' as it is a 'no hot drinks in the playground, ever, effective immediately'. *Do I make myself clear?*" '

Gail nodded. This was the correct response. It was well known among the prep-school staff that the nursery was its own fiefdom. Some of the junior nursery staff – average

age about nineteen – were especially sullen and unlovely graduates of a local college's BTEC in Children's Play, Learning and Development. With, thought Gail, a distinction in sulking. We probably get what we pay for. And that isn't very much.

'So, to cut a long story short – no pun intended – they've both been given warnings.' Eve sighed again. 'Christ, Gail, it's all starting to fall apart. And I'm so bloody distracted, I've just let my seventeen-year-old daughter fly to New York on a private jet with people *I don't actually even know*. Like she doesn't have teenage delusions of grandeur as it is!'

Gail laughed. Eve's ability to weasel out the humour in the most unlikely circumstances was, in her eyes, one of the things that set her boss apart and made her a truly *brilliant* head teacher. Gail wondered if Eve actually knew she was brilliant? On balance, she suspected not.

'OK, so you're off in a minute, Gail?'

'Yes, I'm actually going to be there when Harry gets in tonight. It helps not to have to physically prise him off the Xbox.'

'I bet. I feel so lucky we never had all that screeny stuff with the girls. Mind you, the latest studies are saying that gaming might even be *good* for them. Before you know it, it'll be part of the national curriculum. I can't keep up.' A shrug. 'Look, I'm going to stay late tonight. Simon's with Alice, and Zoe's probably halfway across the Atlantic in a turbo-charged cigar tube, so . . .' She smiled wanly.

'Shall I leave you the Indian takeaway menu? They'll deliver.'

'That would be great, Gail; thanks so much. You are a marvel.' Eve looked at Gail quite intently, which Gail didn't find entirely comfortable. 'I don't think I tell you that enough, do I?'

'Stop it. Part of the job description.'

'Thanks so much. And, anyway, what are *you* up to tonight?' Eve simultaneously reached for her favourite black Pentel Sign pen and Moleskine notebook and Gail momentarily considered launching into a detailed description of this *fantastic* American drama series she'd recently come across, about a high school chemistry teacher who gets cancer and decides to provide for his family by becoming, of all the most ridiculous things, a manufacturer of a class-A drug called crystal meth, when she realized that this sounded very nearly as absurd as Zoe hightailing it to New York in a private jet. And, anyway, she could see that she was already losing Eve, who was now scribbling very fast in the Moleskine in her distinctively elegant, graphic hand.

'Oh, just a quiet night in with some terrible crimes, I think.' In truth, Gail was expecting to see a friend.

Eve glanced up briefly and smiled distractedly. 'Sounds blissful!'

19

As was her habit, after dropping Harry at Breakfast Club, Gail was the first into Ivy House the following morning. She made herself a frothy coffee in the staffroom, fired up the gas log fire in the entrance hall and noted that the faux-Tudor fire-surround needed a good dust. This was not part of her job description but, after all these years, nobody – and least of all Gail – was sure where Miss Prince's job description began or ended. Though it ostensibly meant looking after Eve, it had over time grown organically to encompass part-time bursar, booker of flights and restaurants, occasional online mid-century modern furniture shopper for Tony, not to mention chief confidante to many members of staff. Gail occasionally wondered how Ivy House might function without her . . . and then she pushed the thought away. After all, everybody was dispensable.

She popped her head around Eve's office door to check that it was as immaculate as usual and was surprised to find that it wasn't. There were two dirty coffee mugs and a pile of papers and Eve's desk light was still switched on. Late night . . . On the floor by the sofa there was an open copy of *Hello!*. Gail set to tidying, noting the picture of Mr and Mrs Sorensen looking fabulously glamorous at a pre-Christmas black-tie event. Then, as she arranged the pile of papers on Eve's desk, she couldn't help noticing, too, that Eve had written and printed out something considerably longer than her usual weekly newsletter for the Ivy House website. It wasn't snooping, exactly, to take a closer look – Eve had left it right here in the middle of her desk, after all, and the middle of Eve's desk was very much a part of Gail's world. Gail glanced at the grandmother clock in the corner of the office, which had been in situ long before Ivy House became a school: almost five past eight – Eve won't be in till half past . . . She sat down at the desk and started reading.

OUR CHILDREN

I've been in teaching for half my life and can quite honestly say that it has never been harder, inasmuch as the goalposts seem to be moving all the time. When I started out in the mid-1980s, it was an entirely different world. While we'd had punk rock and a female prime minister, we hadn't had 9/11 and the internet. These days, working in an independent prep school with so-called 'traditional' values – the three Rs, hard work, discipline, sportsmanship, kindness, politeness – seems to be so left field as to appear radical. The generation of children I once routinely shepherded off to good independent secondary schools and grammars are almost a dying breed. Whereas I used to push round pegs into round holes with relative ease, now it seems that the square pegs are starting to outnumber the round ones by maybe as many as two to one. My gut instinct is that, as both independent educators and as parents, we must adapt our teaching methods to this fast-changing modern world for which our children seem to be better equipped than we are – or we 'die'.

Intrigued, Gail read on, speedily. And finally:

Finally, as an independent school head teacher for nearly a decade and a teacher for a quarter of a century, I have flattered myself I know what is best for my pupils. Would that I thought my pupils – or even their parents – felt the same way.

While it may not yet be time to (wo)man the barricades, I do feel very strongly that there is something of an education revolution in the offing – whether we like it or not. For those of us, however, who continue to care passionately about our children's futures and indeed are actively engaged in shaping them, the prospect of radical change is both terrifying and exciting in equal measures. More importantly, however, this change is essential – and it can't come soon enough.

EVE STURRIDGE, Ivy House School,

January 2011

'Ah! I thought I'd get in early and see if it needed a bit more work, but it looks as though you've beaten me to it.'

Eve dropped her bag on the sofa and shrugged off her coat, while Gail blushed deeply. Was it more embarrassing to be caught reading Eve's papers or to be caught doing it in Eve's chair? Both were fairly mortifying and Gail noted that she really must shut doors. Eve's stealthiness was legendary at Ivy House; she could materialize anywhere in the building at any time. 'God, I'm so sorry, Eve, I really am. I wanted to tidy and then the title caught my eye and it looked so interesting that I couldn't resist.' Which was perfectly true.

Eve flopped on to the sofa and rubbed her eyes. 'It's fine, Gail, really. In fact, I'd very much value your opinion. I was here till well after midnight, which is most unlike me.'

Gail felt no need to lie or flatter. 'Eve, it's brilliant, it really is. Somebody needs to say these things and who is better placed than you? What are you going to do with it?'

Eve roused herself from the sofa. 'I don't know yet. Obviously it would be great to get it published, but . . .' She broke off, shrugged and yawned. 'But maybe a *coffee* first? A big one.'

'Coffee it is,' said Gail, exiting the office. A second later she popped her head back round the door. 'Er, just had a thought? What about speaking to Cathy?'

Eve nodded and smiled, a big nose-crinkling smile.

Blimey, she looks just like Zoe, thought Gail.

'You're a genius, Gail.'

By the time she'd re-read the article three times and added a few amendments, Eve was sufficiently pleased with her 'rant' to want to do something with it. *Carpe diem*: by mid-afternoon she'd emailed it to Cathy Gower, her old friend and former uni room-mate, and Zoe's godmother, who was now the editor of a successful Sunday newspaper magazine supplement. Eve's accompanying note was brief:

Hello, lovely Cath, whom I miss. Here's something I enjoyed getting off my chest! Any use to you?! Eve xx

The reply came quickly:

Hello, YOU! How great to hear from you. And I loved your 'rant' – so many interesting points well made – and I speak as a mother of three sons! Unfort the piece is not 'magaziney' enough for me, if that makes any sense – but I have passed it on to my colleague, John Nicholson, on our comment desk. Good luck. And PLEASE let me know if you're going to be anywhere remotely near Kensington in the foreseeable? Visiting your impossibly glam little sis, for eg?! Did you know we belong to the same gym? I occasionally catch sight of her in the changing rooms and invariably skulk away without saying hi because she makes me feel like a wrung-out dishcloth! I know she's younger than us, but not by much, so how does she get that killer bod? Rhetorical Q! Anyway, it would be so great to see you – tho am obv not holding my breath. Love, Cath xx

Eve replied immediately:

Ooh, that's so kind of you, Cath! Am excited by even the remote possibility of getting published – daren't even think about how many people might read it as a result, but will cross that bridge as and when! Oh, and Sonia not only spends most of her non-working waking hours in the gym, but she won't mind you knowing she's had a bit of work, too – plus, not having kids obviously helps immeasurably! Personally, I think tampering with anything below one's neck is unnecessary – I just dust the cobwebs away occasionally! But seriously, would LOVE to see you. Sonia and I are actually meeting this weekend; Zoe's meant to have been staying with her this week while she's on work experience with one of my richest parents (you'll know all about the Sorensens!), but in fact she's just about to return from a couple of days in New York with Stefan Sorensen. In our day, work experience meant a fortnight in the stockroom at Lilley & Skinner – if we were lucky! E XX

And, if Eve thought Cathy's previous response had been lightning fast, it was nothing compared to this:

You're telling me that our little Zoe with the braces and plaits
(and, I recall, exactly the same eyes and eyebrows as Simon) is
currently in New York with Stefan Sorensen?! Are you sure you
trust me with this info?! This is the kind of stuff that shifts
newspapers! Cxx

Right! Should I NOT trust you, Cath?! Zoe is hell-bent on a
career in finance and Anette S suggested she might enjoy work
experience – sorry, an 'internship' – at Odense Holdings. So off
she went to make tea, but has now somehow landed herself in
New York with the boss (and, I might add, the boss's middle-
aged female PA). I mean, what's the prob?! 'Little Zoe' is
seventeen, five foot ten and . . . OK, fair enough, looks like a
model. Should I be worried?! E xx

I'm a mother of sons, so what do I know? But, speaking as
someone who used to be a seventeen-year-old girl . . . yes,
almost certainly! But seriously, good luck! Don't be a strang(l)er.
Much love, C xx

Hurtled straight back to the late 1970s, Eve smiled at
Cathy's in-joke reference to the Stranglers. She also felt
slightly worried about Zoe, and was still worried when she
got home that evening. However, instead of pouring herself a glass of something comforting, Eve went upstairs to
her room, taking her phone with her. She was hoping for a
text from Zoe soon, because she must already have arrived

in New York. Still, Eve didn't want to look too *needy-mommy* by texting Zoe first, given that major teenage rites of passage tended to occur without the assistance of a helicopter parent busily hovering around, cramping their style. Eve thought of herself at seventeen, of her free-range, unmollycoddled, risk-taking generation. She supposed Zoe took her own kind of risks within the limits of her world, which in turn probably meant sex and drugs – but maybe not so much rock 'n' roll? Though, come to think of it, Zoe was planning to go to Glastonbury – sorry, *Glasto* – this year with Rob. Apparently Muse were playing.

Eve, imagining her daughter's introduction to New York via private jet, took a moment to marvel at Zoe's easy, charmed life. There were occasional stresses, of course – exams, mostly, and occasional fallings-out with her friends – but when she looked back on her own adolescence and teenage years, Eve was sure they had been far more obviously and *externally* fraught. As Eve sat on her bed, appraising her toes – pedicure required soon, methinks – she figured that it must have helped that Zoe bypassed Ugly Duckling and arrived at Swan without so much as a zit, much less an existential crisis to rival David Bowie's Berlin years – something with which Eve had identified rather strongly, despite the fact that the closest she'd ever got to Berlin was watching Liza Minnelli in *Cabaret*.

I'll paint my toenails for Simon, thought Eve, rummaging through the cabinet in her bathroom. No, not for Simon. Eve glanced at the half-dozen bottles of uninspiring varnishes. Not boring red or pink; something cooler than that. What, she wondered, was the current version of Chanel's Rouge Noir? There was only one place to look.

Eve sat on her daughter's bed – something she did so rarely she couldn't recall the last time – and glanced, slightly guiltily, around the lovely, light space. Though it was also, she saw now, a space which reflected an eleven-year-old Zoe rather more than it did the seventeen-year-old version. Those primrose-painted walls, for example, had once looked so sophisticated but were now in need of a rethink. That roller blind looked dated, too – not to mention a bit grubby.

Maybe some warm blues and old whites . . . something shabby-chic, thought Eve. And plantation shutters at the windows. Or maybe things have moved on? Eve thought she might pick up a copy of ELLE Decoration and find out. In the meantime, though, she sat in Zoe's bedroom, taking in the chaos of the dressing table with its clutter of make-up and wet wipes and brushes and clips and bottles of perfume and unguents with their tops off; the wastepaper basket full of lipstick-printed tissues, the scattered pairs of virtually identical skinny jeans, balls of minuscule undergarments and many pairs of shoes, unpaired, not to mention the hairdryer, straighteners, crimpers and some kind of a tool called 'Big Hair' – a must-have last Christmas – which lay in a tangle of wires on the floor.

Eve glanced at the cork pinboard over the built-in desk, and the notion of a pinboard also seemed suddenly old-fashioned, though she could neither put her finger on why nor think what might have replaced it. On the board, there were yellowing flyers for parties and gigs and pictures of shoes and jewellery and bags torn from *Grazia*, and a few computer-printed phone-snaps of Zoe and her friends, and Rob . . . What did Zoe call them? Selfies? But nothing very recent . . . Of course, thought Eve, they pin the stories of their lives on electronic boards, not cork. I must look at Zoe's Facebook . . .

As she took in the evidence of her daughter's busy life, Eve realized with a start that she didn't really know her. At some point – maybe in the last year or two – Zoe had not so much changed – she was still, to all intents, recognizably the Zoe she had always been – but had become unknowable. Is this inevitable? Eve wondered. Or have I somehow let her disappear from right under my nose without even noticing? Eve suddenly felt that letting Zoe go was a big mistake. And she didn't even mean letting her go to New York. No, that bit was simply unfathomable. If you really love them, let them go. Who said that? And was it only in the context of lovers, or did it include teenage daughters too? Eve suddenly felt that this was very bad advice. If you really love them, hold them close . . .

Eve cast her mind back to her own teenage years and recalled being seventeen from the enviable vantage point of a confident (mostly) and successful (happily) fiftysomething. Had she not, in fact, 'made something of herself' – to coin one of her father's favourite phrases – she

may very well have had a different – and differently select-
ive – set of memories. She wondered whether other women
who had made 'less' of themselves – or even women who
had made much of themselves while remaining child free,
like her sister Sonia – clung on more tightly to their memories of being seventeen. Were they perhaps more romantic
and rose tinted? A bit 'she doth protest too much'? Eve
didn't think about being seventeen very often, admittedly,
and, when she did, it was invariably through the prism of
motherhood and specifically here, now, in Zoe's bedroom,
as the mother of Zoe.

Distracted, Eve forgot all about nail varnish and went
back to her own bedroom. It too was a lovely light-suffused
space, decorated in cool greys and warm whites, with
reclaimed oak floorboards, a splash of lime on a feature
wall and an en-suite wet room – all designed for Eve by her
ex-husband with a little bit of guilt and a lot of love, not to
mention an intimate knowledge of his client's taste. It was
a space to treasure – and Eve did. Yet, as she stood in the
centre of the room, she noted, not for the first time, that,
several years after the last tradesman had downed his
tools and left the Barn well and truly converted, nobody
other than her ex-husband and her daughters had ever set
foot inside her bedroom. And maybe – Eve allowed herself
to think – that was a shame. Maybe it would have been
good to share it with someone, even if only occasionally?
No, that wasn't right; maybe – and Eve shifted tenses
uneasily – it would *be* good? And she stood in front of the

full-length mirror, appraising her fifty-three-year-old self, briefly: not too bad. She turned to look at her reflection side-on: a slight, barely perceptible thickening around the middle, but thankfully no need to resort to elasticated waistbands just yet . . . Still slim-ish, fit-ish, with good-ish legs, great hair, lovely eyes, no jowls, a brow that was a great deal smoother than it might be . . . Eve was neither horrified nor delighted by the reflection; she was what she was: a woman of a certain age, not in bad shape at all . . . and yet . . . More yoga . . . ? Maybe some fillers?

But the thought of all of this bored her too, because wasn't the great joy of the – whisper it! – menopause the fact that you could either struggle to maintain yourself like a classic car, with your panels regularly beaten and re-sprayed, or you could simply let rust take hold of your bodywork before you ended up crushed and compacted and recycled and . . . ? At which point Eve had had enough of her reflection and looked away.

Although her own generation's youthful risk-taking usually involved actual *physical* risks – horse riding, white-water rafting, heli-skiing, ballet dancing, chasing the dragon, whatever had floated one's boat, frankly – Eve had long recognized that her daughters' risks would be – were already, presumably – entirely different. Raised mostly behind closed doors, the kind of risks they were most com-fortable with tended to be emotional and sexual risks. Of course, thought Eve, the irony of teenage risk-taking is that it's all about what those risks tell your peers, and teenagers choose which risks they take in the same way they might pick out a new pair of shoes or jeans. Eve recognized that her kids, and those she knew at school, saw no problem with being both intensely secretive and overtly, publicly, boundary-free, to the point where it was becoming increasingly clear that young people's lives were only properly lived if they had been validated by a lens.

Eve smiled as she recalled a recent, disconcertingly amusing conversation with Alice while they'd shopped together. Pointing to a branch of Jessops, Alice had said, 'I have literally, like, never even *seen* that shop. What does it sell?'

'Are you serious?' Eve sighed. 'Cameras. And camera equipment.'

'Who buys cameras?' Alice said.

'Er . . . People who enjoy taking photographs!'

'I enjoy taking photographs, but I've never been to Jessops.' Alice shrugged. 'Or any other camera shop.'

'Ah, but you don't take photographs with a camera, you take pictures on a phone. It's totally different.'

'What's the difference?'

'Well, to take good pictures with a camera requires a degree of skill – and it's not one I've mastered, though your dad is a dab hand. But taking a picture on a phone calls for an ability to point it in vaguely the right direction, touch a button and then upload it to Facebook. In that respect, it's a bit like comparing an original Hockney with a Hockney painting-by-numbers.'

'OK.' Alice digested this while they entered Marks and Spencer. 'What's a painting-by-numbers?'

At which point, rather than jump straight in, Eve had been forced to step back from the edge of the twenty-first-century generational chasm – if only in order to avoid calling her daughter an idiot. 'So, knickers or food first?'

Alice grinned. 'Knickers!'

Thank God, Eve had thought, a subject about which we can actually communicate . . .

As soon as she heard the front door slam, Eve slipped back out of her reverie, relieved, and scrunchied her bob into a scrappy ponytail. It was a timely intervention. Simon, Alice, Barney + energy, love, warmth = *family*: her favourite equation. She all but ran down the stairs.

'You look stunning!' said Simon sarcastically, removing his boots. 'So good to see you're still making an effort on my account after all these years.'

'You look, like, *twelve*,' said Alice, hanging up Barney's lead.

Eve smiled. 'And that's the nicest thing anyone's said to me in ages. How does chicken and oven chips sound?'

'Loving your work,' said Simon. 'On the subject of which – Alice, *homework*. We'll shout when dinner's ready. Your mum and I have some proper grown-up parental talking to do.'

'I am *so* outta here,' said Alice, heading up to her room.

'So,' said Simon, in the kitchen. 'How're things?'

For Eve, that tiny conversational nudge was all it took;

out it all it came. 'Oh, *God*, Simon. It's a *nightmare*. I think I'm very close to resigning. No, make that I *know* I am. And do you know why? Jordan! For some reason, your, uh, son has helped me to see things in an entirely different light. It's kind of hard to describe.'

'OK. But try me. I'm interested. *Obviously.* In fact –' Simon grimaced – 'I'll go first, if you like.'

'OK, shoot!' Eve was slightly thrown; she wanted – needed? – Simon to be *completely* on top of things. That's how it had always worked. That's how it needed to work right now . . .

'I have confessions. Things are not only intensely difficult with Jordan, but –' a deep sigh from Simon; Eve noted that whatever was coming was clearly an even more difficult admission – 'my practice probably has another six months in its current incarnation, unless something *very* unexpected occurs.'

Eve instinctively reached for a bottle of wine. 'OK. So no word from the Sorensens?'

Simon shook his head. 'No. Not yet.'

'And would that change everything?'

A nod. 'It might, yes. We'll have to see. Of course, things can change at any time – the phone suddenly rings or an email bounces in – but if that doesn't happen then I'll have to let people go. It'll just be me and Ed.'

Three hours, a chicken, plenty of chips and another bottle of wine later, Simon and Eve had talked through most of their stuff and had found a way to remain as mutually supportive as ever. When things felt as if they may be falling apart, they invariably cleaved together. Some people would call that co-dependent, they preferred *comfortable*.

Alice had been in bed for at least an hour and the second bottle was all but drained when Simon eventually texted Ed to say that, with a lot of conversational ground still to cover, he was going to crash at the Barn tonight, if that was OK? And how was Jordan?

Simon showed Eve the reply:

> All fine. Jordan good – and tired – and early to bed without so much as a peep. I'm off myself in a mo. Love to all.
> C U 2moz. X

So consuming had the evening been, indeed, that Eve had failed to check her phone. She did so right now, close to eleven p.m. – and saw this:

> OMG NYC awesum mum! ☺. Will phone 2moz. Luv U!!! Z xx

'Look.' She showed the text to Simon, who smiled.

'Still alive, then, albeit far too psyched to use proper grammar. Glad we don't have to send Snake Plissken in to rescue her from a post-apocalyptic Greenwich Village.'

'*Snake Plissken!* Kurt Russell! *Escape From New York!* God – *when* did we see that?'

'I dunno. Early eighties? A lifetime ago.'

'I *loved* that theme tune. Do you remember?' Eve started singing it, badly: '*Dur-dur-dur, dur-dur-dur; dur-dur-DUR, dur, dur, du—*'

'Yup, you're pissed.'

'Yes, I do think it's probably bedtime.' Eve stood up and wobbled a bit. 'You know where your quarters are.' Eve leaned against Simon to steady herself and he held her, gently, firmly. *Comfortably.*

'I do, yes —' Simon paused – 'but I'm not entirely sure they're where I want them to be.'

Eve, unsteady on her feet, squinted at Simon. His potential intention was starting, slowly and rather foggily, to dawn on her. 'What do you *mean*? Do you want me to call you a cab?'

'No, I want to share your bed.'

'You do? OK.' Eve didn't consider herself drunk, just comfortably swaddled in alcohol, and, despite the fact that it had been a long time, the prospect of Simon sharing her bed seemed neither surprising nor scary. It's not as if he wants to have sex.

'Are you sure? Evie – I mean, I want to *fuck* you.'

Eve was so surprised that she giggled. '*Whoooa!* Really?'

'Really. Sorry! I've obviously. Um . . .'

'No, it's OK. But, I mean, you're a married man.'

'Ah, well, I was your husband too.' Simon shrugged. 'Look, I've clearly overstepped the mark. Heat of the moment – sorry!'

'You have – but I don't mind. Come on.' Eve took her ex-husband's hand, gently but firmly. 'I'll take you to *your* quarters. We both need to sober up. And sleep.'

Simon nodded and squeezed her hand. Was that a *blush*? They leaned against each other comfortably, tiptoeing the length of the suspended walkway that separated Eve's bedroom and the guest room from the girls' rooms at the opposite end of the Barn.

'Good night, Simon. *Sleep* well. And thank you.'

'For what? I've clearly made a total arse of myself.'

Eve stood on tiptoes and kissed her very ex-husband on the forehead. 'I mean thank you for, um, *wanting* me? That's sort of sweet.'

Simon grinned lopsidedly. 'I never thought I'd say it but I'll settle for being described as sweet. *Sweet* dreams, Evie.'

20

'Oh. My. *God*,' said Gail as soon as Eve walked through the door, an uncharacteristic fifteen minutes late, the following morning. 'I mean, you could have *said*! Phone's burning itself off the hook already!'

'Sorry, Gail?'

Gail couldn't help noticing that Eve seemed distracted. 'The paper.' Gail pushed an open copy of the *Courier* towards her boss. '*This!*'

'C-WORDS IN THE CLASSROOM? IT'S THE F-WORD WE HAVE TO BLAME'

'So-called feminism has gone too far in our schools,' says Eve Sturridge, head teacher of a top prep school

Eve shivered involuntarily and grimaced. She read the piece. While it still contained the essence, the *germ*, of her argument, the emphasis had also somehow shifted, albeit subtly. Without comparing the article, word for word, with her original 'rant', it was hard to see precisely how this editorial alchemy had been achieved; however, it was very skilful, no doubt about that.

'Ah!' was all that Eve could manage. 'Right. OK. I'm just going to make a quick call.'

'To the sisterhood?' said Gail, rather pleased with herself. 'Coffee?'

Eve smiled. 'A pint, I think. Intravenously. And hold the calls for a few minutes, could you?'

Eve sat down, read the article again – this time deploying a highlighter pen – and then, at the end, she flipped open her laptop, searched her emails and dialled a number. It was answered briskly after just two rings.

'Johnny Nicholson's phone, allegedly!'

'Ah, right, yes, hi, John. *Johnny*. It's, uh, Eve Sturridge here . . . I, uh . . . The *article* – I don't quite recognize it.'

'Ah, yes, Eve – the talk of the town! Well, your "rant" is definitely still all in there, but I will admit that we do have a house style to which our skilled sub-editors will inevitably bend raw copy to fit, as a matter of course. You'll appreciate we're a pretty big machine with many cogs, but you may also be interested to know – that is, if you don't know already – that there's a lot of feedback. If you pop online you'll see there are nearly three hundred comments already. I shouldn't be at all surprised if you got a *Today* out of it. Maybe even a *Newsnight*.'

Eve faltered. Cathy had once asked her to be part of a

feature for the magazine in which mothers of daughters and mothers of sons wrote little first-person articles comparing their parenting techniques and were then photographed together, rather glamorously, with their children. That had been *fun* – but Eve could see that things at the sharp end of newspapers were, well, inevitably *sharper*. No, she couldn't countenance either a *Today* or a *Newsnight*, much less both.

'I don't think I was really expecting this. I mean, I wasn't prepared.'

'I totally appreciate that – *totally*. Tell you what – I'm about to pop into conference with the editor, but how about lunch next week? Somewhere fancy? You're in East Sussex, aren't you? Are you able to get up to town often?'

Eve's gut instinct was to say no, very quickly and force-fully. Therefore she rather surprised herself by saying, 'Yes, that would be lovely. Er, how does Wednesday sound?' She hadn't had a day off in ages.

'Wednesday sounds marvellous. To be honest, I was due a lunch with our restaurant critic and it was somewhere indescribably fancy, just off Piccadilly. I shall simply blow him out and keep the fancy reservation. I'll see if Cath's free too, shall I? How does that sound?'

Eve, who thought that sounded marvellous, ended the call, leaned back in her chair and gently placed both her hands over her solar plexus, which was churning – an excited, edge-of-the-precipice churn. Something was shifting and changing. What *was* that, precisely? Eve stared at the blank screen of her laptop and then, very slowly and methodically, typed *John Nicholson the Courier* into Google and started to read. When her phone rang, she ignored it; this was going to be a long day and she planned on continuing it in much the same fashion that she had started it – which was to say *in charge*.

'I am the boss,' muttered Eve under her breath, despite the fact that there was nobody around to hear. 'I am the boss . . .'

She buzzed through to Gail: 'OK, I can talk now.'

'Oh, good, because I've just had the organizers of that conference you're going to on Friday on the blower. They're really hoping to shuffle their schedule around and persuade you to make a keynote address.'

'Make a keynote address at the Independent Schools Conference? Are you *sure*?'

'I'm sure. Apparently Eleanor Hill has pulled out at the last minute and they appear to be *very* excited about having you fill her shoes.'

'I know her shoes – they're very stylish.' Eve sighed. 'Every single fibre of my entire being is saying, "Don't do it" . . .'

'So I can phone them back and say it's a yes? Fabulous! They'll be thrilled – and you'll be great at it. You have the fire in your belly.'

'Well, I'm not sure about that, but yes, OK, I will be there.'

As the day unfolded – and much to Gail's excitement – Eve not only accepted the Schools Conference speaker role but found herself fast-tracked through a small-to-medium media storm. Spookily, John Nicholson turned out to be correct and both *Newsnight* and *Today* did come through with interview requests. With the assistance of the *Courier*'s press officer, who sounded about the same age as Zoe, Eve turned down the chance of being lightly grilled by Jeremy Paxman on the perfectly reasonable grounds of it simply being 'too bloody scary for words', but after much cajoling from the *Courier*'s PR, she finally caved in and agreed to do *Today* at 8:35 a.m. the following morning, albeit on the phone from home rather than in the studio.

'Total pussycat, Humphrys – honestly!' said the *Courier*'s PR unconvincingly.

'Actually, it's not John Humphrys I'm scared of – it's Sarah Montague,' confessed Eve.

During a brief lunch break taken at her desk in the Odense Holdings office, Anette Sorensen paused to scribble a few words on a Post-it note, which she then stuck on to a ripped-out page from that day's *Courier*.

Look at this, S!
A X

Still smiling, Anette buzzed through to her PA. 'I have something here for Stefan. Can you scan it and email it to him straight away, please?'

*

Meanwhile, in the staffroom at Ivy House, Gail was re-reading Eve's article. It was an odd thing, this admission of apparent failure from a successful traditional prep school head – the school was Ofsted 'Outstanding', after all. Gail knew that, even allowing for the article being 'spun' to fit with the paper's fairly right-wing agenda – and she'd read the original – it was still a bit of a curate's egg. But intriguing nonetheless – so much so that the staffroom copy was looking decidedly dog-eared; even though there were three copies of *The Times*, two *Guardians*, an *Independent* and a *Private Eye* all in circulation, today nobody at Ivy House appeared remotely interested in *them*.

Gail waved the paper. 'Anybody *not* read this yet?' Everyone shook their heads.

And over at Eastdene Community Primary School, the *Courier* was also doing the rounds, though Mike Browning, not a fan of either the paper or its politics, was the last to read it.

'Have you ever met Eve Sturridge?' said Year Six's Mrs Jenkins.

Mike barely missed a beat. 'We were introduced very briefly in the Bell, by her PA, Gail Prince – Harry in your year's mum. Anyway, by all accounts she's a passionate, dedicated and gifted head teacher.' Mike glanced down at the page. 'And she's prepared to put herself on the line, so, while we may not sing from the same educational hymn sheet, hats off to her.'

'She's very glamorous, too,' said Hilary Jenkins. Mike simply shrugged.

Eve surprised nobody more than herself by quite how successfully she negotiated what Tony described on his return from Moscow that afternoon – and not inaccurately – as 'this completely and utterly unnecessary fucking shit-storm'.

'Complete and utter shit-storm, yes,' conceded Eve, in Tony's office at five p.m. 'Unnecessary, not so much.' Eve was feeling emboldened in a way she couldn't recall feeling ever before.

'Don't talk crap. I take it this is your elaborate version of a resignation note, hm?' Tony was pacing now.

'It wasn't formally a resignation, no, but if you'd like to take it as one –' Eve shrugged as Tony paced – 'then so be it. Sack me if you like.'

Tony may have been angry – was, if the throbbing veins in his temples were any indication, incandescent – but Eve knew he wasn't stupid. Sacking her right now would clearly create its own media shit-storm. And, of course, media shit-storms were very often bad for business.

21

Zoe Sturridge woke up in her – *her!* – bedroom in the Sorensens' pale, elegant, light-filled triplex apartment, right opposite Central Park and the Metropolitan Museum on Fifth Avenue, fully refreshed by eight hours of deep and dreamless sleep, ready to face her very first full Manhattan day.

Even allowing for a residue of jetlag, rewinding the events of the previous day in her head after a power shower – with jets that came at you from the sides – had Zoe literally hopping from foot to foot with excitement as she inspected her full-length naked reflection in the long glass diagonally opposite her bed. Having originally packed only for a few nights at Auntie Sonia's Notting Hill flat, she'd forgotten to bring anything to sleep in. Oh, well.

Zoe reached for her phone and held it in front of her face while she snapped her reflection. The result was a headless naked body that was, nonetheless, slightly more clinical, more *forensic* than it was sexy. Zoe deleted it and struck a different pose, this time sitting on the side of the bed with her legs slightly apart. Holding the phone in front of her face again, she snapped at the reflection in the mirror and inspected the results: much better this time – *sexier*, but also kind of anonymous, too. Zoe knew that Rob was cavalier about the whole concept of privacy – after all, every single person she knew, excepting her parents, was cavalier about privacy. But it didn't hurt to be aware, did it? Just in case? After all, it was one thing to give her boyfriend an early-morning hard-on via some spontaneous sexting, quite another to do the same for all her boyfriend's mates. It was probably just as well her face was, quite literally, out of the picture and though Zoe suspected it was just a tiny bit weird to care more about her face being seen than it was her admittedly not-so-private parts, that was just the way things were. She enjoyed imagining his expression when he checked his phone during his lunch break:

Ta-Da! Morning from NYC babes! Thinking of U! xxx ☺

After this, Zoe blow-dried her hair, applied her make-up and pulled on a different pair of near-identical skinny jeans to yesterday's, teaming these with biker boots and a pastel pink crew-neck cashmere, with a slightly Princess-Diana-circa-1981 pie-crust-collared blouse underneath. She finished off the look with an oversized mannish blazer with rolled up sleeves and a mint green satchel hung across her body. It was a little bit Alexa Chung, a little bit

Kate Moss and a whole lot of Zoe Sturridge. It was also very 'London Girl'. Having a look that said 'London Girl' on your first trip to New York seemed to Zoe somehow essential. Albeit she wasn't a London girl at all, she was flying the street-style flag, right down to the tips of her (slightly chewed, but . . .) matte grey nail colour.

She was conscious that she was also dressing to be seen by her boss and hoped that this effort would not go unnoticed, either by her boss or her boss's PA, Tina. She liked Tina, who, as a mother of three daughters herself, presumably had a great deal of experience around teenage fashion crises. As she finally emerged from the bedroom, Zoe caught sight of Tina coming out of her own room further down the parqueted hall.

Tina smiled at Zoe. 'Morning. Sleep well?'

Zoe beamed. 'I did, thanks, yes. *So* comfy, that bed.'

'It's definitely a very comfortable apartment. Now, are you all set for a busy day today?' Tina didn't wait for answer. 'Mr Sorensen has already left for his first breakfast meeting – he usually squeezes in two, back to back – and I have got a few errands for you to do. We'll be hooking up back at the Odense offices by eleven a.m., so I suggest grabbing yourself a bit of breakfast in the kitchen. There'll be croissants and Danishes and fruit salad and granola and salami and ham, if you happen to like cold meats in the mornings –' Zoe stood there silently, wide-eyed, drinking in every word – 'it's a *Nordic* thing, really.' Zoe carried on listening intently while Tina explained that neither she nor Stefan were 'breakfast people but, nonetheless, Modesta always does a lovely spread, so she'll be delighted if *you* eat.'

Zoe nodded. She'd met the Sorensens' silent but smiling housekeeper the night before. Modesta was married to the chauffeur, Ignacio, who had picked them all up from JFK airport the previous afternoon, and the couple lived in and kept house whether the Sorensens were in town or not. According to Tina, Modesta doted on Anette and the Sorensen children, but in their absence would make do with doting on whoever looked the most dotable-upon.

And so, straight after breakfast, Zoe's New York morning evolved, and then after a quick sandwich-in-a-brown-paper-bag lunch, eaten at the deli three doors along from the Odense Holdings NYC offices – situated in a chic brownstone on a quiet street downtown, just like the one where Carrie Bradshaw lives in *Sex and the City*, thought Zoe – came a New York afternoon punctuated by, mostly, yawns. Zoe had felt fine this morning, running on adrenaline and excitement, but now her day was starting to catch up with her. The office had its own espresso machine but, when she asked around, it seemed that everybody preferred Starbucks so she volunteered to go on the afternoon run. As she placed a lengthy list on the Starbucks counter and started ordering, a voice behind her interrupted:

'And you can make mine a skinny latte with an extra shot.'

She spun round. 'Mr Sorensen? Sure!'

'And I'll help you carry these back, too.'

'Right!' Zoe didn't know quite what to say, at least until she remembered. 'Thanks!'

'No problem. You've stolen my job. Hasn't she, Debee?'

'*Shohaz!*' said the barista. Zoe concentrated hard to pick up her words . . . 'Any excuse ta ged ouda dat awfice, right, Mr S?' Debee winked.

'You got it,' said Stefan Sorensen.

Zoe didn't quite know what to make of the cheerful banter between her boss and the extremely pretty black girl behind the counter. They seemed like old friends, but maybe this was just how people did stuff in New York. She also realized how embarrassingly few exchanges she herself had ever had with somebody who wasn't white, what with her neighbourhood being *very* racially un-diverse. Nonetheless, she also couldn't imagine Stefan Sorensen having this kind of amongst-equals conversation in, say, the Starbucks in Piccadilly. Yeah, it was clearly a New York thing, this kind of chatty friendliness. Mr Sorensen hadn't even been this friendly to Zoe until now – the plane journey had been notable for the fact that he'd spent all of it on his laptop, speaking to her just once ('How you enjoying executive travel, Zoe?' Answer: 'Very much!'). For her part, Zoe had been thrilled by the take-off and landing, which she discovered you felt much more keenly in a little jet than you did on an ordinary plane, and spent the bits in between reading magazines and staring at the clouds and chatting with Tina. Now, however, she felt sufficiently emboldened and caffeinated to attempt some small talk with the boss.

'I guess being the boss means there's always someone else to get your latte, but maybe it's fun to do it yourself?'

Stefan Sorensen narrowed his eyes and, for the first time, Zoe felt, took a proper look at her.

'Oh, it's not only *fun*, sometimes it's essential.'

'Keeps da feet on da ground – right, Mr S?' said Debee.

'Sure does. Head in the clouds, feet on the ground – that's me.'

Zoe grinned, Stefan grinned at Zoe and Debee glanced between both of them, in a rather knowing sort of way, Zoe felt.

'Debee here has a degree in Child Psychology from New York State University and is currently studying for her master's. Am I right, Debee?' said Stefan.

Debee nodded. 'Yup, thas right, Mr Sorensen.'

Wow, thought Zoe. But what she said was, 'That's awesome.'

22

As far as Stefan Sorensen was concerned, getting to know Zoe was not yet on his schedule. However, having noted her prettiness, smartness and cutely feisty, if ham-fisted, attempt to understand her environment, the emphasis was very much on *yet*. As he moved through an afternoon packed with the usual whirl of meetings and phone calls that involved pacing the office while barking instructions, Stefan's thoughts kept drifting back to Zoe. And, occasionally, one of these stray Zoe-thoughts would segue into a thought about her mother, with and around whom his children spent their days. And so Stefan successfully pushed those thoughts away.

As an 'alpha male in an alpha city' (Anette's description; he had liked it and laughed when it had originally been delivered, tongue firmly in cheek), Stefan Sorensen knew that he was fairly predictable in his alpha-male habits. He liked to work hard and work out harder; he liked to relax in upscale surroundings among his similarly blessed peers, and his distractions from the business of making money were inevitably the distractions of the super-rich – yachting, scuba diving, heli-skiing, playing poker and polo; all of these things were *fun*. And a life without fun was just another late night alone with a spreadsheet. Anyway, even if there was the time, there would never be the inclination to spend a quiet night in with, say, a pizza, sprawled in front of *Breaking Bad* on TV. No – with only a very occasional twinge of regret, Stefan Sorensen accepted that his downtime was uptime, that black tie was his sweatpants-and-a-hoodie – unless he was at the gym, of course, which he was, most mornings, by six a.m., if he wasn't on a plane, or otherwise engaged. It helped to have a trainer on speed-dial and a gym in his own home.

Stefan Sorensen knew himself to be the opposite of risk averse. Just as his talent for making money created apparently infinite opportunities to make even more of it, so he understood that good looks and charm created infinite opportunities to meet and seduce women – which in no way distracted from his relationship with Anette, which was its own special and unique entity, entirely self-contained and utterly impregnable. Stefan had loved his wife intensely from pretty much the first moment he'd seen her, which had been from quite a distance on their first day at university. Sex with women other than his wife was, nonetheless, a regular occurrence – either as one-offs or what Stefan described (discreetly, among the right kind of male friends) as 'six monthers', six months being the cut-off point wherein something invariably ceased being casual and became somehow indefinably more complex and committed. Stefan knew that Anette knew all of this went on – and he also knew that as long as these fun and fleeting distractions never in any way threatened the fabric of their marriage then they would continue indefinitely.

And so today was turning out to be the sort of frenetically busy day that demanded some proper downtime. And, like the unwitting fish in a restaurant tank, today's 'downtime' had already been selected and would soon be removed from the shoal to be prepped. In relation to his New York schedule, Stefan relied on Tina to organize *everything* – it was simply his job to follow through. Downtime arrangements were no exception.

At 5:30 p.m., Tina appeared in his office wearing an uncharacteristic frown. 'Very sorry, Stefan,' she said, 'but I've just had Steve Dershowitz's PA call to cancel your dinner tonight at Locanda Verde with him and Alan Dohenny.'

'Shame, I was looking forward to that. They say why?'

'Urgent business back in London, apparently.'

'OK. So what do I do tonight?'

'Well, I booked the table in your name and it hasn't been cancelled.'

'OK. You fancy dinner?' Stefan enjoyed the occasional fallback dinner date with Tina, though sex was never on that menu. There were certain professional boundaries never to be crossed, and sleeping with your PA was very much one of those.

'You know I'd love that, but I've actually got a ticket tonight for *Memphis*. Hard to get!'

'Oh, no – you've got to see that. No problem. I'll just swing by Verde after work and grab a bite. Early night could do me good.' A pause; a narrowing of the eyes. 'Or how about I show young Zoe the bright lights?'

Tina hesitated. 'Uh, well, *yes*, why not? Your table's booked for eight p.m. . . .' She paused, as though wanting to say more.

Stefan thought about the exceptionally pretty girl in Starbucks whom he'd barely registered on the plane. She was young, maybe nineteen or twenty – but not *too* young. He had seen in her eyes quite clearly that she was not too young *at all*. Stefan Sorensen was not a man who wrestled with his conscience; he famously – in business and in life – made decisions fast and stuck by them. 'Might be fun. Tell her to go home now and get changed and get Ignacio to drop her off at Verde. I'll go straight from here.' Yes, that was a plan. He had been looking forward to a fun business-meets-pleasure evening with the guys, but there was no reason why he couldn't paradigm-shift his way into a fun evening with a pretty young woman. No reason at all.

23

Three hours later, via a minor fashion crisis that was averted simply because she only had one dress with her (very little and black and grown-up and belonging to Eve), Zoe found herself sitting opposite Stefan Sorensen at one of New York's most fashionable restaurants, inspecting their respective starter plates: blue crab with jalapeño and tomato crostini for Stefan and salad with dried cherries, American speck and hazelnut vinaigrette for Zoe, despite the fact that the only ingredient on the menu she had actually recognized was 'salad'. As she watched Stefan eat, she considered how very dramatically her day had reconfigured itself.

'Sorry?' she had said to Tina when she'd been told she was having dinner with Stefan Sorensen. 'I *am*?'

'Yes. You can leave at six and grab a cab uptown to the apartment. Ignacio will drop you at the restaurant for eight p.m.. It's not formal, but it is fashionable, OK? And in the meantime I'd try and brush up on the multi-syllables, yes?'

Tina had been brisk and so Zoe could barely speak: 'Uh!'

'You can do better than that, Zoe! Mr Sorensen has a very low boredom threshold.'

'Absolutely! No problem, Tina!'

Tina had laughed. 'That's better. And have a fun time.'

Zoe had nodded because if there was a more fun time than having dinner with Stefan Sorensen in one of New York's most fashionable restaurants then, at that precise moment, she couldn't really imagine what it might be.

And now here she was, sharing an actual bottle of red wine with Stefan Sorensen. Like, mental! As Zoe nervously took her first sip of something delicious called Lonardi Taurasi, she relaxed slightly and knew with the perfect certainty that comes of being seventeen that this was going to be a night to remember *forever*. Especially as Stefan had smiled as she'd arrived and said, 'Zoe, you are as beautiful as you are smart. Great dress!'

'Thank you.' She'd very nearly confessed that it belonged to Eve but had bitten her lip just in time.

'So, how you liking New York so far?'

'A lot!' Zoe looked around the room – cosy, buzzing, New Yorky, just like she'd pictured it. 'Like, this is *great*.'

Stefan smiled. '*Like*, Robert De Niro owns it. He's often in.'

'*The* Robert De Niro? From, like, *Meet The Fockers*? No way.'

Zoe didn't think she'd been *that* funny; however, Stefan threw back his head and roared with laughter. '*Way!* And, as far as I know, there's only the one.'

'Wow. That is so awesome.' Zoe reached for her wine. It really was delicious.

'And speak of the devil . . . Hey, *Bobby*!'

'Hey, *Sorensen*! Long time!' The two men embraced. 'How's your beautiful—?' De Niro broke off and glanced at Zoe, who swiftly clamped her gaping mouth shut and tried to smile a normal smile. The first time she goes out for dinner in New York and *this* happens! Wait till Rob hears about this . . . Rob, whose parents had actually *named him after* Robert De Niro.

'Ah, I'm afraid Anette's in London, taking care of business,' said Stefan with a shrug. 'However, I have the lovely Zoe here to keep me company. She's interning at Odense and, as it's her first bite of the Apple, I thought I'd show her the bright lights.'

De Niro winked. 'Nice!' He turned to Zoe, held out his hand. 'And where better to see 'em, huh? You enjoy yourself, Zoe.'

Zoe tried to remember Jay-Z's rap from 'New York' – *Yeah, yeah, I'm out that Brooklyn / Now I'm down in Tribeca / Right next to De Niro.* Ha! She nodded. 'I shall, yes, thank you very much, Mr De Niro.' She hoped she didn't sound too stupid; she felt slightly lobotomized. Maybe it was the wine?

When they'd finished dinner, Ignacio was waiting for them in the car, right outside the restaurant. As soon as he spotted Stefan, he got out and ran around to hold open the door for Zoe, who slid into the back seat, smiling broadly. Seconds later, she could feel Stefan beside her, the heat of his leg next to hers as the car pulled away from the kerb and eased its way smoothly into the New York night. As the car carved its uptown groove through the city's canyons, Zoe felt – suddenly, but not surprisingly – the warmth of Stefan's hand as he took hers and started tracing circles slowly on her palm with his index finger.

'That tickles!' She giggled. Zoe noted her giggle with slightly detached surprise; she wasn't by nature a giggler *at all*. In fact, she kind of despised giggling, generally speaking. Then again . . . she considered the possibility . . . perhaps I haven't led a very giggle-inspiring kind of life until now.

'Say again?' Stefan looked quizzically at Zoe.

Zoe squirmed. She thought she'd only *thought* that giggle-related thought, but apparently enough of that divine-tasting wine had made her *say* it. Zoe couldn't recall ever feeling quite as relaxed as she did right now. She was also very tired but absolutely wasn't going to let that stand in the way of anything at all. This, she decided, is probably what it means to be 'in the moment'. She turned towards Stefan Sorensen and looked him straight in the eye. 'I just said that I feel giggly but I'm not usually much of a giggler.'

'But tonight you are? There is a time and a place for giggling and maybe this is it.'

Zoe didn't answer but instead leaned her head on Stefan's shoulder – where it felt just right – and stared out of the car window at the city speeding past. What a great city. She sighed and closed her eyes, felt Stefan turn towards her, felt his lips – *his lips!* – on her ear as he whispered, 'Welcome to New York, Zoe.'

Back at the apartment, there was no sign of Modesta and Ignacio had disappeared with the car. Nobody was in evidence, yet Zoe felt sure that somewhere behind closed doors, or maybe on a separate floor, the well-oiled cogs and wheels of Stefan Sorensen's behind-the-scenes world continued to turn. But, in the moment, here and now, he was pouring her a glass of champagne and, as she sipped her Perrier-Jouët (such a gorgeous bottle!) from a crystal flute, Zoe was feeling just the wrong side of sober. When Stefan said, 'Come on up and check out the view from the terrace,' Zoe said, 'I didn't know there was a *terrace!*' and then stumbled very slightly as she followed him to the elevator, and then giggled, at which point Stefan held out an arm to steady her and then snaked it around her waist and pulled her closer to him. Zoe found that she fitted very well, so she stayed.

'I think I'd better look after you,' said Stefan, gently placing a kiss on her forehead.

Zoe nodded mutely. She felt very safe and special and somehow *chosen* and knew that if it weren't for the bubbles she might have felt nervous, too – but not *that* nervous. 'Yes, please,' she said. And, against the backdrop of the twinkling lights of Manhattan, she held her breath and closed her eyes – you will remember this always, Zoe

Sturridge – and then she felt exactly what she'd expected to feel: Stefan's lips, surprisingly soft, on hers, and his tongue licking her lips and then probing her mouth and it was just . . . just . . . She sort of buckled internally, felt herself very happily letting go . . . Stefan Sorensen wants to fuck me and I want to be fucked by Stefan Sorensen, and . . . A fleeting image of Rob popped into her mind's eye uninvited. And she knew that Rob would be angry at her betrayal but that, then again – you were never quite sure with Rob – maybe his anger would be outweighed by his being impressed. I mean – Stefan Sorensen! In fact, Zoe thought, he'll probably want to see what we get up to. And then Zoe pushed away all thoughts of Rob and was right back in the moment, feeling Stefan's hands moving up her legs, gently but firmly pushing between her thighs. At which point she decided she also wanted to see what this new New York version of Zoe Sturridge was going to get up to.

Snapshot memories from a New York night:

Being carried – yes, *carried*! – through rooms and down halls to a huge and dimly lit (but not dark) bedroom, being placed on a huge bed – made of clouds? This bed is made of clouds, right? – and giggling again as Stefan removed her shoes and tights – omigod, tights with a ladder! – and her knickers – best knickers, thank God! – and as she pulled her dress over her head and he undid her bra he was smiling at her giggles, and then . . . and . . . Ooh, a bit blurry after that, mostly. But not horrible blurry – dreamy blurry. And then eventually, *finally*, curled in Stefan Sorensen's arms, sleepy blurry . . .

Zoe Sturridge woke and stretched and then, just for a moment, wondered where she was, which bed she was in and where, and then, as her tummy gave a tiny flip of pleasure, she turned over, very slowly, and, half squinting in case she woke him, in which case she would of course pretend to be asleep, Zoe peered at Stefan Sorensen, who was currently very definitely deeply and dreamily asleep beside her. She couldn't help smiling, nor could she help gently stretching her arms above her head and arching her back with pleasure, though she stopped just short of an audible *purr*. Lying on her back, she was far enough away from Stefan in the super-king-size cloud-bed to be able to move without waking him, but close enough to feel the warmth of his body and the steady exhalation of his breathing – deep, relaxed, untroubled.

From her comfortable vantage point, Zoe looked at the bedroom for the first time in daylight. It was appropriately large without being grotesquely Master-of-the-Universe – maybe twenty feet square and set at the corner of the apartment building with two walls of, mostly, windows, from which Zoe could, at this angle, see just sky. She knew you had to be pretty high up to see just sky in Manhattan, where 'sky' presumably cost even more than 'tree', and she knew that 'tree' wasn't cheap. The room reminded her of one she had seen once, briefly, when she was ten – at

Claridges, where her aunt had stayed for her fortieth birthday and where Eve and Sonia had taken Zoe and Alice for tea to celebrate. Zoe noted that this room felt equally unlived-in, as if the Sorensens treated their apartment as a private hotel with knobs on, with some of those knobs being permanent staff and your own, uh, *elevator* straight into the entrance hall.

Zoe suddenly thought of Rob and, more specifically, what he would think if he could see her here, now, lying spread-eagled in this absurdly giant bed, next to a *billionaire*, like something out of a trashy miniseries. Except that there was no point in imagining any of this, really, because Rob wouldn't ever see her here. Wouldn't, indeed, ever *know* she'd been here.

As far as Zoe was concerned, this was easily the best and most beautiful bedroom she had ever seen in real life – and possibly even inside a magazine. It was Nordic-stylish without being too in-your-face groovy. It wasn't, for example, as obviously 'cool' as her dad's bedroom – with the emphasis on 'obviously' because, oddly, from this vantage point, her dad's room (hitherto the uber-bedroom benchmark, closely followed by her mum's) was suddenly looking a bit try-hard. This place, however, was just *perfect*: the right amount of art and objects and light and shade and fatness of quilt and plumpness of pillow and correctness of temperature. There could have been an entire field's worth of frozen peas underneath the deep mattress and Zoe would never even have suspected, for all that she felt like a particularly contented princess. At which point she yawned and turned again to look at her bed-mate who, she was startled to see, had his eyes wide open and was inspecting *her*.

24

Ten minutes later, Stefan Sorensen watched the tongue of this beautiful young woman moving up and down, up and down . . . and pushed any nagging thoughts of wrongness – she is very young but not younger than twenty, surely? – to the back of his mind and abandoned himself entirely to this very distracting moment. And then, after they'd had sex for the third time in eight hours – the first time, frenetic and relatively selfish on his part, the second far more generously about Zoe and now this third occasion, which turned out to be somewhere comfortably between the two extremes – Zoe was lying in Stefan's arms, apparently entirely relaxed. He liked that she felt so comfortable with him – felt so comfortable, full stop. He liked this young woman – which wasn't necessarily a given – and he liked that he had so evidently given her such pleasure. The calm, post-coital silence in which they breathed in tandem ended, however, when he finally spoke.

'So, you lovely, intoxicating . . .' He broke off, appraised the woman – *girl!* – in his arms. 'This has been absolutely great in every way, believe me.'

Zoe squirmed and nodded. 'Uh, *yes*, Mr Sorensen.'

'And you can stop the "Yes, Mr Sorensen" routine – cute though it is.'

'Sorry – *Stefan*.' She rolled her eyes and pushed herself playfully into his chest, at which point Stefan very gently eased her away from him by mere millimetres. Zoe stopped squirming, stilled herself.

'So, here's the deal. I have been with my wife for a long time. We met at university, we fell in love and we married just after we graduated. We are partners both in life and in business and we are devoted parents to our beloved children. In short, we will never, under any imaginable circumstances, let anyone or anything come between us. Got that?'

'I've got that. Are you going to, like, ask me to *sign* something?'

Stefan was amused. 'You've seen too many movies, I think. What do you suppose you'd have to sign, anyway?'

Zoe shrugged. 'Um, by the way, you do know how old I am, right?'

'Twenty? Twenty-one? You're at uni, right?'

'No, I'm seventeen. I'm not at uni; I'm doing my A levels.'

Stefan lay on his back, stared at the ceiling and sighed. Jesus Christ! Seventeen! All these years of playing away *by the rules* and now he'd finally broken Anette's Rule Of Rules: no under-eighteens, *ever*. Why hadn't Tina said something?

'OK, so I knew you were a student intern. I didn't realize you were a *high school* student intern. That is very young – seventeen. I'm so sorry. Please tell me you weren't a virgin?'

Zoe giggled – her new default setting. 'I'm only young on the outside – and no, don't worry, definitely not a virgin. I lost it when I was, like, fourteen?' Which, from the vantage point of seventeen, suddenly sounded to Zoe quite young, and maybe a bit slutty – and she didn't want Stefan Sorensen to think she was slutty, just that she was not a kid. Anyway, it was still a whole year later than her best friend, Carmen.

As if to underline the point that she was now very much a young woman of the world, equally at home among her peers in the sixth-form common room of Westdene Girls' Grammar or under the duvet in the New York cloud-bed of a forty-something billionaire, Zoe turned on to her side and traced her finger up Stefan's abdomen, along the whorl of blonde hair that stretched above his pelvis and onwards, up to his chest and his neck and over the hill of his chin and, very gently, barely touching, on to his lips. He groaned and opened his mouth just wide enough to receive her slim finger, sucking on it greedily and, with eyes closed, very nearly abandoned himself to the moment . . . *but not quite.*

He removed the finger and turned to face Zoe. Pretty, pretty *girl.* It actually hurt to say this, because, until Zoe's bombshell, he had imagined there might be a very pleasurable six-monther in the offing. 'OK, Zoe, I had no idea you were seventeen, which means this can't happen again, right?'

Zoe pouted. It was, noted Stefan, a very small, slight pout, but nonetheless the pout of a seventeen-year-old suddenly not getting her own way. This made him yet more determined to do the right thing now. Better late than—

'I don't know what difference me being seventeen makes.'

Stefan sighed. 'It makes a lot of difference. It may seem hard to quantify from your perspective, but –' he shrugged – 'there we are. We have had an absolutely *beautiful* night and we will both remember it always.' Zoe fixed him with her big dark eyes. As trusting as a bloody puppy, thought Stefan.

'Is it finished right now, then – our beautiful night?' she said.

Stefan found this question quite astoundingly and unexpectedly arousing. He sat up and turned towards Zoe, grasping her wrists firmly and rolling her on to her back, hauling himself up until he straddled her. He lowered his lips towards hers and whispered, 'Actually, *no* – very nearly, but not quite yet.'

Jesus. I must be mad, he thought. But somehow Zoe's giggle and all the impending pleasure appeared to cancel out the inexplicable, unexpected, bafflingly illogical *insanity*.

An hour later, he considered deleting the phone number Zoe Sturridge had just given him and which he had dutifully keyed into his phone in front of her, and decided against it. After which none of Stefan's intelligently-measured post-coital rationalization managed to stop him from impulsively hurling a mug of coffee – just handed to him by Modesta – against the kitchen wall while he read a freshly arrived text from Anette. '*Fuck*! I'm so sorry, Modesta,' he said immediately. 'I'm *really* sorry. Lot going on.'

After this, Stefan went straight down in the elevator where, settled in the backseat of his car, being driven downtown by Ignacio, his thoughts circled themselves into such a chaotic vortex that the only escape was to close his eyes and dream of being re-enveloped by a fat white cumulonimbus of a duvet, heralding rain.

However, even as he power-napped en route to the office, there was a small but important percentage of Stefan's brain that was sufficiently engaged to remind itself to sack Tina before lunch – albeit with a *very* generous severance package.

Rob was awoken suddenly from his late-morning lie-in by the *ding* of an incoming text:

> Yay, babes, sending BIG LUV from the concrete jungle
> where dreams are made . . . oh! WOT A NITE!
> ;-) XXX

Rob couldn't get back to sleep after that. He didn't reply to the text, either – instead, he got up and went down to the kitchen, made himself a strong cup of coffee and smoked a roll-up. After about twenty minutes of pacing and smoking and coffee consumption, he went back upstairs and switched on his laptop. Using Final Cut Pro, it didn't take long to edit the footage he knew so well into something that looked, tantalizingly, a lot like a movie trailer. Try as he might to block them out with his work, unwelcome thoughts and their concomitant emotions kept bubbling up. Jealousy, for starters. Rob was jealous of Zoe, having it large in New York. He hated cities, but still: New York. And a fucking *private jet*. And hanging out with a fucking *billionaire*. And ... And ... Rob really didn't want to lose Zoe. Not yet – and definitely not on *her* schedule. *Fuck it*. He slammed the laptop shut and decided to, of all the fucking ridiculous things, go for a walk. Rob really didn't like the way that losing Zoe made him feel.

25

On a surprisingly mild February morning, Gail fell into an easy and spontaneous neighbourly conversation with Mike over their respective mugs of tea and pairs of secateurs.

'You know what, Gail? I like this place more than I ever expected to.' Mike dunked his Rich Tea.

'I'm *so* glad,' said Gail. 'You could easily have found it insanely boring here. I mean, it's not like Eastdene was going to offer you some sort of a big professional challenge or –' she giggled – 'a relentless social life.'

'And luckily that suits me fine, because I'm not after either of those. I'm embracing middle age with a frankly terrifying amount of relish. These days I am all about –' Mike waved his secateurs – '*this!*'

Gail's laughter was slightly over-compensatory, longer and louder than it might have been. Far from being ready to 'embrace' middle age, Gail wasn't even ready to give it a brisk handshake. 'OK,' she said, 'so what kind of shape is your new gardening lifestyle taking?'

Mike raised an eyebrow. 'Hm . . . maybe a stellated dodecahedron?'

'Stop it.' Gail only just managed to restrain herself from overstepping the mark from friendly neighbour to flirty neighbour by punching Mike gently on the arm. Instead, much as she wanted to stay and tease out a little more of the off-duty Mike Browning, she reluctantly made her excuses, shrugging: 'Supermarket, Harry, football.'

'Ah, yes, important stuff. Have a good weekend, Gail.'

Gail filled the rest of her 'good' weekend ferrying Harry from football pitch to friend's party to another friend's Xbox, from the cinema to McDonald's. In between, there was still a surprising amount of time left over for a bracing walk around Hastings by herself. Gail wished she had a dog for company, while knowing that she would never have one unless somebody genetically modified them to not smell of dog.

There were excellent charity shops in Hastings and its environs, quality bric-a-brac to be acquired, if Gail could only steel herself to overcome the *grubbiness* of it all. She knew the area well, and she could see that, these days, it was suffering more than a little from the blustery economic storm. After her charity shop browse, Gail walked along the seafront, past the burned-out pier and up Conquest Road, past the Lottery-Fund-revamped public gardens, peering en route into the windows of the lovely big, slightly careworn houses which attracted new financially downsizing/architecturally upsizing 'down-from-

Londoners' looking to inject some chic into the area's shabby. These people were, Gail knew, particularly greedy for sea views and too many expensive to heat bedrooms, and in their enthusiasm for a low-mortgage lifestyle were happy to overlook the fact that, however big their houses and however gorgeous their views, the town itself was a not-very-commuter-friendly ninety-five minutes from London by train, and at least two hours by car.

Idiots, she thought.

Though her orbit and those of the DFLs had previously never collided much beyond Ivy House (to which they were inevitably drawn) and the occasional supermarket checkout queue, she didn't generally warm to these women, who seemed prickly and shallow and spoke too loudly in public and always looked over her shoulder when they talked to her, apparently searching out something more stimulating and fashionable. They would as often as not rock up in the school playground at drop-off and pick-up wearing big sunglasses *in winter*, as though they were on the slopes, carrying Costa coffees (while bemoaning the lack of local Starbucks) and touting rolled-up copies of *Grazia* like cudgels to ward off the parochially unstylish. They also tended to talk a lot about London as if they lived there; they still got their highlights done in Mayfair, apparently, and met girlfriends for lunch in places like Selfridges.

'Stop it, Hugo! Mummy can't hear herself *think*!'

Gail heard her before she spotted the typical DFL

mother in the gardens, pushing a grizzling toddler strapped tightly into a Bugaboo, while she barked into a BlackBerry. Why do you lot always refer to yourselves in the third person? wondered Gail.

'Look, are you *absolutely* sure you can't get to Waitrose in Tenterden on the way back?'

Gail smiled an entirely fake smile as she approached and the woman glanced at her, still talking into her phone while returning Gail's smile with one that never quite met her eyes, either. 'Really? Well, Sainsbury's might just have it at a pinch, I suppose.' A pause. 'Is it *important*? Well, it's not exactly life-or-death but I can't cook it without it!' The woman rolled her eyes at Gail, as if seeking empathetic sisterly support.

Your poor bloody husband, thought Gail, who had never been to Waitrose – or Selfridges, come to that. If she'd allowed herself to admit it, the truth was that Gail was half afraid of London. And, at her age, the contrast between Selfridges and Debenhams would probably be so mind altering she'd start visiting smart department stores like . . . like . . . *crack dens*. She smiled at the woman in what she hoped was the right kind of way – Gail was, after all, proud to be a *woman's* woman. And then she realized she recognized her – Carol? Caroline? Carola? Whatever. She had a five-year-old in the pre-prep department at Ivy House. Gail widened her smile much further than she wanted to and tacked on a cheery sort of nod and a raised eyebrow. Empathy. Sisterhood. And sound business sense.

'Ah, hello! It's Ivy House Gail, isn't it?' said the woman, slipping her phone into her pocket.

Is it? thought Gail. Am I somebody without a surname who is entirely defined by her place of work? What kind of person would even say that out loud?

'I'm Sarah Fellowes, Edie's mum.'

Gail's smile was now so warm Sarah could have toasted marshmallows, yet ... Sarah and Edie Fellowes? The names registered only vaguely and Gail realized that this was almost certainly the first time in the best part of two decades she'd got any parent's name quite so wrong. And very clearly and suddenly she knew exactly what this meant. It meant that, somehow or other, and without even noticing, she'd probably stopped caring. She smiled brightly at Sarah.

'Hello, Sarah. You're quite close, except my name's not Ivy House Gail, it's Gail *Prince*.'

26

For Eve, a long overdue lunch up in the Smoke with Cathy Gower and Cathy's colleague John ('call me Johnny') Nicholson turned out to be fun and revelatory. The fun came of eating in such chic surroundings; their restaurant had only been open a fortnight and was therefore full of the sort of shiny clientele Eve felt she recognized, even if she couldn't quite place all the faces, though both Graham Norton and Mary Portas (not together) were easy enough to spot. Johnny helpfully pointed out a couple of actors, a senior member of the Cabinet and two well-known restaurant critics.

'That's the smug one –' Johnny indicated a table that was clearly one of the best in the room – 'and, over there, pretending to hide behind a pepper grinder and failing, is the annoying one.'

Eve laughed. 'Not a fan of restaurant critics, then?'

'Actually, I am. I was at uni with the smug one and worked alongside the annoying one on the subs' desk at the *Telegraph*, back in the day.' Johnny leaned forward, conspiratorially. 'They're both brilliant writers, with the kind of morals that'd have alley cats suing for defamation.' Johnny waved cheerfully across the room at each of the critics, who waved back equally cheerfully, and then, affecting mock-horror and clearly playing to the room, waved at each other.

'I'd always imagined journalism to be this vastly complex world, but it seems almost cosy.' Eve drank in the scene, feeling desperately provincial.

'Well, I wouldn't go quite *that* far, but it's a smaller world than you might imagine,' said Cathy. 'I suppose it's like any industry – if you're in it for long enough you inevitably end up knowing more people than you'd probably choose to.'

'And do you love your industry, Johnny?'

Johnny raised an eyebrow. 'Hm. There's an interesting question.' He turned to Cathy. 'Do you? Put it like this – I *know* my industry.'

Eve was genuinely interested. 'So, familiarity breeds contempt?'

Johnny and Cathy smiled; Johnny spoke for both of them. 'Well, I didn't say that, precisely, but now you come to mention it. Although, hang on, we're the journalists, so surely we're supposed to be the ones asking the questions?'

Eve and Cathy laughed. And so they all started asking questions of each other and managed a meaningful bit of business talk, too, which included Johnny telling Eve – to her very considerable surprise – that her little 'rant' went down so well, the paper would be interested in seeing more articles from her in the future. After this, and having discussed their respective children – Johnny had none but, thought Eve, feigned interest quite brilliantly when Eve showed him pictures of the girls on her phone ('My word, supermodels both!') – quite suddenly it was 3:15 p.m. and they hadn't even noticed they were the only diners, aside from the 'annoying' restaurant critic, left in the elegant room.

'Blimey,' said Johnny as he called for the bill. 'I genuinely cannot recall the last time that happened. What a fun lunch!' He turned to Eve. 'I hope you weren't in a rush?'

'Not at all, and I've enjoyed every minute. Though I'd always assumed long lunches were part of a journalist's job description?'

'Ha, well, you would have been right about fifteen years ago – these days, not so much.' At which moment the 'annoying' critic, who'd clearly also had a glass or two, appeared in front of their table, grinning broadly and extending a hand.

'Good to see you two looking so well, Johnny Boy and the fragrant, not to mention *multi-award winning* Cathy Gower, all obviously still on decent expenses. Delighted the *Courier*'s still coughing up in these straitened times. Remind your excellent boss that I'm always available during the transfer window, yeah?' He grinned at Eve. 'But, now, you definitely *aren't* a hack.'

'Is it really that obvious?' asked Eve.

'In the best possible way,' said the critic, whom Eve found rather charming.

'Ah, this is Eve Sturridge, one of my newest contributors,' said Johnny, which made Eve colour slightly. 'And, Eve, this is Gordo McBride, the world's most annoying restaurant critic.'

'Talented and modest too. *Lovely* to meet you, Eve, though I still don't see you as a hack. But here's a tip – whatever they're paying you, ask for double.' And he winked. And Eve winked back. At which point she realized she hadn't drunk so much at lunchtime this entire *century*. But before she could say anything, Gordo was gone.

Johnny pushed back his seat. 'So, that was a lovely lunch.'

'Absolutely magnificent and *madly* overdue. Thanks for letting us crash it, Johnny,' said Cathy, rising.

'Always a pleasure – and I really hope we can do it again.' As Cathy left the table to fetch her coat, Johnny continued, 'Or maybe, Eve, even dinner, sometime soon – if you were planning on coming up to town again? Or, in fact, even if you weren't, maybe I could persuade you?'

Eve could feel a blush rising. The moment clearly demanded to be seized yet what came out of her mouth surprised her: 'I'm not in town much, really, what with the daughters and the day job and all the rest of it, so . . .' Christ, what am I saying? This very nice man is asking me out and I'm batting him away . . .

'Well, now you're a *Courier* contributor it's entirely justified, so if you ever find a window ajar, you know where I am.' Johnny smiled, gave an easy shrug and then there was a beat of silence as Eve and Johnny locked eyes, very briefly. She liked Johnny Nicholson.

On the train home, armed with a bottle of Evian, sobering up, station by station, Eve thought about how she must not let her friendships slide – she would arrange to see Cathy again soon, just the two of them, or even invite her and the boys and, of course, Cathy's husband, Peter, down to the Barn for a weekend. Yes, that was a good idea – they hadn't had a weekend together since all their children had been toddlers. Which, as Eve recalled the consecutive sleepless nights, epic hangovers and fractious kids, was probably *precisely* why they hadn't done it since. But then the toddler years were long gone. This time around they'd probably be drinking wine *with* their kids.

And then her thoughts turned to John Nicholson . . . Who has just turned me into a journalist! Eve contemplated the prospect of a dinner with Johnny and there was no aspect of that that didn't appeal, other than the three-hour round trip. Though perhaps she could stay at Sonia's? Yes, that was a definite plan . . .

Eve took another ladylike swig from her bottle of Evian and was about to close her eyes when she heard the ping of a text arriving. She unearthed the phone from the bottom of her bag. Ah, Zoe. At last!

OiOi CARMEN OMG! U can SO NOT blv wots goin
down here! NewYork – concret jungle where dreems r
made. OH! Have I got NEWS for U?! XXX

Eve firstly felt a wave of irritation at her perfectly intelli-
gent eldest daughter's inability to apparently *ever* send a
text without sounding like a moron, though she supposed
this was yet another Teen Thing. And then she was even
more irritated by the fact that this text was clearly mis-
sent, aimed at Zoe's 'BFF', Carmen. And then, before she
had time to respond, another *ping* –

MUM! SO SOZ! Just havin a Gr8 time. Love u loads. CU
Sat! ZoXXX

– which was fine and nice, and everything. But *still*. There
was no sense of Zoe needing to share that previous 'Have I
got NEWS for U?!' and Eve was suddenly rather keen to
know what this 'news' might be. However, as Zoe's mother,
she reckoned she'd probably be the last to know. She sighed
and tapped out a reply.

EXCITING! Enjoy yourself, take care, work hard and I
look forward so much to seeing you at the weekend! Love
you MORE! Mum xxx

It was somewhere between Wadhurst and Frant that Eve
decided she ought to spend more time reacquainting

herself with her eldest daughter. Perhaps we could do something nice together – and maybe for even longer than twenty minutes? Perhaps we should go to a spa? Though the thought of that made her feel a bit like her sister, Sonia, who – *urgh!* – was pretty much a posh spa season-ticket holder. Then, as the portly, suited-and-booted gentleman in the seat diagonally opposite caught her eye and smiled an amused sort of smile, Eve realized that she'd actually just *pulled* the face she thought she'd only *thought*.

Daylight wine doesn't agree with me at all. And Eve closed her eyes, all the way to Battle.

27

Friday morning. It was still far too early and far too dark when Rob heaved himself out of bed reluctantly – it was a very warm and comfortable bed – and got into the shower.

Ten minutes later, he was weaving up the A21 on his bike. With the London-bound rush-hour traffic, it took Rob just over two hours to get to his preferred parking space, close to Starbucks on Piccadilly, and by 8:29 a.m. he was sipping latte and flirting with the pretty Eastern European barista. Suddenly, the thought of having sex with the barista – a thought that had arrived entirely unbidden but very graphically in his head just as she had handed him the latte – made him feel giddy. And then a picture – an actual real *photograph* – of Zoe had jumped uninvited into his head, too. Rob sipped his coffee and scrolled through the texts on his iPhone until he found the latest image of Zoe sitting naked, legs slightly apart, on the edge of her bed. It had been taken on Tuesday morning, apparently, just after her first night in New York. Rob inspected it closely. For one fleeting moment, he wished that she'd included her head, and then he decided that, in fact, it was just as well she hadn't. He had lots of naked pictures of Zoe but, right now, this one was the best. He squinted at it while mentally superimposing the barista's head on to Zoe's naked torso. Mental Photoshop. Mental . . .

Rob shook his head and pulled himself back together, tucked his phone away and retrieved his camera from his rucksack. 8.39 a.m.: time to get round the corner to see what, if anything, was going down in Bond Street. As far as Rob could tell, it was mostly pretty shop girls – and boys – heading to work alongside upscale business-types in expensive suits. There were lots of ambling tourists, too – even in February; they were all casually unstylish, wearing bad-brand trainers and taking up far too much pavement.

And then, at 8:45, a navy blue Bentley Continental – a car that, Rob noted, managed to be both discreet in its colouring and bling in its sheer *Bentley*-ness – pulled up opposite his vantage point in the doorway of Alexander McQueen. On the other side of the street, a man emerged from a discreet doorway at the same time as a blonde woman, wearing a cream coat, high black boots and carrying a very big handbag, exited the driver's side and another woman, fifty-something, brunette, much smaller handbag, exited the passenger door. The two women spoke earnestly on the pavement for a moment or two and then the brunette woman appeared to drop her head and wipe her eyes, after which the blonde kissed her warmly on both cheeks and handed her an envelope. Without so much as the briefest exchange of words, Rob watched as the man – thirty-something, smart-casual – took the woman's place in the driver's seat, the brunette woman got back into the passenger seat and the Bentley drove swiftly up Bond Street, while the blonde glanced left and right and then let herself into the discreet door. So stealthily efficient were all these manoeuvres that no traffic was held up for even a moment and no hazard warning lights flickered as a kerb was mounted; a small thing, maybe, yet Rob considered it to be a *telling* thing, too. This was presumably how smooth your life could be when you were very rich and thus spared the arse ache of stuff like hunting for parking spaces in central London's rush hour.

Rob wondered idly if maybe the blonde woman – Anette Sorensen; he had no idea who the brunette was but she looked secretary-ish – had a secret thing for stubbly twenty-year-olds in bike leathers? Being both blonde and curvaceous, Anette wasn't *technically* his type, but hey, *whatever* – exceptions could be made. Yet, as much as this idea appealed, Rob doubted that Anette went for skinny biker boys when she was basically married to a bloke who made Brad Pitt look like a bit of a spacker.

As Rob walked up Bond Street, he used his camera as a shield and trusted his instincts – which paid off; within just ten minutes there was no mistaking a smiling and immaculately tailored Stefan Sorensen striding up Bond Street from Piccadilly, carrying a take-out Starbucks coffee. Just as there was no mistaking the young woman walking beside him, either. Rob's first sight of Zoe for a week made his heart lurch. While the temptation to race across the road, hopping over cars like some sort of mad CGI superhero, was overwhelming, Rob counter-intuitively held back and slunk into the doorway of Alexander McQueen. And watched, through his lens.

And what he first saw was this well-dressed, good-looking forty-something guy carrying a takeout coffee down a busy London street, accompanied by a beautiful younger woman in a pinstriped skirt suit . . . I haven't seen that suit before . . .

Yet, within a nano-moment, Rob sensed that the way Sorensen and Zoe were going out of their way not to walk too close together marked them out, albeit only to a very interested party, as co-conspirators in an act of conspicuous ordinariness. To Rob's eyes, indeed, it was all just too 'ordinary' to be true. He aimed his camera, focused and fired: a proper pap's long-distance kiss-kiss, *bang-bang-bang-bang*, unseen and unheard by its victims. And then, within moments, both had disappeared through the same door as Anette.

It was over. Rob's blood rushed and his heart pounded in his ears, deafeningly. He felt light-headed, adrenalized. Five minutes later, back inside Starbucks, he scrolled through the images he'd captured and noted how, in the first few, taken in just two or three seconds, Stefan and Zoe had been walking right beside each other and carrying their coffees, elbows touching, but after an almost imperceptible exchange of words, Zoe had then dropped back a pace or two, moving closer to the buildings, while Stefan had instinctively moved ahead, nearer the kerb.

It was immediately obvious to Rob that they had been decisively distancing themselves from each other. Though obviously in conversation while they walked together in the earliest frames, by the end of the sequence they were far enough away that they could have been strangers who just happened to inhabit the same busy London street. But, mused Rob, who trusted his instincts, you wouldn't go to the trouble of doing that unless you had something to hide, right? And indeed a forensic examination of that final shot paid off: in the super-confident tilt of Zoe's chin and her level, amused gaze – a look he knew so well – Rob could instinctively see the truth, which was that the billionaire financier, Stefan Sorensen, was not only *fucking* his girlfriend, but that she was relishing every single thrilling second of it.

Bitch.

It was at precisely this opportune moment that the pretty barista appeared at the table next to his, cloth in hand, wiping – wiping and smiling at Rob. 'Hiya. You back?'

Rob managed a grin. 'Yeah – apparently I am.'

She smiled. 'Ohkay. Enjay your caffee.'

He liked her accent and he liked her smile and he liked

the thought of superimposing her head on to a naked picture of Zoe. 'Yeah, I will.' Rob could feel a blush rising. What could he say to seize the moment? 'Um. Do you live far away?' Christ! What was he on about? 'I mean, does it take you long to get to work?'

Barista Girl smiled. 'No, not too long. I share a flat near Brixton.' She paused. Rob felt her gaze was searching for something, *reading* him. 'I'm finishing work at four p.m.'

'Cool. Can I meet you after?' Moment seized.

She nodded. 'Sure. But now I have to . . .' She shrugged, smiled, waved her grubby cloth in the air.

'Yeah! You get on and don't mind me.' Rob watched her back as she retreated to her till – it was a lovely dancer's back – sinuous – and beautiful legs. And in between the back and the legs, a peachy little arse . . . Yup, Barista Girl was totally Rob's type. He closed his eyes for a moment, savouring that fact. As he picked up his rucksack, he glanced over at Barista Girl, who smiled back. He gave her a little wave and mouthed the word '*Later!*' She nodded. Rob left the coffee shop and crossed the road where, inside Green Park, he found a bench beneath a tree. Using his rucksack as a pillow, he closed his eyes, lay back and thought about . . . Albania? Romania? Lithuania? Serbia? Wherever the fuck she's from . . .

It was pretty cold, but, nonetheless, Rob dozed for a while – maybe half an hour – and woke with a start to sense a small drool of spittle on his cheek and an aching neck. He sat upright, watching the late morning to and fro through the paths of the park. It was good, people watching. London was growing on him. Maybe it was even possible to extract some order from its chaos? At which moment, a stray thought about Zoe in bed with Stefan Sorensen insinuated itself into his mind. This made him suddenly angry and then, just as suddenly, sad. Maybe there's no order, after all – only chaos? Rob glanced at his phone: still only eleven a.m. Then he scrolled through the phone's camera roll until he found the image he was looking for and, after a moment or two, closed his eyes again.

At lunchtime, Rob wandered along Piccadilly to the big flagship Waterstones. He was so bored, he thought he might even buy a book, but either way there was a nice café.

The afternoon unfurled, slowly. By 3:45 p.m., re-caffeinated and book free, he was once again outside Starbucks, holding his spare bike helmet and waiting for Barista Girl, who was inside the coffee shop, mouthing 'One minute!' at him through the plate glass. At 4:11, they were both on Rob's bike and Rob was enjoying the sensation of Barista Girl's legs tucked into the flying-V shape of his own, her arms wrapped tightly around his waist.

At 4:36 – having pulled up a couple of times so that Rob could take directions – he and Barista Girl had finally stopped outside a modest terraced house in a quiet back street that was more Herne Hill than Brixton. At 5:16 p.m., after the minimum of polite small talk lubricated by half a can of a very cold and very good Czech beer that Barista

Girl had extracted from her grubby fridge, she was on her knees, naked – glory be! – in front of him. Her eyes were closed as Rob looked down at her and muttered, 'Bee-yoo-ti-ful Ba-rista Girl.'

Barista Girl took a break and glanced up. 'Fuck me, Bike Boy?'

Oh, OK then . . . if I must. The sex was absolutely and unequivocally the very best sex Rob had ever had. Nonetheless, it seemed quite extraordinary that it could be possible to have such an awesome time while simultaneously feeling so dementedly miserable. Still, it was good to know you could.

At nine p.m. Rob figured he'd probably better start extracting himself from this pleasantly distracting situation and get back down the A21. He would gladly have stayed curled up on the thin mattress, smelling Barista Girl's deliciously foreign aroma with its base note of freshly ground coffee beans; nonetheless, he hauled himself out of bed.

'You got to go?' Barista Girl pouted slightly. 'Stay?'

'Nah, babes, sorry. Work.' He shrugged as he pulled on his jeans. Naked Barista Girl propped herself up in the bed on one elbow. It looked as though she planned to stay put. Rob snapped the image with his mind's-eye lens.

'So what's your job, Bike Boy?'

Rob indicated the camera bag on the floor. 'Pictures. I take photographs.'

'Of?'

Rob shrugged. 'People.'

'Take mine?'

Rob grinned. 'OK.'

An hour later, Rob finally readied himself to leave while Barista Girl scribbled her number on a piece of paper. Rob took the paper and made a great show of zipping it inside his biker's jacket, then he kissed Barista Girl on the forehead and let himself out of the flat. While he strapped on his rucksack and put on his helmet, he glanced up at the second-floor window. He trusted his instincts and – of course – she was watching him. Barista Girl smiled and waved. Rob waved back. He smiled, too – not that she could see his face beneath his helmet – and then he kick-started the bike and rode away. As soon as he was round the corner, he pulled up, unzipped his jacket, retrieved the piece of paper and dropped it into the gutter.

28

Back home, in the so-called Real World, after spending the final night of her work-experience week with her aunt, Zoe was now facing apparently endless late nights hunched over text books with zero in the way of private jets or billionaires, and she was demonstrably not happy. An aptitude for exams had ensured that, even if Zoe had always forged herself a life beyond revision, the majority of her friends – even Carmen – were too busy to notice that she was opting out of a social life. Indeed, it seemed to Zoe that nearly *everybody* in her life was currently too busy to notice very much that was going on outside their own orbits. Even Rob had apparently disappeared into a permanent edit suite with 'some, like, proper urgent business, babes.' As if. She'd only spoken to him briefly since she'd got home on Saturday morning and it was now Sunday evening, and still no sign. Even her last resort of a little sister was out of the family loop, living in jodhpurs and coming home tired and smelling of horse. And then, all weekend, her mum had kept on trying to instigate *proper conversations.*

'So,' said Eve, during a proper sit-down roast Sunday lunch, which Zoe considered a bit weird, given it was just the two of them, 'assuming you do get the grades, are you planning on going up to uni this year, or are you thinking about a gap year?'

Zoe pushed away the carbohydrates on her plate and shrugged, attempting to look casual. 'Dunno, Mum. I've been offered a gap-year job at Odense, if I want it.' A pause. 'Uh, Tina – you know, Mr Sorensen's PA – has just left.'

'Has she? Well, I doubt you have acquired an executive secretary's extensive skill set after one week, but if Anette and Stefan think you can be useful then that's *great!* Well done!'

Eve looked thrilled, while Zoe flinched. *If Anette and Stefan think you can be useful . . .* Little do you know, Mum. 'I was going to talk to you about it this week. No biggie.'

'*Yes,* biggie! Well, that's marvellous – assuming you don't want to backpack around Asia, that is?'

'Nah, I'm OK with not backpacking around anywhere. And I think there would probably be some more travel, anyway, at Odense.'

'Well. Isn't that *great!*'

Zoe struggled to make the exchange a bit more conversational. 'It's a pretty tight team, so it's nice that they've found room for me. I'm sort of the office go-to girl, really – stationery, phone chargers, new pairs of Fogal tights if Anette gets a ladder, takeaway coffees for everybody all the time – that kind of stuff.'

'Have you told Rob yet?'

'Not yet.' Zoe scrunched up her nose.

'He hates London,' said Eve, misreading the scrunched nose.

'He'll get over it.' Zoe shrugged. 'Anyway, I'll be back.'

'So, Zoe, I've had an idea. To relieve the stress of all that revision, I wondered if you fancied going on a –' Eve paused momentarily, the silence clearly waiting to be filled by a *Ta-da!* – 'weekend spa break? Just the two of us, no Alice! Maybe over Easter?!'

In her mother's voice, Zoe could hear an unusual and disconcerting fake cheeriness, a sort of kindness laced with neediness, which made her feel quite inexplicably *furious*. She scrunched her nose and levelled her gaze at Eve. 'Er, like, *no*, I wouldn't. But *thanks anyway.*' And then Zoe got to her feet and deliberately pushed her plate away instead of taking it to the dishwasher, and stalked towards the door, where she paused and turned and added, knife-twistingly, 'To be honest, I can't really think of anything I'd like to do *less* than that, because I'm nearly eighteen and – guess what? – I no longer want to hang out with my mum for a whole weekend.'

And with this, Zoe rather enjoyed leaving Eve sitting in – presumably, shocked? It was hard to tell – silence, alone at the dinner table, while she went upstairs to her room, where, just to ensure she'd rammed the point home, Zoe slammed her door and roared, 'Just *fuck off*, Mum! LEAVE ME *ALONE!*'

In her bedroom – always her safe, happy space – Zoe checked her phone for messages for about the fiftieth time that day. Nothing from Rob, which was just strange, and nothing – more importantly – from Stefan, either. He had her number because she'd given it to him on her last day in New York – and, even though he hadn't asked for it, she'd actually watched as he'd keyed it into his phone. Or at least – and she felt a small wave of embarrassment as the thought occurred to her for the first time – she *assumed* he'd keyed it in, simply because it *looked* as though he had.

As the days passed – silent, empty days that increasingly passed in a dull blur of revision and chocolate – so Zoe found herself more and more comfortable inside her new angry skin. Caterpillar to raging butterfly – that's how it felt to emerge from her chrysalis right now. Yet this life-changing shift wasn't particularly painful, difficult or remotely beyond her control. Zoe had spent a little bit of time – the bare minimum, really – trying to analyse why this was. Despite carrying around a lot of secrets and therefore having to tell a few too many untruths, Zoe was far from being in some kind of inner turmoil; was in fact *fine* with the secrets. The lies not so much. Just as fat can marble an otherwise lean steak, Zoe's outward coolness well disguised her streak of conservatism. Much as she hated anybody to know it, she was probably, she conceded – if only to herself – fundamentally, a 'good girl' who had rather suddenly, and possibly slightly behind schedule – unfashionably late, even – decided to *hate* the mother she loved, simply because she could.

29

While reading the *Courier* article in her presence, it had, Eve noted, been the uncharacteristic silence that best revealed the scale of Tony's anger. The following week, over an emergency kitchen-based wine summit (called to discuss Zoe becoming 'a nightmare, practically overnight', and Jordan, and then, guiltily, 'not forgetting Alice . . .'), Eve told Simon that, 'If the throbbing veins in his temples were any indication, he was *incandescent*; however, if he sacks me, it will create its own shit-storm. And he's been fielding several phone calls from confused parents as it is. I suspect he thinks it's some sort of menopausal meltdown.'

'And is it?'

Eve punched Simon gently on the arm. 'Shut up.' Then, 'Actually – *fuck* – who knows? Maybe it is. Maybe that's the problem with me and Zoe, too: we are at opposite ends of the hormonal spectrum. I barely know who she is anymore and it upsets me.'

'Of course it upsets you. It upsets me too. But the

father-daughter relationship is different; we're not actually *expected* to know each other – it's just a bonus if we do.' Simon refilled Eve's glass. 'Look, I think she'll be *fine*. And Alice will be fine as long as she has a horse – which will be the last thing I ever bloody sell, if it comes to that.'

'I don't think it'll come to that. Anyway, the horse goes before Heatherdown's fees go – you have my blessing on that. So how *is* Jordy getting on?'

And, as Eve listened to Simon enthusing about Jordan's new school, she was touched by the fact that, although she didn't necessarily fully subscribe to Heatherdown's educational ethos, it seemed to work in its own sweet way. And not just for Jordan – clearly for Simon too: 'So, Wednesday mornings are spent making and playing "musical instruments" constructed from *objets trouvés*. Then the rest of the day is about making and listening to music – just as the whole of Tuesdays is about problem solving and fire building and bivouac constructing in the woods – which apparently falls under the *science* umbrella.'

'I'm sure Bear Grylls would approve, but I'm not sure how it translates into GCSEs.' Eve shrugged. 'Look, the main thing is that it's working for *Jordan*.'

'It's working unbelievably well. And they do proper sport, as it happens. Jordan is apparently *very* good at football.' And Simon explained how sometimes all the lessons were combined so that 'it looks like a hot mess to me, but the kids love it when Madame Smith, who is actually French, takes charge and football is *played in French*.

Heatherdown's pupils are probably the only kids in the country who get *la règle de hors-jeu*.'

'*La* what?'

Simon laughed. 'Yeah, I don't understand the offside rule either. The thing is, Jordan is coming home exhausted in all the right ways, stimulated but not *over*-stimulated, and run out like a dog. I can't pretend he doesn't still have some major moments, but they are slightly fewer and further between.' A pause. 'Thanks *so* much, Evie.'

'For what?'

'For recognizing that Heatherdown was right for Jordan. And for not being afraid to admit it. That takes professional courage.'

'Well, maybe we could all learn a few things from Heatherdown?'

'Yes, I did read your article. It's bang on – and you know it.'

'Sometimes I know it. Sometimes I might need to be reminded. And –' as Simon leaned in to top up her glass, Eve placed her hand over the rim – 'now I need to remind *you* that we've both had enough. Or God knows where we'll end up.'

Simon laughed and laughed, and Eve marvelled yet again how great an ex-husband he was. And how great it was, too, that the trials of the last few months hadn't really changed anything. That even the potential embarrassment of Simon briefly imagining that he wanted to sleep with her again hadn't blurred the edges of their relationship for much longer than it had taken their respective hangovers to subside. It occurred to Eve that, in fact, this had been the very last box they had both needed to tick to ensure that there could never be any regrets – and now the whole issue needed no further clarification, spoken or otherwise. What a profound relief. In a schedule heaving with problems, Eve felt this was one less thing to worry about; that after all these years she was now entirely free and ready to get on with the rest of her life . . .

At the end of the week, the Friday before half-term, Gail brought in doughnuts for her and Eve to have at elevenses. However, elevenses were cancelled when Tony asked Gail to tell Eve, who was on the phone to Simon, to come and see him *right now*.

'What do you think he wants?' Eve pulled a face at Gail. 'I fear the *Courier* thing may not be blowing over quite as quickly as he would like.'

'Why? What's he been saying?' Gail sat down opposite Eve.

'Well, nothing much – surprisingly, for Tony – but I'm just reading between the lines and, uh, the phone calls.'

'Anyone interesting?'

'By "interesting" do you mean Sorensen-and-Dershowitz interesting?'

Gail nodded.

'No, not them, but plenty of other parents; if we had any actual governors, or even a proper PTA instead of the tedious, meddlesome, semi-professional cake-baking "Friends of Ivy House", I think it's fair to say they'd be calling for a meeting.'

'And maybe calling for your head on a plate? Oh, and by the way, don't forget you're seeing Ellie after Tony?'

'Thanks, I had forgotten about that.' Eve got to her feet. 'Right, I'd better start thinking straight.'

Gail smiled. 'Yeah, remember it's not always all about you.'

'Good advice – thanks. Any chance of coffee?'

'Consider it done, boss. And –' Gail leaned forward conspiratorially – 'and I really want you to know that I totally have your back, but, even so, you may want to glance over your shoulder occasionally. Just saying.'

Eve smiled. 'Thanks, Gail. I'm *fine*. Two sugars today though, please.'

Eve was prepared for her weekly meeting with Tony to be sticky because, if there was one thing – actually two things – Eve knew he really hated, they were (1) surprises. Of any kind. Ever. And (2) not getting his own way – *especially* when he was paying for his own way to be got.

Yet, to her great surprise, Eve found Tony to be positively chipper. He wasn't a skilled emotional-temperature taker so, normally, if he needed the heads-up about anything school-related he went straight to Eve, who could be relied upon to tell whatever it was exactly the way it was – and in language he appreciated. Now that Eve seemed to be less of a *solution* than she was a *problem*, that was no longer an option, so Eve guessed that Tony Salter was feeling pretty much the way Napoleon must have felt after the Treaty of Fontainebleau: i.e. busy doing not very much at all, on Elba.

Not, Eve discovered, that he wasn't doing *anything* – far from it. In the pursuit of boarding-school excellence, much of the coppice had now been razed – along with some inconvenient environmental concerns that had been raised by the children, for which compensatory bird boxes had been duly commissioned for other parts of the wood and a new coppice planted on the far edges of the rugby pitch. Meanwhile, heavy plant trundled its way up and down the greensward from morning till dusk as construction got underway on the new boarding facilities in order to meet autumn's immovable deadline. And then, thanks to InterEduSol, the overseas recruitment drive had gone very well, too, so Tony was suddenly quite optimistic about the long-term future of Ivy House.

'According to the bursar's office, there have also been an intriguing number of enquiries from parents of children with – and I quote – "their needs not being met at other local schools",' Tony told Eve. 'We haven't probed too deeply into what this means – like whether these are actual "needs" that are in any way also "special" – not that I object to a special needs provision, per se.' Tony levelled his gaze at Eve. 'Because you know I am happy to fill the classrooms with kids of all shapes, sizes, colours and creeds. I'll take Jews, Muslims, Hindus – *whatevers.*'

'Just as well, seeing as we have a reasonable selection of those already,' said Eve calmly.

'You know what I mean. Buddhists, Sikhs, Zoroastrians, Scientologists – bring 'em all on. I am totally an equal opportunities educator – at a price.' Tony paused and rubbed his hands together, à la Fagin. Which, Eve very much hoped, was in jest, but may not have been. 'Though, on second thoughts, you can strike the Scientologists because they're all fucking mad! I'm happy with all the religion stuff, but I still do *not* want to be the go-to guy for the spazzers.'

'Ah! It's actually "spackers" these days, Tony. Honestly, if you don't keep on top of trends in terms of abuse, you sound just like a sad old bloke.'

'Hm, yes. Maybe even the sad old Principal of a rural prep school?'

Eve laughed. This comparatively cheery mood of Tony's was, he revealed, because he'd just had confirmation from Moscow that there would be fourteen new bells-and-whistles Russian boarding pupils pencilled in for September, to add to the twelve he'd already secured from the Far and Middle Easts. Eve marvelled at how very briskly he seemed to have moved on from the article, even as Eve was still struggling to get a handle on the fallout. As far as she could tell, media opinion was divided. When she'd spoken to Johnny Nicholson at lunch on the Wednesday after publication, he'd said that 'some columnists and commentators think you're a heroine for simply saying the unsayable.'

'*Really?*'

'Really! While the rest – well, the *Guardian* – consider you to be a private-school pariah who dares to stick her head above the parapet of her ivory tower and, as a result, pretty much has whatever is coming. So it's all good!'

But is it really 'all good'? Eve wondered.

Meanwhile, here and now, it was good to know that her other, proper boss was back in his comfort zone. 'Right then,' said Eve, 'if we're all done, I'm going to have to go. I have a meeting with Ellie.'

'OK, Mrs Sturridge. Get out there and boost staff morale sufficiently to deliver us another Ofsted "Outstanding" or . . . or –' Tony stammered slightly – 'you're *out* on your fucking *outstanding* ear.'

Eve hadn't seen that one coming, in itself slightly unnerving. 'Jesus! And precisely who are you being today? Tony *Soprano*?' She just about pulled off a spin on her heels, but sensibly resisted slamming the door.

30

Johnny Nicholson had first seen the set of photographs by accident on a casual trip past the picture desk's screens on the way to the water cooler. Destined for the *Courier*'s online edition, the images had caught his eye because he immediately recognized that the girl – the *young woman* – was Eve Sturridge's daughter, Chloe? No – Zoe. He had only seen pictures of Zoe once before, on Eve's phone at that pleasant lunch with Cathy, and had never met her in the flesh, but nonetheless her beauty had meant that Zoe Sturridge had carved herself a tiny memory-sized niche inside Johnny Nicholson's head. Johnny was not, after all, entirely immune to the beauty of young women, even if he had to occasionally remind himself that he was old enough to be a young beauty's father.

It didn't matter that the nascent friendship with her mother appeared to have stalled – charmed though he had been by Eve, in relationship terms, it had always been a bit of a geographical long-shot – he'd felt compelled to persuade the picture desk that there was no editorial interest whatsoever in Stefan Sorensen and his leggy new Alexa-Chung-alike PA ('No, *really*! Nobody's interested in these hedgie guys – even if they are married to former beauty queens!').

Johnny now wondered, a day or two later, how best to tackle the problem – with which, he recognized, he was becoming slightly obsessed. While Johnny had a very real desire to save the teenager from herself and earn Brownie points with her mum, the journalist in him – the *non-parent* journalist – also wanted to see how this particular little teen-drama might play itself out. Because it was blindingly obvious, just by looking at the set of pictures, that the billionaire hedge-fund genius and alleged all-round great guy, Stefan Sorensen, was fucking – or had fucked – *seventeen*-year-old Zoe Sturridge. And that, even if Eve didn't know about it – which she presumably didn't – or, indeed, even if she didn't *want* to know about it – which she almost certainly wouldn't – she most definitely needed to. If there was one thing of which Johnny was fairly convinced, it was that this little situation had the potential to become very messy indeed.

So, after a day of internal debate, Johnny did the obvious thing – he went down the corridor to visit Cathy Gower, carrying a printout of one of the pap snaps and affecting an air of disinterest.

'Got a minute, Cath?'

'Why do you always choose press day to pick what passes for my brain, Johnny? I'll be so much more fun tomorrow.' Cathy sighed. 'OK, literally a *minute*. What can I do you for?'

'Thanks, darling. Now, this . . .' And Johnny thrust the printout right under Cathy's nose and watched her eyes widen as she processed the visual context – and indeed subtext – of the image.

'OK, so that's my teenage god-daughter, Zoe. What *is* she doing?'

'Aside from sleeping with her boss during her work experience?'

Cathy glared at Johnny. 'You said that, not me.'

'Come on, Cath – it's bloody obvious from their body language.'

Cathy appeared to consider this as she scrutinized the picture. 'Yes. OK. It does seem that way. Jesus. That's my oldest friend's teenage daughter. What the fuckety-fuck?'

'And you a top newspaper journalist, too. Horns of the proverbial dilemma!'

'No, actually, it's not, because, unlike you, I'm forty-nine per cent journalist and fifty-one per cent *parent*. Listen, Johnny, I've got to get this bloody magazine to bed, but then we're going to sort this out.' Cathy shrugged. 'Some-how. Pub at seven, yeah?'

31

'Ah, Ellie!' Eve arrived in Ellie's classroom – the nicest in the building, on the south-west facing corner – and glanced around approvingly. 'My favourite room, this. I'm sure Brahms appreciate it too, albeit probably without quite knowing why.' Ellie nodded, and Eve noted her deep breath; she'd clearly been steeling herself for *something*. 'OK, so hit me with whatever it is.'

'Ah, so, here's the thing—' Ellie paused and took a deep breath. 'Now, you may not be aware that my class is a particularly odd one – for lots of reasons – but it is, and one of the reasons is because twelve out of the eighteen children were born post-May.'

Eve nodded. 'Yes – I knew it was an unusually high number of summer babies, but I hadn't realized it was quite as many as that. So what's going on?'

'Well, we've just done our mid-year tests and, uh, the policy of giving kids born after Easter the previous year's papers seems to be backfiring with the current bunch of Year Fours.' Ellie shrugged. 'It *may* be an anomaly because they're not exactly a control group – the brightest children in the class are, confusingly, also the very youngest of the youngest, the July and August kids.'

Eve furrowed her brow. 'Including Petrus Sorensen?'

'Yes, Petrus is July, but he's definitely in there. Anyway, the thing is –' Ellie sighed – 'all of my A-group in maths – five of them, including Petrus – scored less than sixty-five per cent in their maths tests, despite the fact that they could do it – an old Year Three test, of course – blindfold. And in fact Petrus, who is probably the best—'

'Probably genetic,' Eve said wryly. 'Go on.'

'Probably! But the thing is, he only got fifty-six per cent. Or, more accurately, he got one hundred per cent of the fifty-six per cent of the paper that he actually bothered to do, but then he stopped just over halfway and did a few drawings instead. They're very good; he calls them his "Deadlies".'

Ellie pushed Petrus's test paper across the desk. It was covered with pencil drawings of intensely detailed landscapes scattered with battle scenes featuring what appeared to be robots fighting tanks against a backdrop of castles and mountains. It was very impressively male, just as impressively messy and reminded Eve of something else, too, only she couldn't quite put her finger on precisely what that something was.

'So, anyway,' Ellie continued, 'the point is that my brightest kids ended up doing worse than the less bright kids, which really screws with the statistics. And the thing that is even more interesting is that, when I started getting feedback from parents of the A-group – inevitable, really, given these were disappointing results from our smartest kids – it was alarmingly similar. All five of them were asked by their parents why they'd done so badly, relatively speaking, and all of the kids answered with variations of "I got a bit bored and stopped doing the test and did something else instead".'

Eve smiled. 'Right! *Why don't you just switch off your television set and go and do something less boring instead?*'

'Excuse me?'

'Sorry. It was an old kids' TV show – before your time, Ellie. And, actually, rather *after* my time, but anyway –' Eve exhaled – 'this is all very interesting. So, apparently the youngest kids in Year Four, who by some statistical anomaly are also your brightest, have all revolted independently against a test specifically designed to ensure they did *better* than average.'

'That's about the size of it, yes. To put it another way, the technically least-clever, pre-Easter-born child in the class scored *higher* in their maths test than the *brightest* child.'

'Is the brightest child, by any chance, Petrus Sorensen?'
'Yes.'

'And how un-bright is the least bright child – and is that child a Percy?'

Ellie nodded. 'You assume correctly, bless him! Piers Percy is, well . . .' Ellie struggled for the right word; Eve knew she was fond of Piers.

'Going to have the mickey taken out of him mercilessly at big school – and not just for being called Piers Percy?' said Eve.

'Well, yes, probably. He's a terribly sweet boy, though. I'm sure he'll make it to agricultural college.'

'By hook or by crook.' Eve snorted. 'Forgive me!' Ellie smiled at Eve's joke. 'I suspect both Piers and Petrus would technically be "special needs" if we had a special needs provision – and, obviously, at pretty much opposite ends of the scale, too.'

'But we don't, so . . .' Ellie shrugged.

Ah, but we will, we will, thought Eve, looking intently at the younger teacher. 'It must be hard work?'

To Eve, Ellie seemed immediately relieved – and grateful – to be invited to say, 'Yes, it *is*. I've only been teaching seven years but I've already seen a few extraordinary children. This year's lot, though, are . . .' She tailed off, grimaced, shrugged again.

'*What* are they, do you think?' Eve encouraged.

'*Very* different, incredibly challenging, extremely rewarding and *impossible* to predict. I never know each morning quite where we'll end up by four p.m. And I also feel very strongly that our usually infallible strategy of giving easier exams to the younger children so the school's grades – as well as *theirs* – are kept up has entirely backfired with this year's bunch.'

Eve was interested. She had always struggled with the ethics of the school's long-time strategy of dumbing down tests and exams for even the brightest kids, albeit that better results simply meant more children joining the school, which meant, in turn, better financial results and a bigger salary. 'It's as if they've *intentionally* subverted it. I mean, I don't think they have, and not because they're not bright enough to do it – they *are* – but because they're nowhere near as cynical as us!'

'Hm. As *some* of us,' corrected Eve before she suddenly blurted, '*Stephen Wiltshire!*'

'Sorry?' said Ellie.

'I've been trying to think what – or, indeed, *who* – Petrus Sorensen's drawings reminded me of and it's Stephen Wiltshire.'

Ellie shrugged. 'I don't know the name.'

'Google him. He's probably in his mid or late thirties by now – autistic savant, brilliant artist from the age of maybe seven, noted for his landscapes. He might even be an OBE. Anyway, thanks very much for all of this, Ellie. It's fascinating. And I'd like to pop by your classroom right after half-term and have a closer look at this Year Four in action, if I may?'

'Of course! We'd love that.'

It was with a head full of jostling thoughts on the drive home – about Gail's comments and Johnny's, about Tony's and Ellie's – that Eve pulled into the Esso garage just outside Battle. Unusually, she suddenly craved a can of Diet Coke, a bag of cheese-and-onion crisps and a Snickers, all of which she consumed uncharacteristically fast, and slightly guiltily – she would hate to be spotted by a parent or a pupil – while sitting in her car at the side of the forecourt.

As Eve reached the end of her crisps and slightly regretted that she hadn't bought two packets, she noticed a smart black Land Rover pulling into the petrol station. When the driver got out and started filling his tank, Eve decided, in a move as uncharacteristic as the crisps binge, that she would pop into the petrol station's Tesco Express and sort of, somehow, engineer a casual 'Hello'. Suddenly, right now – and despite their inauspicious start – Eve couldn't think of a person she wanted to talk to more than . . . Mike Browning. And it was remarkably easy. In fact, it was – pleasingly – Mike who spotted her, standing apparently transfixed by an abundance of semi-skimmed.

'Oh, hello again – *Mrs Sturridge*.' He smiled broadly and held out his hand, which Eve took while affecting what she hoped was a convincing *goodness-what-a-pleasant-surprise* sort of expression. 'How nice to bump into you, and in such glamorous surroundings. My compliments on what was a truly excellent article – especially given it was in the *Courier*.'

Eve, clutching too much milk and utterly distracted – by what? Pheromones?! – found it was impossible to respond appropriately without looking like Basil Fawlty, mid pratfall. It seemed to Eve particularly absurdly British to be making polite small talk about one's work while standing in Tesco holding an udder's worth of full-fat milk.

'Thank you – *Mike*.' It suddenly seemed very appropriate to be on first-name terms. 'And, of course, I owe you an apology – for jumping to conclusions. Although, you jumped to yours before I jumped to mine.'

'Guilty as charged.' Mike paused. 'And I, ah, well . . . I'm sure you're very busy.' Mike eyed the milk. 'You certainly *look* busy, but, uh – and this is terribly forward, even head teacher to head teacher – but I don't suppose you fancy a quick coffee?'

Eve felt she'd learned her seizing-the-moment lesson with Johnny, so she nodded. 'I fancy a coffee very much.'

Mike smiled very broadly; it made Eve want to punch the air.

Fifteen minutes later, they had reconvened over cappuccinos in nearby Battle, and politely – and repetitively – reiterated their apologies. And then, blessedly, they both agreed it was time to move on. At the beginning, Eve did most of the listening while Mike shared – and speedily. 'It's probably been a long time coming, leaving London. I love Eastdene – the school and the kids *and* the village. In the last couple of years, I'd started feeling out of step with the times.'

'Or maybe the times were out of step with you? Not to mention *The Times Educational Supplement*.'

'Well, that's kind of you, Eve, but either way it's fairly academic.' Mike mimed a cymbal-crash as Eve grinned.

'For my part, I know that a school like Ivy House has to adapt to survive – and, in many respects, what my boss, Tony, has been trying to do is absolutely correct. There's a certain logic to this, um, *globalization* of education.'

'But . . . ?'

Eve couldn't quite believe how easy this was or quite how much they had in common, despite operating at opposite ends of the educational spectrum. What an unadulterated pleasure it was, finally, to talk about work with Mike Browning . . .

'But? Well, yes, there *is* a but – several buts. OK, so here's an analogy – somewhere between the health-and-safety madness of, for example, those "no-playing-outside-when-it's-raining" kind of rules that you increasingly find at, well, state primaries like yours, and a school like Ivy House's "no-staying-inside-ever-if-it's-Games" ethos, I think there lies a middle way. Call it the "if-we-want-to-go-out-in-the-rain/hail/snow-let's-go-out-and-if-we-want-to-stay-in-let's-stay-in". Does that make *any* sense?'

'Of course it makes sense,' said Mike. 'It's called flexibility. It's called treating each child as an individual. It's what we *try* to do at Eastdene, inasmuch as we can within the state system's constraints. It's what makes every day different and keeps the kids on their toes and also *engaged*. Usually it works, sometimes it doesn't – but, either way, we bend with it.'

Eve looked closely at Mike. 'Do you know Heatherdown?'

Mike nodded. 'I've not visited, though I've been tempted to crash an open day, but of course I know all about it.'

'Well, I used to think Heatherdown's sort of approach was a load of hippy nonsense.'

'Ha! Me too.'

Eve smiled. 'But the thing is that now I very much *don't* think that. Though I have no idea why I'm telling you. It's just that my ex-husband's adopted son, who is somewhere on the spectrum—'

'As most of we boys are, of course.' Mike raised an eyebrow.

Was he testing her? Eve wasn't sure. 'Well – maybe. Anyway, his son was at Ivy House and it wasn't working for him at all – or us, to be fair – and I suggested Heatherdown and, of course, he's thriving.' She shrugged. 'So what do we make of *that*?'

'I think what we make of that is that there is room for all of us. Between you, me and the excellent Adam Thingummy over at Heatherdown, we probably cover most of the bases. Even though none of the schools are perfect, we do all have something quite unique to offer.' Mike shrugged and also let slip a small sigh. 'And would that we could all get on with doing what we're best at. You don't think about leaving Ivy House, do you?'

'Sometimes. Anyway, the thinking may be done *for* me at some point. None of us is indispensable, we just like to think we are.'

A wry laugh. 'Oh, believe me, I'm *very* dispensable.'

Eve scrutinized Mike. So bloody handsome – and, more than that, so obviously a *good* man, too. It was with a start that Eve realized – God, how can I be so slow? – of whom he reminded her: Simon. Her blush – a hot flush sort of a blush, as became a fifty-something's crush – was instant: bright red, right from her chest up to her eyebrows . . . It must be so obvious! 'I find that very hard to believe,' said Eve, raising her cup in a fairly futile attempt to disguise her colour.

Mike Browning met Eve's gaze over the rim. 'Uh . . . look, um, Eve, I apologize in advance because I seem to be feeling very *carpe diem* today, but are you by any remote chance free for dinner? Tonight?'

Before she replied, Eve counted to three in her head and breathed deeply, inhaling some froth from the top of her coffee . . . Fuck. Mike Browning has just asked me out . . . and I've got a milk moustache . . . 'Yes, I am free. That would be lovely.' She wiped her top lip in as blasé a fashion as it was possible to muster, which was not very blasé at all. Then Mike Browning leaned forward and, very gently, brushed her top lip with the tip of his forefinger.

'Bit left. Gone now.'

'Yes. Thank you.' Eve smiled at Mike.

And so Eve Sturridge and Mike Browning talked for another fifteen minutes and then Mike paid their bill and they left the coffee shop and paused briefly on the pavement outside, making arrangements for the evening.

Mike: 'I know it's nearer mine than yours, but the Bell does do an excellent steak pie and chips.'

Eve: 'It does. The Bell's steak pie and chips is *perfect*.'

And then Eve reached out and gently touched Mike's upper arm. 'I *was* going round to my ex-husband's house for dinner tonight, actually – but I don't think he'll mind.'

Mike grinned. 'Thank you for sharing.'

Eve could feel Mike's eyes on her departing back – literally watching my back – as she crossed the road to the car park beside the Abbey. She sat in the front seat of the car and retrieved her phone from her bag, scrolling through the names in her address book until she reached Simon's number. She touched *Call*.

'Simon? It's me. Listen, I'm blowing you out for dinner tonight.' A pause. 'Yes – even for sausages and mash and onion gravy. I know!' Another pause. 'Pie and chips at the Bell.' Another longer pause. 'No, darling, you and Ed can't come and crash. It's a bloody *date*.'

Laughing, Eve had to hold the phone away from her ear to avoid being deafened by the screams of delight as Simon shared the news with Ed. 'Oh my God, Eve,' said Simon, when the screaming subsided, 'until now I'm not sure that Ed and I knew we were quite this *gay*!'

Eve heard Ed's voice loud in the background – 'Speak for yourself, honey!' – and thought she might actually die of laughter. Die of laughter *and love*. Could there *ever* be a better way to go?

Later, over their respective gin and tonics, Mike Browning told Eve that he felt he had 'adjusted pretty well to English village life' and that it clearly helped if you both lived and worked inside 'the community' and were perceived to be one of its 'pillars'. Eve nodded emphatically as Mike confessed he didn't really get the whole 'pillar' thing.

'Well, you're an urban boy, after all – and who knows how many pillars a small community like Eastdene is expected to have?'

'I'm not exactly up there with the vicar in terms of my "village pillarage", but this seems to be the way of things in villages, even in the twenty-first century.'

'Even though it bears more than a passing resemblance, Eastdene isn't exactly Midsomer. I think there's been a fairly negligible number of murders in its history – possibly even none – and it is a tiny bit more racially representative of multicultural Britain.'

'Tiny's the word. There is the lovely Rupasinghe family, who run Londis.'

'And who regrettably send their four fiercely bright, good-looking and exceptionally charming children to Hartsmere.'

Mike laughed. 'Yes, that must be galling. But I do like this place more than I ever expected to like it.'

'Well, we offer both leisurely village pub lunches and bracing beach walks. And property is still cheap by the standards of the south-east. Personally, I love the fact that this little corner of Sussex has an off-the-beaten-track vibe that belies the fact it is only sixty-odd miles from London.'

'Blimey. Are you on the local council payroll?'

Eve laughed. 'If only. No, I'm just so glad you get it – get us. I mean, it's not like moving here was ever going to offer you a hugely exciting life.'

'Well, I didn't want an exciting life so much as I wanted a *life*. I do still have all my old friends. And a few new ones.'

'OK. But –' and Eve was conscious of fishing for details, though it was a conversation she felt they probably needed to have – 'there's no significant other you've had to, uh –' she could feel an uncharacteristic blush rising – '*abandon*?'

Mike Browning shook his head. 'I had a long-term partner for many years. We never got round to marrying but, to all intents and purposes, we were married. She died of ovarian cancer four years ago. She fought and fought; she was an extraordinary woman. She'd first had it in her twenties and then she beat it and was in remission for a decade, and then . . .' He shrugged.

Eve grimaced. 'I am so sorry.'

'Thank you – so am I. But, to give it a positive spin – which isn't easy – Sophie's death has been part of my life's journey, and it's brought me here to Eastdene.'

'And, of course, no children.'

'No – no children.' A pause. 'Apart from the *hundreds* of children.' Eve nodded. 'I've always been a one-swan guy, really. But I'm fine. I'm pretty happy. I'm actually growing things in a *garden* and I would never have thought that would happen.' Mike paused, looked intently at Eve. 'And if that other kind of stuff comes along then great. And how about you?'

So Eve told Mike about Simon and the girls. And, as she expected, he was non-judgemental, understood when she explained that, for many years, she had felt there was potentially far too much to lose by looking for a relationship – especially if you were a swan kind of person who had been lucky enough to find their soulmate for life and then lost them. 'So, anyway, another drink, or a pie?'

'Now you're talking,' said Mike.

So they had their pie and chips and then walked through the village, past the green and the pond with its pair of swans – a big strong cob and his elegant pen and their six peapod cygnets. Eve was briefly tempted to say something about the perfect swan family as they passed, but a quick glance at Mike told her not to. He was clearly thinking about the birds too.

'Just because someone very close to you dies, it doesn't mean they're not still very much a part of your life,' Mike said, suddenly and emphatically.

'Yes,' said Eve. 'My mother died too soon.'

Mike took Eve's arm and slipped it through his, where, to Eve's surprise, it felt entirely right. 'So, my place – or mine?' he said, gesturing towards the house.

Eve laughed. 'Shall we make it yours, then? Lovely house, but of course I can't stay long on a school night.'

'Well, *obviously* not.' Mike fished in his pocket for his keys.

Meanwhile, next door, as she put out the bins, Gail suddenly found herself very distracted indeed.

32

Johnny Nicholson and Cathy Gower did indeed hatch a plan in the pub, although it was left to Johnny to carry it out. Thus he acquired from the picture desk the email address of the paparazzo who had taken the original set of pictures of Stefan Sorensen and the anonymous girl. A swift, businesslike exchange of mails then brought forth a mobile number which, when Johnny dialled, was answered after just three rings.

'Neil Taylor?' said Johnny.

'Ah. Right. Yeah! Who's this?'

Johnny noted that Neil sounded very young. 'Hi, Neil, my name's Johnny Nicholson. I work at the *Courier*. Any chance of a quick coffee sometime in the next twenty-four hours?'

'Ah, yeah, sure. How about the next twenty-four minutes? I'm in Knightsbridge. Can easily get to you by half past.'

'Make it forty-five minutes and we'll call it lunch, yeah? Wagamama at one p.m.? I'll wear an old Comic Relief red nose and carry a rolled-up *Courier*.'

'See you at one.'

Johnny pressed *End Call* and tipped back in his seat, imagining Neil harassing sulky WAGs outside Harvey Nicks.

During the following forty-five minutes, Johnny attempted to distract himself by googling *Stefan and Anette Sorensen* and sifting through the thousands of results. Even though he was normally on top of this kind of research, Johnny was surprised by quite how many column inches had been generated over the past few years by Denmark's highest-profile exports since Bang & Olufsen. By the time he left for his date with Neil, Johnny was up to speed on all things Sorensen-related – right down to the fact that, just last week, planning permission to build what was described as 'a whimsical yet modernist tree-house-cum-folly' had been applied for by the fashionable all-female London architectural practice, Browning and Cox.

Johnny had also been very interested to discover that Anette Sorensen was a great deal more than a mere trophy wife, and that, even aside from her academic qualifications, she was (according to an interview with her 'Best British Friend', Anna Dershowitz) 'not only far more beautiful, but also much smarter than nearly everybody I know – and I know some *very* smart people.'

As Johnny scrolled through numerous images on Google – of Anette in evening dress at Elton's white-tie-and-tiara do for his AIDS foundation, laughing with George Clooney at the wedding of a mutual friend in the

Italian lakes and having an earnest-looking tête-à-tête with Prince Charles at a Prince's Trust fundraiser – he started wondering, What precisely does Anette Sorensen do all day? Johnny had read enough to know that, while undoubtedly a devoted wife and mother, even the excessively well-compensated CEO version of mum-and-wife seemed unlikely to be quite enough to fill the days of a woman like Anette Sorensen. There was a great deal more to Anette, Johnny suspected, than the super-rich version of making the kids' packed lunches, doing the school run, helping on the PTA and dropping hubby off at the heliport in the morning. Yet precisely what that 'more' might be, he had no idea. While sucking on a Singha beer in Wagamama, he was still busily distracted by ordnance-surveying a Sorensenville landscape that seemed ever more complex the more he unearthed, when he heard a cough and, glancing up, took in the sight of the scruffily handsome – in an off-duty Robert Pattinson sort of way – young man, motorbike helmet in hand. He plonked himself down on the bench opposite Johnny.

Rob stuck out his hand. 'Neil Taylor – nice to meet you.'

Johnny furrowed his brow. 'Right. so I'm going to cut straight to the chase here, Neil. You look as though you could do with a few quid, so tell me how much it would take for you to lose those images of Stefan Sorensen and the girl that you passed on to our picture desk a few days ago.'

Rob-as-Neil looked surprised. 'Um. I dunno. What's the going rate?'

'For the memory card? You tell me. But try not to take the piss. It's not Beyoncé and Jay-Z having a foursome with Kim and Kanye.'

Rob/Neil grinned. 'Nah, but she is my girlfriend and I've got *lots* more of her, so that's got to be worth a bit, right?'

Bingo! 'Your girlfriend?'

'Yeah, and there *is* no Neil Taylor. Or, I'm sure there is a Neil Taylor somewhere, but he's not me. Pleased to meet you; I'm Rob.'

Johnny shrugged 'So what's the story, Rob? You're living a secret double life? Student by day, pap by late afternoon, international playboy by night, that sort of thing?'

Rob half grinned. 'That'd be a triple life, but yeah, I guess. I've been doing it for about a year, on and off. A mate got me into it, said it was easy money sometimes, so I thought I'd give it a go. I already had a motorbike and a camera and a scary student loan.' Rob shrugged.

'OK. Score any hits?'

'Yeah, a few. I got a couple of great Ashley Coles earlier this year; sold 'em to you lot. I tick over and I'm paying off my debts. But it's not like I can do it every day.' Rob shrugged.

'So explain this to me, right? You're papping Zoe and Sorensen *with Zoe's knowledge* – I assume she knows what you do for pin money – or you're just stalking your girlfriend for pervy kicks?' Johnny stared at Rob; Rob stared back at Johnny. To Johnny, Rob seemed momentarily flustered. 'C'mon, Rob; I mean, I've seen the pictures in context, shot after shot after shot, not just one picture in isolation.

270

So here's another question – what narrative did *you* impose on all those pictures when you looked at them? What's *the story*?'

Rob shrugged. 'You know the story. They're *fucking*. It's obvious.'

'Keep your voice down.' Johnny felt the age gap, already set to 'chasm', shift to 'Grand Canyon'. 'Right, so you're trying to get revenge by selling these pictures?' Rob shrugged again. Johnny wanted to pick him up and shake him. What was it with young people today, precisely? Why didn't they ever seem to give a shit about *anything*? Why were they so weirdly disconnected and *alien*? Or had middle-aged Neanderthals grunted precisely the same questions about their own tricky teens?

'Yeah, that was basically the plan.'

'Do you love Zoe?'

'Yeah.' Rob looked affronted. 'Of course.' Then he paused, ran his hands through his hair and raised his eyes to the ceiling, puffing out his cheeks and exhaling loudly. 'OK, I dunno anymore. Maybe.' He slumped back on his chair.

'So you were prepared to fuck that all up by getting these pictures published, were you? Not to mention, fuck things up for Sorensen, too? And his wife and kids, who I believe go to Zoe's mum's school?'

Another shrug. 'I didn't think it through. I was just angry.'

'Ever think of maybe just having a conversation with Zoe? Or –' Johnny couldn't contain the sarcasm – 'is that a bit retro, the whole concept of a conversation that isn't on Facebook or Twitter?'

Rob shook his head in exasperation, as if the ethics and morals of the situation were just irrelevant. 'Look, Zoe's *gone*. But maybe I can pay off my student loan and put down a rental deposit on a flat in somewhere shit at the end of the Central Line, or something. Can I have a beer?'

Johnny was dumbfounded. 'Yes, you can have a bloody beer. But do you youngsters actually believe in *anything* other than yourselves? Or is it all about the sex and the money? Can you do real emotions or just *emoticons*?'

'Yeah, fine, whatever – you go ahead and judge us because obviously you totally get what it's like to be young in, like, 2011, right?' Rob scowled.

Sitting there all sulky in his cheap leathers with his beer, Rob looked to Johnny like a very Poundland sort of anti-hero. 'Please, spare me the sob story. That's the other thing about young people – you're all so fucking self-righteous! Next thing, I suppose, you'll be demanding *respect*?'

'Oh, fuck off. Anyway, it's a complete *whatever* now because it's all backfired.'

'Really? And why's that, precisely? Because I'm about to offer you lots of money – how does two grand sound? – for your crappy pictures.'

Rob raised his eyebrows and looked at Johnny. 'Fuck off, two grand! Make it ten!'

Despite his best efforts, Johnny couldn't help snorting a laugh. 'Right. Yes, of course ten grand. Because your girlfriend is also the reincarnation of Princess Diana! Dick-head! Three grand – best and final.'

'Forget it, mate. Eight.'

From Johnny's perspective, it seemed that Rob was more furious at being patronized than he was about any other aspect of the whole sordid business. 'Oh, please, get a bloody grip, Rob. Sophisticated global player risks every-thing for pretty teenage intern? I really don't think so. This is a non-story to everybody except Zoe and her mum.'

Rob didn't miss a beat. 'You've not heard of Bill Clinton, then?'

At that moment, Johnny actually seriously considered slapping Rob, but bought himself a bit of time by hailing the waitress. 'Another two Singhas, please?' Yet, one look at Rob's face and Johnny knew the kid was simply brazen-ing it out; he was completely crushed. 'OK, so what's the plan now? Throw yourself into work and pick up a World Press Award for photography by 2040?'

'Like I said, fuck off! It may just be some big joke to you, but then you've probably never been fucked over by some-one you thought loved you.' *That* pulled Johnny up short. 'So, how much will you pay for the memory card?'

Johnny sighed. 'Five? And that's it.'

'Five is good. Cash. Tomorrow? I'll bring the card and we can swap. Same time, same place, yeah?'

'You've watched too many movies, Rob.'

'You can never watch too many movies.' Rob shrugged. 'See you tomorrow.'

As Rob left, Johnny motioned for the bill, picked up his phone and made a call.

'Cathy? Johnny here. OK, so the deal is done – five grand in cash, handover tomorrow, in return for the memory card. You sure you're all right for the money? Fine. I wish *I* had a few old mates like you. Oh, and by the way, and you'll love this, Cath: our enterprising young freelance paparazzo turned out to be – wait for it – Zoe's jealous boyfriend! Yeah, some chancer called Rob . . . I know, it's all very classy. So have you thought about telling Eve?' A long pause while he listened to Cathy's eloquently argued side of the argument. 'Fair enough, that's very much your call. As a mother, you inevitably have a much better idea of how to play it than I do.'

SUMMER TERM

33

'Thanks so much for all this, Cath – I think it's the best thing to do.' Johnny stirred his soupy coffee while Cathy dunked a bag of something herbal into a mug of hot water. The resulting aroma of damp, Middle-Earthy sticks made him gag slightly, though presumably a cup of hot, wet, Hobbity wood was the price Cathy had to pay to maintain that enviable figure. Johnny was conscious of the stodgy layer that had lately settled around his midriff and which was no longer negated by his morning routine of crunches in front of CNN. He sighed. 'At least I hope it is.'

'It definitely is.' Cathy sipped her drink and, Johnny was pleased to note, wrinkled her nose; no gain was clearly a pain. 'Much as I don't want to give this little shit so much as a quid, if we do, I think we'll be completely shot of him. And, more to the point, so will Zoe.'

'Well, it's incredibly generous of you. And are you really not going to flag it up to Eve? Don't you think she'd want to know? Plus, you know, five grand . . . ?' Johnny shrugged.

Cathy shook her head. 'OK, so five grand *is* five grand,

but I have more than five grand kicking around and, well . . .' A pause. Cathy levelled her gaze at Johnny and took another sip of her sticks. 'The thing is, I feel I owe Eve something.' Then, having perhaps given too much away, Johnny noted Cathy changing her mind about this conversational tack. 'But I want to do it mostly because I'm Zoe's godmum.'

Johnny was intrigued. He knew Cathy wasn't short of cash; she was one of the highest paid members of staff on a well-paying newspaper and her husband was a big deal in commercial property. 'But that's not the only reason, very good reason though that is?'

'No, though it's mostly the reason and right now I think that's all that matters.' Cathy shrugged, smiling sheepishly – the kind of body language Johnny had never associated with the cool, controlled Cathy Gower. He noted that an expert in neurolinguistic programming would probably have had a field day.

'Come on, fess up!'

Cathy winced, closed her eyes and exhaled loudly. 'Look, Eve was my best friend for many years and, in some respects, still is, even though we hardly ever see each other. It's always been the kind of friendship you can pick up and put down at any time, so we do. But the fact is, I'm fifty-three and well paid and we're mortgage free and five grand is basically two *very* nice handbags or a few days skiing.' She shrugged again. 'And I have quite enough very nice handbags and I find I mostly prefer the après to the actual ski these days, so it's worth it because Eve dotes on the girls and she is an excellent human being and one hundred per cent doesn't deserve any of this kind of shit. And of course it goes without saying that, if you ever breathe a word of this to *anybody*, I will have you killed.'

'And rightly so. Trust me, Cath – I'm a journalist.'

Cathy laughed.

'Ah, hello, here comes trouble,' and Johnny nodded towards a young man wearing damp and slightly steaming biker's leathers, holding a helmet and standing in the doorway, scanning the room. 'Good-looking lad,' muttered Johnny to Cath. 'Doesn't look like a loser at all, does he?'

'No, quite remarkably un-loserish. A mini Robert Pattinson, in fact. But still – what an utter dick.'

Rob was scowling deeply by the time he reached their table, which made him look, to Johnny's eyes, entirely slappable. 'Who's this?' Rob flashed a fresh scowl at Cathy and plonked himself down on a bench opposite the booth in which Cathy and Johnny were sitting side by side.

'Charmed, I'm sure.' Cathy held out her hand. 'I'm Cathy, a colleague of Johnny's and a friend of Zoe's mum, Eve. A very good and longstanding friend – not to mention Zoe's godmother.'

Rob's scowl evaporated. 'Oh. OK.'

'That's all you can manage?' Cathy rifled through a large and expensive-looking red leather tote, extracted a Jiffy bag and pushed it across the table towards Rob. 'Now, here's your five K. Don't spend it all at once. Or, in fact, *do* spend it all at once. Maybe on scratch cards?'

'Ah, that reminds me – memory card, please,' prompted Johnny.

Rob pulled a small brown envelope out of the inside pocket of his leather jacket and handed it to Johnny. 'It's all on there.'

'Excellent! Well then, I think that concludes our business. Have a nice life!' Cathy got to her feet. Rob didn't move.

'You can go now. I'm not buying you a beer,' said Johnny cheerfully.

Rob rolled his eyes. 'I'll donate some of it to Children In Need. But there's something else you probably need to know.'

'And that is?' Cathy was shrugging herself into a very chic camel coat.

Rob said, 'Dontchawish dot com.'

'Come again?' said Johnny. 'We're hacks, not bloody MI6.'

'Dontchawish dot com. It's a website. After the Pussycat Dolls song?'

Johnny and Cathy looked equally blank. 'Right. So?' said Johnny.

'Zoe's on it. She's been on it for forty-eight hours. When you got in touch yesterday – after we spoke, and that – well, I tried to remove the footage, but apparently it's too late. It's already viral. Like, it's all over the net, if you know where to look.'

'So, am I reading this correctly? There's moving footage out there on the interwebs of Zoe walking down Bond Street with, uh, Stefan Sorensen – is that what you're saying?' Cathy shook her head, bemused. 'Well, I don't suppose that's the end of the world. I'm sure we can do something about it.'

Rob shook his head vigorously. 'For fuck's sake!' he hissed. 'You two are like something out of the Dark Ages. It's *not* Zoe walking down fucking Bond Street with Mr Sorensen.'

Johnny noted how it was simply 'Stefan' to the grown-ups but 'Mr Sorensen' to the youngster who, just maybe, was better brought-up than he seemed to be.

'It's a fucking *sex tape*. It's Zoe giving me a . . . a . . .' But Cathy shook her head briskly and held her hand in front of her face, palm outwards. Rob fixed her with a hard stare. 'Whatever. But it's your precious god-daughter having sex on camera, for fuck's sake!'

'And *you* did this?' Cathy asked. 'And it's all over the net now?' Rob nodded. ' "Revenge porn", that's what they call it, yeah?'

Rob snorted. 'Well, that's what the *Courier* would call it. But that's not what I'd call it.'

'So what would you call it?' asked Johnny.

'It's more about, well, sharing Zoe with a wider audience.'

At which point, Johnny, to whom this sounded equally offensive *and* lame, snapped. He stood up, leaned over the table and grabbed Rob's jacket, wrenching him half way across the table . . . maybe less like Brad Pitt in *Fight Club*, more Bob Hoskins in *The Long Good Friday*. 'Like fuck it is! Now look here, Sonny Jim.' Yup, definitely Bob. 'Firstly, um –' he caught sight of Cathy's expression – 'sit the fuck down and –' Johnny pushed Rob away again, sat down himself and extracted an iPad from his rucksack – 'let's have a look at this website.'

Rob looked abject. 'I'd rather not.'

'Bit late for an attack of the shys, isn't it, Rob?' said Cathy brightly, holding out her hand. 'And, while we're at it, I'll have that five grand back, yeah?'

Rob shook his head. 'I can't. I need it.'

'I bet you do! About as much as a *seventeen-year-old* girl-friend needs to be perved over by a million faceless onanists for the terrible crime of, basically, choosing to be consentingly hot, in private, for the lens of her beloved boyfriend!'

Rob winced. 'She fucked Sorensen. That wasn't part of the deal!'

And, though Cathy was still speaking *sotto voce*, she thumped her fists on the table. 'I bet it wasn't. It rarely is. But life isn't all about making deals, dick-for-brains. Only an actual fucking sociopath enters into a relationship with an agenda! So did you and Zoe sit down together in the first flush of your delightful young love and decide that, if one or other of you went off and shagged somebody else in the heat of the moment, then the other had an automatic pass to post their most private moments on the interwebs for potentially the *entire fucking world* to look at, laugh at and get off on?!'

'Of course not!' Rob stared intently at the tabletop.

'Right! Of course not! But that's what's happened. Zoe fucked up a bit – which, incidentally, we all do – so, as a result, she – and indeed her family, her mother and father and sister and auntie and grandparents – actually deserves this appalling humiliation, which may, in turn, just destroy all her teenage self-confidence before she's even acquired it?'

Rob shook his head and stared at the table, apparently refusing to be drawn. Is that, Johnny wondered, a tear on his cheek? It was. Rob glanced up, red eyes damp, his colour rising. He fixed his gaze on Cathy. '*She* fucked up first – then *I* fucked up. Oh, and by the way, Cathy, both me and Zoe know exactly how *you* fucked up.'

'Right,' said Cathy, smiling tightly. 'Of *course* you do!'

'Yeah. I was round Zoe's mum's one night and we were all talking over dinner about, like, relationships and stuff – me and Zoe and her mum and her sister – and Eve told us that once, years ago, before the girls were born, she thought she was going to lose their dad to, and I quote –' Rob wiggled his fingers in the air – ' "someone very close to me. About a year after we were married." And, of course, Zoe and her sister begged their mum to say who it was, but she refused. All she would say was that it was somebody close to her who was "leading a very different kind of life, in London". We talked about it later and it was Zoe who guessed.' Rob leaned back in his seat. 'So, *you* basically fucked up by fucking Zoe's *dad*.'

A riveted Johnny had just pulled up the Dontchawish website on his iPad, but stopped looking at the screen now to watch Cathy appraising the young man sitting opposite her, who was revelling in his revelation. Cathy nodded slowly. 'Clever. Nice work, Sherlock. And very close –' she leaned over the table, lowered her voice to whisper – 'but no cigar! It wasn't *me* who nearly destroyed Eve's marriage to Simon before it had found its feet; actually, it was somebody even closer to Zoe's mum.' As far as Johnny could tell, Cathy appeared to be hugely enjoying playing games with Rob. 'No, indeed, *my* biggest mistake was telling Eve all about it. It is to her eternal credit that she dealt with it like the class act that she is and always has been. But right now we shall let that particularly ancient sleeping dog lie.' Cathy turned to Johnny. 'So, what do *you* have to share with us, John Nicholson of the *Courier*?'

'Right, well, are you sure?' said Johnny. Cathy nodded and Johnny swivelled the tablet so that she could see her god-daughter doing the sort of things no godmother should ever witness.

Cathy watched, squinting slightly, for probably less than ten seconds before she tapped the pause button on the screen briskly. 'OK. I pretty much get the gist of that. Nice lighting there too, dickhead. Thinking of going into porn production professionally, are we?'

Rob shook his head, barely perceptibly. 'No. I want it

gone too, all right? I want all of this behind me. I just want to get on with my life. Here –' Rob pulled the envelope containing the money from his jacket and dropped it on the table – 'have this. Fuck it, I'm off.'

Johnny and Cathy watched in silence as Rob picked up his bag and strode across the room and out of the door without a backward glance. Cathy exhaled deeply. 'Goodness me. That went well!'

Johnny laughed. 'Come on, it could have been a lot worse. You've got your five grand back *and* we've got the memory card. All that remains is the, uh, Zoe problem.'

Cathy furrowed her brow. 'Actually, I've got an idea, but I think it will involve confronting both Eve and Zoe. This is going to be a . . .' She sighed, rolled her eyes heavenward. 'Well, it'll be a big deal. But it could just work.' A raised eyebrow. 'I lied to Rob just then, Johnny. Quite straightforward, really. I didn't need the little git gloating; I needed to be the boss of him. So, yes, a hundred thousand years ago, I had a fling with Simon Sturridge and then I fessed up to Eve and she, uh, dealt with it. And we moved on. And here we are now.'

Johnny's eyes widened. 'Right, so Eve just shrugged and forgave you and you all merrily stayed bezzy mates and she stayed with Simon and polished her halo on Friday nights? *Really?!* That kind of shit doesn't even happen in Jennifer Aniston movies.'

'Well, OK, it wasn't quite like that. We didn't speak for a few years. But when we did – which, incidentally, was just after Simon left Eve – we worked it out between the two of us. Eve's sister, Sonia, helped – she was our go-between. It feels like ancient history now, to be honest, but it does also account for the five grand.' Cathy looked at the fat brown envelope lying on the table and then slipped it into her bag. 'But now I have a plan for that, too.'

'Let me guess? Charity?'

'Yes, in a manner of speaking. So,' Cathy got to her feet, 'can I enlist your help in the Great Upcoming Eve-and-Zoe Kitchen-Table Showdown?'

Johnny was flattered. 'Of course – but really? You sure?'

Cathy nodded emphatically. 'I am very much surer than sure. I really want you on my team. Need you on it, really.'

Johnny grinned. 'I bet you say that to all the boys.'

34

9:58 a.m. on the twenty-ninth of April – which was also the morning of the Royal Wedding – and Gail was panicking. Not blind panic exactly, but still. She had announced to Harry that she was 'quickly popping into school – your school!' and had packed her 'satchel' with a lovely fresh new notebook and some sort of sexy turbo-Biro with go-faster stripes – a birthday present from Harry. This year Gail's birthday had fallen on Easter Sunday, which had also conveniently excused Harry's purchase of excessive amounts of chocolates for his mum, the presence of which she could still feel in all the wrong places around her middle. They'd had a good day together, much of it spent in and around the Bell . . . and, on that topic, Gail had decided that guilt was an entirely pointless emotion. However, here and now, guilt free, though in a state of panicky faff, Gail couldn't seem to find anything she needed. It was irrational, obviously, but she suddenly craved a new pencil case and a set of pristine pencils with her name embossed on the side – and it wasn't even September.

'I swear to God I put a bunch of highlighter pens in that bloody bag last night.'

'You didn't, they're here,' said Harry, calmly retrieving the fluorescent markers from a dining chair. 'I used them last night. Mum, are you, like, panicking?'

'No, not panicking, just . . .' Gail paused, looked her son squarely in the eye. 'Yes, yes, I think I probably am.'

'Don't panic.' Harry shrugged. This was, in the eyes of an eleven-year-old, presumably all the advice a panicky mother could conceivably need.

'Yes, well, thanks for that, Haz. And you are OK here, then? I won't be too long. You can probably watch weddingy things already.'

Harry rolled his eyes. 'I'm not watching weddingy things, Mum. Girls like weddings, boys just put up with them.'

Gail snorted with laughter. Yeah, that's about right. 'Well. Designing a treehouse *is* a brilliant idea, but I think you might need a bit of adult assistance with that, so can we default to the Xbox for an hour or so?' Gail registered Harry's expression: resigned, bemused, with a hint of fondly patronized. 'Sorry, I'll shut up now.' She leaned towards him, instinctively half grazing his cheek with a distracted kiss that was ninety per cent breath, ten per cent skin. Gail felt as if the quasi-air-kiss had somehow transgressed a subtle new Year Six boundary, even if Harry himself didn't seem fazed by it. Perhaps he hadn't even noticed.

'I'll be fine, Mum, really – go.' And Harry looked, Gail thought, suddenly very tall and positively adolescent and, as she headed for the front door, she smiled to herself.

It was 10:05 a.m. and, despite living less than two hundred metres from her appointment, Gail was already late, which was unprofessional. With a hint of a springy breeze in the air, she found herself shivering as she walked up the path to Eastdene Community Primary School. She rang the bell.

'Hello, Gail – welcome,' said Mike.

As she'd expected, the staffroom was full of the governors, seated in a circle. Gail was momentarily tempted to take the remaining empty chair and say, 'Hello, my name is Gail Prince. God, grant me the serenity to accept the things I cannot change, the courage to change the things I can and the wisdom to know the difference.' Instead, she said, 'Hi! So sorry I'm late!' Ten warm, smiling faces turned towards her.

'No problem, Gail,' said Mike. 'We all know it's those children who live closest to school who are the last ones in the door every morning.'

'Yes, and it was precisely comparisons with the children that I was hoping to avoid.'

There was warm laughter from all around the room. Phew! thought Gail. Maybe this will all be fine . . .

35

Just after ten a.m. Eve swung the Volvo out of the Barn's drive. Within fifteen minutes, plus three sets of traffic lights, two mini-roundabouts and an apparently mushroomed-overnight Morrisons, Eve was on the outskirts of Battle and turning left into the drive of a large, rambling, gone-to-seed (but pretty, she had to admit, even if that roof looked a bit dodgy) Victorian mansion with a vaguely institutional air. She parked, took a moment to inspect her make-up in the mirror and, as she rang the doorbell, suddenly and inexplicably – but mostly, she felt, absurdly – suffered a surge of something not unlike nerves, which hurtled her, shivering slightly, straight back to school in about 1973. Ridiculous.

After a brief interval, the heavy oak door swung open to reveal a smiling man with quite a lot of beard, wearing cargo pants and a faded 'The Clash – *London Calling*' T-shirt. Smiling warmly, he held out his hand. 'Ah, hello there, Eve! Adam Vine. Welcome to Heatherdown!' Eve noted a surprisingly firm grip.

Five minutes later, she was settling into a beaten-up old leather club chair in Adam Vine's untidy office, nursing a mug of strong, sweet tea.

'I'm sorry about only calling you yesterday, Adam, despite meaning to for literally weeks, but many thanks for agreeing to see me at such short notice. I'm very grateful. So, I want to know everything about this place and how you run it,' said Eve.

Heatherdown's head teacher raised an eyebrow and smiled. 'Well, obviously we're flattered, though I'd have thought you had this educational lark pretty much down pat by now.'

Eve laughed. 'Look, I was so glad to hear how good Heatherdown has been for Jordan that I thought, if you didn't mind, I'd try to see how right you're clearly getting whatever it is you're doing.' Eve paused. 'I mean, it will come as no surprise to you that I don't entirely share your educational ethos. If I did, then I suppose I should have sent my own daughters here.'

Adam nodded. 'Or be doing my job?'

'Well, quite. And, of course, it's not personal. It's just, well, I . . .' Eve paused, looked at Adam, a man-of-beard, early forties-ish – hard to be entirely accurate because of that beard – and wearing a pair of (and Eve felt this was not a good look for men) something Ugg-alike in the boot department. 'Well, that's just not the way I've done things. Call me old-fashioned, but I'm very much of the reading, writing and 'rithmetic school of head teachers, forgive me.'

Adam raised an eyebrow and smiled. 'With Native American sweat-lodge-style drumming just a tiny bit further down your dream curriculum? Perhaps just past quantum physics and Mandarin?'

Eve laughed. 'Something like that, yes.'

Adam nodded. 'But you want to see what it is we do, and why? And, indeed, the kind of results we get? And by "results" I don't necessarily mean the sort of thing that floats Ofsted's boat – or yours?'

Eve nodded, intrigued. 'I get that. League tables are not really your bag, right?'

'Not really. I appreciate they are an indicator of some sort of success for those who define success in that kind of way, but that's just not my – our – definition of success, educationally speaking.'

'And your definition is?'

Adam frowned and peered quite closely at Eve. 'You really want to know? Or you're humouring me?'

'To be honest, I'm not sure I have it in me to humour anyone, Adam. No, I genuinely really want to know. Despite all the Native American drumming and your lack of Suzuki violin and non-contact rugby, my ex-husband is singing your praises and you are apparently doing wonders for his –' and there was only the very slightest pause – 'son.'

'Jordan is great and has a lot of potential. So, what are you doing for the rest of today?'

Eve shrugged. 'Well, you know, there is a wedding on TV I thought I might watch.'

'Ah, yes – we emailed our parents to ask if they'd want to have the children off school, sitting at home, watching some young people they don't actually know getting married and all of them said, effectively, "Not really, since they've only just gone back to school – and since you've asked!" So we told the children this morning that if anybody *did* want to watch it, the TV would be on in the library. However, to be honest, I'm not expecting much take-up, even from our princessiest girls, because we've got a bumper crop of lambs, including a Kate and a William. So why don't I give you the tour and I guarantee you'll learn pretty much everything you need to.'

'Really?'

It was Adam's turn to shrug. 'Well, you won't have a qualification at the end of it, but I can give you a head teacher's sticker.'

'Only if I deserve it. I'd hate to be getting any special treatment.' Eve grinned and stood up. 'Come on then.'

'I think half the school's down in the fields this morning,' said Adam, shrugging himself into a very un-woolly, non-ethnic smart-fabric over-garment and a pair of Hunter wellies. 'They'll have built a camp by now.'

Eve's day was enlightening, and fun, too. She could see perfectly clearly that everybody – staff and pupils alike – enjoyed themselves while they learned. However, she remained to be convinced that an entirely free-range education was any more than a glorified kids' camp. Not that everything was al fresco. The afternoon was spent making and playing musical instruments constructed from *objets trouvés*. Then there was, Eve was surprised to see, some 'proper' music being played – with actual instruments – and singing, too. Meanwhile, the whole morning had been about problem solving, fire building, whittling, cooking and camp construction in the woods. There were so few pupils that all the age and ability groups were mixed, which Eve realized immediately created a family dynamic, with all the good (in-this-together-ness) and bad (sibling squabbles and rivalry) that inevitably entails.

Eve had watched the children with great interest – and particularly Jordan, who was very neatly lining up sticks for the roof of the bivouac, in length order, while singing. At first, she couldn't quite make out the song, though his pitch appeared to be perfect. She edged slightly closer and then, with a smile, picked up the lyrics: 'Don't stop me now, I'm having such a good time . . .'

'Satisfied customer, there, clearly,' said Eve, jerking her head towards Jordan.

Adam grinned. 'The Queen stuff is good, but just wait till you hear his Michael Jackson medley. He's pretty much inches away from the final of *Britain's Got Talent*.' There was a one-beat pause. 'Not that I've ever watched that show, obviously.'

Eve laughed. 'So Jordan is doing well?'

'Very. We seem to speak his language. We really don't mind if he only wants to toast the *pink* marshmallows and not the white ones.'

'The first time I met him, I straight away thought he was . . .' Eve paused and stumbled; there was a catch in her throat. 'I thought he was properly *special* – not as in special-needs special. I haven't been able to get him out of my mind, really.'

'Come on, let's grab a cuppa,' said Adam.

Back in his office, with more tea, Adam said, 'So, what do you think of our "special" kids?'

Eve considered this for a moment. 'That they were obviously all "special" in their different ways.'

'Yeah, but let's face it, some kids are more special than others. You don't have to slay me with faux political-correctness – not everyone is born equal and nor, in my humble opinion, should they be. Could you pick out which ones were most "special"?'

'Well, there was definitely the little boy called Mohammed and another called Jack, and a girl called, er, Melody, or Harmony?'

'Liberty?'

'That's the one. But those are the only names I can remember.'

'Interesting. You're good at this. Mohammed – Mo, to most of us – is currently being formally assessed for an autistic-spectrum disorder. Jack has already been diagnosed as Asperger's and Liberty is almost certainly somewhere on the spectrum, but her parents don't want to play the "labelling" game and they've already decided to home school from eleven.'

'Wow.'

'Yes, wow. But we have a lot more Mos, Jacks and Libertys by-any-other-names – believe me. In fact, probably more than fifty per cent of our kids are quantifiably "different" or somehow "special". We're known locally for that, without having any formal remit to teach these more challenging or just plain *different* children.' Adam shrugged. 'We just crack on with it.' He paused. 'Or, rather, we will crack on with it until we close.'

'Yes, I was going to ask you about that.'

Adam shrugged. 'In a nutshell, we currently have forty-eight pupils and ten full-time teaching staff. Each pupil's parents are paying £2,750 a term, which is arguably about two to three thousand less than they should be paying, and staff salaries average out at about thirty K, while our annual heating and electricity bills currently run well into five figures, never mind any of the other maintenance required by a fifty-acre site.' He paused. 'So, as the Americans allegedly say, you do the math.'

'Yes. I can do the math.'

'I used to occasionally suggest to the owners that we did something ruthlessly capitalist like, I dunno, sell off ten of our fifty acres to some property developers to build a bunch of executive Tudorbethan detacheds. They actually looked into it, but it turns out we're an "Outstanding Area of Natural Listed Conservation", or whatever. And, inevitably, we've got a lot of bats.'

'Oh, dear. I know all about bats. My house is a converted

barn and we had the bat police – Batman, basically – hovering over our shoulders every time we even talked about moving a bloody tile.' Eve smiled. 'You haven't a snowball's in hell.'

Adam grinned wryly. 'My thoughts precisely. Anyway, we've got enough in the kitty to see us through another year, and after that –' a shrug – 'who knows?'

Eve sighed. 'Yes; of course, I wish you very well – if only, selfishly, for Jordan's sake.'

And then the conversation turned to other things that even the head teachers of schools as fundamentally unalike as Heatherdown and Ivy House have in common – notably the children, and the staff. And then, after a refilled mug of tea, Eve glanced at her watch and grimaced. 'I genuinely had no idea of the time. I really must stop taking up so much of yours.'

Adam got to his feet. 'It's been an absolute pleasure, Eve – really.' Eve knew he meant it; the feeling was mutual, and she told him.

'That's very kind of you. And I hope you catch up with that wedding.'

Eve laughed. 'I'm sure there'll be nothing else on TV for days.' Eve leaned forward conspiratorially, to confess. 'And I know I shouldn't care about seeing the dress, but I care almost as much as I did about seeing Diana's. Does that make me ridiculous?'

'Far from it; I think it makes you female,' said Adam. Eve smiled.

An hour later, Eve recounted her day to Simon on the phone, with, very uncharacteristically, her mouth half full while she ate a quick stand-up supper of defrosted chilli and kept half an eye on the royal-wedding highlights on the news. She spoke non-stop for the best part of five minutes without a break, if not quite zealously, then certainly extraordinarily enthusiastically.

'And so,' said Eve, finally winding up, 'Jordan really is in the best place he could possibly be, in case you were in any doubt. And that really *is* a lovely dress.'

'Sorry?' said Simon.

'Princess Kate, or whoever she is now. Lovely frock. Apparently it's Alexander McQueen, as favoured by my lady hedge-funders and venture capitalists. Anyway, as I was saying—'

'OK. No, we were not in any doubt, because the results have been palpable. And I'm delighted by your frankly rather sudden and passionate conversion to a Bear Grylls-ish approach to education. In fact, I think it's bloody marvellous that you're now embracing your destiny so wholeheartedly.'

Eve was swallowing the last of the chilli as she blanched at this. 'I'm not sure it's Bear Grylls-ish, precisely. But what *are* you on about, Simon? Destiny?'

'Come on, Evie, you know exactly what I mean!'

'But I don't.' Eve sounded as perplexed as she felt. 'Really, for probably the very first time in God knows how many years, I genuinely *don't*.'

'Oh, well, you're pretty smart, you'll work it out,' said Simon. 'And now, Mrs Sturridge, I have to go. Oh, and while you're admiring Kate's wedding dress, the rest of the world is, according to Ed and his social media, apparently wholly fixated on her hot sister's arse.'

Eve squinted at the TV, feeling obliged to have an opinion. 'Yes, well, it is a very nice arse.'

'Indeed. Oh, and before you go, how's our Zo?'

'Hm.' Eve considered her answer. 'Reserved, maybe? Ever since she returned from New York, she's kept pretty quiet, slept late and mooched around the house, whether sulkily or simply distractedly it's hard to tell, but all very *teenage*. Obviously life at the Barn doesn't quite measure up to Park Avenue, but I'm pretty sure she's revising her head off, so maybe that's all it is.' Eve didn't bother mentioning that Zoe consistently evaded answering questions, habitually shut conversational doors in her face and generally acted like a pain in the butt. 'Oh, and there's another thing. Alice tells me she makes these videos, alone in her bedroom – just her, talking to the camera on her laptop about girl stuff. Alice said she's seen one Zo made about revision and it's really funny. I haven't seen them yet, but apparently they're on . . . er . . . YouTube. Anyway, her friends watch them and comment on them. It seems to be a *Thing*, probably because they're all equally grounded with their revision, so it's a way of keeping in touch.'

'Sounds suitably twenty-first century, albeit harmless,' said Simon.

'That's what I thought. Still, it makes me feel old.'

'I imagine that's probably the point – as indeed that young Mr Bowie made our parents feel old. Give her a bit of space and I'm sure she'll be fine.'

'OK, will do. And now that's the front door. How one very slim teenage girl and a fat old dog can make quite such a commotion, I have no idea; anyway, I'm off now, Simon. Talk soon.'

In truth, Eve wasn't sure how convincing a liar she was, but no matter. There was nobody at the door; she was blessed with an empty house and all the peace and silence she wanted, which, in turn, would give her ample time to think about Simon's peculiar phraseology: *I think it's bloody marvellous that you're now embracing your destiny so whole-heartedly* . . .

Nope – no idea at all. Eve turned back to the television, where that nice Kate Middle-Class with the dull dress sense, until now, that is, and the upwardly-mobile and high-maintenance hair was apparently a duchess. And, remembering Kate's dead mother-in-law's wedding as vividly as if it had been, say, fifteen years ago, rather than nearly thirty, made Eve feel old. Still, Kate's dress was much better than Diana's.

36

A naked and backlit Zoe shifted position so that she was now straddling Rob, who was sitting on a small, hard chair adjacent to the window of his bedsit on the ground floor of a solidly suburban street, close to his campus. Zoe leaned her cheek on the top of his head. 'Babes. Let's move this chair a little bit to the left so that it is, like, *right* in front of the window, yeah?' A pout. 'Cos it'd be mean to deprive random passers-by of the sight of us fucking, yeah?'

Rob grinned. 'What would you say if I bought you a mortarboard and gown and we played, uh, teachers?'

'I'd say,' Zoe paused, giggling, 'see me in my office after class!'

And then Zoe and Rob had surprisingly languid, leisurely and show-offy sex right there, in the window. And Zoe half watched an elderly man exit the house opposite with a miniature schnauzer, and very much enjoyed the startled look on his face when he glanced up at Rob's window. She enjoyed it even more when, slack jawed, he dropped the dog's lead.

'Just a minute, babes.' Zoe got off Rob, whose back was to the window, and sauntered casually over to the door, where she flicked the light switch. The room was suddenly very dark; the old man could obviously no longer see a thing; however, Zoe could see him – and he remained riveted to the spot and staring at the window, nonetheless.

'Look at that poor old perv over the road –' Zoe climbed back on to Rob's lap – 'staring at us. We probably just made his day!'

At which point, Rob came, very suddenly and oddly mechanically; Zoe noticed the difference, even if she'd have found it impossible to articulate what that difference might be. All she knew was that there was a palpable, swift and shocking disconnection between them and, involuntarily, she let out a startled little cry and moved swiftly away across the room, curling herself into a ball on Rob's grubby old IKEA sofa, previously the scene of the opposite sort of sex to whatever this had been.

Rob, on the other hand, knew exactly what this had been: the *end*. He had the decency to actually blush as he recalled the best sex he'd ever had, with Barista Girl, even as he looked at this crumpled and pathetically unsexy and reduced version of Zoe, who was now also inexplicably wracked by sobs. What were they all about? Was she feeling guilty? Sad? Whatever . . . He shrugged; emotional empathy had never been his strong suit. Anyway, in a phrase he would use later, during post-match analysis down the pub, Rob figured that, all things considered, when it came to shafting each other, he and Zoe were probably just about equal.

'If you make coffee, I'll have a shower, yeah?' said Rob, businesslike as Zoe sniffed and nodded. And then, thank fuck, thought Rob, I can dump you. In the shower, his mind wandered away from the Zoe problem, such as it was, and towards the EasyJet booking he'd made that afternoon, while Zoe had been glued to that bloody wedding. Marrakech. Cool. In the shower, washing Zoe away, Rob started whistling.

37

On Monday morning, Eve was in school by 7:45 a.m., 'pimping, primping and prepping for Ofsted', as she described it in her text to Gail, who, with unfailing professionalism, turned up at 8:00 a.m.

The Ofsted inspector herself arrived on the dot of 8:45, bearing a crumpled copy of the *Courier*, and asked Eve for 'a few words alone, prior to the inspection proper, if that's possible?'

Eve ushered the inspector into her office. Her name was Jean Starling and she had inspected Ivy House on two previous occasions, during which she and Eve had struck up a professional rapport.

'Mrs Starling! Good to see you again – and welcome to Ivy House at a time of, I think it's fair to say, a degree of transition.'

'Yes, indeed, good to see you too, Mrs Sturridge. So, there's obviously a lot going on. Heard you on *Today*, by the way. Definitely held your own with Humphrys, though I hear he's a complete pussycat in real life.'

'Thank you! I wasn't actually in the studio, though, so we didn't meet. I was what they call –' Eve made air quotes with her fingers – ' "down the line".'

'Well, either way, it was very interesting. The whole thing was – is – interesting.'

Eve took this as a cue to take a deep breath. 'And, in the context of your inspection, possibly challenging, too?'

Jean Starling, Eve noted, had a brisk air but very kind eyes. 'Mrs Sturridge, you know as well as I do that, as an independent school, you are subject to what we call a Section 162A inspection every three years. But given what I'm hearing about Ivy House – about the imminent development of a boarding facility and a provision for special needs, which has not previously been a part of the school's offering – well!' Jean Starling paused. 'There are two ways this could go. We could just do the full inspection and – this is very much off the record, I hasten to add – given some of the quite dramatic changes I had not hitherto foreseen, I could conceivably end up not automatically rubber-stamping an "Outstanding" for Ivy House. In fact, there's a chance that it could be effectively demoted to a "Good".'

Eve nodded. She thought she knew where Jean Starling was headed with this. 'A "Good" is not really an option for the school's Principal, I think.'

'Yes, I thought it probably wasn't. And I can see why that would be, too. Especially,' Jean Starling paused and made eye contact with Eve, '*especially* as you do such a good job.'

303

Eve could easily have hugged her but instead settled for a heartfelt, 'Thank you.'

'Anyway, given there are so many changes already underway –' Jean waved towards the window of Eve's office at the precise moment a bulldozer trundled past on its way to the building site – 'we can put it off until a later date, at which point we would do an inspection of both the educational and the boarding provisions. In fact, we could spend this morning doing an inspection so you can implement an action plan that, in turn, will –' she paused and appeared to be choosing her words carefully – 'or rather, *might* – possibly even *should* – result in Ivy House maintaining its excellent reputation.'

'Right. Yes, I hear you,' said Eve. 'And I'm very grateful. I really am.'

'That's all fine, then. So the team are already inspecting your Early Years provision, with the help of, ah –' Jean thumbed through some papers attached to her clipboard – 'Mrs Charteris?'

'That's right, yes.'

'OK. So we can carry on simply in an advisory capacity, if you like?'

Eve nodded, emphatically. 'That would be great, yes.'

'Good, well –' Jean slipped her clipboard into her briefcase – 'that's all sorted, then.' She offered Eve an outstretched hand. 'Keep up the good work, Mrs Sturridge, either here or, indeed –' she paused – 'elsewhere. And I probably shouldn't say this, but ... Well –' she smiled – 'I may be an Ofsted inspector, but I am also a mother and I have a thirteen-year-old daughter who is on her third school and we still haven't got it right.' She shrugged, and sighed. 'There's never any point forcing square pegs into round holes. We do what we have to do for our children, don't we?'

'We do, yes!' Tempting though it was to throw her arms around the inspector, Eve resisted. 'Seriously – thank you.'

'No, thank *you*,' said Jean. 'We'll be in touch. Good luck, Mrs Sturridge.' And then she was gone and, as the office door closed behind her, for the first time in her life, Eve air-punched a *Yeeeees*! And then she thought of Jean Starling's words – *We do what we have to do for our children, don't we?* – and . . . God, I really must call Zoe.

Eve stuck her head round her office door and said to Gail, 'Remind me that I really must call Zoe at lunchtime.'

Gail was very hands-on with a Krispy Kreme doughnut. 'Mmmm, will do! How is Zoe, anyway? Indeed, more to the point, *where* is Zoe these days?'

'Good questions, both of them. She is fine, I think – albeit in A-level revision hell. I haven't seen her all weekend, actually; she's hunkered down at Simon and Ed's, says she can focus better there, for some reason.' Eve shrugged. 'Teenagers are a law unto themselves. You have all this to look forward to.'

Gail smiled wanly. 'Righto. And, before I forget, you might want to turn your phone back on, now that Mrs Starling has left the building. Oh, and you've had a message from Cathy Gower and another one from John Nicholson at the *Courier*.'

'Really?' Eve looked baffled. 'That's terribly enthusiastic of them both!'

'Yes, they seemed very keen to speak to you. Asked me if you were going to be around later. I got the impression they meant later later, like this evening.'

'Curiouser and curiouser. And, on the subject of Alice, I've got to speak to her too. God, today is already far too much.' And, much as I love them, I'm not around later for Johnny or Cathy, thought Eve. Very much not . . .

That evening, Eve opened the Barn's front door to Mike Browning for the first time, with a rather self-conscious desire to show her home off to its best advantage. This wasn't hard; the garden – pretty enough in midwinter – was just starting to come into its own in May. Eve attempted to interpret everything through Mike's urbane eyes: the hall with its mussed and faintly smelly dog bed and ranks of the girls' gumboots standing to attention, many long out-grown; the expansive kitchen and dining room that could easily absorb a far bigger family than Eve's small unit of three; the view out on to the terrace with its inspired-by-Japan planting – albeit from a distance, as Eve had never been to Japan; and the steps down to the lawn and that gloriously bosky, green and pleasantly Blakean view right across the Dene valley. The view, unexpectedly special, always came as a surprise to first-time visitors. Eve pushed the bifold doors leading from the kitchen to the terrace wide open and stepped out. Mike was obligingly impressed. 'Wow, that is some view.'

'Isn't it just? I never get tired of it.' It was somehow extremely important to Eve that Mike should like where she lived. 'There's a swimming pool just round that corner, too. Did I tell you that I had a swimming pool?'

'No, you neglected to share that. That's terribly posh. You are patently the head of an independent school. Nobody I knew in Islington had a swimming pool, though I bet there are a couple now, tucked away in some excavated basements.'

Eve laughed. It was entirely possible that the nicest thing about Mike – aside from all the other very nice things about him – was the fact that he made her laugh. It was probable she hadn't laughed quite as much as this since her earliest years with Simon, which augured well, obviously, even as it scared her a little too. But for now, at least, it was all about the laughter. Well, mostly the laughter.

'I think, if I hadn't been down here already for a few months, I might be quite thrown by the casual glamour of some of these rural lifestyles hidden behind high gates. Everybody seems to have a *Grand Design*.' Mike shrugged. 'My comfort zone was a small chunk of North London in which I was lucky to buy a tall, skinny townhouse with a patio garden on a mixed sort of street way back when I landed my first proper job with a decent salary, in the eighties. Twenty-five years later, having never felt the slightest inclination to move, I watched the street reinvent itself from mostly pretty shabby to insanely fashionable and full of your big media cheeses, *Newsnight* stalwarts, the cooler sort of merchant bankers and ethical venture capitalists.'

'Well, perhaps that's why the media gave you such a hard time? When they saw your London pile.'

'Yes, "London pile" – very much a *Courier* sort of phrase. And I'm sure you'll be using it yourself if – or when – you write for them again.' Mike smiled easily but Eve winced slightly; she had hoped to keep politics off the getting-to-know-you agenda for a little longer. 'But yes, obviously they were jealous of my smart property moves. And now, at the age of forty-nine, having spent years never more than a two-minute walk away from the perfect cup of coffee, a ripe mango, an Ayurvedic massage and some cognitive behavioural therapy, I am – *finally* – entirely charmed by the countryside.' Mike turned away from the view. 'And, indeed, many of those who sail in her, too.'

'Even the fifty-four-in-a-few weeks'-time-year-olds?'

'*Especially* the fifty-four-in-a-few-weeks'-time-year-olds.'

And then they both swivelled round at the sound of a door slamming. Alice, in jodhpurs, trailing a distinctly foxy-smelling Barney, breezed into the kitchen and gave Mike only the briefest of curious glances, as though there were strange men hanging out in her kitchen every day.

'I'm sorry he smells so gross,' said Alice. 'I'll put him in the shower. Hello.' This last was to Mike.

'Yes, do give him a shower, darling. And this is Mike, Alice. He's also a head teacher.' As if that explains anything, thought Eve.

'Right. Is it some sort of club?' said Alice, smiling. This was clearly about as interested as she was going to get.

Which suited Eve fine. 'Maybe. Maybe it is!'

'What school do you go to, Alice?' said Mike, though of course he knew the answer; it had, noted Eve, been one of the very first things they'd talked about over their pub supper.

'Westdene Girls' Grammar. We have no idea how I passed the eleven plus, do we, Mum?'

Eve smiled and shrugged. 'You worked very hard, Alice. Don't be so tough on yourself.'

'Yeah, well. I'm probably about to fail a load of GCSEs, but luckily I want to work with horses, which doesn't need GCSEs, just horse-sense.'

'My sister rode very well when she was your age. She was into eventing,' said Mike, wholly unexpectedly.

'Really?' said Eve.

'Yes, we have horses in the Black Country.'

'Cool. Eventing's my thing, too.' A beat. 'Where's the Black Country?'

Mike laughed. 'The Midlands. Near Birmingham.'

Alice shrugged. 'See what I mean? I'm practically a spacker.'

Eve raised her eyes and threw her hands into the air while Mike laughed, mostly at Alice's slack-jawed look of horror. 'Um, I think we head teachers tend to prefer the term "special needs", don't we, Eve?' Eve was shaking her head, speechless.

'I cannot. Believe. I just said that,' said Alice. 'I'm actually, like, grounding myself. Like, now.'

'Actually,' said Eve, covering her shame while peering through her fingers, 'would you mind awfully grounding yourself right after you've fumigated Barney?'

Mike waited until Alice had left the room. 'Great kid!'

'God!' said Eve. '*Spacker*? What was she thinking?'

Mike laughed. 'I suspect that's the least of it, frankly.'

'Do you think?' Eve shook her head. 'Sometimes I have a sneaking suspicion that I don't know my daughters at all. Which reminds me, I must call Zoe; I tried at lunch and couldn't get through, and I haven't seen her in an age.'

38

However, it turned out there was no need for Eve to call Zoe because – quite unexpectedly and very suddenly – by the time Eve and Mike were on to their second glasses of wine and into double figures with the olives, there was the sound of a slammed door and then Zoe was right there in the kitchen, while behind her was, inexplicably, *Cathy*. Eve hopped off her stool, firstly attempting to hug her daughter – who stood rigid and unsmiling and submitted only grudgingly to a maternal display of affection – and then transferring her attention to Cathy, whom she kissed warmly on both cheeks.

'Gosh, what an absolute thrill to see you too, Cath. But why on earth didn't you say you were coming?'

Cathy glanced at Zoe. 'Well, the thing is, I kind of had a date with Zo – a godmotherly sort of bonding thing – didn't I, Zoe?' Zoe nodded, though her poker face revealed nothing. Cathy continued, 'And so I wasn't even sure if I would have time to see you, Eve. But then one thing led to another and Zoe suggested I come back to the Barn and I, uh, thought that we three might have a chat, if that was possible. But, um . . .' Cathy tailed off and glanced quickly across at Mike, fortunately quite a skilled taker of emotional temperatures and reader of evolving situations, but who was also, at this point, as unsure about where the evening was headed as was Eve. In one area, however, he was definitely a step ahead of his date; he knew that whatever the evening was about it was most assuredly not about him, and so he would extract himself from the situation, though preferably not before he'd reached the bottom of this excellent glass.

Meanwhile, Cathy felt ever so slightly foolish; even her best-laid plans hadn't included Eve potentially entertaining a handsome man at her home on a Friday night – even though there was no reason on earth why she shouldn't. Cathy was, in fact, delighted that her friend appeared to be doing this very thing . . . but how to get him to go? Zoe, meanwhile, was wriggling uncomfortably on a bar stool and picking desultorily at the olives, her expression still unreadable.

Mike looked from Cathy to Eve. 'Right, the evening has been a total pleasure thus far, Eve, and we are going to do it again very soon, I hope, but right now . . .' Mike held out a hand to a slightly surprised-looking Zoe, who took it reluctantly. 'Hi, I'm Mike, by the way, and I think I may be surplus to requirements, here –' a very slight smile from Zoe – 'so I'm going to shoot off now, Eve.' Mike leaned forward and kissed Eve on both cheeks. He took the opportunity, too, to inhale her scent, which was something he vaguely recognized but couldn't place and which he liked very much. 'No need to see me out, really. I'll call you tomorrow, if I may?'

Eve nodded mutely. She was glad of Mike's social skills, though she recognized that the evening had taken a turn she would not have chosen. 'Yes, do please call tomorrow, Mike – and thanks.' The front door hadn't even shut behind Mike before Eve was glancing between her oldest friend and her eldest daughter, her brow furrowed in puzzled bemusement. 'So, what's going on?'

'Is that your boyfriend?' asked Zoe.

'Well, who knows? Maybe. But we're not there yet.' Eve shrugged while Zoe grimaced. 'But enough about me. How's *your* boyfriend?'

'I don't have a boyfriend. He's dead to me. He's a bastard.'

'Oh, honey, I'm so sorry.' Eve reached for her daughter again, but Zoe flinched.

'No. Leave me alone. You don't know anything.' Zoe practically spat the words at her mother.

'Er, can I have a glass of that Dutch courage, Eve?' This was from Cathy.

'God, I am so sorry, Cath. I am just completely thrown by your presence – in the nicest possible way, believe me. So,' Eve poured a big glass of the delicious red and pushed it across the island towards her friend, 'to what do I owe the pleasure?'

'It's not a pleasure, Mum. It's a nightmare!' muttered

Zoe, who then very suddenly broke down in tears. Rather than Eve, it was Cathy, sitting next to Zoe, who was in the best position to put her arm around her. For a moment, Eve wasn't sure how that made her feel, precisely, but feared it was something unexpectedly close to envy.

'Your brilliant and beautiful daughter has, I'm afraid, made a few mistakes and is currently paying the price. Which is why I set up the godmum date, so we could talk about it between us first. It's quite a high and not very nice sort of price and, if you sit down, Eve, she and I will try to explain.' Cathy nudged her silent god-daughter gently with her elbow. 'Won't we, Zo?'

Zoe nodded, between sobs, while Eve simply did as she was instructed. She was not only entirely flummoxed but also, somehow, nervous. 'Come on, then; out with it.'

And so Zoe started talking, slowly and very, very quietly at first, but becoming louder and more vociferous as it unfolded, and Eve strained to listen, desperate to interrupt but forcing herself to sit in silence. Eventually, after what felt like forever to Eve but was probably less than three or four minutes, Zoe started to run out of steam: 'And so I just, like, went – but I turned around at the door and Stefan just looked at me blankly, and . . .' Zoe just broke off suddenly, as if she'd just realized that nobody listening had actually forced her to confess, and suddenly she clammed up tight, eyes wide and scared, as if shocked by how far she'd allowed herself to go.

Eve stared at her eldest daughter, uncomprehending.

But Zoe gathered herself, momentarily: 'And you don't know anything, Mum. You don't have a fucking clue about me and . . . and . . . *anything!* You think I'm, like, Miss Pretty-Perfect-Straight-As, with my whole fabulous life ahead of me, and –' properly uncontrollable sobbing now – 'you have no fucking idea! No fucking idea at all!'

And suddenly it was clearly too much for her. Zoe slid off the stool and walked over to the vast old sofa, burying herself in a corner, balled up like a used handkerchief, howling.

Eve wanted to go to her daughter but knew she wasn't wanted. Instead, she shook her head at Cathy, misery and confusion etched on her features.

'Now, come on, Zo. It's not quite the end of the world, it just feels like it.' Cathy turned to Eve, who looked entirely stricken. 'The thing is, you see,' she spoke slowly, as if explaining something rather complex to a toddler, willing all the information to both go in and stay in, 'that the Sorensen situation is one thing, but–'

At which point Alice appeared in the doorway. 'What's going on?'

'Go away, Alice, please!' Eve's tone did not invite disagreement; Alice raised an eyebrow and turned on her heel. She sat on the stairs, just out of sight but well within earshot. 'What?' Eve continued. 'So there's worse stuff than my teenage daughter sleeping with *Mister* –' she all but spat out the title – 'Sorensen? Is that right?'

Cathy nodded. Then she explained slowly and carefully

about Rob's nasty, petty, cruel act of revenge, explained about Dontchawish.com and about 'revenge porn' as a concept.

As she listened, Eve shook her head again and again. She could hardly process what she was hearing. It was entirely unfathomable. It was the kind of stuff that happens to other people, different sorts of families. Not mine. One thought kept crowding her head repeatedly: Who is Zoe? Who is my daughter?

It was, thought Eve later, as though her life, which had previously been moving at an ordinary pace, had at that moment been put on fast forward, become hyper-real, like a tsunami in a disaster movie, and everything she thought she'd known now turned out to be, if not entirely wrong, then somehow misaligned, out of sync, at odds with what she had come to recognize, rightly or wrongly, as the norm. And so it was that Mike's wry comment earlier in the evening – *I suspect that's the least of it, frankly!* – turned out to be alarmingly prescient. Albeit, that had been way back in a different world, one in which her teenage daughter hadn't had sex with Stefan Sorensen – *Stefan Sorensen!* – after which her jealous and malevolent – I never liked him! – boyfriend had uploaded a sex tape – a bloody sex tape, for God's sake! – to a revenge-porn website. Revenge porn? My God, who knew?

And then there was the fact that she was being told this by . . . Cathy Gower! And Cathy had known of it all before Eve. And, of course, she had always been at the centre of most of the important events in Eve's life; however, right now, Eve couldn't tell if Cathy's presence made all of this much worse, or much better, or, in actual fact, made no difference at all. If only because, for once, this wasn't about Cathy.

Having listened in virtual silence to both Cathy and Zoe's versions of this sorry, smutty, ugly little tale, Eve finally decided to take control and be the boss of a situation she was, in truth, still a long way from fully comprehending. She turned to Zoe. 'Right. That's enough from you, young lady. I will speak to you again in the morning, but now – bed, grounded. And hand over your phone, too.' Eve walked over to the sofa and held out her hand expectantly.

'But, I—'

The still-sobbing Zoe got no further before her mother exploded. 'NO BLOODY BUTS! Upstairs! *Now!* Grounded until further notice and *no phone!* I will talk to you in the morning.'

As the sound of her daughter's running footsteps were punctuated by a 'Fuck off and leave me alone, Alice!' and the inevitable bedroom door slamming, Eve turned her attention to Cathy. 'And I suppose I'm meant to be all grateful and gracious, right?' She took a large sip of wine. 'But, you know what? I'm not feeling either of those things. What an utter bloody disaster.'

'Ye-es.' Cathy cleared her throat. 'Well, of course, I can go, if you'd like.'

Eve snorted. 'No, of course you're not going! As you very well know – and you better than anybody, frankly – if you're going to bear some bloody bad tidings, then you'd better have a very smart solution in mind. More wine?'

It was Cathy's turn to nod mutely. But, even from their tangential positions, both women instinctively recognized that the person with whom Eve was angriest wasn't Cathy, or even Zoe – not even stupid fucking Stefan Sorensen or the idiotic Rob. No, both women knew that the person Eve was most angry with was Eve. It was at this point that she put her head in her hands and her shoulders slumped. She felt utterly diminished and hopeless and a failure as a mother.

'Jesus, Cath. I'm sorry. I'm really, *really* sorry – you're try-ing to help and I'm just so out of my depth. I not only don't seem to know my own daughter – daughters, probably – but I have not the faintest idea where to go with this, how to sort it out. How to mend things.' She looked at Cathy intently. 'Do you?' Eve reached tentatively for her oldest friend's hand and squeezed it gently. She was extremely pleased to discover the squeeze was reciprocated.

Cathy nodded. 'As it happens, I think I do. Let me make a quick call?'

Eve glanced at her watch – the much-loved Rolex Simon had given her for her fortieth – and was surprised that it wasn't yet nine p.m. It felt like midnight.

'Go ahead, of course. I'm going to have a word with Alice. And then I might call Simon. Family summit?'

Cathy nodded – 'Yeah, good idea' – and scrolled swiftly through her iPhone's address book until she found the number she sought. 'Johnny? Hi.' A pause. 'No. Really?' Another pause. 'Are you sure? When was this? When was he arrested?' Eve paused on her way out of the kitchen doorway and turned around. 'Just a minute.' Cathy cupped her hands over the phone and looked at Eve. 'According to Johnny, Stefan Sorensen's just been arrested in New York.'

Eve shook her head, bemused. 'Excellent. So there is a God?'

'He was arrested at lunchtime – that is, lunchtime in New York, which would have been about six or seven p.m. tonight, our time, so basically just now. He was, uh, arrested alongside his friend, Dershowitz.'

'The plot thickens,' said Eve. 'Need I lock up both my daughters? Is Dershowitz sleeping with teenage girls too, then?'

'Not as far as we know. The arrest is very much for financial, not sexual, misconduct – apparently.'

Dershowitz! thought Eve. Ivy House may as well just pack up right now. 'OK, so I'm calling Simon.' She paused for a moment and met Cathy's eye. 'You OK with that?'

Cathy blushed. 'Of course I am, Eve. I'm only sorry –' Eve was already out of the kitchen door, but Cathy finished anyway – 'you felt you had to ask.'

39

Zoe was sitting at the head of the long refectory table in her mother's kitchen. She was wearing a baby blue onesie and her feet were pulled up on to the seat of the chair as she hugged her knees, tired and washed out. She felt about twelve and arguably looked even younger. To Zoe's right sat Cathy on the long bench, with Simon opposite her. Next to Cathy, was Eve, while Alice had been dispatched, very grumpily, to join Ed and Jordan.

'So, anyway, just to recap, Zoe,' said her father in a sort of faux-jaunty tone she barely recognized, 'while on work experience, you had an affair with a forty-two-year-old man – your boss, whom I'd like to punch in the face – who has just been arrested in New York in conjunction with his friend and fellow financial wizard, Dershowitz, and they are currently being investigated, according to Cathy's journalistic sources, by . . . well, who knows? The FBI? And, above and beyond this piece of cleverness, your charming ex-boyfriend has posted footage of you and him having, uh, sex on a revenge-porn website and, shortly before leaving the country last week, he not only dumped you, but he posted the link to the site on your Facebook page, where it has now gone, as they say, viral.'

Zoe nodded, but barely. 'What is this, an intervention?'

'Probably.' Simon sighed. 'So, just where did we go so terribly right here, precisely, Eve? How did we get to be such brilliant parents? Any ideas?'

'Yeah, make it all about you, Dad,' muttered Zoe.

'I'm sorry?'

'You heard.'

Simon dropped the faux-jaunty in favour of the plain angry. 'I think you are very lucky, young woman, that I am being quite as calm and level-headed as I am. I've a mind to smack you and send you to your room without supper.'

Zoe semi-sneered. 'I'll phone ChildLine.'

She watched Simon turned puce and Eve shake her head despairingly at both her ex-husband and her daughter, while Cathy simply raised a hand. 'Simon, Zoe. Stop, both of you. Not helpful.'

Eve nodded. 'Let Cathy speak. She has a plan.'

Zoe watched Simon glare at Eve. 'Be my guest. I have no plan at all. Or, rather, none that doesn't involve me getting arrested too.'

'OK, OK, everybody,' Cathy interrupted. 'So. I suggest that we contact the Odense lawyer, whoever that is.'

'I can tell you who it is – Anette,' said Zoe.

Cathy was only momentarily thrown. 'Right. But she

can't be acting for him right now, as his wife? Odense must have someone else?' Zoe shrugged. 'Anyway, we'll find out. And then we'll tell them that we – in this case, "we" is a national newspaper – have information that casts Sorensen in an exceptionally bad light. Yes, an even worse light than the one in which he finds himself already. However, if he were to make a substantial donation to the charity of our choice, we would conceivably be prepared to sit on that information for an indefinite period, agreed?' There were nods from around the table while Zoe remained both still and silent, intrigued but not wanting to show it. Cathy continued. 'OK, so that broadly takes care of the regrettable Sorensen situation, per se – happy charidee to be decided. Now, Zoe, all we need is for you to agree to become the poster girl for . . .' Cathy paused, searching for exactly the right phrase.

'Sleeping with your boss?' muttered Eve, sighing. 'Jesus. Where did we go wrong?'

'As I was saying,' said Cathy, 'the poster girl for the horror of revenge porn, which is, in effect, a particularly grotesque form of bullying, a sort of offshoot of domestic violence, even, being as it invariably involves men dishing on women – and one about which most women know nothing and are therefore vulnerable to precisely the kind of situation in which Zoe has found herself.' Zoe listened, fascinated. 'So, whatever the moral issues around making homemade porno in the first place, the fact remains that Zoe was over the legal age of consent and in a committed long-term relationship with her boyfriend – and he abused her trust in the most craven and cowardly way.'

'To put it mildly! Fucking bastard,' said Zoe.

'Language!' said Simon, pointlessly.

'Right,' said Cathy, cheerfully. 'Now, this is the point in proceedings where we're coming over all modern.' She reached for her laptop, which had been sitting, closed, in front of her.

'Please, not the bloody website!' groaned Simon. 'There are some things a father really does not need to see.'

Cathy smiled. 'Don't worry, Simon, it's just Skype.' She flipped open the MacBook and tapped at the keyboard. 'So, by the miracle of zeros and ones, *heeeere's Johnny* . . .' Cathy pushed the computer back into the middle of the table so it could be seen by everybody. On screen, Johnny Nicholson waved. 'Hello! So sorry I can't be with you tonight – I'm slaving over a hot news desk in darkest Kensington. However, I'd like to thank my agent, my mother and, of course, God. But mostly I'd like to thank Cathy Gower, whose brilliant idea this was.' Everybody laughed; Johnny's digital presence had successfully dissolved the tension.

'This is proper mental,' said Zoe.

'Oh, now, don't you worry, young lady – we've barely started. So, let me tell you exactly how mental this is . . .'

And he did. He explained to the room – but specifically an entirely riveted Zoe – how he and Cathy had decided that the *Courier* should work with their own IT geniuses to permanently remove the footage from the Dontchawish website and then, after this had been achieved, the paper would break the story of Zoe's betrayal in an exclusive magazine interview with a trusted female journalist . . . who just so happens to be Zoe's godmother . . . and, because all newspapers are obsessed with multi-platform and 'click-bait', the *Courier*'s own wildly successful website would simultaneously carry an exclusive filmed blog – a vlog, apparently – with Zoe, on the same subject, which would itself link to Zoe's own YouTube channel, where she could either continue to discuss the subject or draw a line under it, but either way the *Courier* would drive new 'fans' to her site. It would, in short, explained Johnny, be a way of redeploying the precise technology that had been used against her to Zoe's own advantage. And it would work brilliantly, he assured everybody, 'precisely because Zoe is beautiful and clever. Sure, she's going to start off being the poster girl for revenge against revenge porn – but she'll probably finish up with a modelling contract with Storm and her own reality TV series.'

More laughter. Simon spoke first. 'Wow. That is actually brilliant. Who knew you journalist types were quite so bloody smart?'

Without missing a beat, both the on-screen Johnny and the bench-bound Cathy answered together: '*We* did!' Around the Barn's kitchen table, Zoe noted that the laughter took ages to die down and that, when it did, the mood had shifted from disaster management to something approaching creativity. After a few more minutes of round-the-table and through-the-ether discussion, Cathy ended the Skype call and everybody looked at everybody else and then, inevitably, everybody looked at Zoe.

'You want me to say something?' She shrugged. 'Well, yes, I can do all that. I think it's a brilliant idea too.' She paused for a tiny beat. 'And it's not like I'm fazed by cameras.' Everybody laughed again, clearly relieved. Even, she was quietly delighted to note, her mum and dad.

Twenty minutes later, Simon had left the Barn, Eve had gone upstairs, and Cathy had made a cup of camomile tea, which she took over to Zoe. 'Your mum was going to make this for you, but I think she just forgot.'

'She was? Really?' Zoe looked up.

'Yeah – she's your mum and she loves you, Zoe. But I told her to go and have a soak, because she's had a long day.'

'OK, thanks.' Zoe sighed and wiped away a tear. 'She's brilliant, my mum. Look after her, yeah? Can I take this tea to bed? I'm, like, really tired.' Zoe untangled her legs and stood up, wobbling slightly.

'Of course.' Cathy leaned in for a hug.

Zoe smiled a very small smile. 'Thanks.'

'No problem. Well, OK, a bit of a problem, to be frank, but I think we're sorting it. And I must say that, mostly, you have handled this evening very much like a young woman who is about to turn eighteen and leave seventeen a long way behind – by which I mean you've been mature. And it must be so tempting to just cry and ask for a hug.'

Zoe shrugged. 'The thing is, I'll grow up whether I want

to or not. When do you think we'll do all this interview stuff, then?'

'As soon as possible. Turn it around in the next week or so, if you're up for that?'

Zoe nodded. And then she left the room and stumbled up the stairs and down the corridor, towards her room – her safe place – and, within five minutes, she had slipped into a deep, dream-littered sleep.

40

Monday morning – early – and Gail sat at her desk. She opened a new blank document file on her computer and started to type a letter. It wasn't a very long letter; nonetheless, every word of it was particularly well chosen.

'The Lawns'
Eastdene
East Sussex
Monday, 23rd May, 2011

Dear Tony,

After much deliberation, I hereby offer my resignation. I have been hoping to get back into teaching for quite a while and have just been offered a job as a teaching assistant at Eastdene Community Primary. Mike Browning is also letting me study to qualify as a SENCO and update my PGCE. The job starts in September – when, of course, Harry will also be starting in Year Seven at Eastdene Community College.

I will take away many happy memories of my time at Ivy House.

(No longer) Yours,
Gail Prince

Gail re-read this several times before printing it out, adding her elegant flourish of a signature and putting it into an envelope, and then there was the *ding* of an incoming text. It was from Eve, who was apparently going to be off sick today. Gail couldn't remember the last time that had happened. She texted Eve –

All fine here, don't worry about a thing, get well soon!

– and circulated an internal email to all the staff, saying Eve was off work.

Two hours later, paperwork sorted and in tray emptied, Gail slipped discreetly past the staffroom's open door without making eye contact with any occupants, and knocked on Tony's door.

'Come in! And it goes without saying that all ye who enter here should abandon hope!' shouted Tony Salter. 'Ah, Gail. Smashing! Shut the door behind you, would you, darling?'

Gail shut the door. 'Er, so I just wanted to give you this, Tony.' And she put the letter on his desk.

Tony stood up and grinned and said, 'Now, before I find out what the hell this is all about, is there any chance you can rustle me up one of your excellent frothy coffees? And what news of Eve?'

'Well, yes, I can do that, but I'd rather you read it first. It won't take a minute. And I think it's a twenty-four-hour noro sort of a thing. I'm sure she'll be back in no time because Eve doesn't really do ill.'

'Good-oh. So, is this letter what I think it is?'

'That depends, obviously.' Gail shook her head in mild exasperation.

'Sit, please, Gail.' Tony opened the envelope, unfolded the paper and scanned it quickly. He glanced up, smiling. Gail was slightly thrown by this. 'Don't know what took you so long. I've been expecting – dreading – this for years, Gail.'

Gail blanched. 'Really?'

Tony exhaled deeply. 'Yes, really. I know why you stopped teaching and I know it was my fault. I know I undermined your confidence. And I know I behaved like a shit after Harry was born. And I know how I had you over a barrel when I said that, if you wanted a year's maternity leave, you could only come back as admin staff. That was pretty despicable of me, but—'

'But, Tony—' Gail attempted to interject but Tony held his hand up, palm outwards.

'If you want the truth, I was irritated by how little help you seemed to need. Overnight, you'd turned into the

Dame Ellen MacArthur of parenting – determined to do it all single-handed, all the way. So I left you to it.' A shrug. 'Which was all I could do, really, seeing as you wouldn't return my calls and I didn't much fancy myself as a stalker. And then, when you came back, it seemed to work out so well between you and Eve – you are a real powerhouse of a team – that I just allowed myself to forget you'd ever even been a teacher, and a good one. For ages, literally years, I figured you'd just moved on.'

Gail shook her head. 'No, Tony, I have never moved on. I love working with Eve, but I've always just been biding my time, busy being a mum and paying the bills. And I've talked to the staff here, of course, and then I read Eve's article and I just saw immediately that she's right. And that made me think again about my own career and my own future, for the first time in years. For ages I thought I might try to go to uni and do a degree in forensics. But then I realized I'd just watched too much TV . . .' Gail broke off and shrugged.

'I don't want to lose you, Gail.'

Gail didn't want to think about this – not right now. 'OK, so I'll just go and make you that coffee.'

Tony sighed. 'Gail, I accept your resignation. OK?'

Gail smiled and nodded. 'Thanks, Tony. Sugar?'

Michael Percy unlatched the nursery playground's gate and started to walk home along a route he knew very well. He circumnavigated the car park and the wood-chipped play area, passed the sports hall and the tennis courts and walked along the edge of the cricket pitch towards the furthest corner of the fast-shrinking coppice, where the big diggers were moving backwards and forwards . . . This wasn't the first time that Michael had decided that the actual real tree-house in his own actual garden just over the stile on the other side of the coppice was infinitely preferable to a school called the Tree House, which wasn't a tree-house at all; it was just that, on the couple of previous occasions he'd attempted it, he'd always been caught in the act.

Diggersaurs, thought Michael as he watched their long necks bobbing up and down. Big, yellow diggersaurs!

Just past the diggersaurs stood the stile, which separated his mum and dad's farm from his school. Beyond that was one small pony paddock before the gate to the farm's walled kitchen-garden, which meant that he was almost really home – home to Mummy and something warm and buttery-tasting in the kitchen, and a homely hug instead of a school scolding. Yes, Michael was definitely looking forward to getting home, but first he thought he might stop for a while and watch the big, yellow diggersaurs rolling back and forth across the place where there used to be trees. Back and forth, dipping and bobbing their big, yellow necks, back and forth . . .

And nobody saw that the little boy of not-quite-four, who didn't like 'school' and took his 'blankie' every day in his book bag and missed his mummy each morning and still had lavatory accidents and whose favourite book was *Harry and the Bucketful of Dinosaurs*, was sitting at the edge of the coppice, pretending he was being chased by a digger-saurus . . .

And then the first person who *did* see him was the diggersaurus's unfortunate driver, whose name was Tom and who had a five-year-old lad himself, and who held Michael in his arms as he tried to resuscitate him and, when he failed, howled and swore and dialled 999, scream-ing into his mobile, 'FUCKING WELL GET HERE *NOW!*'

And by the time the helicopter was making everything windy over by the rugby pitch, an hysterical Tom was being restrained by the site's foreman while another diggersaurus driver had gone to fetch Tony Salter.

From the cricket pitch, meanwhile, a small crowd was starting to descend on the coppice at the same time as the remaining workmen were frantically trying to shoo them away from the sight of Michael Percy, who was alarmingly still and broken-looking, lying within the footprint of one of the dormitory blocks. Tony Salter, shocked into silence as he stood next to the site foreman surveying the chaos, felt tears – of pity? Regret? Shame? *Fear?* – prick at his eyelids. He tried very hard – and failed – to blink them away.

41

Having already bunked off work 'sick', it was equally unlike Eve to have a bubble bath rather than a shower in the morning, and to be reading her iPad while she did so, but needs must. It had, after all, been a very exhausting weekend, all things considered.

Eve had continued the logistical chats with Cathy, who had stayed over on both Friday and Saturday night before driving back to town on Sunday morning, after which Eve had gone on a long walk to the stables with Barney and Alice. This was allegedly to see Monty, though in truth she was only really interested in Alice, whom she very much didn't want to neglect. Afterwards, Eve had also finally found time for a talk on the phone with Mike, explaining everything. He had then been invited for Sunday evening's spag bol, and, with the house still reverberating from a weekend's worth of emotional fallout, he had drunk two glasses of wine, dispensed what little wisdom he claimed he could add, and then left by ten p.m. Eve very much hoped he wouldn't tire of all of this domestic clutter getting in the way of the getting-to-know-you phase of their still-impending relationship, but if it did, it did. For what felt like the first time in a long time – since Alice was a toddler, probably – Eve was putting parenting first. She could only hope that Mike, as a non-parent, was sufficiently interested in the novelty of it all to stick around.

And then, after Mike had left, Eve had – nervously – gone upstairs and quietly tapped on Zoe's closed bedroom door. Zoe had been around all weekend, but mostly as a spectral sort of presence, barely speaking, helping herself to cereal, defrosting pizzas, refusing offers of more substantial fare – about which Eve had reluctantly bitten her lip, overcoming the temptation to speak maternal clichés such as, 'But you're far too skinny as it is.'

Eve had quietly congratulated herself for this. However, hovering on the landing, carrying a mug of very likely to be rejected Horlicks and, of all unlikely bedtime offerings, a Tunnock's Teacake, she had been nervous about further rejection from her eldest daughter – the daughter that, since Friday, she barely recognized.

'Come in, Mum,' said Zoe's small voice.

Eve opened the door. 'How did you know it was me?'

'I can hear Alice watching *Secretariat* for, like, the nine hundredth time, next door.'

'*Secretariat*? Isn't that an eighteen?'

'No, Mum – that's *Secretary*. This one's a Disney movie about an American racehorse.'

Eve smiled. 'Right. I knew that.'

334

Zoe smiled back. 'Thanks for the Horlicks and the Tunnock's.'

'How can you tell it's Horlicks?'

'The smell?'

'Right. Yes.'

'Do you want to talk, or something?' Eve noted that Zoe's tone was neither combative nor submissive – just colourless. 'Cos I'm a bit tired, to be honest.'

'I bet you are. No need to talk, no, if you don't want to. Just checking you're OK.'

'I'm fine. It's all fine. I don't want to talk but, just so you know, Stefan didn't like seduce me. It was totally mutual. Consensual – that's the word.' Zoe shrugged.

'Right, well, whatever, thanks for sharing. But that won't stop your father wanting to punch him, I expect.'

'I'm not sure he'd come out of that on top, to be honest. Stefan's very, um,' Zoe paused, chose her word carefully, 'fit.'

Eve smiled. 'Good night, Zoe. Sleep well.'

'Yeah, you too, Mum.' Zoe's mouth was full of Teacake. 'Luff you.'

'Luff you too, Zo.'

And Eve shut the door, still smiling. It would indeed, she suddenly believed, all be fine, in time. No rush . . .

And now here she was, bunking off work on a Monday morning, and relaxing in the bath while attempting to catch up with an article she'd half heard mentioned two days previously, as she'd lain in bed, still slightly stunned from the events of the previous evening, and therefore only half listening to the Saturday morning edition of *Today*. With her iPad precariously balanced on the rack, it was only now that Eve finally started to read the article in the *Telegraph*.

> After announcing she is to leave to run a school in Switzerland, the headmistress of the leading independent girls' school, Wessex Park, has voiced frustration about attitudes to private education in Britain.
>
> Eleanor Hill told the *Courier* that Britain could not celebrate the success and heritage of its independent schools, which are increasingly sought-after among parents across the world. Mrs Hill will leave in the summer to become Director of L'Institut Villa Alpin in Switzerland: 'In the UK, the independent sector has gone through a tough time,' she said.

Eve read on, eagerly.

> Mrs Hill predicts more closures and mergers of private schools: 'We probably have too many boarding schools left over from the nineteenth century. There was a boom period when local British people decided that boarding was the best thing, but that is now changing and these days parents want their children at home.' But, according to Mrs Hill, demand from abroad for a British education still booms. 'I cannot say it strongly enough: this is the future.'

With a solar-plexus lurch, Eve realized that, as she had contentedly busied herself for years with her business, which was educating children, Tony had primarily been *running* a business. Why hadn't she realized that all along? Could she really have got quite so far past life's halfway mark and remained so comically naive? Events of the last few days seemed to suggest that this may indeed be the case. Despite a reasonably convincing veneer of sophistication, Eve suddenly felt unprecedentedly gauche. Hadn't she, for example, always simply assumed that Zoe was a Teflon teen, that problems rolled away from her, even as they often clung to Alice like burrs, that Zoe seemed, if not quite blessed, then certainly somehow charmed. And how wrong had that assumption turned out to be? She carried on reading.

Mrs Hill last week criticized schools that increasingly rely on fees from overseas students, making independent schools the preserve of only the very wealthiest. Our survey reveals that a majority of foreign pupils are currently from Hong Kong (almost 6,000 in the UK), followed by China (3,636), Germany (2,281) and Russia (1,695).

We spoke to one head teacher at an independent school where twenty-five per cent of pupils are from overseas. Wishing to remain anonymous, he told us that some schools recruit foreign students in a 'desperate attempt to fill their empty beds'. He said, 'That's not the case here, however, because we recruit successfully from all over the world.'

Finally:

Many families of foreign pupils are hiring agents or consultants to secure places at good British boarding schools. Some wealthy Russian parents pay £50,000 per child, though commission charges are more usually equivalent to a first term's fees: about £10,000. These agents, currently widely used by British universities, are facing tighter controls in an attempt to squeeze out rogue operators; it also risks creating 'ghettos' of children from the same country at boarding schools, some head teachers have warned.

Fascinating, thought Eve.

Most of the rest of Eve's day passed pleasantly and indulgently – albeit a little guiltily. She'd not quite dared to leave the house in case she was spotted, clearly norovirus-free and footloose, so decided to catch up with the kind of tedious domestic tasks that would assuage any guilt about playing hooky, while leaving her free to think. So it was that Eve had deep-cleaned the oven, tidied the utility room and hand-washed three identical pale grey cashmere sweaters before she picked up Gail's anguished phone message just after three p.m. – she'd been in the garden and hadn't bothered taking her mobile and hadn't heard the landline ringing. She listened in guilty horror – maybe this would never have happened if I'd been there? – before phoning Gail's mobile. She picked up immediately.

'Gail. It's me. My God. I'm going straight to the hospital.'

'But you can't, Eve, not with noro. And, anyway, Tony's there, with the Percys.'

'Fuck noro – I haven't got it. I lied. I –' Eve paused momentarily – 'I bunked off today.' Even as she spoke, Eve was aware that this was a sentence she'd never expected to say. 'Look, I've had a … *testing* weekend, but nothing compared to what the Percys are going through, so I'm going right now. Hold the fort at school, Gail, would you? Until further notice?'

'Done. Harry's in After-School Club till six and then he can look after himself. The phones are burning off their hooks. Look, I'd better go. And I can't believe you bunked off.'

'I can explain, Gail. But do we know how Michael is? Is he going to be OK?'

'I have no idea, Eve. No idea at all.'

The following Sunday was, to all intents, a perfect summer's day. Eve was sitting in the garden of the Red Lion, nursing half a lager and lime and popping dry-roasted peanuts as she waited for Simon to arrive. She knew Simon had been surprised when she'd suggested 'Le Lion Rouge'; it was rare for them to meet anywhere other than on their respective home turfs; however, Eve had chosen the venue with care.

As she waited, she flipped through the *Courier on Sunday* and watched families lingering over their al fresco Sunday lunches – mostly fully loaded roasts, with salad as a seasonal nod. Eve briefly acknowledged people she recognized; *Le Lion* was very much inside the Ivy House catchment, so she'd parked herself in a far corner of the garden in order not to cramp the children's – or, indeed, any of their parents' – style. The children who knew her kept a predictable polite distance; nonetheless, she was sought out by a few parents.

'Hello, Mrs Sturridge – sorry, *Eve!*' said Susie Poe. 'And so sorry to interrupt your, ah, drink, too, but I was just wondering if you'd heard any more news about Michael?'

Eve looked up and smiled. 'No need to apologize at all. My date, that is, my ex-husband, hasn't turned up yet. And I hear that Michael's doing marvellously, all things considered. According to his mother, whom I saw yesterday, he's very chipper and thoroughly enjoying the attention of the nurses, who dote on him. Mrs Percy said that it was, of course, unusual for him to be the centre of attention as a member of such a big family, and that he clearly thrives on it – which made her feel terrible for not giving him enough attention. I told her not to beat herself up; after all, hadn't Michael been heading home when he had the accident? Home to his mum?' Susie Poe nodded keenly. 'Of course, it's too early to know if he'll make a complete recovery. But he is an extraordinarily stoic little man; if his body will let him, I have no doubt in my mind that *his* mind will make it happen.'

It occurred to Eve that perhaps Susie hadn't been expecting quite so much information; however, Eve was becoming used to her role as unofficial mouthpiece for the Percy family. She spoke to them every day and had popped in to the hospital to see Michael three times since Monday. The matron on the children's ward was ex-Ivy House – before Eve's time, of course, but still, old school ties, and whatnot. 'And how are Charlie and Lula getting on at Eastdene? Well and truly settled in, I hope?'

Susie smiled. 'Very well, thank you. They love it. There were a few minor teething problems, of course, which were to be expected, but they came through and now they're just part of that "Eastdene family".' Susie waggled her fingers as air quotes. 'You do know I never would have moved them from Ivy House if it hadn't been a financial issue . . .' Susie paused. 'But, either way, they're very lucky to have had *two* such brilliant head teachers at two such different schools.'

'That's very kind of you, Susie. I'm delighted they're doing well. And they're in very safe hands at any school run by Mr Browning.'

'I suspect you're right. And thanks for the update on Michael – the children know some of his siblings, you see, and have been asking after him every day.'

'No problem; we've all been very concerned. And how are you, Susie?'

'Ah, well, fine. Happily flying solo, no longer single-handedly keeping Kleenex in business, you'll be glad to know –' Eve smiled – 'and enjoying some new challenges. I'm already a parent governor at Eastdene, which is marvellous. And, of course, we're all so thrilled that Gail will be joining the school in September. She'll be such a huge asset.'

Eve raised an eyebrow. 'Yes, I'm sure she will.'

Susie Poe grimaced. 'Oh my god, I'm so sorry! I'd assumed she'd handed in her notice.'

Eve realized she'd done a bad job of disguising the fact that she'd had no idea Gail was leaving. 'Well, I suspect she has, just not to me. I was off on Monday and it's been a very busy week, obviously, as we've all been so distracted by poor little Michael.' Eve paused. What followed came surprisingly easily: 'But, the thing is, Susie, it's not a problem because, strictly *entre nous*, I'll be leaving soon too.'

Susie's eyes widened. 'Well, that is quite a local scoop I've just landed. But, of course, I shan't breathe a word, even though it's what everybody has been expecting, really, ever since your excellent article in the *Courier*. And I heard you on *Today* with Humphrys, too. You did a terrific job – with Humphrys, I mean. You're still doing a terrific job at, uh, everything else.'

It was Eve's turn to be wide-eyed. *It's what everybody has been expecting* . . . Everybody except, apparently, me . . . But, anyway, now I've said it. And to Susie Poe – a journalist – too. So, it's on the record. That's it, then. I'm *off* . . .

'That's very kind of you, Susie. And now here's my ex-husband. Perfect timing! Please, don't let me keep you.'

Eve noted that that particular old headmistressy trick wasn't lost on Susie Poe, who smiled. 'You're not. I'm keeping you. But thanks for the update – and good luck.'

Having just missed being introduced by moments, Simon sat down and watched Susie Poe's retreating back. 'That's a very good-looking woman.'

'Yes. Susie Poe. Down-from-Londoner, journalist, former Ivy-House mother turned Eastdene parent governor, apparently. Oh, and divorced and available – if curvaceous blondes happened to be where your proclivities lay.'

'You know I am very partial to a curvaceous blonde, Mrs Sturridge. Anyway,' Simon raised his glass, 'cheers!'

'Fair enough. In a week when there hasn't really been much to celebrate, I'll raise a glass. Cheers!'

'How is Michael Percy doing?'

Eve repeated what she'd told Susie Poe. 'I believe he's doing very well. Meanwhile, Tony has been worrying himself sick about being sued by the Percys, despite the fact that – the Percys being the Percys – they've told him it will never happen; they are of the opinion, old-fashioned though that may be, that accidents happen, and they therefore have no interest in destroying the school which has done the right thing by all their children. For which we are all very grateful, of course.' Eve sighed. 'But that hasn't stopped Tony shutting down the building works and saying he's having a rethink about, well,' Eve shrugged, '*everything,*

343

apparently.' She paused. 'And that mindset seems to be infectious, because I want to sell the house.'

Simon started; he was clearly thrown. 'But I made that house for *you*. It's a Forever House.'

Eve smiled at the slight tremble in Simon's voice. 'No, Simon. You made it for the person you wanted me to be – or at least the one you hoped I might become – and that's not who I am. And "forever" is a very long time.'

'So who are you?'

'I'm not sure yet, but I'm going to find out.'

Simon sighed. 'So much has changed this year. I can hardly keep up. Do you think you'll move far?'

Eve considered this. 'No, not far physically, I think, maybe just metaphorically.'

Simon smiled. 'Anyone would think you had an A in English at O level.'

Eve rolled her eyes. 'Unlike our youngest daughter.'

'On the subject of which, how are the daughters?'

'Fine, I think. Of course, you know Zo has done her interview with Cath?' Simon nodded. 'And they're doing the photo shoot tomorrow. It'll all be out on Saturday, amazingly. Zoe is very focused.'

'I'll bet. I still fully plan to punch both Stefan Sorensen and the appalling Rob.'

Eve nodded. 'Yup. Good idea. I'm not sure about Sorensen, but, yeah, I think you could probably take out Rob.'

Simon raised his eyes heavenwards. 'Gee, thanks, honey – I'm only twice his size.'

Eve laughed. 'And in all the wrong places, too.'

Simon gasped. 'I cannot believe you just said that, Eve. I am properly shocked and appalled.' But, even as he did his best to disguise it, Eve could see a slight smile playing around Simon's lips.

'Hold that thought, because you ain't heard nothing yet – I'm resigning, too.'

42

In the light of recent events, there had been some talk of cancellation; however, the Percy family – enthusiastic upholders of the 'tradition' – would have none of it. Thus, the Wednesday of the last week in June was, indeed, Upside-Down Day at Ivy House, as advertised. Which also meant that Monday and Tuesday, though nominally normal school days, were mostly just the excitable run-up.

At this time of year, post exams, the majority of the school's academic work was done and the focus was on play – sporting play, acting play or just plain old-fashioned playing play. And there was an atmosphere of expectation around this year's Upside Down, a pervasive sense throughout the school that it ought somehow to be made even more fun than usual, for Michael. Thus there was a general feeling of infectious sunniness in the air. The weather helped; it was definitely properly summery. Sports Day – the weekend before Michael's accident, or BMA, as Gail had it – had been a triumph, with more picnic hampers than ever lining the perimeter of the athletics track to witness Dickens winning the House trophy for the third year running, while the cricket pavilion was host to some hard competitive work by the indefatigable Friends of Ivy House, the bunch of closely knit and tireless 'professional parents' (as Eve referred to them, meaning women who made parenting their profession; Gail's preferred description, on the other hand, was 'the sisters of Stepford') whose previous lives as lawyers, PR executives and academics effectively ensured that the cricket tea's Victoria sponge was as unbeatable as the school's first eleven.

It was this atmosphere of fun-by-any-means-necessary that had unexpectedly – to Eve, at least – hastened Eve's decision making. She'd spent quite a bit of time with her boss over the last couple of weeks and had been surprised to discover aspects of him she'd never known: a vulnerability closer to the surface than she could have imagined; a sensitivity around the Percy family that hinted at the possibility of hitherto unprecedented kindness. As emotions had run high in the week after Michael's accident, these discoveries had been baffling to Eve, though not unwelcome.

Even so, it was hard not to break the news she needed to break in as brisk a fashion as possible. So, after tapping on Tony's office door at 9:30 a.m., that's exactly what she did.

'OK, so I shan't beat around the bush; I'm resigning, Tony. I'd like to leave at the end of term, though I appreciate that may be too soon, so, if it's at all helpful to the school, I am happy to work over the summer. But, either way, I'm done. I'm off. And I'm sorry to spring this on you on Upside-Down Day, especially with everything that's happened recently. And what's all this about Gail too, while I'm at it?'

It was rare that Tony's expression gave absolutely nothing away, but, unexpectedly, this was one of those occasions. Tony gave Eve a very long, level sort of stare and then said, 'Actually, I'm not accepting your resignation because I'm sacking you instead. And, as for being any alleged –' he wiggled fingers in the air as quote marks – ' "help", well, that's a bit rich coming from you. So you can sod off right now, today, if you like. Gail's going at the end of term, anyway. She handed in her notice on the day Michael . . . whatever. Anyway. End of an era, onwards and upwards.' He sighed.

Eve hadn't quite expected this. 'You think that that would be good for the school? For the pupils? For staff morale? You really think I should just walk out? What message would that be sending the troops, Tony? Am I going to be escorted from the building carrying my cardboard box of personal effects? Christ, this isn't some steely sort of financial services corporation stuck in a Canary Wharf tower. We're not bloody Enron!'

Tony listened to Eve, cocked his head to one side and said, 'Yeah, I think now is probably as good a time as any. Steve Bryant can be acting head teacher for a fortnight.' He paused and, to Eve's astonishment, suddenly buried his head in his big hands. 'Oh, fuck it, Eve, who am I kidding?

I'm selling Ivy House. I'm done. I can't have little boys being run over by fucking diggers in a school I own. If it was anyone other than the Percys' little boy, I'd be having my arse sued, anyway. Just imagine if it had been a Dershowitz kid, or a Sorensen?'

Eve winced. 'On the subject of which—'

'I know, I *know*. Our last Dershowitz leaves in a fortnight, anyway – I believe they're currently torn between Haileybury and Harrow – and if Sorensen goes down, I expect Anette will move away.'

It was Eve's turn to sigh. 'Who knows, Tony? I shall miss the Dershowitzes; I like them. But the Sorensens I –' she stammered slightly – 'I . . . barely know. Anyway, if you need to sack me for some peculiar control-freaky reason, then go ahead, but please don't mess up Steve's end of term. As Head of Games, he more than delivered with Sports Day – and, anyway, I'm not sure he actually owns any clothing other than tracksuits.' Eve paused, attempted to read Tony's expression. 'Look, Tony, I may as well stay for another couple of weeks, for God's sake.'

Tony pursed his lips and squinted at Eve. 'Up to you. You can either stay for another fortnight, pointlessly, or you can leave right now with six months' salary. Here –' Tony opened a drawer in the Scandi-desk, pulled out a cheque book and scribbled on it with his large, childishly looping handwriting and his illegible flourish of a signature. And, even from where she was standing, Eve could see the noughts . . . Sod it. I'm not too proud to take that! And she surprised herself with how good it felt. Tony handed her the cheque. Eve took it, glanced at it and nodded, folding it carefully and placing it in a pocket. Tony remained standing. 'Uh, the thing is, I have it on very good authority that you bunked off work on the day of Michael's, uh . . . We've had the *Battle Observer* sniffing around about that. Perhaps if you'd been around it would never have happened? So, not a fucking word of any of this to anyone in the, uh, media – OK?'

Eve, astonished, couldn't think of a response. Of course, she knew that the only 'very good authority' Tony could possibly mean was Gail. And how extraordinarily unlike Gail it was to whistleblow to Tony against her. Yet that was apparently exactly what had happened. Why?

And then she realized. Of course! It was all so suddenly, completely, comically, staring-you-in-the-face bleeding obvious that she let out an involuntary 'Ha!' Swiftly followed by an 'Omigod!'

Yet, even as all these new and distracting thoughts crowded for her attention, Eve suspected her overriding memory of this moment would be of Tony Salter, standing behind his desk, wearing a tweed skirt suit, American-tan tights, a pair of scuffed brogues and a thin smear of frosted-pink lipstick, with that distinctive messy cowlick protruding from his Margaret Thatcher-style wig. It was all she could do not to explode with laughter.

End of an era, indeed . . .

Back outside Tony's office, Eve paused, drew a very deep

breath and then rushed as quickly back to her office as possible, without actually running. Inevitably, Gail was in situ behind her own desk, just outside Eve's office. Eve affected a bright smile that very much belied her true, confused feelings.

'I've just had a quick meeting with Tony and I'm leaving, Gail – right now. So that makes two of us!'

Either Gail hadn't picked up on her last comment or she'd chosen to ignore it. 'What do you mean? Do you have an appointment? Are the girls OK?'

'The girls are fine, but, yes, apparently I have an appointment with the rest of my life. Tony's, um, sacked me, effective immediately. Apparently he's unimpressed with the reasons for my, um, absence on the day of Michael's accident. Talk about Upside-Down Day!' Eve felt that she'd given Gail every opportunity to say *something* . . .

But Gail's jaw went slack. 'What? You're kidding?'

'Nope, not kidding – leaving. And can I ask you a huge favour?' Conscious of being let down – and indeed hurt – by her right-hand woman of the past decade, Eve was now all brisk focus and adrenaline.

'Of course. Jesus, Eve, it goes without saying.'

'Does it? Well, anyway, don't mention this to anybody, if you can avoid it. Say I've gone down with that violently contagious norovirus again, if you absolutely have to.'

Eve paused, met Gail's eye. Gail nodded. 'OK.' And then she carried on nodding. And then her eyes widened: 'Oh no! *Omigod*, Eve! I just let it slip when I was talking to Tony.

I think it was the Tuesday or the Wednesday night, I can't remember. I meant no harm! Tony was, uh, round mine and we were just talking about everything, and – God! Why would he *do* that? Why would he use that against you?'

It was Eve's turn to look bemused. 'I have no idea, Gail. And I had no idea you were so close, you and Tony – until just now, that is, when I did. Anyway, whatever. It would be great if you could pack up my desk a bit. I'm just going to grab my laptop and phone and some correspondence and stuff.'

'Right. OK. But, Eve, this is all mental. Are you OK?'

'Fine. I'm fine. Really. At least, I'm fine at the moment. Tomorrow –' Eve shrugged – 'who knows?'

And as she stuffed random paperwork into her Mulberry first-day-of-the-new-school-year 'satchel' and grabbed her phone and raced through the highly adrenalized final moments before she left, Eve suddenly recognized that she would probably never set foot in this room – her home from home for the past decade – ever again. Of course I won't. This is it. All that work, that passion and dedication, all those hours of worrying and trying to get it right – and for what? To be forced to walk out on children and staff she cared about. The unfairness – the wrongness, frankly – of now leaving *her* school in the hands of the man who actually owned it made Eve, to her surprise and horror, actually cry with fury, fat cheque notwithstanding. A hot tear slid down her cheek – and then very many more as the dam burst. Jesus! I can't let anyone see me leaving like this. I'll have to sneak out, round the back. After ten years, I have to make my exit like a bloody thief.

A knock on the door, swiftly followed by ashen-faced Gail. Her dismay at the sight of Eve in tears was obvious.

'Sorry, Gail, I'm just having a moment – I'll be fine.' Eve sniffed. 'Look, I'm going to leave by the back door, nip down to the sports hall and then round to the bottom car park. That way, nobody will be able to tell that the noro is fake and that what I'm actually suffering from is leaking eyes and –' she glanced at Gail – 'a breaking heart.' Which was all it took to set Gail off, too. 'Stop it,' said Eve. 'One of us has to be the grown-up and, as I've been relying on you to fulfil that role for the past ten years, it would be great if you could carry on for just a few more minutes, thanks.'

Gail smiled wanly. 'I don't know how you retain your sense of humour.'

'Nor do I. But have you actually *seen* Tony all cross-dressed-up in his Joyce Grenfell rig? Just hold on to that mental image. Right, I'm off.'

'Where do you think you'll go?'

'Oh, God, I don't know. It's a bit too soon to think about it, really.'

'No, I mean where will you go *now*?'

'Oh! Yes, of course – er, home?'

'Right. And is anybody there?'

Eve thought for a moment. Alice was probably at the

stables; Zoe was staying at Simon and Ed's this week. Mike was at school, obviously . . .

'Nope, nobody's there. I'll probably be in the pub, slumped over a bottle of Glenmorangie. Anyway, congratulations on your job at Eastdene.'

'I was going to tell you before I told Tony, Eve. But you weren't there, and then everything else happened.'

Eve nodded briskly; she'd been wondering why Mike hadn't told her, too. Then again, she'd hardly seen Mike. 'One day playing hooky off school in a whole decade and I'm certainly paying the price.'

Gail blushed and looked away. 'Eve, if you do end up in the pub, may I suggest you get changed first?'

Eve glanced down at her feet and started to giggle, albeit slightly hysterically. She had, of course, forgotten that she had her hair in bunches and was wearing a short-sleeved buttoned-up white blouse with a red tartan tie, a navy knee-length box-pleated skirt, white ankle socks and a pair of red Mary Janes. She clamped her hand over her mouth and snorted.

'I mean, obviously *we're* all used to the Upside-Down traditions,' continued Gail, deadpanning, 'but, out there in the wider world, a mature woman – never mind a head teacher – wearing school uniform is likely to be interpreted in a very different way. And as for the pub . . .' She broke off, shrugged.

Eve couldn't speak. She thought she would probably either faint or explode with laughter. 'Thank you, Gail –

thank you for being the best. Even if you snitched on me to Tony –' a beat – 'having also withheld the fact that he's Harry's dad for a decade.'

Gail's eyes widened. She looked as though she was going to say something and then thought better of it. Eve continued: 'You know you could have trusted me, Gail? I've always trusted you.' Her tone was definitely more in sorrow than anger.

Gail shook her head, a deep blush already rising up her neck. 'Now is not the time for this.'

'Now was apparently *never* the time!'

Gail turned away so she could avoid Eve's gaze. 'You'd better go before the staff cricket match starts and you're spotted – I can already see Year Seven and the sisters of Stepford making picnic lunches in the sports hall. Go! Can I call you in the morning?'

Eve was already leaving the room. She paused. 'Well, I can't stop you. I might even answer.'

And, with that, Eve walked out of Ivy House for the last time. Buzzing with adrenaline, she stuck her head in the door of the bursar's office en route to the back door. 'Hi, Pat. I'm going out. I may be some time. Like, actually, forever.'

'OK,' said Pat, only half listening and without glancing up from her copy of *Good Housekeeping*, 'but you'll want to be back for the cricket match. Tony's umpiring.'

'That's a shame. I'm sure he'd prefer to be bowling maidens over in his tweed skirt.'

Pat glanced up. 'Sorry, Eve, what was that? Reading a really good article on Emma Thompson. I always liked her more than Ken.'

'Showing your age, Pat. Didn't they split up in, like, the eighties?'

'Nineteen ninety-five, as it happens. But you're right – I do still think the eighties were about ten years ago. I'm not sure where my nineties got to, really.' Pat sighed.

Eve looked at Pat's severely unflattering bob and pastel mother-of-the-bride shift dress and the gilt-chained handbag slung over the back of her chair. 'OK, so, anyway, I'm off.'

But Pat still wasn't really listening. 'Okey-dokey, Eve, see you later. Goodness, that wedding dress of Em's really was an absolute horror.'

43

Once she'd reached the Volvo unseen, Eve pulled her hair out of its bunches, rubbed the eyebrow-pencilled freckles off her nose and drove home, deliberately slowly.

As she entered the house, she smelled Zoe's favourite scent – Agent Provocateur, what else? – before she saw her daughter, sitting in the kitchen, wearing pyjamas and eating cereal. Well, it is just about still morning, after all. Zoe waved at Eve and mouthed, 'Just a minute!' as she continued her phone call, so Eve nodded and went to fill the kettle. While she waited for Zoe to finish talking – to Carmen, by the sound of it – her own phone buzzed in her bag. She pulled it out and saw *MIKE* on the screen ID. She swiped the *Slide to answer* icon.

'Mike?'

'Eve! I didn't really expect to get you, but I just wanted to wish you a happy Upside-Down Day.'

'Sweet of you. Couple of things, though – I've just been sacked by Tony, so I'm at home. And, er, why didn't you tell me you'd hired Gail?'

'God, Eve – what with everything else that's been going on, it just didn't occur to me. I assumed Gail would tell you herself, given you're so close. But what the hell do you mean, sacked?'

So Eve explained briskly, editing as she went, conscious that Zoe had now ended her call and was listening, too. She felt suddenly fenced in, claustrophobic. The last few weeks had been . . . exhausting.

'May I come round later?' said Mike. 'I'll take you out for dinner. A proper date dinner that, with a bit of luck, won't be interrupted by any fresh drama.'

And Eve was so tired she simply nodded at the phone.

'Mum, you have to, like, speak!' squeaked Zoe.

'Eve? You still there?' said Mike.

Eve grinned at her daughter. 'Yes; sorry. I'm completely done in. It's all catching up with me. Please, *please* take me out for dinner. I can't think of anything I'd like more, really.'

'Deal. I'll be on your doorstep at seven thirty.'

Eve rang off and shook her head in mock despair at Zoe. 'Crazy days.'

Zoe looked her mother up and down. 'Make sure you get changed before Mike comes, yeah, otherwise he'll think you're a weirdo. And, you know what you need, Mum? A holiday. I think you should go away somewhere lovely, with Alice. I'll stay here and look after Barney and water the garden and be one hundred per cent the kind of daughter you'd like me to be, if only for a week or two – promise!'

Eve narrowed her eyes. 'That's actually not a bad idea. But do I trust you? Won't you just post a party on Facebook and the Barn'll be crashed by a thousand teenagers from all over Sussex – and probably Rihanna and Beyoncé, too, for all I know. Remember, I'm about to try to sell it, so I really don't need it trashed!'

Zoe shrugged. 'No worries. I've come off Facebook for a bit; I'm doing Twitter now. But have you really been sacked, Mum?'

'Depends. It's probably more like "let go". But, yes, I'm gone. Unemployed!'

'But with a nice big cheque. Go on, book a holiday. Then you'll sell the Barn and find us a lovely wonky cottage, hopefully, and—'

'Why do you say, "wonky cottage"?' Eve butted in.

Zoe smiled. 'Because we have the same taste. Don't *you* want to live in a wonky cottage?'

'I totally want to live in a wonky cottage – always have done. But I never dared tell your dad!' Eve smiled sheepishly at her daughter, who had clamped her hand over her mouth and was snorting with suppressed laughter.

'That is the funniest thing I've ever heard. You were married to a modernist architect, so you had to live in a big, shiny *Grand Designs*-y box!'

At which entirely accurate observation, Eve wrapped an arm around her eldest daughter's waist and they leaned into each other, shaking with laughter. 'I know! All I ever wanted was exposed beams and an inglenook fireplace.'

'I'm so telling on you!'

'You're not telling your dad!'

'I so am.'

'I'll kill you!' But Eve was still giggling.

'Do you want me to look after the house while you take your youngest daughter on a lovely mums and daughters spa break, or what?'

'Yes, I do. Very much.'

'So how much is it worth for me not to tell Dad that you want to live in, basically, Ye Olde Curiosity Shoppe?'

Eve giggled. 'Shoes? Is it worth shoes?'

'And . . . ?'

'Um. Maybe more shoes?!'

'Might be!'

Upside-Down Day, indeed . . . thought Eve, suddenly and very unexpectedly enjoying every moment.

After a quick diversion to Tesco Express for milk and something microwaveable, Gail was home later than she'd expected. Harry was out of After-School Club and sitting on the bungalow's garden wall, swinging his legs sulkily and scuffing the backs of his brand-new Nikes. 'Please don't do that, Hazza!' said Gail, feeling a surge of irritation. Fifty quid, even in the sale. Harry was already a size six.

In the kitchen, Gail made herself a cup of tea and picked up the newspaper she'd left folded neatly on the breakfast bar for several days, waiting for the right moment. And now seemed as good a moment as any other to read the *Courier*'s interview with Zoe.

REVENGE PORN – A Victim's Story
Zoe Sturridge speaks to Cathy Gower

A victim of so-called 'revenge porn', seventeen-year-old A-level student Zoe Sturridge has opened up to the *Courier* after sexually intimate filmed footage of her was put online by an ex-boyfriend. Zoe, of Eastdene, East Sussex, is also one of six female accusers from around the world set against American revenge-porn website owners, Brad Hunter and Chuck Williams, after discovering she had been featured on their Dontchawish.com website.

In an exclusive interview with us, Zoe spoke out bravely this week after the two men were indicted in California for running the site.

'You think that it can't happen to you, but it can,' said Zoe. 'I was so damaged by it. I just wanted to stay in my room forever. It just all hit me like a ton of bricks.'

The 'it' she refers to is footage that was uploaded to the site earlier this year. It took nine days to get the images removed, but by then it had been mass-texted and Facebooked to almost everyone she knew. Zoe is now on a crusade and has been joined by her mother – head teacher and occasional *Courier* contributor, Eve Sturridge – who has been dubbed by her daughter 'the Erin Brockovich of revenge porn'.

'I'm so happy that, finally, something's happening,' Eve told the *Courier*. 'Revenge porn is really just about hurting and humiliating people, trying to ruin their lives. It's a form of domestic abuse, an issue of control and coercion.'

So where does the law currently stand?

'Well, it depends what the image depicts, but, in legal terms, I believe it's more a case of harassment and an issue of protection of privacy,' says Eve. 'There is a Protection From Harassment Act, but it's a breach of privacy if someone posts images of you on the internet, and you could launch a civil case on the basis of that, but not a criminal case.'

'A lot of women are being threatened with just the possibility of revenge porn, too,' says Zoe. 'It's invariably from exes – and usually men, too.' It seems that compassion, respect and empathy are not part of the revenge pornographer's lexicon; Zoe will, according to her mum, have to 'monitor the internet for the rest of her life, because this stuff, once out there, rarely disappears completely. There are all sorts of implications around this, not least for potential employers.'

Zoe, who has been studying for A levels and wants to work in finance, found out about the betrayal from her boyfriend just after they'd split up, and was devastated. 'Those images were private – and I'd trusted my boyfriend to keep them that way, forever. He just said to me, "You are on a website called Dontchawish.com,"' she recalls, '"and you might want to do something about that!" And then he told me he was going on holiday. I haven't seen him since and I don't want to. He's dead to me now.'

Zoe warns others of the potential dangers and hopes that revenge porn – effectively the distribution of a private sexual image of someone without their consent and with the intention of causing them distress – will, in the future, be made an offence. 'Revenge porn knows no borders. When my material first started going viral, straight away I was on a site that was outside of this country. And, while I'm determined that this horrible experience won't ruin my life,' says Zoe, 'I'm just as determined it shouldn't ruin anybody else's, either.'

You can find out more about Zoe's campaign via her YouTube channel and you can follow her on Twitter, @ZoeSSays.

Gail looked at the picture of Zoe, who, she realized with a start, was no longer just long and skinny and leggy, but somehow now properly beautiful, and then she refolded the paper neatly and took a sip of tea, thinking about relationships and their unexpected consequences and then, more specifically, about Zoe's experience. Still, thought Gail, a girl as beautiful and as blessed as Zoe can turn even horrible things like this to her advantage. She'll end up modelling, or on *Big Brother*.

Gail peered out at the garden, distractedly noting that it needed a mow, but also . . . Oh my God! Something very exciting had happened that, what with all the recent chaos, Gail hadn't noticed until now. Had it, in fact, just happened *today*?

Gail unlocked the kitchen door and walked across the lawn to the beds that bordered Mike's boundary. Yes! There were six unfurling buds on the rich pink and yellow 'Bowl of Beauty', the 'Sarah Bernhardt' was coming along too and the extraordinary 'Angel Cheeks' was already in full show-stopping glory.

'Hazza? *Harry!* Come and look at these. Your granddad planted them and they've just come out.' Harry was doing keepy-uppies at the other end of the lawn. He was good at football . . . But still, Gail thought . . . 'Second thoughts, Hazza, you're all right – don't come anywhere near here with your ball.'

She kneeled on the lawn and watched the bloated honey-bees hovering greedily above the bed filled with the feminine, fragile-yet-powerful, late-blooming peonies. 'Peonies from heaven,' as her dad always said; you're beautiful. They'd always been her favourites – flowers that rewarded patience and that, on arrival, announced, 'Your summer is finally here . . .'

44

Despite her exhaustion, Eve enjoyed the slightly disorien-tating feeling that comes of boarding a plane in one climate and disembarking in another. She peered out of the window as the plane taxied to a standstill, heat haze shimmering on the runway's tarmac. Outside, on the steps, just inches away from the air con, the heat hit her like a fat, heavy wave and she had the feeling that even a thirty-second walk to the transit bus would allow the sun to leave its mark on her genetically Celtic skin. Eve didn't really do sun directly, didn't sit in it ever, far less prostrate herself on beaches. She was, by nature and inclination, a lurker-under-parasols, but that didn't mean she didn't like having sun around her – preferably just out of reach.

'What do you think so far?' Eve turned to a smiling Alice. Silence. She tugged off her daughter's headphones. 'I said . . . What. Do. You. Think. So. Far?'

'Cool,' said Alice.

Eve smiled. 'And yet also the exact opposite of that – phew!' She fanned herself.

'Hot flush, Mum?' asked Alice, wide-eyed and faux-innocently.

'Something like that, yes. It is about ninety degrees.'

'Is that in old money?'

'Ha! Yes. Anyway, after we get our bags, we're apparently only about twenty minutes from a pool,' said Eve. 'And I shall this say only once—'

'SUNBLOCK!' said Alice. 'I know. And I also know you'll say it, like, nine hundred and thirty-seven thousand times in the next ten days.'

Eve sighed. Alice was right, but tomorrow, with a bit of luck, she might even start to relax.

Both of them slept deeply that first night: early to bed and early to rise, the better to enjoy their morning foray without the searing heat. It didn't take long to slip into the siesta-orientated swing of things when the alternative was being exhausted and frazzled. Yes, today was definitely the time to strike while the iron was merely warm. Eve was given impressively detailed driving instructions from the hotel's front desk, but apparently the drive in their hired Seat should only take about twenty minutes, door to door, even though the natives habitually did it in well under fifteen.

'We're in no rush,' said Eve. 'Just keen to make it one piece.'

'Well, it's a really gorgeous spot there, just outside Portinatx, which is one of my favourite beaches,' said the boutique B&B's English owner – precisely the kind of deeply tanned, glamorously boho, coolly accessorized Jade Jagger-y kind of thirty-something who made Eve feel like a particularly pale and uninteresting fifty-three-year-old mother-of-two from East Sussex. 'The address you're looking for is one of *the* most amazing new houses on the island – El Paradiso, which everybody slows down to get a peek at when they drive past. Enjoy your morning!'

It took Eve and Alice over half an hour to travel the six or so miles to El Paradiso, mostly because they kept slowing down to look at things and even, at one point, stopped to scrump four large oranges from a branch overhanging their side of the road and which were therefore, according to Eve, 'perfectly nickable'. It was just after nine a.m. and definitely heating up when Alice finally spotted the low-key white gateposts and hand-painted sign.

'El Paradiso! Look, *there*!'

'Well spotted!' said Eve. 'And the gate's open, too.'

As they drove up the shady drive towards the large, low, white single-storey building – relatively modest from this angle, but, Eve guessed, presumably less so once inside – Eve was silently nervous. Alice, on the other hand, was not.

'Wow,' said Alice. 'I mean – *wow*.'

'Yes.' Eve sighed.

'Mum, imagine living here?' Alice's eyes were like a Japanese anime character's.

'I can't, really,' said Eve, 'more's the pity. Right, shall we just see if anybody's in?'

Eve parked in the shade beside a beaten-up white

pick-up with its keys still in the ignition. Alice rapped the knocker against the heavy dark-wood door – the house was virtually windowless, impregnable-looking from this angle – and added a resonant *ting-a-ling* on the proper big bell hanging on the wall beside it. They waited, shifting from foot to foot. Then, finally, muffled, from the other side of the door came the sound of a voice coming closer – an English and, more specifically, male, *London* voice. And then quite distinctly there was an amused-but-resigned sounding, 'All right, all right – whatever, don't put yourself out. I'll get this.'

The door swung open to reveal a tanned, smiling, good-looking man in his late thirties. He was wearing denim shorts, a faded pink Superdry T-shirt and black Birkenstocks.

'Morning! What can I do you for?'

'Oh, er – hi!' said Eve. She held out her hand. 'My name's Eve Sturridge and this is Alice. I think we're expected. Anyway, it's lovely to meet you, Mr . . . ? God, I'm so sorry; I realize I don't actually know your name.'

The man smiled and opened the door wider. '*I'm* so sorry, Mrs Sturridge, I didn't recognize you off duty in your summer mufti. I'm Joe Parker; we've not met properly. But I am literally "Parker" to Anette's "Lady Penelope".' Eve grinned. 'I know,' said Joe. 'She's the spit, right? Come in; come in. Everybody else is out the back, by the pool – no surprise, I'm sure. We've been here just over a week, now, and seem to have a routine going.'

'Thanks very much – that's extremely kind of you.'

Eve and Alice stepped into the cool, dark hallway and, as their eyes adjusted, looked around as they followed Joe. The house turned out to be nothing short of astonishing on the inside. Wildly modern with brightly coloured walls, it was a hip interior designer's dream-home-cum-gallery. Perched on the side of a cliff overlooking the sea, the house unfolded over several layers, with a vast glass wall to enjoy the view. Outside, a stone terrace wrapped round the building and led down to a huge infinity pool.

'Oh. My. *God*,' said Alice. 'This is the most amazing house, ever!'

Though modernism was not her thing, in this case, Eve was inclined to agree.

'This is a stunning house, Mr Parker.'

'Call me Joe. "Mr Parker" always makes me feel like I've been stopped for speeding and the Old Bill are inspecting my licence. Not – I hasten to add – that that happens very often.'

Joe led them down a set of sweeping marble stairs and then out through a folding glass wall on to the terrace. At this point, there were more sharp intakes of breath from the Sturridges at the close-up sight of the extraordinary, curvaceous pool, designed to look natural – albeit, thought Eve, natural in the style of, say, Tracy Island. Joe grinned. 'And, yes, you're right, the place *is* very nice. One of the perks of our job, me and the missus, is staying here for six weeks every summer and, instead of *being* the staff, having our *own* staff – though we inevitably end up doing a bit of babysitting for the boss. We're lucky – all the cousins get on. Usually. Well, they are today . . .' Joe broke off and, peering closely at Eve, narrowed his eyes. 'You know that I'm married to Anette's sister?'

Eve shook her head and shrugged. 'I didn't, no.'

But Joe was already moving out of earshot, towards the pool. 'Birgitte! Kids! We have guests.' Five children of various ages and sizes and, apart from one brunette, a similar degree of blondeness climbed out of the pool: three boys and two girls, accompanied by a slim, very attractive, bikini-clad blonde woman in her thirties. The Sturridges, outnumbered, shuffled from foot to foot.

'Hi!' said the woman, smiling and holding out a damp hand. 'You must be Eve? I'm Joe's wife, Birgitte, mother of two of these.' She nodded towards the kids, who, having lined up, now looked like the cast of *The Sound of Music*. 'You could try to guess which were which, but I would forgive you for getting it wrong; from a distance I can't always tell them apart myself. Anyway, from left to right, we have Alvar, Byrge, Petrus, Aija and Chanelle. Joe didn't get a look-in on the baby names, as you can tell.'

Joe shrugged. 'Just as well, or they'd probably have been Kevin and Ron. Anyway, the first two are ours, the second two belong to my sister-in-law and the last one is Aija's best friend, who is here as her guest.'

'Hello, Aija, Petrus, *Chanelle*,' said Eve, smiling at a

lightly tanned and apparently very much at home Chanelle Billings. 'How are you? Having a good time?'

'Totally! It's awesome, Mrs Sturridge!'

'Of course, you all know each other. I am stupid!' said Birgitte, slapping her forehead with her palm. 'D'oh!' The children giggled.

'Don't be silly; no reason why you should remember me at all. But –' Eve waved towards the pool – 'I do feel you ought to know that there's definitely more kids in that pool. Had you not noticed?'

Birgitte smiled and nodded. 'Yup, we have all the Percy kids here too. Anette thought Mr and Mrs Percy – who are her next-door neighbours, of course – would appreciate some time to spend with Michael this summer. And, of course, farming families rarely get to go abroad for holidays, so . . .' She shrugged. 'They all seem to be having a good time, but they do burn very easily, so we are getting through a lot of sunblock. And they're not convinced by the food, but we're working on it.'

'That's so lovely. I'm sure they're having a marvellous time. Which reminds me – Alice?'

Alice rolled her eyes. 'Yup. *Sunblock*. I'm on it – and it's on me. And I *love* the food.'

Birgitte laughed. 'Now, Alice, would you like a swim?' Alice nodded. 'Excellent. We have loads of spare pairs of swimmers in the pool house, if you haven't got any with you right now. Aija and Chanelle, show Alice where to get changed, yeah?'

'Cuppa? Unless you fancy something cooler?' said Joe.

Eve shook her head. 'Actually a cuppa would be perfect.'

'Then I'll stick the kettle on. Sit wherever you like, inside or out, make yourself comfortable. Anette will pop up in a bit. She likes to ride in the early mornings, so she's probably still at our stables.'

As Joe and Birgitte retreated to the kitchen, Eve squinted towards the pool-house cabana, where the kids were hopping in and out, grabbing lilos and noodles and chucking them into the pool. Eve noted with amusement that the fabulously chic pool now resembled an exceptionally well-appointed civic leisure centre. She watched as Alice, who emerged from the cabana in a pretty, *tiny* emerald-green bikini, dived a perfect arc into the deep end and emerged, grinning and spluttering, to applause from the younger kids, and Eve.

As she clapped, she noticed a woman appear through a discreet gate very close to the pool and head towards the terrace. Eve slipped on her shades and squinted some more – the sun was very bright by now – and, though the woman was backlit, Eve could immediately see that it was Anette Sorensen, barefoot, wearing a large white shirt over a black bikini top and denim shorts. Her hair was tied up in a scarf and her sunglasses were pushed up on to her forehead. When she spotted Eve, she smiled and gave a cheerful little wave.

God, thought Eve. Even though this is why I'm here, it's

still potentially pretty awkward. Yet, instinctively, she scrambled to her feet.

Anette was still smiling when she stopped at the table and held out both her hands, taking Eve's and, disconcertingly, squeezing them gently. 'Eve. Thanks so much for coming. And I see Alice is making herself at home in the pool. Marvellous. Ah, tea! Perfect! Thank you so much, Joe.'

Eve noted, not for the first time, how Anette Sorensen's breathily lilting vocal tones had an extraordinarily relaxing effect. She'd make a brilliant hypnotist. Eve felt that, although there might well be some awkward moments to come, things might – just – work out OK.

'You should know – that is, if you don't already – that I removed the children from Ivy House the moment I'd heard you had left.' Anette sighed. The first hint of tiredness Eve had noticed. 'It has been a very busy time, working out what to do next. In so many ways.'

'Yes – yes, it has. And, um,' Eve steeled herself, '*Mr* Sorensen? How is his, uh, situation?'

The sun was so bright that Eve could just detect the hint of a frown behind Anette's big and very dark glasses. 'Well, Stefan has been bailed. He is sorting out some business and then he'll be joining us next week.' A pause. Anette pushed the glasses back on top of her head. 'After you've left. The arrest is in error, I can assure you, Eve. Mr Dershowitz is, however, still under arrest.'

'I had heard that, yes.' Eve hoped she was striking the

right tone, but it was almost impossible to judge. 'It must be very difficult for Anna.'

'It will all be resolved very soon, believe me. I think it has been something of a, er, wake-up call for Stefan, but the inconvenience and embarrassment will be temporary; rest assured, he is guilty of no impropriety.' Another pause. 'No *financial* impropriety.'

Eve chose her words carefully. 'Well, I'm glad this is a temporary professional hiccup for Mr Sorensen.' *Are we going to dance around this bloody great elephant all day?*

At which point, Anette might have read her mind. She gave a polite little cough and took a sip of tea. 'Here is the thing, Eve: I feel very bad for Zoe. For her Odense experience being so, ah –' she broke off, apparently deliberating over her choice of words – 'deeply disappointing and, naturally, very upsetting for you, as a mother. However –' another small cough – 'that's as maybe. We can talk about it; I'm sure we need to. But first, can I tell you a little bit about me, if you don't mind?'

Disarmed, Eve shook her head. She'd meant to nod. 'Please, go ahead.'

So, Anette started at the beginning and told Eve how, as a mysteriously bourgeois child of hippy parents, she had always yearned to live in a shiny executive home with a stay-at-home mother and a father she barely saw, who wore suits to go and do his Important Work. She told Eve she'd dreamed of riding a pink bicycle with handlebar streamers around a cul-de-sac and then returning home to play with a Barbie in an airy bedroom of wall-to-wall carpets, neatly fitted wardrobes and walls covered with posters of ponies. She really hadn't wanted to live in a caravan in a boggy field and have her fringe trimmed with pinking shears or ride to school on a fat little pony with no saddle and spend all day at that school having the mickey taken out of her relentlessly by her fellow students because she was invariably wearing wellingtons indoors, often with no socks, and her jumpers were knitted – badly – by her mum.

And then, Anette told Eve, when her parents had finally left their eco-commune and moved back to Copenhagen, she had begged them to let her try for a scholarship to a posh private school where the girls wore crisp navy uniforms. And so they did, and she won her scholarship and, because her parents weren't at all poor, just slumming, she was therefore able to board – so she did that, too. And then, pretty soon, she'd reinvented herself from the slightly grubby daughter of pothead hippies to the sleekly sophisticated creature who had won Miss Denmark and then, on her first day at university, the heart of Stefan Sorensen – a man who had actually grown up in a shiny executive home in a cul-de-sac. Eve listened, fascinated, as Anette confessed that she had never stopped moving away, very fast, from her quite literally messy childhood ever since.

'And I made myself become that "normal" girl who had grown up in a "normal" home – indeed, almost a parody of that, in fact, when I entered Miss Denmark, which was precisely the kind of thing my parents despised. And nobody knew any different because I never invited them back to my real home. I mean, why would I? By that time, my parents lived "over the shop" – only their "shop" was a notorious hippy hangout, selling bongs and rolling papers and cannabis-leaf bumper stickers. By the time I got to university, I really was my own reinvented woman. It was just incredibly lucky that I met Stefan, too, because I realized not only that, with him, I didn't want to lie anymore, but also that I could probably make the life for myself that I'd never had and always wanted. Because, you see, he *had* had that life, and he knew how it all worked – and, even more importantly, it didn't scare him at all. He didn't want to live in a caravan, either; at eighteen, he wanted to live in a nice neat flat close to the train station. And then, later on, when he'd made his first millions, he wanted to live in a nice big house with a garden – near the airport.'

'Well, it's fair to say he pulled that off,' said Eve.

Anette smiled. 'But, of course, you think the very worst of Stefan – and why wouldn't you?' Eve hoped very much that this was a rhetorical question and that she didn't need to reply. 'In your position, I would too, no doubt of that.'

Eve couldn't help herself. 'But what about *your* position? After all, your husband slept with –' sharp intake of breath – 'my teenage daughter.' And, as she spoke, Eve's eyes followed Alice as she swam a perfect length of the pool at a leisurely crawl. Despite the heat, Eve shivered.

'It's true, and he's an idiot, of course! But both of them admit it was consensual and, as he knows well enough, I have a ban on youngsters. I can only assume he thought Zoe wasn't as young as she is and that, for her part, Zoe did nothing to dispel that belief. Stef and I have an arrangement that works for us. It would not work for everybody.' Anette shrugged. 'Maybe, despite all of *this* –' she waved a hand – 'I am more hippy child than I care to admit. My sister certainly is. She works for me, as does Joe, and they live in a lovely home on the estate, but she'd be just as happy in a tent. I know it. And she's a devoted home-schooler. Me –' she shrugged again – 'I believe in schools. Which brings me neatly to Heatherdown.'

Eve's eyes widened. Anette smiled.

'After a long conversation with your friend, Cathy, who explained very clearly and concisely the terms and conditions surrounding, uh, Stefan and Zoe –' Anette's tone was entirely without animosity – 'well, then I had a conversation with Mr Salter, who had nothing but good things to say about you.' Eve looked baffled, shook her head. 'Yes, Tony Salter. After that conversation and some discussion with my legal team, followed by a call to Adam Vine, I have bought Heatherdown School. So, for every square-peg kid stuck in a nice executive home in a cul-de-sac, dreaming of campfires and climbing trees, woodsmoke and camaraderie – well, there will be a school for them, scholarships on tap.' Anette shrugged. 'But, of course, the real point of this meeting, the reason why I invited you to El Paradiso when Cathy told me you were coming to Ibiza with Alice, was for me to offer you a job, Eve. To, ah, when the deal is done – which I have every confidence it will be, because the terms are attractive to all parties – offer you Heatherdown to run, as head. Adam, meanwhile, is moving to Denmark, where he will help to set up a sister school.'

Still Eve remained silent.

'And this is not just for you, Eve, but for *my* children, too – and indeed for all those other children out there who, whether or not they know it yet, may need a Heatherdown.'

Eve was entirely lost for words. She couldn't quite make sense of what Anette was saying but . . . I must try to sound like a head teacher, at least: 'Well. Of course, I am incredibly flattered – and astonished, frankly, Anette. But—'

Anette interjected. 'Don't "but" me, please, Eve. Don't even bother answering right now. Frankly, you will need time to think, of course. I don't even own the school yet, so there are many things to discuss. The paperwork is underway. I just wanted you to agree in principle. And, while you are thinking about that, I hope you and Alice will relax on the island. And, should you need to talk to me anytime in the next ten days, then I shall be very easy to find. I shall mostly be right here, by the pool, with the kids, or, at sunup and sundown, on a horse. More tea?'

'Thank you, yes.' Eve sat in silence for a moment or two. Then: 'Do you mind me asking you something very personal, Anette?'

'No. If I can answer it, I will. Shoot.'

'Do you think your marriage works because of or despite Stefan's extramarital, uh, behaviour?'

'It's a good question. I think, for most people, it might not work. And I don't say that with any kind of sense of superiority. In truth, a faithful husband would be preferable to an unfaithful one, of course. But the fact is that having a great deal of money can free you up from the pettiness of life. By which I mean that it offers the chance to engage with a bigger, more important picture. Do you see?' Eve nodded. She sort of *did* see. Anette continued. 'By being together, Stefan and I are able to do things we could not so successfully achieve apart. I like to make a difference and if the price I have to pay for that is a husband who sometimes sleeps with other women because he can – and this is, like so many high-achieving men, literally the only thing about which he is lazy – then so be it.' A shrug. 'Hurting people wilfully is entirely unacceptable; hurting people accidentally is also undesirable – which is why there is so much regret with Stefan about Zoe, and for me too – but simply sleeping with people is not unacceptable at all, really. It is a small thing, I think, in the big scheme. There are more important things for us all to worry about, no?'

That's very evolved, thought Eve. I'm not sure I could ever be that evolved, even if I woke up to this view every morning for the rest of my life. 'I think part of me is still angry at Simon, even now, after all these years.' Why am I telling Anette this? 'But I think that might be passing. Finally.'

'I'm glad. Now, can I ask you something?'

'Of course.'

'Are you more angry with your daughter or with my husband?'

Eve considered the question. 'I think I've been angry with both of them for different reasons, but I think that will pass, too – partly because I'm sort of seeing someone and he talks a lot of sense. On your own, it's very easy to lose perspective.'

'That handsome head teacher at Eastdene!' Anette tilted her head to one side.

'Yes, Mike. How on earth do you know?'

'My God – they talk of nothing else at the Bell. I think you need to get out more!' The two women met each other's gaze properly for the first time, and laughed. And carried on laughing. At which point, they were joined by Birgitte. 'Listen, Birgitte, I am telling Eve that everybody knows about her and Mike Browning!'

'The delicious Mike Browning. For ages Anette and I were sure he had to be gay because how else could he not have been snapped up by a sexy single mother – no?'

'Like Susie Poe?' said Anette.

'Exactly!' said Birgitte.

Eve followed the conversation, enjoying the fizz of feminine, sisterly humour. And, apart from banter with the daughters, I really don't get enough of this . . . I must call Sonia.

'So,' said Anette, 'if you turn down Heatherdown, I may just have to offer it to Mike.'

Eve laughed. 'I don't think you'd get very far. He's fairly anti independent education.'

'I'm sure you could talk him round.' More laughter. 'Now, please say you'll both stay for lunch? It would be unfair to drag Alice away from her important new role,' said Anette.

Eve glanced over at Alice, busy throwing a succession of happily shrieking Percys into the deep end of what was almost certainly the loveliest leisure-centre swimming pool in the world. 'Thanks, Anette. We accept.'

Nine days later, Eve and Alice hauled their heavy bags (there had been some shopping during the last few days) down to the 'check-in desk' in the lobby of the boutique B&B – a big, fruit-and-flower-laden table in the hallway, at which 'Jade Jagger' – real name, Anastasia – sat with an iPad, sipping a mug of something fragrantly herbal.

'Hi, Anastasia. We're all good to go, albeit reluctantly. Better settle up.'

Anastasia smiled. 'Nothing to settle. All sorted.' She pointed at the door, through which, right on cue, appeared Joe Parker.

'Hi, Eve. Hi, Alice. We've settled the bill for you – this one's on Anette – and you'll have a nice ride home, too. Mr Sorensen arrived an hour ago – I've just dropped him at the house – and his jet has now refuelled and is waiting to pop you both over to Gatwick.'

'Oh, wow! Awesome!' Alice hopped gleefully from foot to foot.

Eve was not so easily swayed, however. 'Oh, no, I really don't think we can – not after Anette's picked up our tab. And we have perfectly good flights on EasyJet.'

Joe pulled a face. 'I thought you might say that. I've just checked the flight and it's delayed until further notice. Engine failed before take-off on the outbound flight from Gatwick, so it's been grounded. Could be hours.'

Alice was literally hopping. 'Oh, Mum! Come *on*!'

Eve wobbled. The thought of sitting inside Ibiza airport for an indefinite period didn't wildly appeal, so, even though it was terrible self-interest if she caved in, it would still be fun for Alice. 'OK, thanks, Joe. We graciously accept. And do give Anette this, too, when you see her.' She handed Joe an envelope, which he slipped into a shirt pocket. 'No probs, Mrs S. Now, let's go, because, it's a funny thing, but even unscheduled flights like to stick to a schedule.' Alice looked suitably baffled. Joe grinned. 'No, Alice, don't worry, I don't get it either.'

45

Just over four hours later, in Eve's kitchen, Mike was at the sink, filling the kettle, brow furrowed, intrigued by conversational shifts that included Alice's detailed description of the idiosyncrasies of travelling by private jet, right through to Eve's thoughts about Heatherdown. He did his best to keep up. 'So you think you want to make a go of it, then?'

Eve looked Mike in the eye and took a deep breath. 'Do you know what? I think I do. And, before you ask, no – I have absolutely no idea exactly how that has happened.'

Mike smiled. 'This is good news.'

But Eve wanted further reassurance, even if it sounded slightly needy. 'Though, you don't really approve of me or the job, do you?'

Mike shrugged. 'I think one of the great things about growing up, generally speaking, is discovering that maintaining an entrenched position can compromise other aspects of one's life far more than one would, uh, like.'

'That's very gnomic!' Eve teased.

'What I mean is—'

'I know exactly what you mean. You mean that ideology is one thing but that people are quite another?'

Mike wasn't the blushing type; though, if he had been, this would have been the perfect moment to indulge. 'Yes, that's exactly what I mean. I'm just hoping that isn't a compromise too far.'

Eve took the proffered tea. 'Yes, me too,' she said, smiling. 'Me too.'

46

'Surprise!'

As she walked into her father's living room, Zoe dutifully arranged her face into a suitably astonished/delighted/
appreciative expression. It had clearly been a very smart
move to demand, by force, that Alice fess up – on pain of
imminent death – if she heard anything *even hinting* that
there conceivably, may, possibly, perhaps be anything even
vaguely looking like a surprise party in the offing.

Zoe had barged into Alice's room, which was not a place
she felt the need to visit very often, and wrinkled her nose
at the acres of rosettes and posters of random horse people
doing dressage . . . Weirdo. 'If I find out that there is, and
you knew about it, I will . . . I'll . . . um . . .' It was important
that she followed through; however, Zoe wished she'd
given all of this a bit more thought.

'You'll what? Ban me from borrowing your Big Hair?
OMG – my life is totally over! How can I go on?' Alice fell
on to her bed, clutching her heart, eyes rolling, dying.

'No, I'll think of something much worse.' An image

flashed into Zoe's head of that old movie, *The Godfather*, that she'd once watched with Rob. 'Something horrible to do with Monty – just leave it with me.'

Alice sighed. 'You weren't always such an utter bitch, Zo. You used to be quite nice.'

Zoe started and then stared at her sister. 'I . . . uh . . .' OMG. She was literally about to cry. Her stupid little sister had made her *cry*, for fuck's sake. She wiped her eyes. 'You know I've had a weird time.' She corrected herself. 'No, I'm still having a weird time.' She flopped on to Alice's bed.

'Want to talk about it?' asked Alice.

Zoe appraised her sister. Oddly, she felt that, yes, actually, she might want to confide in someone. Alice wouldn't have been top of her list, obviously, but she'd sort of started to tell Carmen everything a few weeks ago, and then she'd bottled it. 'OK. So. Tell anyone, especially Mum or Dad, and I will kill you, your horse, your dog, your friends—'

'Stop right there. If you say "family", it's not going to work.'

'Oh, ha ha.' Zoe slapped her sister's leg, but not very hard.

'So, go on, then,' said Alice calmly, moving over on the bed to make room for Zoe.

'OK,' said Zoe.

And she did. She told her that, after her recent fifteen minutes of tabloid infamy, Stefan Sorensen had texted her, telling her he was proud of her – which meant that he did have her number, of course – and she'd not only not replied, she'd *deleted the number.* Alice was very impressed by this – and Zoe had liked that.

Thus, three weeks later, when Alice had tapped on her bedroom door and hissed through the gap, 'Yup, there's something going on. It's at Dad's,' Zoe had been sufficiently forewarned to arm herself.

Hence she was wearing exactly the right sort of face right now, as she scanned the room, smiling. 'Wow! Omigod! How *amazing*!' Necessarily avoiding Alice's wry smile, she practically convinced herself.

Her dad handed her a glass of champagne and the room filled with a chorus of 'Happy Birthday' – loudly from Simon, Eve, Mike, Ed, Jordan, Alice, Carmen, Father Ted and Gramma Grace, slightly quieter from everyone else. After which traditional ritual embarrassment, Zoe started to circulate among her friends and her parents' friends and some slightly unexpected grown-ups whom she liked, such as her Aunt Sonia, and Cathy and Johnny. Zoe watched as Cathy introduced Johnny to her Auntie Sonia, and grinned – she could practically feel the pheromones flying between them. How awesome would that be? Auntie Sonia and Johnny Nicholson? Cathy caught her watching and winked; they both grinned. And *then* Zoe's eyes lit upon the random but madly handsome square-jawed man-boy of about her own age who was standing next to Cathy. Omigod, Abercrombie Model is, like, one of Cathy's sons. My godbrother?!

Zoe moved fast. 'Thanks so much for coming, Cathy!'

'Not only an important godmotherly duty, of course,

but a total pleasure too.' Cathy grinned. 'Do you remember Ethan? Year younger than you? Skate dude?'

'Oh. Uh, yeah – hi.' Seventeen? Too young. Then, as if by magic, Alice appeared by her side. Zoe noted that her sister wasn't exactly panting; however, as she smiled at Ethan, there was a definite golden-retriever puppy look about her. God. Zoe rolled her eyes and couldn't resist: 'Oh, hi, Alice! This is Cathy's son, Ethan. Is that, like, loo paper? Stuck to your shoe?'

Alice looked stricken, Ethan pretended not to hear and Cathy shook her head. 'Don't worry, Alice – no loo paper. Your sister is just being—'

'Just being my sister?' Alice shrugged. 'Used to it.'

Ethan grinned. 'At least you've only got one annoying sibling. I've got two.'

Alice shook her head. 'No, I've got two. That's my brother, Jordan, over there.'

Cathy smiled, turned to Zoe and leaned in to whisper in her ear. 'Many happy returns. Now, you probably don't know this, but Ethan and I are both staying at your mum's this weekend – and I'd really love to spend a bit of time with you, alone, before we leave. How does that sound? Maybe a drink tomorrow night, or, if you're busy, we can grab a few minutes on Sunday?'

Zoe smiled – why not? 'Yeah, that would be really nice.'

Cathy smiled and nodded. 'One of the great things about godmothers, theoretically, is that they have all the good bits of mums, but without having a mum's agenda.'

Zoe nodded. 'Cool.'

'I hope so. Now, go off and enjoy being eighteen. Little Zoe, eighteen! How can that be?'

Zoe grinned. 'And now you sound exactly like my mum.'

Much later, pouring another glass of wine for herself and her sister, Zoe said, 'Sorry about the loo-paper thing. And I probably owe you for alerting me. Think of anything?'

'Yeah, I can,' said Alice, eagerly.

'Shoot.'

So Alice did. And Zoe nodded. 'It's totally impossible, you know that, but I'll see what I can do.' She patted Alice patronizingly on the head. 'Now, stop following Ethan around like a saddo. I'm going off soon to, er . . .'

'Find something you're entitled to vote for? And then get a tattoo?'

'Lunch is served!' shouted Simon.

Zoe laughed — she already had a tattoo, but not one that Alice was ever going to see — and Alice smiled. She liked it when her sister found her funny, which she used to do a lot. 'Exactly,' Zoe said. 'But first, obviously, lunch.'

As they queued for the buffet, laid out under a gazebo in the garden, Zoe found herself standing next to her mother. 'So, have you thought any more about what you'll be doing this academic year?' said her mum, in the new, slightly formal, adult-to-adult sort of tone she'd started using ever since all the *stuff* had happened.

Zoe nodded. 'Yeah, I think I'd like a gap year, after all.

Bit of travelling? I've got my savings, and Father Ted says he'll top me up. Mike says that, if I don't have a gap year now, I never will. He says that they didn't even exist when he was a teenager, but he quite fancies having one when he's fifty.'

'Did he now?' Eve smiled; Mike's fiftieth was in six months' time.

'He also says that I could do modelling in my gap year.' Zoe shrugged. 'Lucrative, but I dunno. Standing around pouting? Boring.'

Eve looked at her daughter, who generally did a very good job of standing around pouting, entirely unpaid. She was currently wearing the very tiniest cut-off denim shorts Eve had ever seen and a barely-there sequinned halter top. On this evidence, there was no doubt in Eve's mind that Zoe could 'do modelling'.

'Well, yes,' she said. 'Though, if high finance is a high-stakes, cut-throat business, I suspect it has nothing on fashion.'

Zoe raised an eyebrow. 'Mum. Can I tell you something about Alice?'

'Of course – as long as it's not telling tales.'

'Look, she knows that five very average GCSEs are never going to be enough to get her a place in the sixth form at Westdene. The thing is, what she really, *really* wants is to do a BTEC in Horse Management.' Zoe waited a beat. 'At Hartsmere.'

Eve raised an eyebrow and nodded slowly. 'Is that so?'

'Yes. She wants a career with horses and she doesn't see any point in wasting anybody's time – not least her own – doing stuff she isn't remotely any good at, and doing it badly.' Zoe shrugged. 'And I kind of see her point, even if you won't. And the other thing – and she won't tell you this herself because she doesn't want to hurt your feelings, but I can – is that she wants to live here, with Dad and Ed, so she can see more of Jordan. Jordan loves horses; a total natural with them, apparently. Alice is teaching him to ride Monty.' Zoe paused. 'Did you even know that?'

Eve raised her eyes and shook her head. 'No, I didn't know that.'

'Well, you do now.'

It was a lot for Eve to take in; however, there was no opportunity to do so at that precise moment because Zoe and Eve were distracted by a small commotion from the direction of the kitchen and, with it, the arrival – accompanied by an excited 'Ta-da!' fanfare from Alice, who announced, 'This just arrived with its very own chauffeur!' – of a vast and glamorously boxed bouquet of flowers.

Eve smiled, fabricating a disingenuous, 'So what's all this, then?' – because she knew what this was – as she watched Zoe park her laden plate on a table in order to inspect the flowers and open the accompanying fat envelope.

Zoe stared at the card inside the envelope for the longest time; Eve and Alice and Simon and Ed stared at her. 'It's from my godmother!' Zoe glanced up. 'It says, *With my very best wishes for a perfect eighteenth birthday! Love Cathy.'* Zoe wiped away a tear and then glanced up in time to catch a fleeting nod and a wink and a smile from Cathy, who mouthed, 'Happy birthday!'

'And that's a very fat envelope for a card,' said Alice. 'What's in it? Like, a million pounds?' Everybody laughed.

'Shut up, Alice,' said Zoe warmly, extracting a pretty, pink leather document-wallet from inside the fat envelope. She opened it. 'Omigod!' said Zoe. '*Omicompletelybloodygod!*'

Alice: 'I was right. It *is* a million pounds!'

'No, no, it's not a million pounds, but –' Zoe's face lit up; it was the first time anybody had seen that proper big, beautiful Zoe smile in a long time – 'it *is* a gap year! It's a cheque for, like, five thousand pounds!'

Alice's eyes widened. 'For, like, real?'

'For like *totally* real!' Zoe looked around for her friend. 'Yay, Carmen! We're *totally* having a gap year!' And then she looked around for Cathy, who, very keen to avoid a fuss, was nonetheless doing a very bad job of trying to hide behind one of the gazebo's spindly legs. Zoe ran towards her godmother and threw her arms around her neck. 'My God, my godmother! Thank you!'

Simon raised an eyebrow and a glass and clinked it against Eve's. 'Well! Let us heartily congratulate ourselves on picking the right godmother. I hope to God Sonia comes through as impressively for Alice in a couple of years' time. Cheers!'

Eve smiled and rolled her eyes. 'Yes, that would be lovely, wouldn't it? I'll flag it up.'

Glancing at her ex-husband, Eve wasn't entirely sure if Simon had picked up on her sarcasm, but realized, to her mild surprise, that in fact she wasn't really bothered either way.

47

It was just past nine on the first evening of Ivy House's summer holidays, when the doorbell rang. Gail disliked cold callers generally, even friends, and liked them a great deal less in the evenings, when she was halfway through a fine episode of *Nurse Jackie*. However, she didn't want to be a curtain-twitcher, so she paused the TV reluctantly, took a deep breath and opened the door. At which point she quickly arranged her face into the correct sort of expression while noting that, regrettably, she was wearing an XXXL grey marl onesie and Harry's Christmas present to her: novelty Rudolph slippers, complete with red nose and antlers.

'Hi, Gail, sorry about turning up on your doorstep unannounced like this – I just needed a quick word, if I could?' said Tony Salter, with, Gail liked to think, only the very briefest of glances at her slippers.

She coughed slightly. 'Yes, that's fine, Tony. Um, Harry's in bed – done in after cricket club – and I'm just watching a bit of telly –' Gail could hear herself prattling and willed herself to stop – 'but, yes, come on in. I might even have a beer kicking around somewhere. Or wine? Or tea?' Shut up, Gail!

Tony nodded. 'Yes, any of those – all of them, maybe. Shall I take my shoes off?'

Gail nodded. 'If you wouldn't mind.' In the kitchen, she reached for the kettle, then thought better of it. 'Actually, do you fancy a wine? I've got some in.'

'But is it drinkable?'

'I think so. It's a 2006 white Bordeaux. Mike Browning gave it to me for Christmas.'

'Did he now? Your next-door neighbour, am I right?'

'That's right. Lovely bloke – great head teacher, too. Harry loves him.'

'I bet he does.' Tony heaved himself on to a stool at the breakfast bar. 'But, more to the point, do you?'

Gail blushed; however, because she was facing away from Tony, she could at least attempt to brazen it out. 'Well, I think the whole of Eastdene is a little bit in love with him – even Dave, over at the Bell.'

But Tony had already lost interest in Mike Browning. 'Well, I'm sorry to miss seeing the boy.'

'Yes, it's a shame, but he is usually asleep by now. You should've texted.'

'I always assume they're up till two a.m. these days, surfing porn on the internet.'

'No, Tony, that's just *you*.'

Tony laughed. 'Not totally lost your sense of humour

then, Gail? We don't see too much of it in the office, these days.'

Gail ignored this; Tony might not see much evidence of her sense of humour, but other people certainly did. 'OK. So? What can I do for you, Tony?'

He sighed. 'OK, so I'll never give up asking you to marry me, Gail, but if you won't do that – and I'll assume it's still a no – then at least tell the boy the bloody truth, for Christ's sake. He's eleven. He needs a dad.' A pause. 'Actually, he needs *his* dad – and I need *him*, Gail. I need my son in my life.'

Gail could not entirely ignore the beseeching tone. It wasn't the first time Tony had come begging, but it was the first time he'd sounded quite so . . . desperate. What's brought this on? She felt very calm. 'We get on fine without you, Tony. You know I still haven't touched a penny of the maintenance? It's all still there in a savings account, for when he's eighteen.'

'Lousy rate of interest – I've told you over and over I'd invest it better.'

'It's fine. It's a lot of money – it'll be getting on for two hundred grand by the time he's eighteen, I suppose. And, of course, he'll get this house off me, too, one day. Look, he's a good kid; he won't go bonkers and blow it all down Slots of Fun or end up on *Jeremy Kyle*.'

'Don't change the subject, Gail.'

Oh, for fuck's sake, Tony! thought Gail. 'Why not? You spent years and years changing the subject and, now you've

396

decided you want to have the conversation, I'm just expected to fall in? Well, I'm not.' Gail's voice was somehow louder than she'd realized. She saw Tony frowning and running his fingers through his hair, that messy dark cowlick.

'Mu-um? I can't sleep.' Harry was standing in the doorway wearing pyjama shorts, his still-damp shower-hair all over the shop – that needs a trim – and he was clutching his favourite bear. My man-boy, thought Gail, my Mowgli . . . Her heart lurched with love. 'Hello, Tony,' said Harry.

'Hello, Harry,' said Tony. 'Uh, your mum and I were just talking. How are you?'

And then, quite suddenly, looking at them both standing awkwardly in her kitchen, together but apart, Gail was struck forcefully for the first time by the utter absurdity of the entire situation. Bloody hell, this is mad!

'Hazza? Actually, I'm really glad you're awake, because Tony came round hoping to see, er, you!' Her heartbeat quickened.

'Yeah?' said Harry, now leaning against the breakfast bar, rubbing his eyes with his bear-free hand.

'Yeah –' deep breath, one, two, three – 'and that's because he's your dad, Harry. Tony is your father.'

At which soap-opera-style bombshell, albeit (Gail couldn't help noticing) sadly lacking in *EastEnders*-style cliffhanger-signalling *doof-doof-doofs*, Harry simply smiled and yawned and stretched his skinny arms above his head. 'Yeah, I know, Mum.'

Gail turned to Tony, eyes wide in shock. Tony shook his head vigorously, as if to say, *No, I didn't tell him!* She shrugged. They both stared at Harry, baffled.

'Fuck's sake! I've always known, since whenever – because I'm eleven and look at us!' Harry turned to Tony. 'But it would've been better if you'd said –' he affected a deep voice and a truly terrible American accent – 'Harry, I'm ya FADDER!'

'What, like Darth Vader to Luke Skywalker?' said Tony. 'And if I ever hear you say the F-word again, I swear to God, you'll regret it!'

'Yeah, exactly like that –' Harry grinned – '*Dad.*'

At which point Gail didn't know whether to laugh or cry, so, in no particular order, she did both.

48

A perfect autumnal morning in late September and Eve threw her bag – last year's bag – into the passenger seat and turned the Volvo out of the Barn's gravel drive, driving past the new *For Sale* sign and on, towards Heatherdown.

Fifteen minutes later, she and Anette were wearing hard hats provided by Simon and half watching numerous topless young men swinging around Heatherdown's scaffolding, like a tribe of depilated primates. Both women stood in front of the building for a minute or two in a companionable sort of silence, which was broken by Eve.

'Please don't let me put you off at this extremely late stage, Anette, but I just want you to know that there really is no such thing as the perfect school.' She paused. 'Mind you, having brilliant staff helps a bit. On the subject of which, I spoke to Ellie just before I left. She's on her way.'

'Good.' Anette smiled. 'And don't worry – I didn't imagine there was such a thing as the perfect school. Not yet. It's probably a lifetime's work.'

'Yes, we'll be learning something new every day,' said

Eve, 'which is OK because, actually, if there's *one* thing I've learned in the past fifty-three years, it's that all of life is school.'

Anette nodded and put her finger to her lips. 'But *shhh* – for God's sake, don't tell the kids. Let them find out themselves, yes?'

Eve smiled. 'Definitely.'

POSTSCRIPT

OFSTED: RAISING STANDARDS,
IMPROVING LIVES
16th September, 2011

Dear Mr Browning and Students,
This letter is provided for the school, parents and carers to share with their children. It describes Ofsted's main findings from the inspection of their school.

Inspection of EASTDENE COMMUNITY PRIMARY SCHOOL, EASTDENE, EAST SUSSEX

Thank you for making the inspection team so welcome when we visited your school. We enjoyed having the opportunity to meet you and your teachers. You told us that you enjoy your school and particularly appreciate its family atmosphere.

You are especially well served by an interesting and diverse curriculum and a wide range of extra-curricular activities. Your attendance is excellent and we were extremely impressed by the fact that your teachers know you as individuals and teach you very well. You are also exceptionally well behaved and clearly get on well with each other.

So, in summary, I am delighted to be able to say that you go to an outstanding school. You make outstanding progress in your subject areas and the provision made for your spiritual, moral, social and cultural development is also outstanding.

Congratulations on all your hard work. We wish Eastdene Community Primary School the very best for the future.

Yours sincerely,

Jean Starling
Lead Inspector

ACKNOWLEDGEMENTS

Many thanks to my editor, Jane Wood, for her great skill and continued patience. This one took a bit longer than either of us had hoped but hey, sometimes life gets in the way.

Above-and-beyond thanks to my wise and witty Special Agent, Jonny Geller. Sorry about all those ranty emails, re 'life getting in the way'.

Thanks are also due to everybody at Curtis Brown and Quercus for all their secret agenty/undercover publishery stuff. You are all very clever and exceptionally kind. And so good-looking, too . . .

Thanks to my delightful not-quite-but-nearly-as-good-as 'stepsons', Archie and Noah, for recognising that 'the X-Box room' is, indeed, also my study.

Thanks to all the teachers in all the schools with which I've ever collided. Mostly for having A Proper Job and (mostly) being brilliant at it, but also for taking the boys off my hands between 9 am–3.30 pm so I can do stuff like this. Grateful.

ACKNOWLEDGEMENTS

While it turns out that I am absolutely no fun to be around when I'm writing a book, arguably I am even less fun than that when I'm *not* writing a book. So, very big love and extra special thanks to Julian Anderson for putting up with me (nearly) all the time.

Finally, mega Mum-thanks to my extraordinary sons, Jackson and Rider, who not only inspired this book but are (of course) the very coolest, cleverest and handsomest of 'square pegs'. I love you both far more than you will ever know.